# A HOME IN THE SUN

Sue Moorcroft writes award-winning contemporary fiction of life and love. *A Summer to Remember* won the Goldsboro Books Contemporary Romantic Novel Award. *The Little Village Christmas* and *A Christmas Gift* were *Sunday Times* bestsellers and *The Christmas Promise* went to #1 in the Kindle chart. She also writes short stories, serials, articles, columns, courses and writing 'how to'.

An army child, Sue was born in Germany then lived in Cyprus, Malta and the UK and still loves to travel. Her other loves include writing (the best job in the world), reading, watching Formula 1 on TV and hanging out with friends, dancing, yoga, wine and chocolate.

If you're interested in being part of #TeamSueMoorcroft you can find more information at www.suemoorcroft.com/street-team. If you prefer to sign up to receive news of Sue and her books, go to www.suemoorcroft.com and click on 'Newsletter'. You can follow @SueMoorcroft on Twitter, @SueMoorcroftAuthor on Instagram, or Facebook.com/sue.moorcroft.3 and Facebook.com/SueMoorcroftAuthor.

By the same author:

# A Home in the Sun

## Sue Moorcroft

avon.

Published by AVON
A division of HarperCollins*Publishers* Ltd
1 London Bridge Street
London SE1 9GF

www.harpercollins.co.uk

HarperCollins*Publishers*
1st Floor, Watermarque Building, Ringsend Road
Dublin 4, Ireland

This paperback edition 2021

1

First published as *Uphill all the Way* in Great Britain by Transita 2005

A catalogue copy of this book is available from the British Library.

ISBN: 978-0-00-843043-6

Typeset in Sabon LT Std by Palimpsest Book Production Limited, Falkirk, Stirlingshire
Printed and Bound in the UK using 100% Renewable Electricity at CPI Group (UK) Ltd

MIX
Paper from
responsible sources
FSC
www.fsc.org  FSC™ C007454

This book is produced from independently certified FSC™ paper
to ensure responsible forest management.

For more information visit: www.harpercollins.co.uk/green

# Acknowledgements

Thanks to Sue Dukes for answering fifty emails about sub aqua diving without a single complaint.

To Tony Bosson for his advice on hand injury, and for letting me touch his scar.

Especial gratitude to *all* on the Malta Global Friends website, but especially Tom Restall, Paul Vella, Louis Risso, Peter Birkett, Mark Caruana and Bill Coxhead, for patiently answering my many and varied questions about my beloved Malta and for making the translations. If any of the words are naughty, it was them, not me!

And to Salvinu Lombardi of Sliema, for very kindly doing much the same.

I would never have got this far, or, indeed, very far at all, without the Romantic Novelists' Association, and in particular the New Writers' Scheme run, at that time, by Margaret James, who always knew just what to say.

Author's note:

The above is most of the original Acknowledgements attached to Judith and Adam's story, which was my first published book. I hope you enjoy revisiting that time with me. I'd like to add huge thanks and appreciation to my wonderful editor Helen Huthwaite and all on the Avon team, my awesome agent Juliet Pickering and everyone at Blake Friedman Literary Agents, Team Sue Moorcroft, everyone who follows me on social media and, most of all, you the reader.

Thank you.

To Michael,
For never suggesting that I get an ordinary job.

# Part One

## Giorgio and the House of Cards

# Prologue

*August 2000*

Judith was glad to her bones that she'd come to live in Malta. She was forty and it was early in a new millennium – the perfect time for change. Her marriage to Tom was over. Her uncle Richard had offered her the chance to buy into his estate agency on the island. Perfect.

Now, in the beating summer heat, she was spending her lunch hour at Ghar id-Dud, strolling between the tourists on the broad promenade high above the rocky foreshore. Behind her lay the open-air cafés known as kiosks, a busy road and tall hotels; before her stood the stone skeleton of a derelict pier reaching out into the sparkling blue sea. The pier was probably thirty feet tall and four teenage boys and a girl were leaping from the top with blood-curdling shrieks, plummeting through the salty air to shatter the waves below. Leaning on the guardrail between promenade and the drop-off to the sea, Judith grinned as the teens resurfaced in circles of foam, whooping their exhilaration as they swam back to the ladder attached to the rock. Her stepson Kieran was at university in Sheffield. If he saw these teens on his next visit to Malta, he'd want to hurl himself off the pier, too.

It did look inviting. If Kieran tried it then Judith knew she would too, jumping into thin air to slap down into the sea with leg-stinging force, waiting for gravity to stop bearing her down before kick, kick, kicking, ears aching, for the surface.

A deep voice at her shoulder observed, 'It's a little crazy but nobody dies.'

Judith turned in surprise. A man smiled at her. He looked Maltese, his shirt white against skin that was several shades more golden than hers. His eyes were as dark as damsons and his black hair well cut and neat. At the open neck of his shirt glinted a gold crucifix on a thick chain. He settled his elbows on the guardrail a foot away from hers. 'This I have done.' He gestured at the foolhardy teenagers clambering back to the upper level. He spoke good English as many Maltese did, it being one of the official languages of the island. He looked at least a decade younger than her.

Judith returned his smile politely. 'You've jumped off it?'

His soft, husky laugh seemed to trickle across her skin. 'When I was a stupid teenager. But it is unsafe for many years. You see there has been a fence to keep people off. It's broken, and the children climb.'

The teenagers' howls of glee began again as they sprang joyously into nothingness and smashed down into the waiting blue waves.

'It's called The Chalet,' he said, gesturing towards the ruined pier. 'It used to have a dance floor and an open-air café on two levels, for celebrations, for dances. A balustrade ran all the way round and there was a grand entrance, here.' He indicated a spot close to where they stood.

Judith gazed at the skeletal structure, trying to envision such imposing flesh to what were now very bare bones. 'What happened to it all? A bomb?'

He smiled. 'No. A storm, a *grigal*.'

She glanced at him. '*Grigal?*' She'd begun to learn a little Maltese but this was an unfamiliar word. 'I'd assumed it happened in the war.' World War II had been cruel to Malta and ruins, such as those of the Royal Opera House in Valletta, still dotted the island.

'Storms on the north-easterly wind,' the man explained. 'They can bring enormous waves. You've seen the break-water in the mouth of Grand Harbour? It is to keep the shipping protected from the *grigal*.' He nodded towards The Chalet. 'Now, the government wishes for this ruin to become something safe and new but there is nothing decided, I think.'

Judith stared at the crumbling remains of balustrades supported by immense pillars planted on the base that ran out into the water. Richard had told her about the Maltese winters being mild compared to English, but that they brought violent storms. Judith, though she had an affinity with the sea, had difficulty imagining waves so monstrous they were capable of sucking masonry off such a big structure. Her Sunday scuba dives would certainly slow down in seas like that. If she was going to take an instructor qualification, she'd need to get on with it.

''Allo, Giorgio!' a woman called from behind them, above the buffeting of the breeze.

The man looked around and waved in acknowledge-ment. Turning back to Judith, he said, 'I must work now.'

Judith turned and saw a cream coach with a rainbow

arcing over a big Z on the side. It waited, engine running, outside The Preluna Hotel, a popular pick-up point for tourist trips. 'You work for Sliema Z Bus Tours?'

He nodded. 'I am Giorgio Zammit, a tour guide.' He pulled a navy tie from his pocket, flipped up his collar and began to tie it as he hurried in the direction of the tour bus, tossing back a, '*Ciao*,' over his shoulder to Judith.

'*Ciao*,' she returned, quite sorry to see him jumping aboard the idling bus, taking a clipboard from a female tour guide waiting on the steps. As the bus pulled away, he ducked to wave goodbye to Judith.

Shyly, she waved back. Then she checked her watch and realised it was time for her to return to work, too. She crossed the promenade then turned left to follow Tower Road to the sea road and Richard Elliot Estate, where she had an appointment with a Scots couple who were looking for a holiday home. Selling apartments didn't exactly make use of her qualifications as a surveyor but she was enjoying the change, as well as the chance to live in Malta.

She met Giorgio on her lunchtime stroll several times, after that. He'd materialise beside her, either off duty or waiting for a one o'clock pick-up by a distinctive Sliema Z Bus. They'd spend a few minutes on a bench, sipping water or licking ice cream.

One afternoon, he told Judith he was about to escort a trip to Ta' Qali Handicrafts Village in the centre of the island. 'It's what remained of the RAF airfield where the famous Gloster Gladiator biplanes, Hope, Faith and Charity, flew against the Germans,' he explained. 'Craftworkers have moved into the old Nissen huts and created a thriving tourist attraction.'

'I've heard of it. Do they sell Mdina glass there?' she asked, thinking of the jewel-like colours of the glass she saw frequently about the island. 'And filigree jewellery? I keep meaning to visit.'

'Come today,' he suggested, treating her to his boyish smile. He let his arm touch hers, his skin hot. It was common for Maltese men to wear short-sleeved shirts, even with a tie, and his tour-guide blazer was folded beside him on the bench.

She laughed. 'I haven't booked.'

His head shifted closer. 'There is space.'

Tempted, she glanced at her watch. She was responsible for her own schedule and had no meetings that afternoon. She withdrew her phone to call Richard. 'I'll pay my fare. You won't get into trouble with your employer, will you?'

'No.' His eyes gleamed with amusement. It took her a month to discover that he was one of three partners in the business.

'Richard,' she said into her phone, when she'd dialled the office of Richard Elliot Estate. 'I'm taking this afternoon off to join a trip to Ta' Qali. There's nothing in my diary.'

'Have a good time,' he answered comfortably. Richard was fantastic; she had such a great relationship with him. It was sometimes difficult to remember that he was her mother Wilma's brother because he was much younger than her, not just in years, but in attitude. Whereas Wilma had lived in Northamptonshire all her life and had a 'bootiful' accent, Richard had married pretty Maltese Erminia and moved here in his twenties. The relaxed pace of Malta suited him and Judith couldn't imagine him ever returning to the UK.

The modern coach arrived, cream paintwork gleaming, a contrast to the island's bright orange route buses, some of which had been trundling the island's roads for fifty or sixty years. Judith felt almost shy as Giorgio took her hand to cross the promenade. They climbed aboard the modern vehicle and Giorgio introduced Judith to his colleagues. 'This is Peter, our driver, and the other guide today, Victor.'

Peter and Victor, in the same white shirt and navy tie as Giorgio, looked interestedly at Judith and smiled. Then Giorgio installed her in a front seat, grabbed a clipboard and began to work his way around his passengers, who looked relieved as the doors closed and they got the benefit of air conditioning.

'Hallo, madam, I am Giorgio, and I am your guide today. Your name, please?' His charm was effortless. It flowed from him, coaxing out smiles and laughs. Then the bus pushed its way out into the busy Maltese traffic, following the coast road past apartments and restaurants, palm trees, kiosks and the rocks beside the sea.

Giorgio spent most of the journey on his feet beside the driver, facing the passengers and, via a microphone, providing a commentary about himself, the bus, the tour company, the areas through which they passed and Malta's history, swaying easily with the bus's motion, his smile flashing.

After disembarking half an hour later at Ta' Qali, he and Victor took a group of passengers each around the warren of curved, corrugated Nissen huts to watch the making of filigree jewellery or glass-blowing. Then he gave his group an hour to shop, pointed out their bus number, explained where to get an ice cream and reminded them not to neglect to drink. 'The sun we give respect, in August.' He conferred with Peter the driver, filled in a couple of boxes on a form, then jumped down beside Judith where she waited on the weed-strewn concrete. 'Today is an easy job. Everybody will shop. Maybe they spend too much money, but that is OK.'

She laughed and didn't protest when he once again took her hand. It was pleasant to make a slow circuit of the huts, seeing the sunlight strike the jewel-like colours of the glassware and jewellery in display cases and admiring the intricacies of the Malta lace, *bizzilla*. And always she was conscious of Giorgio and the smile in his eyes.

He was . . . unsettling. His eyes told her he desired her but she was cautious. She'd already discovered that Giorgio was a decade younger than her. Ex-husband, Tom, had succumbed to the temptation of Judith's replacement, Liza, and he was ten years Judith's senior.

After the shopping hour was over and the passengers all safely back in their seats, Judith learned that the trip continued with a visit to the magnificent Mosta Dome and a folk evening in Qormi. Giorgio's eyes laughed when she showed surprise. 'I've tricked you into spending longer with me than you meant to,' he murmured.

His expression was so mischievous that she felt herself smile. 'I could call a taxi.'

'That,' he replied gravely, 'would make me very sad.'

She stayed with the tour group for the visit to the famous dome, through which a bomb had dropped during the war but hadn't exploded, followed by a visit to a restaurant for *brogioli*, which was beef wrapped around mincemeat, and steaks of the local fish, *lampuki*, with spinach and bitter olives. The guests wound down over deliciously moist cakes and cold wine and the majority of Giorgio's duties had been discharged.

He sat with Judith on wooden chairs in a dim corner of the courtyard, a table between them. She told him about her mum and older sister Molly in England, and about Kieran, who she still called her stepson, despite the divorce.

He listened, smiling. Eventually, he said, 'Did you enjoy yourself today?' His voice was low, obliging her to lean closer to hear.

She smiled into his dark eyes. 'Oh, yes.'

'I would like to meet you again. I would like very much.' His voice was deep and intimate, his gaze intense.

'OK,' she repeated. 'I'll book on your trip to Gozo in three days.'

He laughed. 'That is not quite what is in my mind.'

She sat back and reached for her glass of wine. 'It's enough for now.'

The next day, she found Richard in the office before her, his light grey jacket hung up carefully behind him. He frowned when she told him about her outing, absently rubbing his balding head. 'What do you know about him?'

Surprised by the small frown that had gathered up the skin of his forehead, she shrugged. 'His name's Giorgio Zammit—'

Richard rolled his chair closer to her desk, his eyebrows knitting. The office didn't open until ten and though people hurried past the agency's glass windows or gazed at properties for sale on the display, they were alone. Richard's daughter Rosaire would be showing potential clients around a villa in Lija soon, but she hadn't arrived yet. Judith's other cousins, Raymond, Lino, were also out with clients. 'Bus tours bloke?' he demanded.

She agreed warily, nettled by his tone. 'Why?'

He sighed, reaching out to place his hand over hers. 'His wife Johanna lives in Sliema, too.'

Her stomach dropped.

Her uncle's round face was solemn and sympathetic.

He hesitated, choosing his words. '*Some* Maltese men are attracted to British ladies because they're brought up more liberally than many Maltese women.'

'I don't think that's it,' she protested, although she heard uncertainty in her own voice.

He looked uncomfortable. 'I think you're just a trifle older than him?'

She refused to voice the word *yes*. 'I'm grateful, in other words?'

He squeezed her hand again. 'I think you're wonderful and don't deserve to be hurt again, like Tom hurt you with Liza.'

All morning, Judith thought of Giorgio's smile and the warmth in his dark eyes, the curve of his eyebrow and the way his cheekbones made her want to stroke his face.

That lunchtime, she loitered on the promenade near The Chalet, taking sips from a water bottle and observing her surroundings from behind her sunglasses. When Giorgio arrived, hurrying towards her, eager smile blazing, she stopped him. 'Giorgio, I don't think you're a single man.'

Though he didn't drop his gaze as he joined her at the guardrail, his answer was circumspect. 'Why do you say this?'

Her heart contracted. She'd hoped he'd burst out with a denial. 'Someone told me you're married. There's no divorce here, I know that. So unless your wife's dead, you're still married.'

He crossed himself at the mention of death. Then his fingertips tapped gently on the rail. 'You are right,' he said sombrely. 'There is no divorce in our country. But some men live apart from their families. Many, many men. Shall we walk?'

She agreed and they strolled along the broad paved promenade between the rumbling traffic and the drop to the rocky beach where children waded in the rock pools and the blue waves broke in white froth.

Judith's heart knocked uncomfortably in her chest but she wasn't scared of the confrontation. She'd been the wife cheated on and it hurt. 'So, you have a wife.'

Gravely, he nodded. 'Johanna. We married when we were very young – sixteen.' He sent her a sheepish look. 'Our daughter, Alexia, she was already to come, you understand?'

'Ah. I see.' A teenage Giorgio had got his girlfriend pregnant. She could imagine marriage being expected. Her aunt Erminia was Maltese and Judith was aware that the Maltese church held its members to certain standards.

'Lydia followed, four years later but after a few years . . . we are all very unhappy when we live together. It's better not. I have lived alone for five years and now Alexia is fourteen, Lydia is ten. I love my children very much and see them very often. But I do not love their mother and I have not loved her for a very long time. I doubt whether she ever love me, ever.'

His emphatic tone and the glitter of his eyes moved her but she wasn't about to let him off the hook. He hadn't told her about his wife. He hadn't explained the situation. She felt empty at the deception. 'Giorgio,' she said, carefully. 'I *am* divorced. My husband found another woman while we were still married. I know that kind of pain. And I don't think we should go out together again.'

'I am separate,' he declared forcefully. But he made no attempt to detain her when she said it was time for her to return to the office, hurrying down the narrow pavements of Tower Road and along The Strand.

From then on, she changed the route of her lunchtime exercise, turning right out of the agency instead of left, following Sliema Creek to the yacht marina at Ta' Xbiex. It was only two days before he materialised at her side as she sat watching the boats bobbing on the glittering, calm sea.

'You're booked on the trip to Gozo tomorrow.' He looked tired, strained, but his shirt and tie were immaculate as always. 'It's your day off. Come and enjoy it. It will be a busy day for me and I will be occupied. I will not bother you.'

'How did you find me?' she demanded, ruffled at the way he popped up like a genie let out of a bottle.

He pointed towards the road behind them and she turned to see a big cream bus decorated with a rainbow. 'I saw you sitting,' he said simply. He smiled sadly and left her.

Next day, despite her better judgement, she took him at his word and mounted the gangplank of the boat to Gozo, the largest of the neighbouring islands. It was a beautiful day. The sea crossing was calm and Judith enjoyed the coach tour around the island, much quieter than Malta, with more terraced farms and narrow roads. She sat at the back while Giorgio stood beside the driver and held the tourists spellbound as he told them about the Neolithic Ggantija Temple ruins.

Despite his promise not to 'bother' her, at the end of the day he halted her as she made to follow the other tourists from the ferry. The other guide, a woman, must have been forewarned because she herded the rest of the passengers down onto the quay, leaving Judith and Giorgio alone with the creaking of the mooring ropes and the chug of small motor boats making their way up the creek. He gave her a small smile. 'Tomorrow is my rest day. I spend it on a beach. To help me enjoy this, will you be my company?' He thought for a moment, then amended himself. 'My guest. I am sorry that I did not explain I have not lived with my wife for a long time. I was ashamed. My parents are so embarrassed my marriage did not work that I have grown used to not talking about it.'

Judith failed to resist his sad, brown eyes.

A trip to the beach wasn't a commitment.

And he *was* separated . . .

They spent the day on the white sand of Anchor Bay at the north end of the island, talking, swimming in a sea barely ruffled by the breeze. In the evening they ate in Rabat, in the centre of the island, in a small cellar restaurant aromatic with goat's cheese and herbs and lit by the dancing light of red candles in wine bottles.

Judith enjoyed herself but doubts plagued her.

He drove her home in the early hours, the stars bright against a black sky. Parking outside her flat beside the slack night-time sea, he cradled her face gently and kissed her, a deep, carnal kiss, a kiss of clear intent, a kiss that made her muscles melt. Seriously, he told her, 'It's a big thing we have and I think we should begin a relationship.'

His words forced her to face a truth that had been niggling at her all day and into the evening. She sighed. 'It might be big, if we allowed it. But, although you say you've been separated for years, you took me far away from your home.'

He grew still. 'I do not hide you.'

'I think you do. Your wife lives in Sliema.'

He stared at her for several long moments. 'I apologise,' he said, at last. 'Yes, it is true, a little. Johanna and me have been separate for five years but I do not make people talk of her by making a parade of my feelings for you.

14

Why give her that pain? She and I will be always apart but still we consider our daughters. They are good daughters and Johanna is a good mother. Also, my parents, they are unhappy their son cannot have a good marriage and I try not to make them more unhappy. They are my parents. My uncle Saviour and aunt Cass, my cousins and their children, we all live in this big village that has grown into a tourist town. My parents would hurt to feel the family embarrassed by me. You live in Sliema, you know Sliema. People know other people.'

'Difficult,' she acknowledged, sadly. The streetlights and the moonlight glittered in the ripples of Sliema Creek and Giorgio's eyes. 'I think it's impossible, Giorgio. I'm not the kind of woman to be tidied away, kept secret from your family.' She kissed his cheek in fleeting farewell. Then she jumped out of his car and raced safely through the entry door to her apartment building. The door locked automatically behind her with a soft, final-sounding click.

The next day he surprised her at the office a few minutes before she would normally take her lunch. He'd never visited her there before. Solemnly, he faced her across her desk, ignoring his interested audience of Richard, two of Judith's cousins Rosaire and Lino, and a couple looking at the details of a flat. Giorgio regarded Judith fiercely. 'It is *not* impossible. If you want, we promenade ourselves. We go now to Tony's Bar on The Strand and eat at a table on the pavement where everyone in Sliema can see. Every day, if you want, we do it.'

His eyes were almost black and her head spun with how much she wanted to believe him. 'I can't let you make your life so uncomfortable, either for yourself or for those you love,' she protested.

So, instead, she allowed their love affair to begin – discreet, if not quite secret.

In the UK, she would've thought nothing about a relationship with a separated man. The difference between the UK and Malta was that though it was the year 2000, unless the law changed – under discussion but a political hot potato – Giorgio would never take the next logical step to divorce.

Richard was kind, though he didn't approve of what she was doing. He'd married Erminia, a Maltese woman, when he'd been stationed on the island with the British Army in the sixties, so had some insight into what she was getting into. Probably too much. He frowned over the issue as they worked together at polished maple desks, guiding foreign buyers through the labyrinth of acquiring property on the island.

Then one evening he took the two of them for a beer at a pavement café overlooking the creek that bobbed with boats in blues and reds. 'It's dangerous to go into these relationships half-heartedly,' he warned them. 'If one partner's British and the other Maltese and you want to live in Malta, it's better to embrace the whole thing, culture, religion – and marriage.'

Giorgio grinned at the older man reassuringly. 'I'd marry Judith if I could. I cannot, so we make our own rules.'

Richard sighed. 'If you think that, you're barmy.'

He was right, Judith found out. Although Giorgio moved into her flat after a few months, it turned out that they always worked around the rules of others, a sort of open secret. Giorgio did arrange a meeting at the flat with his parents Maria and Agnello but they stayed only a couple of minutes to point out that Giorgio was married to

Johanna and that Judith was a divorced woman before walking out with cold looks cast Judith's way.

Giorgio saw his daughters, Alexia and Lydia frequently, but Judith was never invited along and she never tried to invite herself.

The only member of Giorgio's family who acknowledged their relationship was Giorgio's aunt Cass, whose husband Saviour was Agnello's brother. She had a soft heart and Giorgio was a favourite nephew so she met them occasionally for quiet meals of pasta and red wine. 'I understand the situation,' she kept assuring Judith.

But their evenings out together were always well away from Sliema.

# Chapter One

*April 2004*

Tired of listening to a mechanical woman's patient explanation, *The phone you are trying to reach may be switched off. Please leave a message . . .* Judith McAllister tossed her mobile phone onto a low table and prowled out into the heat on the open balcony to stare at the early-evening light dancing on the water of Sliema Creek.

The creek, one of those deep fingers of sea that cuts into Malta's coastline, reflected the intense blue of the sky just before it darkened to dusk. Red-and-white ferryboats shimmied lazily, returned from their day excursions around the island or to the sister islands of Gozo and Comino and emptied of early summer tourists. Those tourists had probably all gone straight to the aluminium tables beneath the yellow or blue umbrellas of the pavement cafés to cool off with a chilled Cisk beer.

Although the sun was sinking behind the building, the summer had begun early in Malta and the heat was intense. Judith wasn't much of a sun-worshipper now. In her twenties and thirties she'd basked at every opportunity but maybe wisdom had come with maturity and now, at forty-four, she was wary of blistered skin or pounding headaches.

The Strand, the teeming road between herself and the boats, was busy with cars, orange buses, and *karrozzini* – Malta's traditional horse-drawn carriages. She gazed down into the street, half expecting to see Giorgio demonstrating his knack of parking his bright red MG in impossibly tight spaces. A glance at her watch told her he was much later than expected.

She'd rushed home from work two hours ago but found their flat empty and silent. After showering, she'd slipped into a floaty dress the colour of bluebells and dried her dark hair so that it lay sleek over her shoulders. Still no Giorgio. Maybe he'd stopped for a drink with his mates?

She turned her head and narrowed her eyes to gaze inland up the creek towards the bridge to Manoel Island, the smaller boats bobbing at cheery red or yellow buoys and the luxury cruisers, the 'gin palaces', moored behind the bridge in the yacht marina. She suspected Giorgio was deliberately late. He'd been irritated that she'd worked this afternoon when he wanted her to go scuba diving.

'But it's Saturday, and I have the air!' he'd complained, indicating the newly filled silver oxygen cylinders, dark eyes indignant. 'This dive has been arranged for a week. We have good weather.' She'd recently introduced Giorgio to scuba diving and he was showing the beginner's impatience to be underwater all the time; go further, deeper, push the limits of his Open Water diving qualification without bothering with further training.

She'd stroked his thick, dark hair, satin against her skin. 'It's a pain on your weekend off. But they're important clients, Giorgio. We've been wooing them for months so

I can't let Richard down by missing the meeting. It's not his fault they had to reschedule.' Giorgio was well aware she'd invested part of her savings, including her divorce settlement, into Richard Elliot Estate. Almost all that had been left had recently gone into Giorgio's business, Sliema Z Bus Tours, but even that wasn't enough to prevent him from occasionally testing her commitment to Richard. Giorgio wanted always to be first in Judith's life. He was like a boy, thinking he could get his own way if he pushed her hard enough, smiling into her eyes and trying to charm her. She'd pressed a soft kiss to his lips. 'We can dive on Sunday. The sea will still be there.'

His eyes had softened as he'd accepted her kisses but he'd refused to miss the dive he'd set his heart on. 'No, because I work this Sunday. If you work Saturday then Charlie Galea will be my diving buddy.'

Alarm had lanced through Judith. 'He's not much more experienced than you, Giorgio—'

He'd kissed her again. 'We're both qualified to Open Water Diver, Judith.'

'But so inexperienced—' Her words had been lost in laughter as he smothered each one of her objections with a kiss.

Now, Judith sighed as she watched the small, neat horses whisking their tails in the shafts of the *karrozzini*. Apart from her instincts rebelling at the thought of novice divers buddying up with no experienced diver nearby, her own opportunity to dive this weekend had probably gone. Giorgio would have let Charlie use her air and he'd be working tomorrow, when Judith was free.

The sun had been a demon in Sliema today. She would have loved to escape it by sinking into her beloved, beautiful, hushed turquoise world of weightlessness, to revel in the water gliding coolly into her wetsuit and skin as she signalled all-OK to Giorgio and their bubbles fizzed around them. It was magical to descend slowly over a drop-off to where schools of fish darted like shining rainbows.

Scuba diving was all the more fun now Giorgio had qualified and they could dive together. Even decompression halts had become a pleasure. The cobalt-blue panels of her wetsuit entwined with the scarlet of his as they hung together in the water to watch elongated beams of light filtering down from the surface.

She let her eyes half-close as she enjoyed the memory of combined body warmth and water chill.

Curling her bare toes away from the hot concrete of the balcony, she wandered back indoors to the shady kitchen. The windows stood wide open in an attempt to release the hot air of the oven that contained a kept-warm-for-too-long lasagne.

An open bottle of red wine waited on the worktop. She poured herself a second glass and returned to the sitting room to try Giorgio's phone again. *The phone you are trying to reach . . .*

A fat lot of use that was, she thought.

Restlessly, she prowled back into the living area, pausing before the mirror to fidget with the layers of her dress, selected to complement her golden-brown eyes and the nutty highlights in her hair. Then, after slotting a CD of smoochy songs into the player, she sank into a chair, her bare feet cooling pleasantly on the tiled floor, her head tipping comfortably back. 'Giorgio's playing bloody games, Judith,' she said to herself.

He probably thought she'd be too pleased to see him when he finally sauntered in to be angry. He'd press his body to hers and emphasise his displeasure at being abandoned today in a teasing way. 'So, now the work is finished and you have time for Giorgio?' And suddenly being with him would be more important than making complaints about where he'd been until now.

That's how it was. Being with him was always more important than everything else.

The entry system intercom buzzed, jarring Judith out of her thoughts. She jumped up and she reached for the handset. 'Giorgio, I thought you were never coming! Have you forgotten your key?'

A hesitation. Then, 'Judith, it is Charlie Galea. Can I speak with you?'

Her heart raced at the sound of Charlie's voice. Wondering whether Giorgio was ill, she said, 'Of course, Charlie. Come up.' She pressed the button to release the front door.

Charlie Galea was just younger than Giorgio, thinner and taller. He lived with his wife and three small children in San Gwann, behind Gzira and Ta' Xbiex. She knew him a little; he was another recent addition to the diving fraternity, hanging out at the same bars as her and Giorgio after dives.

Footsteps sounded on the concrete stairs and then Charlie stepped through her pale-green front door and into the entrance area that opened out into the other rooms, his black shorts and flip-flops dusty, dark curls coarse with dried salt water.

He was drawn and ill at ease as she showed him into the sitting room where he could sit down, looking horribly uncomfortable. She wondered suddenly whether Giorgio was drunk and had sent gullible young Charlie Galea to make his excuses. Or perhaps to fetch Judith, so that

Giorgio could sparkle his eyes at her and urge her to join the fun.

'Coffee?' she offered tentatively.

He shook his head. Cleared his throat. Then, unexpectedly, slid a hand across his eyes.

Silence.

Despite the heat of the summer day, Judith felt a chill slither around her. Was Charlie *crying*? She forced her lips to form words. 'What's the matter?'

The young man sucked in a deep, shuddering breath. 'There was an accident, today. With Giorgio.'

Her heart lurched. Judith sat forward, fists balling, heart pummelling her ribcage from the inside. 'How bad?' she managed.

He shook his head, sniffing 'Very bad. There was a jet ski—'

Her stomach tossed like a pancake. 'Oh no!'

The story came tumbling out as Charlie fought tears in order to speak and his command of English faltered. 'There was plenty of sea for everyone. Anchored there was a cruiser but not close to shore. We see it before we go down.

'Under the water, we hear engines as we come up, but we are at the end of our air, waiting at three metres to decompress. We are well within the fifty-metre zone and we send up our marker buoys already. We are safe to surface, we think.' He wiped his face with his T-shirt, his eyes wide and hopeless. 'But there were two jet ski, put in the water from the cruiser maybe. They move so quick, right inside the reef. Giorgio, he surface first . . .'

Judith gasped. Horrific images flashed into her mind: Giorgio mown back under, his respirator torn from his mouth as the roaring beast of the jet ski bounced across the water and too close to shore, ignoring the significance of the colourful surface marker buoys that should have told them there were divers below.

Her heart beating in her throat, she jumped to her feet. 'He's alive?'

Charlie nodded. 'But bad.'

'I should have been there.' She was the more experienced diver. She would have heard and understood whether the telltale buzz of engines was near enough to be a danger. 'Is he in St Luke's hospital, at Gwardamanga?' She tried to control her breathing so she could hear Charlie's reply.

He nodded again, coughing back his tears. 'The helicopter take him.'

Giorgio was alive. He'd reached medical help. That was what mattered. She began to cast around for shoes, her bag. 'I must go to him.'

Charlie climbed to his feet, his eyes enormous with apprehension. 'They say no.' Then, when Judith didn't respond, '*Judith*, they say *no*.'

Her movements slowed. Stilled. The world went quiet apart from a mosquito-like whine in her ears. She sank back down, bonelessly, into her chair. 'Who does?' she whispered. As if she didn't know.

'His wife. His mother. They ask the hospital to make sure you are kept out. You are not family, you not visit, they say.'

'No!' she cried. 'They can't do that.'

But they could. That much became all-too-painfully obvious.

Until the accident Judith hadn't completely appreciated the strength of Giorgio's family's feelings. She'd told herself his parents were old stick-in-the-muds and it was their

24

problem if they refused to acknowledge her; the relationship could go on without their approval. And her existence shouldn't cause too much pain to Giorgio's wife Johanna because it had been years since they'd lived together.

But now the depth of the antipathy towards her became stark.

The family refused to acknowledge that her place was with Giorgio and instructed the hospital not to let her visit and to refuse her calls.

Judith's pleas and demands for admittance to intensive care got her nothing but pleasant, firm blocking from medical staff. 'I'm so sorry. Family only.'

She called twice at his parents' house in an attempt to negotiate, willing to do anything, say anything, to make them let her in to see him. But no one answered her knock at the front door.

She went to Giorgio's aunt Cass, relying on her gentle heart, but even she was unable to help this time. 'I dare not. I cannot,' she told Judith, compassion and grief mixing in her dark eyes. She smoothed Judith's hair. 'It's too difficult at the moment. If Saviour found out I'd interfered he'd be furious. I'm sorry, Judith. But Maria and Agnello . . .' She hesitated. 'They're adamant that it's your fault. You introduced Giorgio to diving, then abandoned him to an inexperienced partner. You could have kept him safe. They say this over and over and tell Giorgio how you have let him down.'

Judith couldn't bring herself to protest because ever since Charlie had broken the news, the same thoughts had whirled through her head. She should have found a way to stop Giorgio diving with another novice. She could have shouted or screamed or cried. *Made* him wait.

Damned well made him.

Giorgio had only just been certified. Judith was qualified to divemaster status and was trained in first aid and rescue. She knew how to limit the damage in bad situations.

Responsibility and guilt rose up in her throat to choke her. 'Tell him I love him. Make sure you tell him, won't you, Cass? And that I should never have let him dive without me. Try to make him listen.'

'I'll tell him,' Cass promised. She hesitated. 'But I don't know if he will hear.'

'Doesn't he ask for me?' Judith cried.

Wordlessly, Cass shook her head. 'He is too ill.' Or he'd fallen for his family's line that she was somehow responsible for him going diving without her steadying presence.

Helpless, Judith went through the motions of her life, barely eating, hardly sleeping. Mechanically, she pinned on her professional smile each day while she showed people apartments and extolled the virtues of roof terraces.

Richard proved to be her rock in a suddenly heaving world. 'You take some time off if you need it,' he said. But she took none because the agency was busy in the summer and what would she do with time? Go hospital visiting? Hardly.

The *Times of Malta* printed the full story of the diving accident: the slow process of Charlie getting help, Giorgio being airlifted to hospital as time filtered away. Journalists explained about the first 'Golden Hour' when treatment to head injuries is most effective.

Almost unbelievably, the jet skier responsible had raced away in the wake of the accident, obviously frightened of being brought to book, and nobody had got the name of his boat. There was a new outcry against jet skis in letters to the editor and diving clubs made statements both of caution and reassurance.

Judith winced at a counter outcry about novice divers. Was it fair to blame only the jet skier? Had the diver had adequate instruction? How about supervision whilst experience was gained? Desperately sick in the heart, night after night in her silent flat she tortured herself by reading every letter and column inch. She didn't tell her family back home in England what had happened. Her mum Wilma would worry herself sick in her retirement home, her sister Molly might offer to come out to 'help' – which would mean try to boss Judith about as she was eight years older and acted it. But Judith just wanted to be left alone to grieve. She couldn't even make herself call Kieran and face his grief for Giorgio, who he'd plainly liked and admired.

After four weeks, she began to realise that there were other things to worry about and, at Richard's prodding, drove to where Sliema met Msida to see Giorgio's business partners, Anton Dimech and Gordon Cassar. The small, over-filled office of Sliema Z Bus Tours was on the end of the large, low shed that housed the buses and she parked in the yard, conscious of an accelerated heartbeat. She barely knew Anton and Gordon but something told her they might not welcome a request for a business update. Her investment in Sliema Z had been an informal arrangement made between her and Giorgio to help buy two new buses to capitalise on ever-growing tourism in Malta.

'Hello?' Anton and Gordon said when she knocked on the office door and strode inside. They looked surprised, even astonished, to see her.

She drew on her people skills and pasted on a smile. 'Good morning.' She sat down and gripped her bag to prevent her hands from shaking in the overheated office, where open windows did little to relieve the oppressive heat. 'I'm sorry to bother you at this awful time. You must be busier than ever in Giorgio's absence.' She waited out the following silence, making it plain that she expected them to take part in a conversation.

Gordon was the first to blink. He was a small man, the more pleasant of the two men, with black-framed glasses and coppery lights through untidy hair. He smiled. 'Of course, we have plans to cope with the unexpected absence of a partner, you need not worry—'

Anton made a shushing gesture and spoke much more formally. 'Madam, what is your enquiry?'

She swallowed, the steeliness of Anton's gaze an uncomfortable reminder that he was used to being in control. He was the one the others deferred to, with his push and focus and faultless English. She cursed herself for not getting Gordon on his own. She might have steered him into giving her information. 'As an investor, I thought it was reasonable to ask—'

'Madam, we appreciate your investment. I can assure you that Giorgio's absence will not affect it.'

She was infuriated by such cold courtesy but, sacrificing the quest for business information, she got to the real reason she was there. 'And how is Giorgio?' She hated to hear herself ask, she who'd shared a bed with Giorgio every night and should now be beside him in the hospital.

Anton cut off the reply Gordon had opened his mouth to make. 'His family will have the most accurate news, madam. The business you can leave safely in our hands.'

Her throat dried, making it impossible to do more than poke out her chin against the humiliation of her reception and nod her curtest goodbye.

She returned to work, shuffling her car into a small parking space and walking the last part. Richard looked up as soon as she stepped into the air-conditioned interior. 'How did you get on?' His kind eyes were troubled.

A lump leapt into Judith's throat. 'They blanked me. Told me to leave the business to them and approach the family for news about Giorgio.' She half-fell into her chair to stare out at the traffic and the creek beyond, feeling powerless.

After a pause, Richard said, 'Your investment should have been put on a proper footing.'

'Yes,' she agreed listlessly. 'Thank goodness for my job at the agency.' At least here, she had Richard, his quiet support preventing her from racing to St Luke's Hospital and hurtling at the doors of the intensive care ward.

She saw no option but to wait for Giorgio to contact her once he was well enough.

The wait went on for weeks. At night she played every nightmare scenario in her head and during the day she called and visited the hospital in the hope of finding someone who wouldn't block her enquiries.

Eventually, after several attempts, she persuaded Cass to meet her in a café in St Julian's, a tiny front room of a place where Cass seemed to feel tucked away from curious eyes. A bead fly-curtain clicked softly in the doorway and the serene young lady behind the little counter hummed under her breath as she put out trays of fresh arancini, balls of rice filled with cheese or bolognese sauce.

On the pale-green table stood two glass cups of cappuccino. Cass lifted hers elegantly and pursed her lips to sip. Her dress was smart, her hair carefully done.

'News?' Judith poked her teaspoon into her froth, too strung-up to even stir properly. 'I read in the paper that he's out of intensive care.' Judith leant closer, as if she could haul Cass's knowledge, her feelings and impressions into herself by sheer proximity. 'So how does he seem? When did you see him last? What are the changes? What do the doctors say? Hasn't he asked for me?'

Sipping again, Cass raised her pencil-arched tan eyebrows sadly into hennaed hair. '*Everything* about Giorgio is changed. There is no energy, no smile, no laugh, no joke to make you smile, no endless conversation. It is a completely different Giorgio.'

Hope sank and settled low in Judith's stomach. 'But he no longer needs intensive care?'

'He has stabilised,' Cass acknowledged, sighing, and shaking her head.

'And has he . . . has he asked for me?' Judith persisted. It seemed fantastic to her that he was lying in bed only a few miles away and hadn't got a message to her, even if his family had secreted his mobile phone.

Another sigh. An aching silence. 'He's not going to.' Cass's voice was very kind. 'If it had happened, don't you think I would've found a way to let you know? To leave a message at your office? You're torturing yourself, Judith.'

Judith tried to lift her cup but her hand shook and her voice came out as a whine. 'I must see him! I might not exist for his parents, but I can't just suddenly stop existing for him.'

Compassionate tears stood in Cass's eyes. 'I'm so sorry. But you do need to accept that Giorgio will never ask for you again. He's too injured. Too changed.'

Judith clenched her hands into fists, making her voice as urgent as she knew how. 'But I must try.'

# Chapter Two

OK. Cass had confirmed it: he was out of intensive care.

Out from behind the locked doors.

Judith demanded and pleaded for Cass's help and finally they arranged a visit when siesta made the streets emptier, the Maltese summer sun blazing down on yellow limestone buildings. Cass told Judith a quiet way to Giorgio's ward then stayed outside to keep watch. Judith was so thankful that the older woman had agreed to help her to see Giorgio that she pushed aside what it would mean for Cass if Maria and Agnello Zammit knew she was a closet Judith-sympathiser. Her whole attention was focused on hurrying in through the hospital entrance.

Inside, the corridors were cool and quiet. Judith stole along, following Cass's directions, avoiding nurse's stations and trying to look as if she had every right to be where she was.

She turned the final corner and there was his name hand-written onto a tile on a door.

*Giorgio Zammit.*

Her heart somersaulted.

He had a room of his own. When she edged to one side of the open doorway she could see him! He lay on his side, his back to her. He was hooked up to a heartbreaking array of machines but she recognised the way his hair lay at his nape and the gold of his skin.

The open window fluttered the yellow curtains, the bed a white island in the centre of the room. Two nurses and a woman in a white coat attended the bed, selecting dressings from a trolley, talking soothingly to Giorgio in gentle Maltese.

Slowly, she stepped back. Giorgio was receiving necessary care. A seat stood a few yards up the corridor within sight of Giorgio's door and she withdrew to wait.

Ten minutes became twenty, then thirty before the nurses finally emerged, gliding the trolley up the corridor, passing Judith as she sat frozen, holding her breath in case they asked what she was doing there. Instead, they moved on to a different white room and another patient. With a soaring heart, Judith jumped up and hurried towards Giorgio's room.

But then she saw a Maltese couple barrelling towards his door from the other direction. The woman's lips were set, eyes blazing. They'd only met once, but Judith had no trouble recognising Giorgio's possessive, hostile parents. Maria and Agnello Zammit.

She halted like a guilty child.

Furious words began to stream from Maria Zammit in rapid fire, her chest heaving beneath her sedate navy belted dress, her voice a frustrated hiss as a concession to the hush of the wards. 'No! Get away! *Away!* Not you here, you, no!'

Judith pitched her own voice low. 'Mrs Zammit, I was only—'

Maria Zammit thrust her short body between Judith and the door to Giorgio's room. 'No! He not speak to you, you go. Leave.' And then, as Judith hesitated. '*Now!* You never see my son. You English. Go England!'

'I love him,' Judith tried, struck by despair so intense that it seemed to suck away her oxygen. She glanced at Agnello Zammit, whose forehead was furrowed unhappily as he laid his hand on his wife's arm and spoke to her in their own language.

Mrs Zammit shook him off. 'Go! I call for the *ners*.'

The ridiculous notion that a mere nurse would scare her away returned Judith to reality. She was tempted to fold her arms and challenge, 'Ha! You do that!'

But she hesitated. Anger wasn't the only emotion in Maria Zammit. A muscle was tugging at the older woman's cheek and a tremor at her lip. 'Go,' she repeated, the tic jumping more fiercely. Judith was considerably the taller of the two but Giorgio's mother didn't give an inch, evidently a tiger when it came to doing what she believed protected her family.

Family was important to Giorgio, too. Judith's conscience twinged because she knew how he'd hate this confrontation. The parents he loved and respected were making his decisions for him, holding all the authority. If Judith wanted to get in to see him, she was going to have to think strategically.

She made her voice calm, although her heartbeat was shaking her entire body. 'I'll go away – after you let me see him. On my own.'

Mrs Zammit snorted. Her husband muttered something.

Calmly, Judith added, 'If not, I'll just keep coming back.'

A tear slowly escaped from one of Mrs Zammit's dark eyes but she showed Judith gritted teeth. 'You teach him to dive under the water. He nearly die. Is because of you! All know this.'

Judith's face drained. Fruitless to protest that Giorgio was an adult who had made all his own decisions about diving because Judith blamed herself every bit as much as the Zammits blamed her. 'If I could change places with him, I would. Please, Mrs Zammit.'

Silence.

Judith dug her nails into her palms, staring at Giorgio's mother, willing her to comply. See sense. Judge the long-term benefit against a five-minute concession.

'You are not his wife,' Mrs Zammit pointed out unnecessarily.

'No. And I'll bet his wife doesn't visit him much, does she? I'll bet she's just signed what forms were necessary and left him here alone.' Such a waste when all the time Judith herself was aching to be by Giorgio's side.

Agnello Zammit made another remark to his wife, softly, palms up and shoulders shrugging. An older Giorgio. His voice went on, gentle, musical; Judith couldn't make out enough words to know whether he was arguing for her or against.

An angry glitter brightened Mrs Zammit's eyes but finally she demanded, 'You go away? Stay away?'

Judith nodded, every muscle willing Giorgio's mother to concede.

Mrs Zammit's lips thinned. 'Five minute!' she allowed eventually, folding her arms. 'He not talk to you. I know this.'

Tears spilled out onto Judith's cheeks and she wiped them away with her palms. Her skin was dry and lined to the touch and she felt a pang that she hadn't made more of an effort before coming to see Giorgio. Lately,

34

she hadn't been taking care of herself, not as she used to. Hand cream and moisturiser hadn't figured in her routine. Her mirror this morning had shown her a woman who was usually reasonably attractive but was no longer bothering, her hair grown out of style and sliding over one eye like a Disney dog.

Relief shook in her voice. 'Five minutes.' She almost ran the final few steps to Giorgio's room and shot through the door before Mrs Zammit could think better of her decision. Then she paused, taking in the stillness of the sickroom.

In the quiet, a machine hissed and peeped. Wires. Tubes. White bedlinen, yellow curtains. The combined smells of antiseptic and body odour. Outside, the distant sounds of a vehicle straining up the hill towards the hospital.

Giorgio, still lying on his side, didn't look up as she walked around the bed. She halted as she caught the peculiar expression on his face, the twist to his lips that wasn't a smile. The dressing above his eyes – eyes that stared unseeing.

For a moment she couldn't speak, sickened by his appearance. Though she'd been warned, somehow she hadn't let herself expect this level of change in him. His face had softened and sagged, although he'd lost weight. He had a jowly, loose look that sent him abruptly forward in years. Though the truth of what she was seeing hit her straight away she still tried to catch his dark gaze, willing him to focus on her face. 'Giorgio?' she whispered. '*Giorgio!*'

But, as Mrs Zammit had forecast, Giorgio didn't reply. Because he couldn't. That's what nobody had explicitly said. He was on some deep, unreachable level of unconsciousness. She took his bare arm, feeling the softness of

35

the hair at his wrist. His flesh felt hot and unresponsive. Even when Judith increased her grip slightly, he remained silent, his face still. The silver that had brushed his hair lately glinted in the light. Surely he must react to her touch when such electricity used to crackle between them? Something? 'Darling,' she whispered. He twitched, as if to shrug her off.

Aware of Maria Zammit gazing in balefully through the glass aperture, Judith stroked his hair. 'I'm sorry you were so badly hurt,' she murmured, her voice catching on her grief. 'I should've stopped you diving without me, it was too soon for your level of experience. I can't sleep for guilt. Forgive me.' He twitched more violently, as if he *really* wished she'd remove her hand. Reluctantly, she dropped his wrist and backed off, her head flooding with images of their time together. His lips at her throat, his body over hers . . .

Where had it all gone? All lost in Giorgio's blank-eyed gaze.

Mrs Zammit opened the door sharply and entered the room, breaking the spell.

Unspeaking, feet dragging, Judith made her way from the room, passing silently between Giorgio's parents. The door closed heavily behind her.

Spinning, she fled. Through long corridors. Down stone staircases, treads worn with age. Striding out into the heat like the backwash from an open oven. *Giorgio hadn't known her. He didn't know anything.*

Cass materialised from behind a couple of parked cars, her face lined with anxiety. 'Judith! Maria and Agnello came early – I had no time to warn you in case they spotted me.'

'Don't worry. I didn't tell them you were here.' Sagging

against the wall, her bones turning to mush, Judith closed her eyes. 'I hadn't realised quite how . . . You were right, I should've stayed away. I'm sorry I hounded you into this, Cass. He didn't know me. He doesn't know anybody, does he? He's just . . . *blank*.'

Cass patted her shoulder. 'I told you, you expect something that can't be there – the old Giorgio, his old feelings. Trust me. It would have been better to have just kept your memories.'

Judith opened her eyes and gazed sightlessly at the china-blue sky. 'But how could I have just written him off?' When there was no reply, straightening slowly, she hugged Cass. 'Thanks for helping me, even if it wasn't any use.' She choked out a sob. 'At least I know now. There's nothing left for me here.'

# Chapter Three

In a very few days, Judith had her life all shut down ready to leave Malta. It wasn't that she was keeping her promise to Maria Zammit to 'Go England!' but Malta just wasn't bearable now that she no longer had Giorgio, his smile, his love, the feeling of being alive in his arms.

Even though she'd loved her time here, adored the golden island set in the sparkling Mediterranean and the heat, the sea, the people, without Giorgio . . . it was no longer the same. Everywhere she looked held a painful memory.

Richard had been incredibly kind, accommodating her frantic need to go home without a murmur. She'd called Molly last night, telling her that she was coming home and would explain when she got there.

On the flight back to England she was silent, ignoring the seat in front pressing against her knees, unable to bring herself to chat with the red-skinned tourist couple next to her who loudly mourned the end of their holiday. Judith gazed out of the window, scarcely seeing the clouds, the sea, the mountains. Eventually, the aircraft descended towards the green and yellow fields of England and the jumbled grey buildings and roads that surrounded Gatwick airport.

It had to be bloody Gatwick, she thought. Luton, Stansted, East Midlands and Birmingham airports were all within an hour or so of Brinham, but the travel shop had only been able to get her a reasonably priced flight to bloody Gatwick on the bloody wrong side of London, though the Maltese clerk's dark eyes had been sympathetic. He knew, she'd supposed; half of Sliema knew Giorgio.

A long journey to Northamptonshire was just another problem.

She and Giorgio had always faced problems: Giorgio was younger than Judith. Giorgio was Maltese and Judith was English. Giorgio was Catholic, Judith was nothing in particular. Judith was divorced, Giorgio . . . well, Giorgio wasn't.

She closed her eyes as the plane descended, remembering his smile as he held her, kissed her, insisting that none of it mattered, it could all be managed, none of it was as important as they were.

And, in the end, he'd been proved right, in a way. There was no longer a 'they' and, therefore, none of the rest mattered.

She eased her seat belt over her sage trousers, chosen for the flight because they were loose and comfortable – although her entire wardrobe was fairly roomy, nowadays.

The plane went through an unhappy landing, its engine note rising and falling and a crosswind rocking the fuselage. The tourist couple became white and sweaty instead of red and sweaty as the aircraft yawed its way through bumpy air.

Watching England rushing up to meet her, Judith

swallowed to equalise the pressure in her ears but felt no threat to her stomach contents because she hadn't eaten. For the last two months, weight had dropped away and now her arms were like sticks on the blue plastic armrests.

The plane eventually beat the crosswind and landed with a spine-jarring bump, engines howling into reverse. Finally, they were taxiing, stopping, passengers rising, jostling, talking, reaching up to empty their lockers.

Judith dawdled over collecting her possessions so that the aisle was empty when she stepped from the aircraft, then shuffled along endless corridors and stairs to queue at passport control before moving into baggage reclaim, her jacket over one shoulder, passing the waiting-at-the-carousel time thinking about how it was going to be to live back in Brinham.

In her mind's eye, she conjured up the leafy, hilly market town in Northamptonshire, in the centre of England. She'd been brought up there and had been contentedly making a career of being a single woman until she met big, brusque, older but surprisingly ardent Tom McAllister. She'd fallen in love with Tom and with dear, sweet Kieran, his son. Tom's first wife, Pamela, had died young and Kieran was delighted for Judith to step into her place. They'd been a happy family for nine years, until Judith had realised Tom couldn't have been all *that* happy because he'd fallen for a woman she'd never met, someone Tom's company had worked for: Liza. It had half-killed Judith to no longer live with Kieran but he'd been almost grown up and, despite his sorrow, he'd seen there was little option but a rapid divorce. By the time that was over he'd been at uni. Judith had quit England early in the new century, convinced of the need to strike out, to *go*. She wished she was now as convinced about coming home.

Her elder sister Molly and her husband Frankie were waiting at the barriers when she battled out through the green channel dragging a stubborn trolley piled high with unmatched suitcases. Molly was much smaller than Judith and at fifty-two was becoming plump, her black hair sporting Morticia Addams-like streaks of silver as it spilled down the back of her red coat. Taller and skinnier, hairline receding, Frankie O'Malley waited at his wife's side, hands on hips, eyes impatient under his dome of a forehead.

'Here she is!' Molly, although sounding pleased, still somehow managed to frown.

Frankie fished out his car keys. 'All right, Judith?' he said laconically.

'Fine, thanks,' she answered just as briefly. Although Frankie took the trolley from her and Molly fell into step by her side, Judith noticed that there were no delighted smiles or hugs to welcome her home, no anxious enquiries. If she'd expected a demonstration of sisterly love, she was unlucky, but Molly wasn't demonstrative by nature and had no way of knowing how much Judith needed hugs right now.

They'd parked in the drab concrete block that was the short-stay car park. Once they'd settled in the car and Frankie had navigated them through the car park and the motorway approach, Molly twisted around within her seat belt. 'So, you're home for good?'

'Whatever good is.' From the rear seat, Judith craned back to look at the fat silver belly of a jet taking off over the M25.

'Where are you going to live? And what on?' Molly's eyes were full of compassion but also a healthy elder-sister readiness to remedy Judith's problems with a dose of good advice.

The plane above banked steeply, white now as its topside came into view, and Judith fell into the younger-sister trap of self-justification. 'I'll live in my house, the one I bought after the divorce. Uncle Richard will be paying my dividends on the shares I own in Richard Elliot Estate, so that'll get me by for a while. He's also selling my car for me, subletting my flat and shipping the last of my stuff on.'

Possessions. What did possessions matter? She'd lost Giorgio.

Her heart clenched.

Sudden, unanticipated doubts sent sweat bursting across her forehead. Should she have left? Perhaps if she'd persisted, sneaking in to see Giorgio, talking to him, forcing herself to his attention, perhaps she could've eventually made his eyes brighten beneath his thick brush of hair, regard her with their old love . . .

Molly's anxious voice sliced into Judith's fantasising. Molly was good at what was known in Northamptonshire as 'whittling', which meant worrying too enthusiastically. 'How can you live in your house? What about your tenant?'

Judith shrugged impatiently, wishing Molly would stop making her think of practicalities. Time enough for that later. Time. Loads of time, now. 'He'll have to go, I suppose.'

Molly glanced around again, looking sceptical. 'Can you just get rid of him, on a whim?'

Frankie flicked on the indicator and swung into the outside lane, rushing up behind an old Metro and flashing his lights. 'I think she can if it's for her own occupation,' he put in. 'With notice. Might depend on the tenancy agreement. I'll find out if you want, Judith.'

Judith yawned and wondered if they'd stop asking questions if she pretended to sleep. She didn't need Frankie to find out the terms of a standard assured shorthold tenancy agreement for her; she'd just spent four years working in an estate agency, even if it wasn't in the UK, and anyway was well aware of her rights and her responsibilities regarding her own tenant. Still, Frankie's offer was well-meant, even if it did hint that he didn't think Judith capable of knowing how to be a landlord. She answered calmly, 'The law is that I have to give him two months' notice, but I'm sure he'll respond to a cash incentive to look for somewhere quicker than that. My friend Melanie found him for me when the last tenants left – he's a mate of her husband. We've emailed – he seems a nice bloke.' She didn't bother mentioning that she vividly remembered Adam Leblond from school, being fifteen when he was seventeen or eighteen and trying to get him to notice her. Lots of girls had wanted to be noticed by Adam Leblond. Molly, like Frankie and Tom, was too old to have been at school at the same time as Judith and Adam.

Frankie snorted. 'Being a "nice bloke" don't mean much if he's in your house when you want to live there.'

She let her head tilt sideways to rest against the window. 'Pity he's always been a good tenant. Bad tenants only get notice of two weeks.'

Molly swung around in her seat yet again, aghast. 'But you wouldn't have wanted a bad tenant, Judith! Friends of ours let to students and they treated the house like a squat. Disgusting, honestly.'

Judith felt her shoulders move in a silent laugh but didn't risk offending Molly by pointing out that her remark had been an attempt at a grim joke. Molly took life seriously. Earnestly, she went on, 'Judith, you wouldn't have been there to take control if things had gone wrong and I wouldn't have wanted to take it on. Frankie's too busy.

43

Tom might've been persuaded, of course, if he was in a good mood,' she said reflectively. 'But it would be a bit much to ask him now you and him aren't married . . .'

'I'd hardly ask Tom to deal with my tenant for me,' Judith observed mildly. 'You're worrying about something that never happened, Molly.'

Frankie swerved into the middle lane to overtake on the wrong side, making Judith's head tap uncomfortably against the glass. She shifted her position.

Molly grabbed the handle on the inside of the door as Frankie raced on to jink the car around a Land Rover. 'Of course. Well, you're welcome to our spare room for as long as it takes,' she added. She didn't sound exactly enthusiastic.

Judith shut her eyes. Molly and Frankie's spare room. She'd tried not to think about it too much until now. Leaving the Giorgio-pain behind and that last sight of him had been her priority. But now she made herself envision the not-quite-a-double room with a single bed and a wardrobe full of the overspill from their son Edwin's old room, tennis rackets and one-man tents, remnants and reminders of his childhood that Molly refused to throw out. Edwin was thirty-three now and lived in Scotland with a girl his parents scarcely knew because he didn't seem family minded. It was doubtful that he'd be back to claim his tent and go camping with the scouts any time soon.

Frankie, like Tom, was a builder. Their house was one he had built himself in the mid-eighties, steeply gabled and the window frames painted forest green. It always looked to Judith like part of a Tesco supermarket. A good big property, roomy, it had four bedrooms. Of these, Molly and Frankie's enormous bedroom was the most impressive, with an en suite bathroom plus a dressing room. The other big room, over the double garage, was Frankie's office, permanently strewn with paper and drawings of extensions. And then there was 'Edwin's room', which Molly kept as it had been when he left it to go to university in 1989, the bed covered with a marbled blue quilt and the grey carpet vacuumed every week. Judith would've liked to be offered Edwin's room because it was pleasant and spacious and had an en suite bathroom, but it seemed the modest spare room was as good an offer as she was going to get.

Maybe she ought to have booked into a B&B. The prospect gained in appeal as she mulled it over and the car swayed and swerved with Frankie's aggressive driving style. Would Molly be offended? Or relieved? She tried to envisage her life as a guest. Was Molly still grumpy in the mornings? Would Frankie feel he couldn't relax and be himself with Judith there? Or, worse still, that he could? He might wear a gaping dressing gown and scratch sweaty bits of himself.

However, against expectations, when they arrived, Judith was pleasantly surprised to discover that Molly had emptied the wardrobe in the spare room. The furniture smelled of lemon Pledge and the fresh peach bed linen of fabric conditioner. By the time all Judith's bags were in the room – carried ultra-carefully up the stairs so as not to mark the new wallpaper – the floor area had shrunk dramatically. Hemmed in by her possessions, she felt a massive heave of homesickness for her own place. The comfortable rooms of her flat on The Strand, the balcony scorched by the sun and overlooking the rippling blue of Sliema Creek and across the harbour to the curtain walls of Valletta rising from the sea. The double bed in the shaded bedroom at the back.

Bit late for those thoughts. Uncle Richard or one of her capable cousins would have her flat sublet in days. She yanked her thoughts away from Sliema and made an effort not to be ungracious. 'Sorry to put you out like this, Moll. I'm disrupting your life, aren't I?'

'Oh well,' shrugged Molly. But her curranty black eyes sharpened. 'Of course, it's been a bit of a bombshell, I'll be honest with you. A phone call yesterday – then today, you're here, bag and baggage.'

She waited, her eyebrows raised. At Judith's silence, she reached behind herself and pushed the door closed to signify that Judith could speak in confidence. Or that neither of them would be leaving the room until a bucket of guts had been spilled.

With a sigh of resignation, Judith sank down on the bed. Some degree of explanation was due to her sister for Judith turning up, leaving her life, her job, the place that had been home for the past four years to dump herself on Molly. It was just that talking about it was going to make it all the more raw.

Molly folded her arms and her face settled into lines that said, '*I could've told you something like this was going to happen.*' She edged closer. 'Is it that man you've been mixed up with? Gino?' Molly hadn't approved of Judith living with a man so much her junior and so Judith had never invited her to meet him, or brought him to the UK.

'Giorgio.'

'Jaw-joe, then. Has it all ended?'

Judith tried to explain her snap decision to flee. 'There didn't seem to be much future for us because . . .' Her voice dried in her throat.

Molly sighed – in exasperation rather than sympathy. 'All that business with his family you told me about, I

46

suppose? Or did he find someone more his own age? I know you've never quite lost that angular, schoolgirl look that means you don't look your age but a gap always seems more when it's the woman who's the oldest, doesn't it?'

Judith winced. 'Neither of those things. I don't really want to talk about it right now.'

Molly's expression softened. 'Well, don't blame yourself—'

'But I think I am to blame. Look, Moll darling.' Judith scrambled to her feet and slid a sisterly arm around the other woman, whether Molly would appreciate it or not. 'I feel as if I'm putting you out enormously, why don't I book into a B&B for now, then perhaps rent somewhere for a few weeks until I can get my tenant out? I'll see him tomorrow and give him notice.' She squeezed her sister's cushiony shoulders. 'I shouldn't have just dropped myself on you like this – you have your own life to get on with. I'm a disgrace, aren't I?' She tried to make it a joke.

Molly hunched a shoulder. 'You're *welcome* here! I'll let you settle in.' She swung out of the room, leaving Judith to flop back down onto the bed. Welcome? She automatically translated the word into Maltese. *Merhba*. She didn't feel welcome. She felt as if she were presuming upon her sister's hospitality. But, with their mother ensconced in a care home now, an automatic return-to-family reflex had sent her to Molly.

At least, now she was 'home', she'd be able to see more of Mum, pay surprise visits to The Cottage retirement home. 'Hello! I've called to see Wilma Morgan, I'm her daughter.' Sit with her. Take her out. Talk. Try not to swear, which always made her mother tut, 'Really, Judith, do we *have* to have that language all the time?'

And Judith not being able to resist. 'Bloody right!' Or worse.

At least Wilma laughed at Judith's jokes. 'Don't you think you're a little old to still be playing the rebellious child?' Judith was looking forward to seeing her mum. The last time had been when she'd visited just before last Christmas.

She closed her tired eyes. Immediately a dearly loved face swam into focus. *Giorgio*. Her heart swelled and shrank sickeningly. *Giorgio*. She forced her eyes to open wide, wide, very wide. *Oh, Giorgio . . .*

After half an hour of unproductive staring at the ceiling and allowing a few hot tears to run down her cheeks, Judith rolled off Molly's spare bed. Better unpack sufficient clothes for a few days, she supposed, cardigans and fleeces included. Northamptonshire's late summer was a different prospect to Malta's. Here the sky was a pale-grey blanket of cloud; no high blue dome, no heat clinging on the breeze or seeping up from the rock. Here she'd sometimes need long sleeves, jeans and socks.

She threw open a case and yanked out a handful of underwear – stretchy, lacy, pretty. She opened one of the small drawers at the top of the oak chest set beside the window. Halted. The drawer was already full of underwear in neat piles – plain, white or beige, and quite unlike hers.

She shut the drawer again, thoughtfully, and tucked her stuff into the empty one beside it.

Later, dinner was served formally in the cavernous dining room. Two Hepplewhite china cabinets and a dining suite for ten covered only a portion of the honey-coloured wool-twist carpet. Judith was convinced that Frankie O'Malley earned enough to provide sufficient furniture to make the room gracious. It was like Molly, however, to not really see the point of furniture for furniture's sake.

Not for her a couple of comfy recliners by the French doors, perhaps in bluebell leather, or plum, with a sexy little stereo and a bulbous lamp on a side table. No jardinière filled a corner and no grandfather clock chimed companionably as they ate.

Theirs was a house that ached for loving touches.

Molly brushed aside Judith's offers to take them out for a meal or buy a takeaway. 'You're our guest.' Molly had an annoying habit of sighing over extra work even as she refused offers of help. That was the way Molly was. 'Also, Frankie will only complain if we were to go out – he likes home cooking.' That was the way Frankie was. Molly ate several bites of her dinner before asking, 'Does anyone else know you're home?'

Judith shook her head and tried to feel some appetite for juicy lamb chops and pungent cabbage. 'No, nobody, yet.'

'Not Thomas? Not Kieran? Not Mum?'

'No.' Judith never rushed to make contact with her ex-husband but she'd never stopped missing Kieran, who'd provided her with nine years of motherhood, even if it were the step variety. 'I'm looking forward to catching up with Mum and Kieran, though.'

Frankie looked up from where he'd been silently engrossed in his meal, his attention caught by the sound of Tom's name. Frankie and Judith's ex-husband, Tom, each running building firms in the town, occasionally combined forces to tackle larger jobs. They were mates and it was through her brother-in-law that Judith had met Tom fifteen years ago. Frankie displayed a fierce loyalty to his mates, to all things male, really. Wilma termed it being a man's man. Judith gained the impression that her mum didn't necessarily mean it as a compliment.

Frankie reached for extra peas. 'He's very cut up at the moment, is old Tom. Had a hard time of it this last year.'

'Because Liza left,' supplied Molly, as if Judith might have somehow forgotten that Tom's third wife had recently abandoned him. Molly had even phoned Judith in Malta especially to tell her, rather than leaving it to the cheaper option of email.

Liza's name had once had the power to slice through Judith, not so much because Liza had put paid to Judith's marriage but because she'd shaken her self-belief. Tom had preferred another woman. Liza had known that Tom was married – Tom had known that he was married – yet she hadn't let it stop her having a taste of his big, bullish body. Liza had proved to have all the attraction of the classic 'new model' that men were always accused of falling for: younger, prettier, more desirable and, for all Judith knew, better in bed. But falling in love with Giorgio had so restored and healed Judith that she'd come to feel grateful to Liza. Without Liza stealing her man, Judith would never have found another.

'Careless with his wives, isn't he? Pam dies, Liza and me leave,' Judith observed lightly, but she was scarcely even thinking about Tom. She was relishing the knowledge that she could ring Kieran tomorrow and arrange to meet him in person instead of relying on the wonders of email to keep in touch. Kieran had finished university and was working in Northampton now. He was living right here in Brinham. At this moment he could be playing squash at the sports centre or having a drink with his mates in one of the pubs Judith had known all her life, his boyish face quick to smile, his toffee-coloured eyes to twinkle.

Frankie, however, hadn't finished with the subject of Tom. He shot Judith a severe look. 'Tom took Liza's desertion very hard.' He stabbed the meat from his cutlet. 'He had no idea that she was seeing someone else.'

Judith brought her mind back to the subject of her ex. 'It's not much fun to discover that the person you're married to is having sex with someone else. It certainly blighted my marriage.'

Frankie pointed his knife accusingly. 'You could've patched things up with Tom, if you'd wanted. He *was* prepared to give Liza up for you – it was you who chose to leave.'

'True.' She stopped pretending to eat and laid down the heavy silver cutlery. 'I'm afraid I'm terribly unforgiving. After all, it only took me discovering his horrid little affair for him to offer to end it.'

Frankie didn't seem to hear Judith's heavy irony. Instead, as if Judith were somehow responsible, he began enumerating Tom's problems on his stubby, grainy fingers. 'That Liza, she took the Mercedes, she took all the money out of the savings accounts, she kept her credit cards, and she took . . .' He stopped and snatched up his fork to resume eating.

'What?' Judith prodded, becoming more engaged in the conversation as she caught the flash of guilt on her brother-in-law's face.

Frankie shrugged and took a mouthful of potato.

Judith grinned suddenly, her cheeks feeling stiff, as if wrenched into unaccustomed positions, then she laughed. There was only one thing Liza could take from Tom that Frankie would suddenly think better of mentioning. 'Has he been stashing away cash again, do you mean? Tucking it behind radiators and underneath drawers so the tax man can't find it?' She threw back her head and laughed again. 'Ha! Talk about hitting him where it hurts. Was it much?'

Frankie grunted, blotting sweat from his high forehead with his sleeve. 'Poor bastard's been left with nothing but the house.'

Judith couldn't resist a jibe. '*Poor* bastard. Scraping by in a seven-bedroom palace.'

'Shall we change the subject?' Molly put in, her brow puckered in worry at the developing tension.

'You can laugh.' Frankie flushed at Judith as if Molly had never spoken, his eyes glittering with irritation. He and Judith often became prickly with each other over the subject of Tom. 'First, he had to extend his mortgage to pay you off and now Liza's snitched all the liquid assets and done a runner to France with her new bit of rough. He bought that house and spent a fortune doing it up and he ought to be able to start planning for retirement. Instead he's got to keep working just to put back what you women have taken out of him.'

Pushing her chair back, Judith rose. If she'd had any sympathy for Tom being left alone, it flitted away. 'Parasitical, are we? And all Tom ever wanted was a housekeeper-cum-cook-cum-gardener for his seven-bed palace, one who would also bring home a full month's salary and give him sex. Rather than leaving him and expecting our fair share of things, I expect he would've preferred Liza and me to die, like poor Pamela, bringing him in a nice fat insurance cheque.'

'Liza never brought home no full month's salary,' Frankie snapped.

'Maybe she doubled up on the sex.' Judith began to turn away, preparing to return to her own room.

Frankie began serving himself seconds of potato. 'All I'm saying is that you never *had* to leave him.'

Judith sighed and summoned a smile for her brother-in-law for Molly's sake, not wanting her sister to have to put up with Frankie in a bad mood. 'No. And I wouldn't have done if he hadn't been unfaithful . . . but he did get several years with Liza, and I got several years in Malta.' With Giorgio. But she didn't say that. The very last thing she wanted was Frankie ferreting out the story about Giorgio and reporting her pain back to Tom.

# Chapter Four

Judith woke to a silent Sunday, early daylight falling on her stack of suitcases and yesterday's clothes strewn over a yellow damask chair. She sat up and raked her fingers through her hair. Two tasks today: take the first step towards reclaiming her house and ring Kieran. Her tenant, Adam Leblond, being a mature man, might well be up and at home. Kieran, being an immature man, would likely be in bed until lunchtime. She'd approach the tenant.

She breakfasted alone on coffee, Molly and Frankie still being upstairs, then stepped out into a sunny morning. It was a twenty-minute walk to Lavender Row at Judith's rapid pace and she strode out of Molly's posh estate and into the more familiar streets of terraces and semis in the older part of town. She must get a car sorted out, maybe one of those titchy, zippy little things – a Smart car or a Seicento.

But, in the meantime, the weather was dry and her smoke-grey fleece was proof against the breeze; a walk would be good. It would get her out of Molly's house, too. She'd heard Molly and Frankie bickering last night. She hoped they hadn't been bickering over her.

The sooner she was back in her own place, the better for all concerned . . . apart, perhaps, for the tenant, who had to be told he'd soon be moving home.

In her bag was a letter, hot off the computer in Frankie's office, formally giving the required notice. She'd printed on the smooth white envelope, *Adam Leblond*. Staring at the once-familiar name, she found herself awash with memories of Brinham Grammar School. Stiff navy blazers, tan leather satchels with doodles all over the inside (because doodles on the outside would get you detention and a sharp letter home). Logarithm books, sensible black shoes, white shirts and striped ties, echoing corridors, quadrangles at break time, hockey in the rain, the A-stream, the smell of chalk dust and plimsolls, crisps from the tuck shop. Boys in the corridors and classrooms. Adam Leblond. It had always sounded like a good name for a pop star; a crooner with golden hair and a repertoire of dance steps. Still, she supposed, the name didn't sound bad on a photographer in the latter half of his forties, as she knew him to be.

As she marched along the Sunday streets, she refamiliarised herself with her surroundings: the greenness of the fields glimpsed in the distance, the trees lining the roads, the flourishing gardens – some so 'flourishing' that a machete and a flame gun would be required to get them under control. Weeds just didn't grow like that in Malta. English town gardens were a real contrast to the palm, cypress, twisted olive trees and grey-green spear-like agaves that dotted dry Maltese earth. Her eyes had become used to stone and flat-roofed buildings, sand-like soil, dust instead of mud. She told herself that she was bound to miss Malta, the constant, mighty presence of the sea and the unremitting glare of the sun.

It would be different, but could still be enjoyable, to live once again in Lavender Row.

After she'd moved out of the seven-bed detached in Victoria Gardens, the erstwhile marital home, Tom had growled and muttered and fought to retain it because it was 'an investment'. In order to also keep his builders' yard, machinery and equipment, he had, as Frankie pointed out yesterday evening, raised capital. He'd tried first to dismiss Judith's contribution to the marital assets from her job as a surveyor, which she'd held for the duration of their marriage, but the lawyers had soon sorted out his misapprehensions. Tom had had to pay Judith a fair sum. As if to punish her, he'd then moved Liza into their old home.

Judith had no longer cared. She'd bought 18 Lavender Row outright, providing her with a stable stake in England, and had a tidy sum left over. The house was terraced and double fronted, the windows set into stone mullions, the rooms large and tall with ornate plasterwork, moulded picture rails and tall skirting boards. Relishing her return to living alone, Judith had enjoyed choosing plain carpets and colours for the walls. A small gravelled area to the front and a long strip of garden at the back completed the property but she hadn't been as interested in those. She'd lived comfortably in the pretty terrace while tying up loose ends, giving notice to her employer and working on her move to Malta. A year there had proved about right to ease through the painful separation from Kieran and see him through his final school days. She'd bought into Richard Elliot Estate once Kieran seemed settled at uni.

She knew from Molly, via Frankie, that Tom was now furious that the house in Victoria Gardens that he'd fought so hard for had plummeted in value when an edge-of-town retail park was built behind it. Instead of looking out on hedges and fields, Tom now looked out on a row of leggy conifers doing an inadequate job of disguising a DIY shop's loading bay. For some reason, the planners had also allowed a nightclub to move into one of the industrial units, providing a noisy, technicolour finale to most Fridays and Saturdays for the nearby residents. Someone ought to have pointed out to Tom that investments could go down as well as up.

Judith swung into Lavender Row, where cars lined either side owing to the absence of driveways, and paused when she reached number 18. The small front garden now boasted a dwarf acer in a cobalt-blue pot in the middle of the gravel. The front door was painted black and the stained glass aperture gleamed in the sunlight.

She wrinkled her nose at the neatness. Broken windows and rubbish piled in the garden might have given her an excuse for early termination of the tenancy.

Pressing the white doorbell button, she listened to the ringing in the depths of the house and prepared to meet Adam Leblond for the first time since her teens. What would he be like, now? Fat? Bald? Grey?

But the man who answered her summons and stood framed in the doorway was none of these things. He was about the same age as Kieran and if he'd told her he was a member of a band, with his long hair and ripped jeans, she would have believed him. A heavy metal band.

'Hey,' he greeted her amiably. She knew from Kieran that 'hey' was the new 'hi'. He pushed dark hair back over his shoulders, scratched his bare chest and tugged tattered jeans higher over his hips.

Judith glanced again at the house. It was definitely number 18. 'Hi. I'm looking for Adam Leblond.'

'Yeah, upstairs. Do you want me to shout?' The young man half-turned as if preparing to do so.

She hesitated, checking her watch. It was eleven o'clock, which seemed a reasonable time to call, even on a Sunday. 'If you think it'll be all right. I'm Judith McAllister, the landlord.'

'Oh, right.' He turned his face towards the stairs. 'Dad? Dad! Lady who owns the house is here.' So the young guy was Adam Leblond's son.

A pause, then a muffled reply, which Judith didn't catch.

The amiable young man turned back to her. 'Can you wait five minutes? He hasn't emerged yet.'

Maybe eleven o'clock *was* too early on a Sunday. 'I'll come back—' she began.

He pulled the door open further. The hall carpet – she'd left all the carpets – looked freshly vacuumed. 'No, come in. I'm Caleb, by the way.'

'Hi, Caleb.' She wondered who Adam Leblond had produced this interesting young specimen with, whether any of the adoring legion of Brinham girls who'd pulled in their stomachs when Adam Leblond blew past on his dark-green racing bike had been the lucky one. After he'd left sixth form he'd faded off her radar and from her memory until a local friend, Melanie, had emailed Judith in Malta after learning the last occupants were moving on. *If you haven't got new tenants yet, would you let the house to a friend of my Ian's? You might even remember him from school – he was two years ahead of us. His name's Adam Leblond.*

Seeing his name had sent a nostalgic shock through her, but, deeply involved with Giorgio at the time, Judith hadn't spared a minute to share those old emotions with Melanie. In any event, her crush, secret and agonising, had been based mainly on a solitary conversation about sweets one day outside the school gates.

*Sure*, she'd replied, glad enough not to have to get involved again with local agents. *If you and Ian recommend him, I'm sure he'll be ideal.*

Now she followed Caleb down the wide passageway to the kitchen with its side window overlooking the patio. Apart from an open bag of Hovis bread and a sprinkling of crumbs beside the toaster, the room was immaculate. She recalled emails from adam@adamleblond.co.uk seeking permission to decorate and him shrugging off her offer to pay towards materials. He'd evidently done a great job. White gloss gleamed on the woodwork, creamy yellow emulsion on the walls contrasted with blood-red curtains and the pine units were freshly coated. The worktops were uncluttered.

Caleb offered her a drink, taking down thick orange mugs. 'I would tell you to make yourself at home but as it belongs to you . . .' He grinned as he checked how she liked her coffee and made instant in the mugs. His grey eyes shone with humour in his tanned face. Every few seconds, he flicked his long hair back over his shoulders.

She sat down at the kitchen table. 'Do you live here, Caleb?'

He slid two slices of bread into the toaster. 'On and off, while I'm deciding what to do with myself.' He paused, glancing at her as if struck by a thought. 'Is it OK for me to stay here with Dad? It's not in contravention of the landlord's rules, is it? It's just for a while.'

Blowing on her coffee, she tried to sound reassuring, but felt duplicitous, knowing she was going to ask this pleasant young guy to leave, along with his dad. 'We have a standard assured shorthold tenancy agreement

– there might be a clause that states Mr Leblond should give me the opportunity to veto any long-term guests or co-tenants.' 'Mr Leblond' sounded overly formal but she hardly felt that she knew Adam and on the odd occasion they'd communicated he'd always signed himself with his full name.

'Oh. Right.' Caleb pulled a conspiratorial face. 'I don't want to screw things up for Dad. I'll push off to Mum's if I have to.' So whoever Caleb's mother was, Adam Leblond didn't live with her.

Caleb reminded her of Kieran. She felt her lips curve into a small smile at the gangly young man, the easy grin, the air of finding everything doable. 'It mainly matters that the house has been looked after.'

He waved a dismissive hand. 'Oh sure, you know what Dad's like.'

'Not really,' Judith said. 'A friend arranged the tenancy while I lived abroad.'

His eyes lit up. 'Where have you been living?' Without waiting for a reply he went on, 'I've just done my gap – Thailand, Cambodia and Australia. Dad had kittens if I didn't email for a couple of days while I was in Cambodia. Australia was cool. *So* cool.' He began to bombard her with stories about hostels and working in kitchens to pay his way, employing the vocabulary of his generation: 'cool', 'crazy', 'wicked'. She wondered whether to tell him that she'd been around his age in the seventies, when the same words had peppered her conversation. She kept waiting for him to throw in 'groovy' or 'fab', to talk about living on a kibbutz, the icon of freedom in her teen years and not attained because she'd sensibly gone to college.

They were interrupted by the rapid rhythm of feet descending the stairs.

'Here's Dad.' Caleb promptly vacated his seat as if he'd only been keeping Judith company out of good manners.

Adam Leblond jumped the final two steps and then swung along the hall. He looked as if he'd come fresh from the shower, his damp hair combed back from a face pink from shaving. His brows were two straight lines, as if he looked as if he spent a lot of time squinting into the distance. He was more wiry than she remembered, quick of movement, flesh taut over his jaw and cheek bones. He wore a plain black T-shirt tucked into black trousers.

Caleb passed him in the doorway, carrying his toast with him. 'See you later.'

After a flash of a smile in his son's direction, Adam Leblond looked at Judith and frowned. 'Sorry, I was reading in bed.' His eyes were piercing, alive. His hair receded a bit at either side at the front. Faint diagonal lines on his forehead cut across horizontal ones when he frowned.

'It's me who should apologise. I should've phoned and made an appointment. I'm Judith McAllister.' It wasn't worth reminding him that she had been Judith Morgan, in the fifth year when he'd been in the upper sixth. If he'd ever known her name, he would surely have forgotten by now. Automatically, she extended her hand.

He recoiled. Hesitated. Then withdrew his right hand abruptly from his pocket, displayed it for an instant before shoving it back. 'I don't, really.' He half-smiled.

'Oh!' Her heart hopped in shock at the glimpse of his hand. Pink flesh had closed over where his first three fingers ought to have been, a yawning gap between his little finger and thumb. Oh, poor Adam! She flushed hotly that she'd embarrassed him with her attempt to shake hands. 'Sorry. I didn't know—'

61

Compassion for her discomfort flickered in his eyes, darker grey than his son's, one corner of his mouth lifting. 'It's relatively recent. Are you here to inspect the house?' He leaned back against the door jamb. 'It's OK if you want to. I expect Caleb's room's a tip, but it's just clothes on the floor and stuff.'

Caleb returned briefly into view, moving from the front room to the stairs, four CDs clamped in his hand. 'You were supposed to tell her that I was living here, Dad.'

'Oh!' Adam Leblond flushed. 'It didn't occur to me. It's only Caleb, he's my son, a guest. It's not as if I'm subletting.' He was still frowning.

'That isn't the reason I'm here.' Her face felt hotter and hotter. All they'd done so far was to make one another awkward, one apology countered with another. His obvious concern for his responsibilities as a tenant made her feel sheepish. She was here to chuck him out of his home, for goodness sake. A deep breath. 'Could we talk?'

'Of course. In here.' He led her into the room that was lounge at one end and dining room at the other. Her grey-blue carpet was still on the floor but he'd added inky damask curtains, a charcoal suite and ivory wallpaper. Everything in the room was functional; no occasional tables or ornaments cluttered the gaps. An Apple Mac computer, large, brand new and looking state-of-the-art was hooked up in the same alcove where she used to stand her rather more elderly PC.

Despite its spare style, the room felt welcoming and lived in. A neat pile of glossy magazines stood on the floor beside one chair, and two empty beer cans beside the other. 'Caleb,' he explained, as he gathered the cans into his left hand. 'I'm sorry. You've caught me on the hop.'

She flushed anew. 'I shouldn't have called unannounced.

But I came home from Malta yesterday, and I need to discuss something with you.'

His tidying ceased. He straightened, bright eyes suddenly wary. 'You come home yesterday; you call on your tenant today? Sounds like a problem.'

His lightning perception forced her into a blunter approach than she'd prepared for but she made herself hold his grey gaze and speak calmly. 'I'm afraid so.' Fumbling, she extracted the envelope with his name on from her bag, and held it in both hands. 'This is probably not what you want to hear but I must give you notice. I've left Malta for personal reasons and I need my house back.' Her throat was dry.

Slowly, he put down the cans and took the envelope, opening it awkwardly, holding it in his left hand while he slit the flap with the remaining finger on his right. He read the letter in silence, folded the page up and returned his gaze to her. 'So I get two months' notice? Two calendar months from today.'

Wishing the news hadn't made him look so bleak, Judith shifted in her chair. If she hadn't been hoping to get him out without full notice she would have sent the letter by registered post and been spared this interview. She cleared her throat. 'To be honest, well, I'd really like you out sooner. If possible. I could offer an incentive—'

He laughed, grimly. 'I've nowhere to go.'

She pushed back her hair. It needed cutting and it was annoying her. 'Neither have I. And it's my house. I'm afraid I need it back.'

He nodded, sinking into the armchair with the magazines beside it and regarded her narrowly. 'But under the tenancy agreement I have two months.'

'Yes, you do. But you haven't precisely been sticking to

the tenancy agreement, have you?' She glanced up, from where thumping rock music was filtering through the ceiling.

He did that half-smile again. It gathered the corners of his eyes into laughter lines and cut grooves at the sides of his mouth. It didn't seem to mean that he was finding things particularly funny. 'I don't think a court would grant you early possession because I had my son to stay for a few weeks.'

Court. She wouldn't take such a trivial matter to court and he probably knew it. 'I suppose not,' she conceded, beginning to feel fatigued and strained. So much had happened in such a short time and now she was back in her own house and it didn't feel like home. It felt like Adam and Caleb's home and she felt like a bitch for asking them to go. But she wanted to live in her house, not as a guest in Molly and Frankie's.

A silence. He frowned, pulling his bottom lip and gazing out of the window at cars passing in the street outside. 'The thing is, Mrs McAllister,' he began slowly. 'The thing is that I've been having an awkward time. I had the accident where I lost my fingers and my marriage broke down. My wife got the house. The woman always gets the house, doesn't she? I hate solicitors and all the nasty procedure of trying to shoehorn the opposite party out, demanding shares of the equity, her solicitor insisting the dog belongs to her even if the dog thinks it belongs to me. So I left when my wife asked me to, making things easy for her because we have a long history and we're still friends. Foolish of me, on reflection, but I do tend to see myself as the guy who wears the white hat. I was relieved when Ian's wife Melanie said she knew of a nice rental and now I'm happy and comfortable here.

'And then you come along and say, "But it's *my* house!"
And it is. But you're out of order – it's my home. Until
the twenty-first of August, in law, this is my home. It's
kept well, you've no grounds for eviction. You can examine
every room if you want to, the empty beer cans are about
the worst you're going to find. Sorry, but I don't feel too
co-operative.'

He twisted the letter over and over between the fingers
of his good hand, the jerky movement the only sign of
any agitation. He switched his gaze back to Judith, eyes
gleaming with anger. 'So if you've run back to England in
a stress because you've had a row with your boss or been
dumped by some man who doesn't realise when he's well
off . . .' He tossed down the letter. 'Tough. I'm not inclined
to roll over this time. Because the woman *always* gets the
house, and I'm sick of it.'

Judith clenched her hands. 'I'm sorry to even ask it of
you.'

'Don't be sorry. You've been refused.' His tone remained
calm, despite the anger in his eyes.

She tried again. 'I can offer financial compensation for
the inconvenience. And the woman doesn't always get the
house. My husband kept the house . . . and I bought this
one.'

'*Inconvenience*? It's a flaming liberty!' He snapped his
lips shut around his words as if regretting the letting of
emotion. Then, more quietly as he seemed to realise what
she'd said, 'Sorry, if your husband got your marital home.
But I'm not going to leave before I need to.'

Her eyes began to burn. She blinked. He was right to
be annoyed. She *was* out of order. She'd entered into an
agreement with him and now she wanted to welch. He
had every right to be cross and recalcitrant.

But, oh, her heart was sore. She wanted to live with her own things, her own phone and computer, where she could decide whether the television went on and what to watch. Her own place where she could lick her wounds and recover from losing Giorgio. And this was her house!

She sucked in a big breath and then let it out slowly, looking away for a moment to reassemble her expression so that it was closed and unemotional. She turned back to him. 'Mr Leblond, would you . . . would you consider just taking my word for it that I had a pressing reason to come home, without me going into detail? That I'm in an emotional state that makes getting settled in Brinham and back on an even keel desirable?' She noticed he was watching her mouth.

Gently, he shook his head as his eyes flicked back to hers. 'Sorry, Mrs McAllister.' As his hair was drying it was lightening, becoming the chestnut colour she remembered, slipping down at one side.

She closed her eyes for an instant and swallowed. The ticking of the clock on the wall seemed suddenly very loud. She opened her eyes and rose, hitching her bag onto her shoulder. 'It's not your business but you're right. It's a man.' She saw a *thought-so* look fleet across his face. 'He hasn't exactly dumped me. But it doesn't look as if there's a future for us.'

And, without warning, tears rose up and choked her.

'Hell,' he sighed.

There were no sobs. The tears just sprang silently from her eyes and poured down her cheeks. Judith opened her handbag and scrabbled for a travel pack of tissues. She'd used a whole rainforest of them in the last couple of months.

She pressed a wad of tissue against each eye in turn and sniffed inelegantly. Another jerky breath, and her voice

66

came out through a throat that felt stretched like wire. 'I'm staying with my sister but I need to be on my own or I wouldn't ask you to start looking for somewhere else immediately.'

'I'm sorry,' he repeated. But this time he sounded as if he might mean it. He hesitated, and then asked gently, 'You don't think you'd be better off with your sister for a while? Rather than being alone?'

Judith gave a strangled laugh through her tears. It was odd to be laughing and crying at the same time. It made her feel as if she might soon be flailing for whatever smidgen of control she had left. 'She's driving me nuts already. I don't even want to look at food but she wants me to *eat*.'

He laughed briefly. He'd forgotten to keep his hand out of sight and, wiping her eyes, she caught a glimpse of zig-zag lines across the palm like white lightning, new pink skin across the strange, shiny knuckles. He said, 'But you do look as if you need to put on at least a stone.'

'I know, I'm a scarecrow.' She wiped her eyes and sniffed again.

'Not as extreme as that. Perhaps a chicken carcass.'

'Thanks a bunch.' She tried a watery smile and he grinned suddenly and winked.

But he didn't offer her the house back. She had little choice but to leave.

# Chapter Five

The Water Gardens were not so splendid now as when
built in the late Victorian era. All the eight fountains of
varying sizes were dry and the people of Brinham were
left with just one algae-ridden, scalloped-edge pond. Either
side, smaller ponds in the same design had long ago ceased
to hold water and had become flowerbeds.

The parks department had planted up the waterless tiers
of the fountains with French marigolds and catmint to
clash gaily with scarlet salvias and purple lobelia. The
weedy grass around the beds and paths was mown and
the benches thick with bright green paint, glossing over
last year's *Baz luvs Katee* and *Northampton Town FC*
carved into the wood.

The park made a pocket of colour just off the town
centre; somewhere for office workers to eat their sand-
wiches on hot days or gangs of teenagers to hang out once
they'd exhausted their money at the shops. Shoppers
nipped through between town and the car park, a bare
line in the grass where they cut diagonally across. And
now, after the exhausting scene with Adam Leblond that

had ended with her no nearer taking possession of her house, it made an oasis of peace where Judith could collect herself and wait for the redness around her eyes to fade.

She'd charged her British mobile phone the evening before and now found a vacant bench and pulled it from her bag to ring Kieran, pushing the little rubbery keys with mounting anticipation.

She got him straight away. He raised his voice over the happy background clamour of a pub. 'Hey!' he said. 'I emailed you this morning. Isn't this call on your English phone? Doesn't that cost you loads?'

'No, because I'm in the Water Gardens,' she said brightly, making her voice level and serene. 'I'm home.'

'Shut up, shut *up*!' she heard him yell into the escalating racket around him. Then, back into the phone, 'What, the Water Gardens in Brinham? You're in *Brinham*? How cool is that? I'm, like, in The Punch. Stay put.'

He rang off and she folded the phone shut, waiting, her gaze on the old black iron arch with *1900* set into the wrought iron, commemorating that the gardens had opened a hundred and four years ago. Beneath the arch, a lane threaded into the town centre. Judith's heart thrummed gently with anticipation. The Punch was a bar in the cellar of The Duke of Brinham Hotel on High Street. When she'd been a youngster it had been a popular venue for discos or parties. They'd tried to pretend it was just like the infamous Cavern Club in Liverpool.

Judith had been Kieran's stepmother from when he was nine until he was eighteen – really important years. Such a little mouse he'd been when she first knew him, an unlikely son for big, bullish Thomas McAllister. While Tom made her the subject of an exciting, conspicuous courtship, Kieran and Judith quietly clicked; the little boy who'd lost his mother, the woman who'd never so far had the kind of relationship that went along with children appearing on her radar.

Her gratitude to his late mother, the unknown Pamela, was boundless. She'd even felt guilty about her joy, as his father settled possessively on Judith for his second wife, to see Kieran dance with joy and demand to be allowed to call her 'Mum'. Pamela's death had gifted Judith a son, a dear little boy with an endless capacity for love.

Tom was a big cattle rancher of a man, gruffly kind to Judith – in those days – and gratifyingly active in bed but on her wedding day Judith probably loved Kieran more than she loved Tom. She loved Tom, of course she did. But, oh, she did love Kieran! At thirty, it hadn't mattered to Judith that forty-year-old Tom hadn't been particularly keen on 'starting again' with a new baby. Kieran had been enough.

During the marriage, she should have pushed harder for the adoption that would have given her parental rights. But whenever she'd brought the subject up, Tom merely pulled her into his arms and kissed her. 'He *is* your son, he's the first to say so. We don't need any fuss in the court.' And so Judith settled down to the novel position of mother.

She remembered how much she'd loved it. Swimming lessons, football club, friends for tea, parties, school open evenings, new school uniform, bedtime stories. She'd invested herself in Kieran and *mother* had been more satisfying than *wife*. Tom had seen her as one of his possessions and it had caused friction.

And when, after almost a decade of Judith being with Tom, Liza came on the scene, Judith was almost relieved. Tom's betrayal had given her back her freedom.

But then Tom tripped her up.

She might have thought twice about removing herself from a suddenly crowded marriage if she'd realised for just one instant that Tom would avenge himself at her lack of forgiveness by roaring, 'You can forget about keeping in touch with Kieran. He's my son, not yours.' To a stunned Kieran, he'd snapped, 'And you can stop calling her Mum.' Would she ever forgive Tom for using highly strung, gentle Kieran against her like that?

Eighteen or not, Kieran had wept. Judith had lost her head, screaming at Tom, 'You overbearing arse! You never have his best interests at heart. No wonder the poor boy's scared of you.'

Her hasty words compounded the damage. If she'd kept herself together and reasoned with Tom he might have calmed down and pretended he'd never shouted the rage-fuelled words. She should have negotiated, cajoling if necessary. Tom, desperate to patch things up, had been trying to force her to heel, and she knew that.

Well, his clumsy strategy hadn't worked. Kieran, growing up fast, sneaked in meetings with her between school and home, meetings he didn't bother advertising to his father. And Judith had certainly felt no compulsion to own up.

Tom's fury at Judith for refusing to pardon his infidelity eased in time, of course, but Kieran had by then been in the habit of keeping secrets from his father. Then, finally, Kieran went to Sheffield University. Judith moved to Malta and funded Kieran's visits to her, as well as timing her visits home to coincide with his.

Thank God for email and telephone calls to fill in the gaps.

Then suddenly Kieran was there, running into the park, multi-coloured trainers on jet-propelled feet, brown spikes of hair tossing over his forehead, eyes scanning the green-painted benches to find her. She sprang to her feet, her lips stretching into a great grin of welcome. Then she faltered. Kieran was towing along in his wake a slight teenage girl in tight turned-up jeans who must, she realised with a spurt of irritation she immediately tried to suppress, be the Bethan he'd mentioned a lot lately. They'd been going out together for about four months and Judith hadn't got a feel for how involved they were. But then Kieran let go of the girl and sprinted the final yards across the grass and Judith threw her arms open wide.

His embrace swept her completely off her feet. 'Mum! Wow! This is so good, so cool! When did you get here? I didn't know you were coming.' He hugged her so tightly that she literally couldn't inflate her lungs and when he set her down she had to cough for breath.

'Let me look at you,' she gasped, brushing his hair back, feeling it like silk against her fingers. 'You look so well, darling! How are you? How's the new job? It's great to see you.' She wasn't a small woman but her stepson towered over her. His height contrasted with his boyish looks so that the impression was of a seven-foot-tall twelve-year-old.

With a final squeeze, Kieran let her loose. 'Mum, you have to meet my Bethan.' He swung around and hauled the slight girl forward. 'Beth, this is my mum. My step-mother, I mean, Judith, who I talk about all the time, not Liza, obviously. Wow, this is so great! I can't believe I'm finally getting to introduce you guys.'

Bethan smiled shyly. 'Hey.' She looked as if she might still be at school, a tiny elf-child in an enormous hooded top, her hair artificially black and showing fair at her centre parting and above her fringe as if someone had

72

stood behind her and drawn a large T on her head. Silver studs ornamented her nose and lip to go with teenage spots on her forehead. Kieran, Judith noticed suddenly, now had an eyebrow pierced.

She made herself smile and offer an enthusiastic 'Hey!' to Bethan, although she felt a swell of disappointment. Was it very mean of her to want Kieran to herself? She normally saw him only every few months, visits she sucked up whole into her memory to turn over and over until the next time.

Still, she was home now and as Kieran was living with his father she'd have loads of time to get him on his own. She made sure her smile remained in place. 'It's great to meet you, Bethan.'

The three settled back down on the bench, Judith ready to enjoy Kieran's company, his news, his excitement and enthusiasm for his new job, which was with the local water authority. But when two of Bethan's friends, as fragile looking as her, wandered into the gardens on wooden-soled sandals and Bethan leaped up to cross the grass to meet them, Judith grabbed her chance. 'I need to talk to you, Kieran.' She swallowed against a suddenly closed throat. 'Later, perhaps. Or tomorrow after work?'

The sparkle faded from Kieran's eyes as they searched hers and he looked suddenly concerned. 'I suppose there had to be a reason for you suddenly turning up. Hang on.' He ran across the grass to consult Bethan, who nodded, waved sketchily at Judith and turned to clomp off with her friends.

Kieran pulled Bethan back for a kiss, a wide-open-mouthed kiss with visibly curling tongues. Her friends watched on casually. Judith looked away, uncomfortable with witnessing the appetites of her stepson.

Then Kieran ran back, his hair blowing above his toffee-brown eyes, his broad top lip creasing laterally with his big, beaming grin. He flung himself back down on the bench. 'What's up?'

Kieran was the only person from Brinham who knew all the truths, both wonderful and awful, about her affair with Giorgio. Kieran, with his teenage values, saw no reason why they shouldn't be together. Kieran thought Giorgio was too cool for words. Giorgio had taken Kieran night fishing, puttering along in a small fishing boat and shining a lamp into the water in search of squid and to drink in atmospheric little Maltese bars run by his friends. He'd also taken Kieran on day trips when there were a couple of empty places on the bus, ensuring he got a seat close to nice-looking girls.

Kieran was going to be distressed about Giorgio.

Shoving away the memory of Giorgio's smile, the feather-light touches of his fingers skimming her spine, the tenderness as he called her '*gojjella tieghi*', my jewel, she took Kieran's hands and told him about the accident, quietly and simply. No amount of wrapping up of the truth would prevent Kieran's grief.

His light brown eyes widened with pain. 'It happened two months ago? He's still unconscious? And you've only just told me?'

She tried to explain. 'It was hard to cope—'

Kieran swore, snatching back his hands to slap the bench with the flats of them. 'And of course you had to cope all by yourself? That's what you've always got to do, isn't it? Keep it all in. Give up on him and come back to England because of some stupid bargain you made with his horrible mother without even letting me know what happened. You weren't the only one to care

74

about him! I deserved to be told if I wasn't going to see him again.'

Voice shaking, she tried to explain. 'I'm sorry if I did the wrong thing in your eyes. It didn't seem like "giving up". It wasn't a "bargain" I made with his mother. I never took any notice of her wishes before! Leaving seemed the right thing to do because it was hard to be in Malta without Giorgio.' Understanding that Kieran was lashing out in sorrow at the situation rather than her, she stroked his arm and tried to offer what comfort she could. 'I made his aunt Cass promise she'd contact me if he woke up. If that happens, I'll be on the next plane back to Malta.'

And then Kieran's shoulders began to shake, and Judith ignored her own pain burning inside her and threw her arms around the person who was the nearest thing she'd ever get to a son, holding him close while he cried.

It was two hours before Kieran had recovered himself enough to leave Judith and hurry away to find Bethan.

Judith, exhausted by comforting him as he came to terms with something she'd yet to fully come to terms with herself, trudged to the taxi rank. Next on her list of important people to visit was her mother, Wilma. Molly had been dubious when she'd heard of Judith's plan to turn up unannounced but Judith was looking forward to seeing Wilma's face. She hoped Molly wouldn't have called ahead to spoil the surprise.

She dropped into the back seat of the first taxi in the rank with a sigh. 'The Cottage retirement home on Northampton Road, please.'

'Righto, duck.' The driver guided the car along the streets she'd known all her life to a tree-lined road out of town. It looked as if it were meant to go somewhere important, but it had actually been superseded by a dual carriageway to Northampton a couple of decades ago. Many of the large, gracious houses were now put to other uses, like care homes, clinics or B&Bs, extensions and parking areas taking up what had once been large gardens.

As age had crept up on her and alone after her husband's death in his fifties, Wilma had sold her bungalow, which had stood half a mile away. Molly had helped her identify the tall, airy rooms of The Cottage retirement home as somewhere she might be happy and where she could access the care her arthritis demanded.

Gazing through the window at the generously sized redbrick or pebble-dashed buildings, Judith smiled faintly to remember Molly had said Wilma should live with her instead. Wilma, typically independent, had thanked her but said with a twinkle, 'You've got your own life and too many stairs. I'll be lovely at The Cottage because it's so expensive – like a hotel but better. You get what you pay for.' That had turned out to be true.

When Judith arrived, she discovered Wilma was enjoying a session of seated yoga, gentle exercises for those without much mobility. Not wanting to disturb that, after signing the visitors' book she took a seat in the no-man's land inside the tall front doors to read the magazines and let Wilma enjoy her exercise session in peace, deciding from the combination of smells that the residents had probably enjoyed shepherd's pie for Sunday lunch, earlier. A couple of copies of *My Weekly* later, a cheerful carer, whose tight lilac uniform rode up in horizontal pleats above all the widest parts of her, popped her head around the corner. Her name badge, high up, near her shoulder, said *Sandy*. 'Are you Wilma Morgan's daughter? She's back in the lounge, lovie, if you're ready. Shall you wait in the corridor while I just tell her who it is?'

Judith followed the carer up the wide corridor and into a sunny, pale-green lounge with an aquarium in the corner and a large television on a stand. Tall, comfy chairs faced the TV, many occupied by elderly men and women watching the happenings on screen or drowsing over a crossword. Quickly, she said, 'I'd rather be a surprise. I've been living abroad so I'm hoping she'll be happy to see me.'

Sandy paused just outside the open door to the lounge. 'As long as we don't get her too much all of a doo-dah, lovie, that's all I need to be sure of.'

Judith ignored the note of warning in Sandy's voice. She wanted to see her mother's face shine with astonishment and delight at seeing her. 'Is she having funny turns or something?' From the doorway she could already see Wilma sitting in a high-backed chair, peering into her handbag. Her heart expanded with love.

'We just find it best to provide a nice calm environment,' Sandy replied.

Judith managed a smile. 'I haven't come to upset her.' She suddenly longed for the comfort of her mother's arms and slipped past Sandy into the warmth of the room. As she covered the last few steps across the carpet she drank in Wilma's hair looking white and freshly washed in the sunlight, her face as soft and gently defined as bread dough. Judith had to swallow before she spoke. 'Hello, Mum! It's lovely to see you.' She felt a beaming smile take hold of her face, though her eyes burned hot.

Wilma jumped, tipping her handbag upside down onto the floor. 'Judith?' Her hand flew shakily to her chest and her mouth dropped open. 'Oh, Judith! Oh, darling. What on earth . . .?'

With a noise that might have been a gasp, a laugh or a sob, Wilma grabbed for Judith's hands, pulling on them so Judith could help her to her feet. Trembling with the effort of standing without a frame or stick, she slid her stiff arms around her daughter and leant heavily against her, breathing in uneven little gusts. 'Judith, my girl! Come here . . . Let me just look at you! My duck, when did you get here? What a shock! But how lovely . . . How lovely, how *lovely* . . . I can't believe I'm so lucky! I just can't believe . . . I've gone as shaky as a lamb. I'd better sit down.'

Alarmed, Judith helped her mother plump solidly down into her chair, then watched anxiously as she tunnelled clumsily up her sleeves for her hanky to catch some of her rolling tears. Feeling guiltily that Sandy might have had a point about getting her mum 'all of a doo-dah' she said apologetically, 'Perhaps I should've rung first—'

Sandy, who'd hung around under the guise of helping untangle a man's glasses chain from his buttons, cut across her in a loud sing-song voice. 'Are we all right there, Wilma? Yes, darlin'? Your daughter was a big surprise, wasn't she? Have you got your breath all right, lovie? Shall I get you a drink of water? Yes, all right, lovie, coming up. Is everyone all right?' She smiled reassuringly at other residents who'd turned to see what the ruckus was about.

Wilma managed to stop laughing and sniffling and blotting her tears, and called after her. 'Thank you, Sandy, just the job.' Then she swung suddenly on Judith and pinched her arm. 'You!'

'Ow!' Judith pulled her flesh out of the uncomfortable grip.

'You,' repeated Wilma, beaming and shaking Judith's shoulder this time. 'Why didn't you let me know you were coming? I could've been looking forward to it for weeks. How long are you here for? Can you pick up my bag and my bits for me, duck? Just look at all my rubbish on the floor, now, what will people think?'

As Judith gathered up Wilma's bag, purse, tissues and pens Sandy returned with the promised water, chiming loud, comforting phrases as she tucked the glass into Wilma's hand. Before she turned away she studied her intently, then nodded to herself as if satisfied that her charge was in no imminent danger of collapse. 'All right then, Wilma, you just take your time now, lovie, and have a lovely visit with your daughter. Just get her to ring that bell if you need another glass of water, all right, darlin'?'

Judith was conscious of being in disgrace, having gone about things the wrong way and ignored advice to the contrary. The staff had her mother to look after full time and didn't need Judith breezing in and upsetting everyone. The residents were entitled to their after-dinner nap or to watch TV without raised voices and upset handbags. 'Sorry,' she whispered, meekly collecting an *I-told-you-so* look from Sandy before she bustled from the room.

Wilma took back her large black bag and gripped excitedly on to Judith's sleeve, making it difficult for her to rise from her knees. 'How long are you here for? Is everything all right? Is Richard all right, and Erminia and your cousins?'

'They're all OK. I've come home.' Judith smiled, gently patting her mum's hand and then freeing her sleeve so that she could get up and at least grab a footstool to perch on.

'Oh, my duck.' Wilma breathed in rapture, eyes shining from behind her glasses. 'Home for good? Are you back in Lavender Row? Have you seen our Molly?'

Judith made sure she didn't bring on any more 'doo-dahs' with an admission that a broken heart had brought her back to England. 'Richard and family are absolutely fine. I'm staying in Molly's spare room until I've got my tenant in Lavender Row out.'

Wilma's smile faded. 'She's a good girl is Molly. What kind of a mood's her Frankie in?'

Shrugging, Judith pulled a face. 'Never changes much, does he?'

'Frankie's Frankie,' Wilma agreed, rolling her eyes. 'But never mind him. It's just so lovely to have you back.' Slowly, as her arthritic spine demanded, Wilma leaned forward and gave Judith the big hug she'd been longing for.

The next hour passed in a happy catching-up on news. Judith told Wilma every detail she could think of about the lives of Richard, Erminia and their children, Rosaire, Raymond and Lino. She was even sufficiently forgiven by Sandy to be given a cup of tea with the residents.

The visit cheered Judith so much that, when it was over, she decided she might as well see her ex-husband Tom and get it over with while she was feeling strong. From The Cottage's lobby, she rang for another taxi to take her back through the town centre and uphill into another one of the older sectors of town. The taxi, piloted by a near-silent driver, carried her past the grey hulk of the bus station, the Sunday market, coffee houses she hadn't seen before, print works, car parks and, presently past a white sign bearing the words *Thomas McAllister Building & Development* in red, arching over double gates to a yard. The gates were closed, as it wasn't a working day, but Judith knew what would stand behind them. A cabin where a couple of long-suffering clerks put up with Tom's eccentric work methods and a yard full of barrows, dump trucks, a skip, trestles and scaffolding towers.

Building equipment had once been a familiar part of her working landscape, too.

Four streets further on, at the house in the generously sized square called Victoria Gardens, it was a different matter because there had been a lot of change courtesy of Liza, the woman Tom had preferred over Judith. Thanking her driver and paying her fare, Judith got out to gaze at what had once been her marital home while the taxi purred away. The extensive front garden of the gracious old house had been paved over, a big, ostentatious urn stuck where the alpine garden used to be and the desert of drive was flanked by variegated topiary balls. Judith had never cared much for variegated plants, which, after all, only made a virtue out of a virus. The low white wooden gates she'd once chosen had been replaced by tall, spindly black wrought iron with golden spikes on top – an unhappy fit with the original ornate Victorian railings around the sunken gardens in the centre of the square.

She gazed nostalgically at the communal garden, remembering sunny days spent beneath its tall copper beeches that glowed in the sunlight. Creamy Russian vine rioted over a series of brick arches. Mile-a-minute, some people called the vine and when she'd been married to Tom the residents had held Mile-a-minute Sundays, forming working parties to cut the vine back to prevent it from smothering the entire district. They'd been loud and happy occasions fuelled by glasses of wine and picnic lunches. Children high on Mars bars and Coca-Cola would give up stuffing the snaky clippings into black bags in favour of screaming and racing around, scaling stepladders no matter how often they were warned not to. Kieran had been one of them.

Judith turned away from the memory and clanged through the fancy, golden-tipped gates.

It was an odd sensation to knock at the door of what used to be her home, especially since it was a different door now, with mock Gothic hinges and an ornate black letterbox. She wondered what had happened to the gracious old one with the stained glass panel. Tom had probably sold it to a reclamation yard.

Tom answered the door and looked stunned to see her. He also looked dishevelled, with food spots on his shirt and his hair on end. The contrast between him and Giorgio struck her like a slap. Tom looked slack and pale and all of his fifty-four years. A cynical person might say she'd done all right for herself, exchanging this husband for Giorgio's dark good looks and fewer years on the clock. Giorgio's body had been firm beneath her hands. Tom's typically English appetites for fatty food and too much beer had combined unhappily with the effects of gravity. He was showing definite signs of wear and tear, his hair leached of colour and both face and body pouchy.

She arranged her features into a smile. 'Hello, Tom. Sorry if I woke you from a Sunday nap.'

A familiar parade of expressions flitted across Tom's lived-in face. Pleasure to see her, then the resentment he harboured towards her so unreasonably. Lastly, resignation, because no matter how angry he'd become it had been futile. She'd left him anyway. 'Judith! What are you doing here?'

'I just came to tell you that I'm living in Brinham again, just so you'd know. I'd hate Frankie to surprise you with the news.' She could imagine Frankie dropping in at Tom's yard with a caustic, 'Your old missus has turned up again,' probably in front of Tom's employees.

82

He blinked and stroked his hair back over his head. She was sure she'd been right about the nap. Perhaps he was wondering whether she was part of a dream.

'I was sorry to hear about Liza.' She congratulated herself for actually sounding sorry, rather than smug at his comeuppance.

'Yes.' He hesitated. 'It was a bad time.' Then, ungraciously, 'Well. I suppose you can come in.'

She remained where she was. She'd never cared for the bluntness of Tom's manners and marvelled that once she'd seen him as a rough diamond, rather than just the rude man she saw now.

After a second he sighed, and amended with overdone courtesy, 'Why, Judith, how lovely to see you. Would you care to come in, perhaps for some refreshment?'

She grinned at his exaggerated air of indulging her. 'A cup of tea would be very welcome. Thank you.' She stepped into the big hall with the dogleg staircase rising from it.

He closed the door behind her. 'You know where the kitchen is. Get me a cup while you're at it.'

She opened the door again and stepped back out. 'You don't change much, Tom.'

'It was a joke!' he shouted after her as she strolled down the drive. 'Judith!'

Her hand on the large gate latch, she paused. Had she overreacted? Couldn't she take a bit of wry humour any more? Maybe she should turn back and have a civilised cuppa with this big bluff bloke who was once her husband.

But Tom yelled on. 'You don't have to be like that . . . you stroppy, awkward mare! You always were flitty or we'd still be together.' Flitty, from Tom, was an insult usually reserved for exasperating female customers who changed their minds mid-job. Flitty was an insult, when associated with Judith deciding to leave him over his infidelity.

She stepped through the gate, calling back, 'I might be stroppy and awkward but deciding not to be married to you doesn't make me flitty. It makes me sensible.' With a cheery wave, she left him behind. Again.

Why had she bothered? Tom never improved.

# *Chapter Six*

For two weeks, Judith continued on in Molly's spare room. It was still odd and uncomfortable. Her sister and brother-in-law, she sometimes suspected, only made the effort to converse when there was a witness.

At the end of every day, Frankie climbed out of the van with *Francis O'Malley Construction* on the side. Molly would have already prepared a meal for him to come home to – a proper, cooked, two-course dinner from fresh ingredients. After eating, Frankie retired behind the paper and Molly sat before the television watching, without any change of expression, soaps, dramas, reality shows and comedies. Judith soon began to spend most evenings reading in her room, which at least gave her hosts the privacy to ignore each other. She wondered how on earth her sister shared a bed with someone she hardly spoke to.

During the day, Judith got out of the house as much as she could and tried to get the hang of living in Brinham again. Brinham was a perfectly pleasant market town in an OK part of Northamptonshire. The town centre had grown up in the era of dark-red Victorian buildings with moulded brickwork and steep roofs and what remained of that period was worth a second look. It wasn't always beautiful but it definitely had style.

Unfortunately, in the seventies it had been acceptable to demolish streets and streets of that Victorian heritage and replace them with an enormous shopping centre like something a five-year-old might make from Lego – if Lego made only mud-brown bricks and long, narrow, wired-glass windows. The Norbury Centre was a development Judith had never cared for but at least the council had paved Market Square and the pedestrian arcade, installing olde-worlde black lampposts hung with baskets of vermilion petunias, so the blemish of The Norbury was less conspicuous.

English weather she was finding a bit moist, even in summer, but there were lovely days, too, with sunshine that caressed the skin. In Malta, summer sunshine could still hit you like a sheet of hot metal.

She visited a hairdresser for fresh highlights – Sparkling Embers – and to have her shaggy barnet cut back into a new low-maintenance feathered style onto her shoulders. She liked it. It swished when she turned her head.

She bought a small car, two years old and bruise purple, then collected Wilma from The Cottage to take her to a coffee shop with yellow café lace and green gingham curtains.

'You're too thin by half,' declared Wilma, struggling out of the car and patting her pearly white perm while she waited for Judith to wrestle her walking frame out of the hatchback. 'I'll have a nice pot of tea because I can't bear coffee in these places – it's nothing but froth. And you only get a dab of jam with a scone.' With a lightning change of subject she added, 'I wish I knew what really made you come home. You never really confide, Judith. You didn't fall out with Richard and family, did you? Isn't it about time Richard retired? He might be my baby brother but he's knocking on.' She smiled as she took the walking frame, her jowls lifting and becoming part of her cheeks. 'I wish you'd brought my wheelchair.'

Judith made sure Wilma had her balance before she let go of the aluminium frame. 'You said you wanted to walk.'

Wilma laughed. 'Don't take any notice of me. I can't walk.'

'Piggyback?' Judith turned and crouched invitingly.

Wilma's chuckle was more of a wheeze. 'Serve you right if I hopped on.'

It was a lovely couple of hours. Wilma's worst fears weren't realised as the scones came with thick jam and the only uncomfortable moment was when Wilma declared loudly that she didn't like the way things were done in 2004 because Judith had to get up to the till to pay instead of the bill being brought by wait staff.

A couple of days later, Judith arranged to see Kieran, who had Bethan by his side. They met at a pub – not The Punch, which had once been her local, because it was now overrun by under twenty-fives. The Prince was more multi-generational. When Bethan asked for a vodka shot, Judith automatically asked, 'How old are you?' Kieran frowned at Judith.

'Seventeen,' Bethan admitted, and pulled at the fronds of the two-tone hair hanging around her face.

Judith bought the vodka shot without arguing but glanced at Kieran. 'And you're twenty-two.'

'I know that.' He took the bottle of strong lager he'd

ordered from the bar and led the way to a table by a window. 'There's no law against it, is there? You don't seem to worry about age gaps in your own relationships.'

Judith stared down into her cold white wine as she took her seat, thinking of the years between her and Giorgio and suddenly didn't want it. She put it on the table.

'Sorry,' he mumbled.

'It's OK. Age gaps are all a question of perspective and . . .' – she fumbled for a word – 'wisdom.' She didn't point out that Bethan wasn't yet lawfully an adult, which Judith found more significant than Kieran seemed to.

He frowned, and she knew he was searching for her meaning and suspecting her disapproval.

When she'd had enough of Kieran and Bethan's in-your-face conducting of their courtship, all those yawning kisses even when Judith was halfway through a sentence at the time, she left them to it, stepping out into the late-evening purple darkness.

It was drizzling. 'Bloody British weather,' she muttered, turning up her collar. She was aware that she might not be wise to wander the streets of this area late at night on her own. This wasn't Malta, where the world and his wife would be strolling in the comfortable evening temperatures along the promenade from Sliema to Spinola. This was Brinham, which had its bad areas like most towns, and a sensible British personal safety code must be followed. It didn't pay to wander back streets with a handbag on show, late at night, alone. She turned towards the taxi rank.

But then her phone beeped and she fished it from her pocket.

A text message from Richard flashed up. *Must speak, can u get 2 landline?*

She stared. It would be nearly midnight already in Malta.

She returned, *Will be @ Molly's house 30 mins* and turned towards the couple of taxis standing in the rank, heart hurrying as fast as her feet. Easy-going Richard never before sent her a dramatic, urgent-sounding message.

# Chapter Seven

When Judith quietly let herself in through Molly and Frankie's front door she found Molly had already gone to bed. Frankie was asleep in his chair, paper collapsed on his lap, glasses skewed, mouth open. The house was dark except for a small reading lamp reflecting on Frankie's head and a weak bulb that lit the stairs.

Creeping quietly, Judith collected the cordless phone from its stand in the hall and carried it to her room. The instant it rang, she pressed the key to accept the call to ensure the others weren't disturbed.

Richard's voice filled her ear, warm, friendly, reminding her sharply of Malta. She pictured him at home with the doors and windows open to the night, stroking his smart little moustache, his feet bare on the tiles. His wife Erminia would be reading a magazine or knitting in the background from the light of the lamp with a pink tasselled shade. He said, 'I rang Molly's and she told me you were out with Kieran – sorry to have to bring you home early.'

She tried to keep her breathing calm. Could he have news of Giorgio? 'No problem. What's up?'

He sighed. 'Are you alone?'

She gripped the handset more tightly. 'Yes.' She could hear a tremor in her voice.

'It's bad news.' Another sigh. After a lengthy pause he added, 'It's just that . . . well, Sliema Z Bus Tours has gone bust.'

*Bust.* She turned the word over in her mind. Bust? Bust. She couldn't, for a moment, see its relevance to Sliema Z Bus Tours. Or, of course, she *could*. But it couldn't be that. *That* would be too terrible. *That* would mean . . .

Her mouth went numb. She fought to remain calm. 'What's happened?'

'As we agreed, I wrote to the directors advising them that you wished to sell your share, and offering them the option to buy it from you. In view of the informal nature of the agreement between you and Giorgio, it seemed the best way. What I got back was a notice about insolvency, and the address of the liquidator.'

'Oh no,' she breathed.

'I didn't bother you at that stage, because I thought it was simply a mistake. I didn't think it could be insolvency. I thought it was probably something to do with structure, because of Giorgio not being able to administer his own affairs. A technicality.'

Her voice echoed oddly in her ears. 'But it isn't?'

'No.' He gusted a sigh. 'I've been to your apartment today to collect the mail. It included a notice to say they're in liquidation.'

Disbelief made her blood thunder. She snapped, 'That's ridiculous. They're not in liquidation, I invested thirty thousand liri. They're negotiating to buy new buses. If they were in trouble, they would've cancelled the expansion and used the money to trade out of their difficulties.'

Richard's voice was heavy as he said flatly, 'Your money's gone.'

Wordlessly, she wiped sweat from her top lip and the base of her throat.

'Your money's gone,' he repeated, as if he thought she hadn't heard. 'I've had a long talk with Giorgio's business partners, Anton and Gordon. I've been with them all evening, in fact. Although you and other individuals supposedly invested to fund the planned expansion, actually one of their drivers had caused a fatal road accident. The company's insurance had lapsed.'

Judith closed her eyes tightly, feeling sick. 'But that can't have taken all the money?'

Richard's voice was gentle. 'Your money was used to meet their legal costs, and it's gone. The liquidator's selling the bits and pieces they owned but the premises were rented and the vehicles leased. You know how these things are arranged. I can meet with the liquidators on your behalf but there's no point until their enquiries are complete.' He paused. 'The liquidator is making the usual enquiries about directorial negligence. Eventually, you might be able to bring action against them but . . .' His voice tailed off doubtfully.

Judith tried to grasp what was happening. 'The business can't be insolvent.'

'It can, I'm afraid. The case has been going on for two years. It's a complete house of cards. I'm sorry, Judith.' A long silence. A slow breath, then he added, in a rush, obviously knowing this would be unwelcome news but that Judith had the right to know it, 'Anton says Giorgio was responsible for insurance matters.'

'I see,' she said dully. Bright, happy-go-lucky Giorgio. She could imagine him forgetting something as mundane as insurance. Or, even more likely, gambling that they'd never need it and the money could be better employed in printing flashy brochures for more luxurious tours. It was like falling on a knife to think that he'd hidden the enquiry into the fatal crash from her. No wonder he hadn't been his usual self in his last days.

'I wish I could offer to return the money you invested in Richard Elliot Estate now, but I don't think I can at the moment,' Richard added awkwardly. 'We bought into that new hotel development in Sliema . . .'

Hollowly, she said, 'I know. It's OK. We agreed a schedule and none of this is your fault.' The knowledge that she was nowhere near as comfortably circumstanced as she'd thought settled heavily in her stomach. They'd been so bloody excited to be involved in the small hotel; she'd been as enthusiastic as anyone. She hadn't realised she'd become so short of capital.

They talked money a while longer. There was about two thousand pounds on its way to her from the sale of her car in Malta and all she had on top of that and her dividend payments was a couple more in savings and Adam Leblond's rent, which wasn't exactly an income. After eventually concluding the call, she scarcely slept. In the early morning, too restless to remain indoors, she let herself quietly out of the house and went out to pace the misty streets of Brinham, hoping the sun would soon burn off the dampness and her whirring brain would quiet.

*Oh, Giorgio. You've let me down.*

But she still loved him. On a massive heave of sadness, her eyes boiled at the memory of the hospital, the tubes and beeping machines.

Cass had been right to say she should never have seen him that way. How much better for her final memories

93

of Giorgio to be of him smiling, laughing, plunging his unbroken body into the sea, spending a raucous day on a fishing boat with his mates, drinking golden Cisk beer or bitter black espresso, eating sun-dried figs. Or swaying with the movement of an impressive, modern, air-conditioned coach, eyes sparkling and hands gesticulating, captivating his passengers with tales of village *festas*, bare-back donkey races, parades and *ghannejja* or folk singers. Had he really been hiding how close disaster loomed as he'd ushered tourists around ancient stone cities, cata-combs and prehistoric temples, old film sets and bustling markets?

The impression Sliema Z Bus Tours gave had certainly been one of prosperity. The shiny cream coaches with rainbows on the sides had plunged visitors into itineraries bursting with fun, history and culture. It hadn't looked, as Richard termed it, like a house of cards, which one bit of mismanagement would send fluttering to the ground.

It *must* have been oversight or false economy that led to the vital insurance policy being allowed to lapse at least . . . mustn't it? But had Giorgio known that she'd never see her invested money again? Had he considered his seeking of private venture capital legitimate?

Inside, she knew it didn't matter. He had left her high and dry and she could hardly challenge him about it now.

Living free at her sister's house could scarcely continue; she was the kind who felt an overwhelming need to pay her way. And when she got her house back from Adam she'd have electricity bills, gas, water, food . . . She sighed. Even without a mortgage to pay, she'd have to get a job, part-time, at least.

Her feet took her into town where the market traders were setting up stalls and the butcher was optimistically winding out his canopy to shade his window display from sunshine. A postman pushed a pram-like mail carrier up the street, pausing to force packets of letters through letter flaps set low in shop doors. Paperboys cycled on the pavement with baseball caps far back on heads of tightly cut hair.

Judith crossed Market Square into High Street, threading her way between people hurrying to work. What kind of job should she be looking for? Before she went to Malta she'd worked long hours for a big construction company on sites that had felt like muddy cities with streets filled with rumbling construction machinery. But she didn't want to go back to that, all the regulations and permissions and head-in-the-clouds architects along with the awful head-aches for junior managers of large projects. In her absence things would have changed; she'd have to get her head around updates and new regulations for things like glazing and insulation. And she'd have to overcome that male-dominated world all over again. She'd met Tom on one of those blokey construction sites but she no longer had the kind of energy needed to deal with his colleagues.

No. She just couldn't hack it at the moment. It was too much pressure for someone whose emotions were all over the place and the income from a decent part-time job should be enough as she had no mortgage. Something interesting . . . not a shop, not a bank, not a big bland office, not a call centre, not a pub . . .

'Judith!'

She blinked herself out of her list of negatives and realised with a small shock that Tom was standing across the High Street, shoulders hunched, a navy baseball cap pulled over his eyes. 'Hang on,' he called. He waited for the lights to stop the traffic, then crossed to her pavement.

She regarded him with misgivings. She wasn't in the mood for more of Tom's grumpiness – or 'being in a mardy' as the local slang would have it.

But today Tom seemed quite genial. 'Fancy a cuppa? There's a new caff up here, Hannah's Pantry, and they do a beautiful brew.'

Lack of sleep caught up with her in a rush, making her head feel light. A 'beautiful brew' sounded just the cure so she said, 'OK, why not?' and let him show her to a small café in High Street, its frontage painted navy blue. A friendly cuppa might improve relations between them. She didn't want to be living in the same town as him in enmity.

Others were already enjoying the fruits of Hannah's Pantry, when they arrived. It was panelled in pine and served tea and coffee in mugs, with milk from a jug and sugar from a bowl. The menu was chalked up on a board and luscious homemade cakes waited in a glassed-in counter. The staff members were young, probably sixth-formers, with one bulky woman – Hannah – in charge.

'Mornin' Tom.' Hannah reached around her capacious chest to pop toast from an enormous chrome toaster.

'All right, Tom?' A tall young man cleaned a table with a quick spray-and-wipe.

'Hey, Tom.' A diminutive girl rapidly set out a range of jams and marmalades, wiping each jar.

'Morning, morning,' he replied comfortably, as he edged between the tables. By the time he'd exchanged greetings with three staff and two customers, Judith had got the idea that he was a regular. They both ordered tea and toast and sat down at the pine table the young guy had prepared near steamy windows. At the bottom of the glass, the ghost of a smiley face beamed out from a previous layer of condensation.

As they breakfasted, Tom asked Judith about Malta. Judith told him a little of her life there but nothing about Giorgio because, apart from being just too weird to discuss him with her ex-husband, feeling as raw and let down as she did, she simply didn't want to let Tom into those memories. Despite Richard's shocking news, Giorgio was too precious, too special, too private to open to Tom's gruff brand of – or perhaps even lack of – sympathy. And, you never knew with Tom – he might even gloat.

'So, if you're back for good, what do you intend to do with yourself?' Tom's large teeth crunched into toast made from thick white bread and running with butter. Awake, washed and brushed, he looked considerably better than he had done when she'd seen him last.

She spread ginger marmalade on her own toast and took a bite, enjoying that particularly British combination of hot toast, cold conserve and a slick of butter between the two. 'A job's high on my list of priorities.' She sipped hot tea from the forest-green mug.

He grunted. 'Back to the hard hat and wellies?'

'Hope not. I don't want to work full time. Don't particularly want the stress of site meetings and trying to make architects understand why their pretty picture won't work on the ground – you know what that's like. I'll have to look about, think about what I can do.'

He talked around a mouthful of food. 'I could look out for something for you.'

She selected lemon curd to spread on her second slice of toast. Tom was already on his fourth. 'That's a nice offer, but I don't want to be in construction, thanks.' And she didn't want any threads to draw her towards Tom. She crunched into the toast and the tart-sweet bite of the lemon.

When breakfast was over and they'd said goodbye, Tom headed for Thomas McAllister Building & Development despite it being a Sunday and Judith headed off to gaze in the windows of three of the town's job agencies, reading the cards in the *Summer 2004 – P/time* columns. Nothing took her fancy. The openings all seemed to do with payroll, warehouse work or driving. She knew she could sign on at an agency for professional people, but then, surely, wouldn't they offer her jobs within her construction management profession? She turned away with the intention to return on a weekday.

All her life she'd decided what to do and then done it. The unsettled purposelessness she was experiencing now was foreign to her and vaguely depressing. She knew she wanted something different. Something . . . well, she didn't understand what. But different. For lack of anything else to do, she headed back towards Molly's house.

Her route happened to take her close to Lavender Row. She slowed, thoughtfully. There would be no harm in calling in to see if Adam Leblond had begun the hunt for alternative accommodation. It might delay the return to the frigid life of Molly for half an hour. She turned left and was soon sauntering up her own street, taking in the geraniums in tubs and windows open to the fresh air now the sun had got the better of the early mist. Soon she was turning onto her short front path and pressing the doorbell.

Adam Leblond answered the door with a phone tucked between shoulder and ear. He gestured her into the house with a flash of his smile. She followed him into the combined sitting and dining room where the computer in the alcove displayed a screenful of thumbnail images and a cable ran between it and a matt black camera. Silver photographer's cases were open nearby and paperwork was laid out neatly across the carpet. 'Two minutes,' he mouthed, gesturing her towards an armchair.

Then he returned to his phone conversation with restrained patience. 'But that wasn't what you asked for . . . Of course I could have done the garden as well, but this is a bit after the event, isn't it? I can't rewind time.' He listened for a minute, performed a small eye-roll then wound the call up with a brisk, 'OK. Let me know tomorrow if you want me to schedule another shoot.'

The moment he clicked the phone off and glanced Judith's way with a, 'Hello—' the phone rang again. He grimaced. 'Sorry. But do you mind if I take it?'

'Go ahead.' She picked up a glossy home magazine to flip through while he entered into another exchange, clamping the phone to his left ear with his shoulder and scribbling on a pad awkwardly with his right hand, the pen lodged between his thumb and the knuckle where his first finger used to be. 'Yes, I said I can. How many? . . .What's the angle of the piece? . . . Well, you must know what the writer's written . . . Email those details to me, please, and I can give you a quote.'

He put down the phone once more, scribbled on for a few moments, then flung himself down on the sofa, shoving back his hair. 'Sorry.'

She closed the magazine. 'No, I shouldn't turn up unannounced. I didn't think you'd be working on a Sunday.'

He blew out his lips. 'I shouldn't be. Unfortunately, I've just lost my assistant so I have to deal with my paperwork myself. And the phone call was from a picture editor of a magazine who can access her computer network from home. Probably sitting on the lawn with her laptop catching up on a few things while her kids play in the paddling pool.'

'You work for magazines?'

'Mostly. Mags schedule features, then contact me to shoot the accompanying pics for them. A lot are case histories, you know, "I had an affair with the cannibal next door" sort of thing.' He grinned, obviously not expecting her to believe the reference to a cannibal. 'I cover the Midlands for several titles. Very busy at the moment.'

She felt like breathing a Kieran-like, 'That's *so* cool!' But restricted herself instead to, 'So you won't have had a minute to start looking for alternative accommodation?'

'No need.' His calm eyes hardened. 'Nowhere near August twenty-first. That's when you can run an inventory, inspect the property, give me back my key money, and I'll go.'

Judith's stomach dipped.

Key money.

She'd forgotten she held his key money. The modest savings she'd thought she still had plummeted by about twenty-five per cent. Rats.

His grin flashed and all the grooves beside his mouth and eyes deepened. 'Do you know you've got marmalade on your chin?'

She jumped up to glare into the mirror over the fireplace. Sure enough, the cleft of her chin was decorated by a smear like a comma. 'Bugger.' She scrubbed at her chin with lick-and-tissue, succeeding in making the skin pink. 'I had breakfast with my ex. His idea of fun not to tell me, I suppose.'

'Breakfast with your ex? Civilised.'

'Accidental meeting.' She returned to her seat, her chin

burning slightly and her cheeks burning a lot. 'Then I went browsing job agency windows.'

Interest dawned in his eyes. 'You're looking for a job?'

She wrinkled her nose. 'Economic necessity, like anyone. Something part time, hopefully.'

'What sort of thing? Because I'm desperate for someone like you to help me on a big shoot, tomorrow.'

Surprise zinged through her. 'Like me? What am I like?'

He gestured vaguely. 'Personable, with a brain. I have a hectic day scheduled. Got to drive to a village near Coventry to take shots of a family with thirteen children ranging from a new baby to twins of twenty. Nightmare trying to keep everyone engaged and happy for the duration of the shoot at the best of times, let alone when there are so many kids. And everything's more difficult since . . .' He indicated his damaged hand. 'I had a brilliant assistant, Daria, a friend's daughter who came on shoots and did my routine phone calls and invoicing and stuff. Terrific. But she's just run off to Northumberland after a whirlwind holiday romance, leaving me stuck.' He sounded disgruntled at Daria's defection.

Judith glanced at equipment cases on the floor of the dining room, gazing at grey felt-lined compartments packed with cables and lenses. 'Doesn't sound too difficult,' she observed.

His face lit up. 'So you'll give it a go? That's great!'

She was taken aback at this leap of faith. 'I actually meant it doesn't sound too difficult so you ought not have trouble filling the vacancy.' Did she want to be a photographer's assistant? How many people did it take to hold a camera anyway? 'Wouldn't you need someone full time? And permanent?'

'Two days one week, four days the next, depending. I

101

can advertise for someone permanent, but in the meantime I've got tomorrow to get through. You'd be doing me a huge favour if you helped out. I pay by the day.' The sum he mentioned seemed to Judith to be worthwhile. 'Please?' he added, brushing back his hair in harassed fashion. 'I'm really stuck.'

'Oh. Um. I have no relevant experience or qualifications but perhaps just while you advertise,' she managed, eventually.

'Excellent.' Decisively, he jumped up and pulled one of the metal cases closer. He fished out a lens in his left hand and a camera body in the right. 'I can teach you what you need to know. Let's start by me telling you the names of all the equipment . . .'

At the end of two hours she was dizzy with changing lenses, taking equipment on and off tripods and putting the settings he wanted on the Nikon cameras. Every item was now tidily back in its compartment.

'Earlyish start in the morning,' he breezed, closing the last case. 'Can you be here by seven? I need to get going about then. The shoot's not till ten but you know what the traffic can be like at that time in the morning.'

She narrowed her eyes at him, taking in the straight hair that flopped across his forehead above an expression of studied casualness. 'You didn't mention a crack-of-dawn start.'

He smiled disarmingly, eyes twinkling. 'Hardly crack of dawn. Dawn's much earlier in summer.'

# Chapter Eight

'About seven' proved to be deceptively approximate.

Judith arrived two minutes after that time on Monday morning, having found it difficult to wake after the sleeplessness of the night before, and arrived to find the gear loaded and Adam in the driving seat of his car, waiting. He started the engine as she plumped into the passenger seat. ''Morning,' she said agreeably.

'Indoor–outdoor shoot,' he replied, as if they were colleagues of long standing and could dispense with anything but the job in hand. He pulled away before she'd even got her seat belt fastened. His right hand had some kind of aid around it that helped him grip the steering wheel and the car had column gears so that his left hand didn't have to dip to a traditional gear stick and leave his right hand in charge of steering on its own.

She managed to click the seat belt home and followed his lead that chit-chat was not required. 'Is that significant?'

'It means we have to carry more equipment. We're heading for a village called Bulkington, north of Coventry.

I know our route is A14, M6, but can you look it up from there, for me? The map book's under your seat.'

Blearily, she found the page and glanced at the network marked in blue, green, red, orange and white that denoted the country's roads. She yawned and tried to focus, her head feeling twice its usual weight. After a few moments' study she said, 'Looks like you take the M69 off the M6, and it's just off that.'

'Sounds easy enough. Find something on the radio that you want to listen to then have another rummage through the biggest equipment case. Make sure you remember how to change memory cards, grip, tripod, etc. Please,' he added, as an obvious afterthought.

She dragged the case off the back seat with an inner sigh. It would have been nice to relax the journey away. Not *sleep*, of course not, that would be an unprofessional way for a photographer's assistant to behave. And, also, she'd probably snore with her mouth open or something equally cringe-worthy. But playing with memory cards wasn't interesting, and she yawned prodigiously all the way up the A14 as they progressed slowly through the morning traffic.

Eventually, he took pity on her. 'How about a coffee stop?'

She gave another face-wrenching, eye-watering yawn. 'Coffee would be brilliant. I'm sleepy.'

'You don't say,' he answered ironically.

They bought coffee in big cardboard beakers and awarded themselves ten minutes on a bench outside the service station, the idea being that fresh air might wake Judith up. By the time she'd drained her cup, she did feel brighter. 'Better get on.' She looked at her watch. A proportion of the time Adam had built in for traffic hold-ups had drained away.

This proved to be a problem when they finally turned onto the M69 and Judith got the map out again to navigate them through the A-roads. She was better able now to focus on the multi-coloured strands that denoted the roads they travelled. She found Bulkington, close to the M69, with her finger. Then her heart sank. 'Oh, hell. We can't exit the M69 where I thought we could. It's one of those places where the roads cross but there's no junction.' At his impatient sigh, she added, 'Sorry.' Her face heated uncomfortably. It wasn't a good start to her day as a photographer's assistant.

'Brilliant,' he muttered. Then, 'OK, we can't turn around on the motorway, so what's our best solution?'

He was obviously irritated but at least he hadn't yanked the car onto the hard shoulder and snatched the map from her hands as Tom would have tried to do. Mortified at her error, she studied the map with a degree of care that would have been useful in the first place. 'At the next junction you can turn right onto the A5, then take the first right. The road curls back beneath the motorway.'

'That doesn't sound too bad.' But he flicked a glance at the dashboard clock and moved purposefully into the outside lane to get a hurry on . . . just as they encountered the first signs indicating roadworks.

By the time they'd navigated the roadworks and the route off the motorway to Bulkington they were fifteen minutes late. Judith, gaining the distinct impression that being late wasn't in Adam's business model, had to ring ahead on his mobile to apologise, hot with embarrassment at making a silly, uncharacteristic mistake.

'Don't you worry, dear, we won't be ready anyway,' was the comforting response from Jillie Lencko, the mother of the impressive family.

And she was right. They arrived at the two semi-detached houses knocked together. Invited in, they discovered one of the eldest female twins had gone to the shop in a huff and the other wasn't back after staying out all night. Jillie Lencko displayed a spectacular quantity of breast through her open dress as she fed a baby who smelled as if he needed changing while a handful of the thirteen Lencko offspring raced around in an exciting game of chase. Having originally been two dwellings, the house had two front doors and two back, allowing plenty of scope for racing in and out of the property. They went back out to the car.

'You're going to earn your stripes organising this crowd.' Calmly, Adam began to unload his gear from the back.

From this, Judith assumed he'd to set up his equipment while she took charge of the personnel. 'I'm not changing the nappy. I'll sort the rest.'

'Fine. Smells don't show up on images.' He grabbed cases in either hand, balanced a tripod on his shoulder and took the path to the left front door.

If Judith had been tired before the shoot, she soon realised she was going to be exhausted after. As Adam opened cases she buttonholed the two oldest-looking Lenckos available, one male, one female, both in the black studded clothes of goths. 'You look like the guys with the authority. How do I go about organising the tinies so we can get this photoshoot underway?'

The male sighed. 'Yeah. Us as usual.' But he set the older half of the family to subduing the younger half, combing hair, washing faces and doing up buttons or hair ribbons, snapping out instructions that ended the game of chase. The baby fed stolidly, throughout. Soon the twins returned sheepishly from their respective sulks and high

jinks and disappeared upstairs to get ready. The baby
burped without decorating his blue outfit or his mother's
black-and-violet dress. Jillie thrust her breasts away and
Pete Lencko, the man of the house, emerged from the loo
with the *Daily Express*.

They were all set for a shoot in the vast sitting room
that had been made from most of the ground floor of one
of the original houses.

Adam took Judith aside. 'We normally do our best to
co-ordinate everyone so that we don't have horrible
colour clashes on the page but we need to work fast
while we have their attention. So do your best – and at
least get that girl with the cochineal hair to stand away
from the lad with the blue plume. Blast, that tall boy's
got a black eye, look. Turn him three-quarters on so it's
hidden. Pull the curtains and we'll work entirely with
flash because the bloody sun beams into this room from
all angles.' So the morning progressed, Adam reeling off
what he wanted, what he envisaged and how he was going
to get it, and Judith fielding toddlers as they made a break
for freedom or getting teenaged girls to pause in their
chewing and *smile*!

While he worked, Judith noticed, Adam managed to
forget about keeping his damaged hand out of sight. He
used it as he needed it and adapted what he had to. With
a mixture of Adam's charm and Judith's gentle bullying
they managed the Herculean task of completing the shoot
before anyone burst into tears or abandoned the shoot.

'Thanks everyone. You were amazing,' Adam told them
when the last shot had been taken – generously, considering
what a sustained effort it had taken to wrangle them.
Then he and Judith had to get all the gear back in the
car, trying to avoid too much 'help' from overenthusiastic

and sticky young hands. Eventually, they were able to shut themselves back in the vehicle and drive away.

'You did great,' Adam congratulated her, visibly more relaxed now the shoot was over.

'It was more fun than I thought it would be.' Judith yawned as she used the map to guide Adam back to the motorway. Then the next thing she knew she was waking up outside the house in Lavender Row, the map still spread out over her lap.

Groaning, she flexed her stiff neck. Her mouth was dry, her eyes were gritty and her hair was flattened over one eye. 'Are we back? We've missed lunch.'

'We can have some soup. Wake yourself up and I'll show you how to download the pics onto my system and then run you through the paperwork.' Adam threw the splint from his hand into the centre console, apparently as fresh as he had been at seven this morning.

'Paperwork?' She trailed indoors behind him. 'What about the soup?'

He pushed into the sitting room. 'My assistant does most of my paperwork. And some phone calls. It's in the day rate, OK? And I'll need an invoice from you for your hours for the month, so you mark the days you work in that black diary, and at the end of the month type an invoice on the computer, print it out and put it on that pile for my assistant to pay.' He grinned.

She blinked at her temporary assistant status being so casually extended. 'But you'll be advertising, soon?'

'Yes, yes.' He waved the question away. 'My assistant gets the soup, too. Is tomato OK? It's all I've got. Now, downloading the images isn't rocket science but it does have to be done correctly or you can lose the work or mess up the settings on the camera . . .'

'Soup,' she said firmly, heading for the kitchen.

He sighed. 'OK. Soup first.'

When she finally left the house, after he'd taught her how to download, label and organise the images, explained his computer system, showed her how to raise invoices and post them to the appropriate spreadsheet – the paperwork was a doddle because Adam was organised and everything was up to date – it was turned six o'clock. She'd also somehow agreed to assist him on shoots on Tuesday (a donkey sanctuary), Friday (a girl who'd done well in *Pop Idol* revisiting her old school) and Thursday and Friday of next week (a couple who'd married each other three times and a windmill turned sumptuous dwelling).

'Just until you advertise,' she reminded him. 'It ought to keep the wolf from the door while I look around for something else.'

'What else?' he queried genially.

That gave her pause. 'I don't know.' But working for her tenant was a bit odd.

Weary from her busy day, she trudged home. And then, groan, groan, she discovered that Molly and Frankie were engaged in a teeth-clenched row, just when all she wanted to do was flop down somewhere and relax. Creeping upstairs, she showered, shut herself away in her room with her radio and a book and tried to ignore increasingly unignorable shouts and slams. Eventually, she put on her shoes, crept back downstairs and slipped back out of the front door.

Not having an abundance of places to go, she opted for jumping in her car and visiting her mother. One of the carers in a lilac overall showed Judith to Wilma's pink-and-white room, where she'd sought the comfort of

*Coronation Street* on TV. 'Hello, dear,' said Wilma uncertainly when she caught sight of Judith, rocking her tubular aluminium walking stick on its three grey rubber feet. 'I'd forgotten you were coming. I haven't put my lipstick on.'

Judith kissed her mother's soft cheek. 'You haven't forgotten, Mum. There was nothing arranged. I just thought I'd like to see you. Is that OK? You said I could pop in any time, now I'm living in Brinham again.' She sat down in an orange plastic chair, massaging an ache above her left eye. Sleep was beckoning madly, but an early night was off the cards chez O'Malley.

'Of course! It's lovely to see you.' Wilma agitated her stick some more and sucked her teeth. 'What shall we talk about? I haven't really had a chance to think of anything to say.'

How odd that her mother should need notice to gather together the ingredients of a conversation with her daughter. Had Judith been very self-absorbed not to notice how her mother's world had shrunk? Now she was back in Brinham she must make more effort to become part of the fabric of Wilma's life. Meanwhile, it would probably be easier for Wilma if Judith got the conversational ball rolling. 'I've got a temporary job as a photographer's assistant.'

Wilma laughed. 'A temporary assistant? You? Does your employer realise that you'll be bossing everyone about in no time?'

Settling in the chair, Judith got herself comfortable. 'That doesn't sound like me at all,' she joked. 'Anyway, it's just one bloke. The one who rents my house, Adam Leblond – he was two years above me and Mel at school. It's just till he gets someone more suitable and I look round for something else. What's new with you?'

Wilma gave the subject some thought. She wore no powder and her skin looked duller than usual. 'Nice lunch, today,' she offered. 'Beans.'

'Green beans?'

'Yes, I don't like baked beans. And a chop and new potatoes. Very fresh and tasty. They look after us lovely, here.'

'That's good.' Late-lunch soup seemed a long way in the past. Stomach gurgling, Judith cast around for more material for discussion. 'Have you read your newspaper today?'

'Most of it. And done the crossword; the crossword's my favourite, I always leave it till last. And the problem page. Me and my friends here all buy different newspapers and pass them around during the day. Florrie read out a problem from a magazine today, ever so racy, and only from a girl of seventeen. We all giggled but I was a bit embarrassed.' She went on, outlining the way the papers and magazines circulated.

Despite her good intentions, Judith's mind began to wander over the recent disasters in her life . . . Giorgio in a stark white hospital room, his gaze not meeting hers . . . Sliema Z Bus Tours in liquidation. Judith's money down the toilet.

Wilma grasped Judith's wrist gently, regaining her attention. 'Today there was a letter from a woman who was awfully worried about her daughter.'

Judith blinked. 'Sorry?'

'A problem, m'duck, on the problem page.'

Like many people, Judith only skimmed problem pages for the snigger-worthy and the salacious. 'Oh?'

Wilma adjusted her glasses with their fancy designs up the side and flexed her fingers on the handle of her stick.

'She's in her forties, the daughter, and a very competent person – on the outside. But she's thin as a rake and the mum suspects she's awfully upset. Something horrible's obviously happened but she hasn't confided. It's quite all right,' she went on softly. 'The daughter's always bottled up her problems and solved them herself, right from when she was a tiny girl. But it doesn't stop the mum worrying.'

Hot tears pricked Judith's eyes. She didn't need to be told that Wilma was fabricating an entry on a problem page in order to tell Judith something.

Wilma shuffled in her seat so that she could lean forward and take both of Judith's hands in her cool fingers, leaving the stick standing alone on its three feet. The light overhead reflected on the lenses of her spectacles, making her expression particularly earnest. 'But the daughter will feel better one day, duck, however horrible whatever it is that's happened. It's just that the road to recovery is uphill all the way.'

Judith found herself unable to speak around the tears that had formed a lump in her throat so just stroked the old fingers that were holding hers, the hands that had cared for her when she was a child, and hoped her mum was right.

# Chapter Nine

The next Sunday, Judith cried off Moll's traditional Yorkshire pud meal (and the traditional washing up that followed). Things had calmed down in the O'Malley household in recent days but Judith still liked to be out as much as possible. Moll had refused point blank to talk things over with Judith or acknowledge that she and Frankie were having issues. Instead, she'd pasted on a smile and breezed, 'We're fine, don't worry about us.'

Judith sauntered through a sunny park, where she watched a football match between teams that evidently didn't know that football was a winter sport, to Hannah's Pantry where she drank a latte and talked to Hannah behind the counter. Her pleasure in a little aimless chatter made her decide to look up old friends and get back in the swim of her English life, soon. Sunday lunchtime probably wasn't the moment for dropping in, when roasts would be out of the oven for carving and gravy thickening on the hob.

Bruised clouds gathered as Judith left Hannah's Pantry and the town centre to make her way to the riverbank thinking she might eventually have lunch at the coffee shop there and watch the narrowboats humming gently by. Fat raindrops splatting on the pavement made her doubt the wisdom of this plan, the more so as they became faster, heavier and were cheered on by growls of thunder. In seconds the rain had soaked her hair and was bouncing up from the pavement onto her bare ankles.

Her jeans sticking clammily to her legs, she changed direction rapidly into her old neighbourhood, along Leicester Road, past the shop on the corner of Senwick Street where the May trees would have been decked with deep pink blossom a couple of months ago. Thunder rolled, lightning flashed and rain hissed from a smoke-grey sky, stinging her scalp and her face as she jogged breathlessly into Lavender Row. She knew Adam was away for the weekend but she hoped maybe Caleb would be home. If not, she had her key. She'd get out of the downpour then text Adam to say she'd cheekily taken shelter from a storm. He surely wouldn't mind. They'd been getting on very well as they worked together and she'd enjoyed being driven around the Midlands this week, journeys filled with undemanding conversation about routes, coffee and photo-shoots. She'd learned he had another son, Matthias, older than Caleb and his opposite – steady and conservative, working on a doctorate in marine biology in Plymouth. He was getting married next year. She'd talked about her mum and that her dad had died from complications after flu not long after she'd left school.

From this direction, number 18 was out of sight around an elbow. As she neared, she frowned. From somewhere, a clamour of noise was overriding even the thunder and rain. It sounded almost like a fairground with pounding music, shrieks, bellows, howls of laughter and girlish cries.

A woman under a golf umbrella coming the other way paused with an angry shake of her head. 'It's been going on all night. All night! My husband wanted to call the police but you don't want any retribution, do you? It might be our windows, next.' Pulling her thin blue mac more tightly around her, she scurried on her way.

Judith listened. Thump-thump-thump-roar. Squeal.

She rounded the bend.

At 18 Lavender Row almost every sliding sash window was open and several had been smashed, allowing curtains to flutter out into the rain. Empty cans and bottles filled the tiny frontage and glass was scattered through the gravel.

'My house,' she breathed as shock shimmered through her. 'What's happening to my house?'

Dispensing with the formality of ringing the bell she flew through the front door, pulling up short at a pool of vomit. A plump girl was sprawled glassily at the bottom of the stairs and looked suspiciously as if the vomit might belong to her.

Judith picked her way past and stamped upstairs where most of the noise was coming from. The house seemed to be shaking with the beat of the music and people bellowing to be heard over it. Cigarettes had been ground out on the carpet and the mixture of stenches made her want to gag.

The bathroom door was locked. In the smallest bedroom, two young men smoked joints and examined one of Adam's silver cases of camera equipment clumsily, cans of beer between their feet.

For now, the equipment she usually cared for wasn't her primary concern. She moved swiftly on to the second room, now Caleb's, and decorated with posters and a litter of dropped clothes. There, a girl cried blue mascara noisily down her face while a lad had passed out crosswise on the bed. The room at the front that used to be hers – presumably now Adam's – hosted at least three couples on the bed or the floor, one of whom was awake and naked. She backed out hastily with a hissed, 'This is my bloody *bedroom*!'

Then a shock of splintering glass. She whirled and sprinted back downstairs, hurdling the vomit to run down the hall.

In the kitchen, eyes wide, hair tumbled around his face, Caleb stood. His lips were moving as he gazed from the broken glass in the back door to the broken glass in the door between kitchen and hall. Judith was almost upon him before she could distinguish the words over the music.

Mantra-like, he was muttering, 'My old man will go mental. My old man will go mental.' Joint in one hand, vodka bottle in the other, he chanted the words, shock stretching his face. Behind him, a lad with a short, square haircut was knocking out the last of the glass with his fists, globs of blood flying from his lacerated arms.

'Stop that!' Judith bellowed, fury coursing hotter and hotter through her body. 'That glass was original!'

The youth with the square haircut shook her off with a snarl.

Swaying, Caleb turned his gaze and frowned as if trying to place her.

A new sound broke through the music from the sitting room, sharp, staccato, metallic. Judith turned and raced in to find a bare-chested youth hitting the cast-iron fire surround with a poker and giggling as the inset tiles shattered. A girl was retching into the seat of an armchair. Two young guys were having a beer-spitting competition,

116

roaring with laughter as they spattered the girl's back and Adam's computer. A further dozen or so people were comatose on the floor or furniture.

It was such a contrast to the careful way she'd kept the house – and Adam after her – that Judith felt anger explode, as if someone had set off a bomb in her chest. Self-preservation stopped her attempting to disarm the poker-wielder so she tore the plug of the booming stereo out of its wall socket instead.

Her ears rang in blessed relief at the reduction in noise.

She stamped her way back to Caleb, who was still standing in the kitchen wearing an expression of comical dismay, his companion meticulously snapping off the final pieces of glass in the back door.

'They've trashed Dad's house,' he told her sadly, his dark eyes desolate.

'No, they've trashed *my* house. Wait till I see your father!' she snapped. 'I'm calling the police.'

Caleb rocked on his heels. 'Grandma's ill. Dad's gone to Bedford to see her.' Shakily, he drew on the fat roach between his fingers, which had gone out anyway. 'Back on Sunday.'

Judith snatched the roach and threw it out through the broken glass of the back door. 'Yes, I know where he's gone. I've been working here this week, haven't I? He'll be back today.'

'Sunday,' Caleb corrected her gently.

'Sunday's today.' She suppressed an urge to shake him, preferably by the throat.

Caleb's eyes grew round. 'Holy crap. He'll go mental.'

'That'll be two of us,' she promised grimly. Should she call the police? It was the sensible option for several reasons. An aggressive party reveller fuelled by God-knows-what might turn on her as she tried to clear the house. Officialese, in the form of a crime report with statements, could very well prove to be necessary for an insurance claim and, on the off chance that some stupid young idiot needed medical help, the police could deal with it instead of her.

But then . . . She studied Caleb, wide-eyed and pasty white. Caleb might well get arrested. Charged. She'd be responsible for getting him a police record. The house stunk of dope – he and most of his unattractive mates were off their faces. The government might've seen fit to downgrade grass but she wasn't sure she wanted to put that benevolence to the test when damage to property was involved.

And how would she feel if it was her stepson Kieran standing there in Caleb's place, knowing he'd messed up in a big way?

She was saved from further heart-searching by the banging of the front door as it slammed back against the hall wall. And, slowly, in stalked Adam, striding down the hall, gazing around himself with eyes that seemed to emit sparks. 'Shitty death,' he ground out dangerously. Judith watched his progress as he carefully skirted the girl at the bottom of the stairs and the evidence of her excesses, peering into the sitting room, wincing, and heading inexorably for Caleb.

Father and son stared at each other. The square-cut man who'd been breaking the glass advanced, fists clenched, but Adam shoved him irritably in the chest and, with a stagger, he ricocheted harmlessly onto the back door. It obligingly opened, leaving him to collapse to the ground outside.

Adam had eyes only for his son. 'Are you all right?'

Caleb nodded, and swayed. 'Sorry, Dad. They, like, got

118

completely out of hand.' For an instant, he looked as if he might burst into tears.

Then Adam spotted Judith. His eyes crackled like a winter sea in a moment of infuriated pride. 'Oh, hell.' They stared at each other. 'I take responsibility. I'll get it cleared up,' he ground out.

She folded her arms. 'You bet.'

It took till mid-afternoon just to empty the house of unwanted bodies.

Luckily, none of the unconscious proved to need hospital treatment. Showing great inventiveness, Judith thought, Adam filled a plant-sprayer with icy water and strode around squirting the slack faces of the comatose young people who didn't respond to a shake of the shoulder. 'Come on! Up you get, son, on your way.' Squirt. 'Wake up, wake up! You must leave. You! *Hey, you!* Wakey, wakey.' Squirt, squirt. 'Time to go.'

Grunts, snarls or squeals greeted his efforts and he was equally impervious to each. 'Out, now. *Now*, I said. On your feet and get out.'

One moment of high anxiety came when the bathroom door remained obstinately locked for all Adam's knocking and he had to kick his way in. There, a waxen girl was out cold on the floor, the room a filthy mess where her stomach had ejected its contents. She did, however, respond to the plant-sprayer treatment. When Adam asked for her home number so he could phone her parents she got up and scuttled out of the house.

Caleb lurched about, gathering cans and bottles into plastic sacks between swigs of water taken at his father's command. Periodically, Adam grasped his son and stared into his eyes, satisfying himself that Caleb was in no

119

immediate danger from any of the poisons he'd put into his body.

Judith patrolled the clean-up operation with hands on hips at this insult to her home (even if it wasn't, strictly speaking, *her* home at the moment). After ejecting the last reveller, Adam swept up the glass then borrowed a wet/dry cleaner from a friend and scoured the carpets, improving the situation but failing to return all of them to their state before cigarette burns and unsavoury stains.

Gradually, the smell of carpet cleaner and bleach began to overpower tobacco, beer and vomit. An emergency glazier arrived to make the appropriate repairs to the windows and doors. Caleb was finally permitted to haul himself upstairs to collapse on top of his duvet and sleep.

Slowly, Adam returned to the kitchen where Judith waited, furious and stunned by everything she'd seen. As it hadn't been Adam's party she managed to ask, 'Is Caleb going to be OK?'

'I think so,' he said, flatly. 'I need him to live so I can ground him for the rest of his life.'

Despite her anger, she almost smiled. It hadn't escaped her that Adam's first words to Caleb had been 'Are you all right?' rather than a screamed 'What the hell have you done?' which she was sure would have been Tom's reaction had Kieran been the culprit.

With brusque movements, Adam made coffee and set out a biscuit tin.

They sat down facing one another at the pine kitchen table.

Adam passed his good hand over his eyes. As so often, his damaged right hand was out of the way in his pocket or beneath the table. He looked exhausted. 'So now you have perfectly good grounds for immediate eviction,' he said bitterly.

'In anyone's book,' she agreed.

He nodded. 'Can I have seven days, Judith?'

She stared into his eyes and saw a mixture of defeat, determination and resignation. She felt sorry for him but she did want her house back and what had happened was more than anyone could overlook. 'Of course. You can use the time to get the repairs done. I doubt the key money will cover it.'

# Chapter Ten

Judith found herself in the odd position of working for Adam at the same time as chucking him out of his home. During the planned shoots on Thursday and Friday, each adopted the policy of speaking only as necessary. their previously friendly chats or exchanges of jokes noticeably absent.

At the end of the week, Adam used the Sunday to move out of Lavender Row, all his possessions piled in a hire van by him and a subdued Caleb. He'd secured a flat to move into in about twelve days but she hadn't felt able to ask him where he was staying prior to that. If truth be told, she was feeling guilty that she hadn't given him longer to sort himself out.

However, she hadn't done that so, on the Monday, she moved back in. The insurance company had yet to stump up for the tiles and the fire surround to be refinished, some of the carpets to be replaced and for the bathroom door to be repaired, but the house was habitable.

Her furniture arrived from the storage unit where it had spent the last few years. She'd half-forgotten her cottage suite in shades of blue and lilac, the bed with the carved wooden headboard, the maple wardrobes and the dressing table with the mirror.

The phone line was returned to her name so she was suddenly overtaken by a desire to ring Giorgio's aunt Cass in Malta and pass the number on. Suppose – just suppose – there was a change in Giorgio's condition, no one would be able to tell her if they had no contact details and, of course, she'd cancelled her Maltese phone contract. She completed the tasks of arranging the furniture with the idea dancing in the back of her mind then, at the first opportunity, nipped into town and bought a house phone with built-in answering machine.

Once plugged in, the shiny grey plastic set seemed to taunt her, waiting to see how long she'd hold out before looking up Cass's number. Judith told herself to be careful, though. If Giorgio's uncle Saviour knew Judith was calling his wife, Cass's life would be made difficult.

Stomach twirling with apprehension, she dialled. The first time, Saviour answered but Judith had anticipated the eventuality and quickly assumed the voice of a confused tourist. 'Oh, dear. Is this the Park Hotel?'

She heard a deep chuckle from the man she'd seen from afar once or twice but never met. 'You call the wrong number.'

Judith – or rather the confused tourist – apologised and hung up.

In the evening she tried again – and this time she heard Cass's high voice. 'Cass, it's Judith,' she whispered. 'Can you talk?'

Cass sounded tense. 'Saviour's not here, if that's what you mean. But I have nothing to tell you.'

Disappointment sank through Judith. What had she

expected? A miracle? 'There's no change at all?' Her voice was hoarse.

Cass's voice held a note of sympathy but also warning. 'He won't suddenly begin asking for you. You know that, Judith.'

'Can I . . .' Judith had to clear her throat. 'Can I give you my new phone number?'

'Of course.' Cass sounded sad, weighed down by the words she didn't speak: *if you think there's any point.*

Judith's breath deserted her so that she could scarcely get the numbers out. After the call, she heeled her hands fiercely into her eyes, holding back the scalding tears.

The tears wouldn't be held. They burst from her eyes and flooded down her cheeks, ran into her mouth, burned the inside of her nose and filled her throat.

It was two hours later when, her entire head aching, she came to a decision.

She would cry no more for Giorgio.

It was pointless now, wasting energy that she was going to need to build a new life that didn't include him. She had to accept that she'd never again see laughter in his dark, dark eyes, or desire as he reached for her. There would be no phone calls to interrupt meetings with long-wooed clients, no waves from the windows of buses returning after a day trip. No waking in the morning to find he'd kicked off the sheet and was spooned around her, sharing her pillow.

No whispers, no laughter, no hanging entangled beneath the waves as they waited out a decompression stop before they could surface.

'That was then, and this is now,' she told herself aloud, treading up the stairs. 'This is Brinham, this is England, this is my life. I'm going to finish unpacking my cases. I live here, now.' She blinked away a fresh burning in her raw eyes.

She'd ring Richard tomorrow and ask him to ship the things that had been too bulky to bring in her suitcases from her Sliema apartment: a few small items of furniture, several watercolours of the island by local artists. Giorgio had bought her two: one depicting the ferry crossing Marsamxett Harbour to the bastions of Valletta; the other showing the promenade along Tower Road with The Chalet projecting starkly into the sea – the place where they'd first met.

She emptied her first two cases, which produced enough stuff to fill a wardrobe and spill over into the spare, and then began on the third, a grey giant filled with what she'd judged she wouldn't need much. She stood for a painful minute clutching the neoprene of her wetsuit, the silicone mask and fins, breathing in the familiar smell, remembering long sunny days when she and Giorgio had dropped together into the quiet and cool green-blue depths.

Then she bundled it quickly into the built-in cupboard in the box room. She wouldn't need it. She doubted she'd go under the waves again.

There were no photoshoots in the following week. Judith felt blessedly peaceful now that she'd winkled Adam out of the house and given Molly and Frankie their spare room back. She had time to do . . .

Almost anything.

She had time to think. Time to grieve, time to be freshly aware of what she'd lost. Time to wish she'd never left Malta but also time to realise that leaving had probably been for the best. Brooding made the time go slowly and left her unable to sleep or develop an appetite.

She needed physical activity. The garden looked a good project. She watched garden makeovers on TV and thought gardening might be just what she needed. She began cutting the long, narrow lawn, which was growing strongly. It took ages with the small lawnmower she'd left in the shed and even longer to neaten the edges with clippers that needed sharpening. The raw smell of cut grass made her sneeze and caused her eyes to run. She remembered how much she hated gardening.

Obviously, getting out and about was what was needed. She abandoned the garden and rang The Cottage retirement home to say she was coming to take her mum out. Even so, Wilma was flustered at her appearance and Judith couldn't decide whether it was with pleasure to have an outing or irritation that she'd miss *Neighbours* and *The Natural World*. Nevertheless, Wilma agreed to her wheelchair being folded up and wrestled in through the hatchback of Judith's car.

Knowing how much Wilma loved a good browse around the shops, Judith whizzed her in the car into the neighbouring county of Buckinghamshire to Milton Keynes. On the ice-smooth floors of the shopping mall the wheelchair bowled along and she began to congratulate herself on making a good choice. 'OK, Mum?' she called gaily.

Wilma folded her arms over the handbag in her lap. 'It would be lovely to go outside to the market, wouldn't it, duck?' Taking this as a request, Judith manhandled the heavy chair through the glass doors and onto the uneven ground of the market place where the chair moved like a bent supermarket trolley through mud. Wilma clung on as they rattled past stalls of fruit or cleaning fluids or jeans and at the end of the first row said, 'It's too much for you over this rough ground.' She wouldn't be swayed

126

from this stance and, truthfully, Judith was thankful to bump the chair back into the smooth-floored mall.

Wilma's eye fell immediately on a nearby kiosk. 'That frozen yoghurt looks lovely. And they've got peach.'

'That's a good idea, Mum.' Glad for a minute to recover her breath, Judith chose strawberry and finished up the tub in record time, licking her spoon and her fingers.

Wilma laughed, still trying to manoeuvre the tiny blue spoon with arthritic hands. 'It's all on my chin and my hands. Have you got a tissue, Judith? Then we can go and look for a new bag for me.'

But after they'd rolled around the mall from department store to department store for what seemed to be hours, Wilma sighed. 'They're jolly expensive, and I don't like any so much as my old one. And you must be getting awfully tired, heaving me about.' She sounded suddenly dreary.

Judith squeezed Wilma's shoulder. The shopping trip seemed to have ended up as more a trial than a treat. She cursed herself for not properly appreciating her mother's world and her lack of mobility. Molly would have known. Molly always knew the right thing to do for their mother. 'Is this all a bit much, Mum? Would you rather I took you home?'

Wilma dimpled, dreariness apparently forgotten. 'We shouldn't leave without having a cup of tea first, should we? And a scone, with lots of jam. John Lewis does lovely scones.'

Two scones later they finally set off home, Judith reminding herself that she really must stop pouncing on her mother on a whim, interrupting Wilma's routine and not giving enough thought to whether she'd actually enjoy what Judith decreed a treat. Wilma reinforced this resolve by looking excessively relieved to be delivered home to her room at The Cottage.

During the following week, Judith met Kieran for dinner, accompanied, naturally, by Bethan, taking Molly with her because Frankie was at work. Then the insurance company paid up and she chose new carpets for the main living room, hall and her bedroom, and was waiting for them to be fitted.

She was glad that next week she'd have her part-time job as a photographer's assistant to occupy her again. She hadn't begun scouring the sits-vac ads yet because helping Adam wasn't demanding, was generally interesting and often fun. Hopefully, the froideur between them would soon thaw because being a full-time lady of leisure gave her too much time for a flea-jump mental process in which she flitted from thought to uncomfortable thought. Also, she needed some money coming in. However much she'd yearned to be on her own, now that she was she felt unlike the self she'd always known; it was like hearing a familiar song with the words changed.

Thinking about Adam made her finally get round to contacting Melanie, the old school friend who'd put up Adam to be Judith's tenant. At Brinham Grammar she'd been an absolute knock-out, the one with a lush figure that all the lads fancied rotten. Her clear skin had tanned beautifully in the days when a deep tan was considered a desirable sign of health and set off her sultry brown eyes. She'd peaked early, unfortunately. Her busty body soon became soft and less shapely and people began to say, 'Shame, because she's got a lovely smile.'

But so far as Judith was concerned, Melanie was still Melanie with a ready grin, a dry wit, and a sympathetic nature. They hadn't seen much of each other in the last decade but she had her phone number.

Melanie was enchanted to hear from Judith and

128

demanded a girls' night out that very night. 'I'll organise tickets online to see the play that's running at the Derngate Theatre in Northampton and book a table in a wine bar afterwards.'

Judith readily agreed and it was *wonderful* to see Melanie again, to be yanked into a big, squashy hug, Melanie's cry of delight ringing in her ears. 'Judith, how I've missed you! How fantastic that you're home!'

Judith felt unexpectedly choked. 'I've missed you, too. I wish we hadn't bothered with the play, now. I just want to go somewhere and talk our heads off.'

Melanie beamed. 'But Ian's waiting outside in the car. He said he'd chauffeur for us to allow me a decent session at the wine bar afterwards.' Sure enough, Ian's eyes twinkled through his big, silver-framed glasses at his wife and her friend squashed in the back seat of his Punto so they could talk without drawing breath all the way to Northampton.

By the time they got there they were ready to settle down and watch the play about murder and betrayal. It was great, although they agreed that they preferred the old Royal Theatre next door, joined on to the Derngate now, and the pantomimes there when they were kids. The ice creams had seemed bigger and the performances even more magical.

After the curtain, Melanie threaded them through the streets to a wine bar with primrose frontage and a grape-vine painted across the windows. 'So,' she said, pouring big glasses of deeply red wine. 'Poor old Adam blotted his copy book and you had to throw him out?'

Judith felt a flush heat her cheeks. 'His son, Caleb, had a party and trashed the place. Adam instantly agreed to leave. Hard luck on Adam, I realise, but it's good to have my own place back.'

'And it's your house, of course. But, yes, hard luck on Adam. And he's had enough bad luck lately.' Frowning, Melanie fanned her face with a beer mat.

Judith's flush deepened. 'I know he's a friend of yours. He's a great guy.'

Melanie's ready smile burst across her face, making her twinkling eyes almost disappear into her laughter lines. 'A friend of Ian's, really, but yes, Adam's lovely. He's moving in to a new place this weekend, a flat.'

Judith didn't say she was all too aware of that. She sipped her wine, realising that all her restlessness and lack of concentration this week had been guilt that in leaping at the opportunity to reclaim her house after Caleb's party, she hadn't much cared where Adam went until the day came for him to go. 'He's been staying with friends, I suppose?'

Melanie fanned herself harder. 'With Shelley, his ex-wife, would you believe. They were never what you'd actually call *devoted*, you know, but they're still fond of each other.'

Judith wondered whether Adam would appreciate this conversation if he could hear it but asked anyway. 'So why did the relationship end?' She'd only heard from him that it had, not why.

A shrug of Melanie's round shoulders. 'Who knows what goes on in a marriage.' She blotted her pink face with a napkin. 'You remember him from school, don't you? A bit of a star attraction in the sixth form, was Adam. Too much sought after to bother with us fifth years.'

Judith let her lips curve up in a tiny smile. 'I think I spoke to him once but, other than that, yes, we were too lowly.' She'd gone to pains to hide her crush on

130

Adam from Mel at the time so wasn't going to give it an airing now.

On Saturday, Adam came to call.

Judith's heart misstepped when the doorbell rang and via the sitting room window she caught sight of him hovering on the path. When she opened the front door his smile was polite but his eyes were wary. 'Are you safe to be spoken to, yet? Or still likely to erupt?' His brows drew down intently.

She decided to begin with a neutral stance. 'Depends what you have to say.'

'That's a typical Judith answer.' He turned and beckoned. Caleb stepped into view, cheeks fiery red and eyes darting to Judith and away. 'Don't be shy,' Adam said. 'This is your conversation, not mine.'

Gingerly, Caleb edged closer. His thick, dark hair looked combed, his jeans were unripped and his T-shirt bore no offensive slogan. Judith could imagine Adam instructing him to make himself presentable. Caleb cleared his throat. 'Hello, Mrs McAllister.' He'd obviously decided calling her 'Judith' as he'd begun to, was now inappropriate.

She folded her arms. 'Hello, Caleb.'

He eyed her, apprehensively. 'Would it be OK if we came in for a minute, please?'

'Of course.' She stood back and let them troop past and into the sitting room, having trouble keeping a straight face at Caleb's hunted expression as he trudged back to the scene of his recent crime.

Once in the room, Caleb and Adam waited to be invited before they sat down on her cottage-style sofa and, after one horrified look, Caleb averted his eyes from the still-damaged fire surround, the Victorian tiles cracked or missing because the insurance company was being tricky about what they should cover there. 'I've come to, like, apologise.'

Judith, seating herself across from him in an armchair, raised her eyebrows. 'Only *like* apologise? Something similar to an apology, but in actual fact not one?'

Adam coughed to cover a laugh, amusement flickering in his eyes.

Caleb looked bewildered. He hesitated. 'No, I have come to apologise.'

'Go on then,' Judith invited him, affably.

He scratched his head and stared at her. 'Um, sorry,' he said, sounding baffled.

'What for?'

'For, like, trashing your house. No!' Before she could open her mouth. 'Not *like*. I *am* sorry for trashing your house. I thought it'd be cool to have a party while Dad was away but it got completely out of hand. People turned up that I'd never met and they were seriously out there. Know what I mean?'

Judith frowned as if perplexed, thoroughly enjoying the conversation and not just because she'd wondered whether she'd ever see Adam and Caleb again. She hadn't indulged in the gentle sport of teasing a teen for a while. 'Not really,' she deliberated. 'Everybody's out there, aren't they? Except we three, I mean, because we're in here.'

He stared at her again, clearly wondering how anyone could be so difficult to communicate with. 'I mean that they were . . . they went mad,' he explained with great patience. 'Smashing stuff up and everything. And I think some people had too much to drink.'

Judith assumed a look of mock-horrified amazement. 'Really? I wonder how that happened?'

Silence. Then, softly, Adam prompted, 'Caleb . . .'

Caleb heaved another huge, mournful sigh. 'Yeah, OK. *Everyone* had lakes of stuff to drink and most people were stoned, too. There's no excuse. I shouldn't have had a party here. It was totally out of order and I'm totally sorry.'

For the first time, she smiled. 'Thank you.'

He looked relieved but still shifted uncomfortably in his seat. 'Dad thought . . . no, *I* thought that I might do something, you know, something to help you out. To make up.'

Beside him, Adam caught Judith's eye and nodded.

Completely on board with the idea of redemption, she cast around for a job she could reasonably expect Caleb to accomplish without taxing him unduly or placing herself or her property in too much jeopardy. The lawn had already grown after her half-hearted attempts at taming it so she said, 'How are you at cutting grass?'

'I expect I could do it,' he admitted cautiously.

'Shall we find out?' She led the way into the kitchen and through the door to the back garden.

Judith and Adam took to the patio bench while Caleb got the mower out, a bench that had been green wrought iron with white slats last time Judith saw it but was now all black, which she rather liked. Adam had been the perfect tenant; he'd decorated everything in sight, kept the house immaculate, then, precisely when she wanted to evict him, had made it possible by fouling up so comprehensively. Or, at least, having a son who fouled up on his behalf.

Her conscience twinged afresh. Poor Adam.

Once settled on the bench where they had a good view of Caleb trying the lawnmower's pull-cord starter, they swatted gnats and drank tall glasses of orange juice that Judith fetched from the kitchen. To her relief, they seemed to slowly rediscover the easy companionship that had developed prior to Caleb's party.

He shaded his eyes as the lawnmower failed to respond to Caleb's energetic efforts with the pull-cord. 'I kept thinking you were going to giggle.'

Judith sniffed. 'I wasn't aware that anything about the episode was funny.'

He swung around accusingly. 'Your eyes were laughing.'

She shrugged, and sipped at her juice. 'Perhaps,' she admitted, her lips curling. 'A teeny bit.'

Adam grinned briefly. Then he touched the back of her hand. 'And now Caleb's made his apology, it's time for me to offer my thanks. Thank you for not involving the police. I'm sure you must've considered it – I wouldn't have blamed you but I'm grateful you didn't. Caleb's wayward enough, he doesn't need a police record, however minor.'

She kept her face straight. 'Really *out there,* is he?'

Adam dropped his head back and laughed, eyes gleaming silver in the sun. She thought, objectively, what a very attractive man he was, especially with his day's growth of beard to emphasise the angle of his lean jaw. Then he sobered and sighed. 'You've been brilliant, and now I have to give you some really bad news and you're going to hate us all over again. And you'll be right to hate us, because it's something really annoying.' He put down his glass on the floor, and leant forward on the bench to look into her face with an expression of concern and apprehension. In fact, he looked a lot like Caleb had in the sitting room.

'Go on, get it over with,' she said, resignedly.

134

He hesitated. 'You're really going to hate it.'

Disquiet stirred in the pit of her stomach. 'You're scaring me.'

He ran his hand over his hair. 'After the party, I noticed something was missing from the smallest bedroom.'

She felt herself relax. Why should he think this would make her hate him again? 'Camera equipment? I'm afraid there were two lads messing around with it but I wasn't in the mood to attempt a rescue at the time. It's up to you if you want to take it further – I could give a reasonable description of the thugs involved.'

But he was shaking his head. 'No . . . although my equipment *was* rather mauled about by those disrespectful bastards. I'd love to get my hands on them.' He broke off, glancing down as if tripped by a sudden and unwelcome reminder of the state of one of those hands. He gathered himself. 'But there was something else I kept in there and I think it must still be in your house, somewhere.'

He blew out a breath. 'Caleb moved the tank when we moved out and obviously funked telling me it was empty. I'm afraid it's Fingers who's missing. My snake.'

# Chapter Eleven

For a moment she didn't absorb the full import of his words. 'You called your snake *Fingers*?' Her eyes flicked involuntarily to his hands. He'd clasped the left one around the right, keeping the damage, as he so often did, out of sight.

He smiled, faintly. 'Caleb's idea of a joke. He bought Fingers for me after I lost mine and at first I thought I'd take him straight back to the exotic pet shop. But then I began reading the book about keeping corn snakes and I got interested. In fact, I got to like Fingers.'

All at once, Judith developed a funny sensation in the pit of her stomach. A pulse began behind her eyes. 'I hate snakes. Is he dangerous? Is he poisonous? Is he *big*?' Sweat broke out on her neck.

'He's harmless, honestly,' he hastened to reassure her. 'He's not poisonous, he's a couple of feet long. Not much longer, anyway. He's still young, his markings haven't changed into stripes, yet. But I'll get him back, I promise. Just don't go around spraying wasp killer or whatever.'

Judith felt her toes curling off the floor as if the snake

might be slithering towards her. 'That would harm him, would it?'

He nodded earnestly. 'Of course. Snakes are alive – they breathe air, drink water and like sunshine, just like us.'

Judith's calm crumbled. 'They're not like us at all. A *snake*, yuck! A snake in my house. And this is what you term "annoying"?' She hadn't even liked the eels she'd come across on dives, and eels weren't snakes. They were fish, even if they had no legs and a lot of attitude.

Adam spoke earnestly. 'I'm really sorry, Judith. But it's not his fault he's a snake. If you'll just give me a chance to find him . . .'

She shuddered, thinking words she didn't like, such as 'slither' and 'coil'. 'Snakes are green and slimy.'

His half-smile tipped one corner of his mouth. 'Not Fingers. Autumn colours. Rather pretty. And snakes are quite dry, actually.'

She shucked this minor point off. 'Where could he be hiding?'

'Well, I've already checked my stuff, inside my sofa and chairs, for instance. So I'm thinking now about under your floorboards or behind the fire. Or maybe under the kitchen units . . .'

'Fantastic.'

'Sorry.'

'*Bloody* fantastic!'

'Bloody sorry.'

She glared. If Adam had once been the perfect tenant, those days were certainly over. 'Don't you laugh about this, Adam Leblond.'

'Never, Judith,' he declared, firmly. 'Never in a million years.' But he looked the other way so she couldn't see his face.

He didn't find Fingers that day. Caleb finished the lawn, then left with an air of virtuous relief, while Adam systematically took the house apart upstairs. 'Good job you haven't had the new carpet down yet,' he panted as he pulled the existing carpet off its gripper and began to lever up the floorboards.

'Yes, good job.' She pulled a face. 'How on earth would the snake get down there?'

He flashed his torch into the hollow he'd just exposed. 'They can squeeze their way into seemingly impossible places.'

Judith backed away. 'I don't know whether to feel safer here or in the sitting room. I don't want Fingers jumping out at me.'

He snorted a laugh, his eyes gleaming as he looked up at her. 'Snakes aren't well known for jumping.'

The hunt for Fingers drew to a close at about nine p.m. By then, Adam had stopped making jokes. He rubbed his jaw sheepishly. 'Shall I come back tomorrow to do the same demolition job on the downstairs?'

She groaned. 'Yes! It's either that or I walk around scared to death in case he appears. He just better not slither into bed with me, that's all.'

'He wouldn't dare,' Adam told her. As he was looking studiously elsewhere as he said it she couldn't tell if his eyes were laughing.

Judith spent a jumpy and wakeful night. She remembered Giorgio telling her the legend of how Malta had no poisonous snakes after St Paul was unharmed though a venomous viper bit him. Fingers wasn't a viper and wasn't poisonous but none of those things seemed to comfort her. Where was he? Snakes were nocturnal, weren't they? Adam had told her Fingers fed on rodents so unless she had a colony of mice beneath the floorboards by now he'd be getting hungry. Looking for food. Coming out from hiding. *Slithering* out. *Coiling* up.

With a shudder she tucked the duvet firmly around her shoulders and left the light on.

Next morning, nerves jangling, Judith found herself examining every patch of carpet before stepping on it as she moved around the house. She had to stay in until Adam appeared as he no longer had a key but the moment he arrived she dropped the spare key into his palm. 'I'm going to have lunch with my stepson. If you find your scaly, slimy friend please lock up after you when you leave.' Grabbing her handbag she scurried out into the street, relieved at the sight of a summery blue sky dotted with cotton-wool clouds.

Adam walked out with her and stood grinning on the top step, watching her unlock her car. 'Snakes aren't slimy. Did Fingers try to slither into bed with you?' His T-shirt blew against his body in the breeze.

Horror wriggled up her body. 'No!'

He swung the key slowly. 'He's a gentleman, evidently.'

'And this lady's going to stay out of the house all day.' She jumped into the driver's seat and, with a wave, was soon on her way. First, she met Kieran at a new pub called The Cider Tree and, for once, he was without Bethan. Kieran didn't seem in a very good mood. He hardly smiled at all and was more interested in gazing morosely at other people in the pub than in holding a conversation.

'Have you and Bethan had words?' Judith tried, gently, concerned to see him so uncharacteristically low.

'No!' he said, as if horrified she'd even ask.

Hmm, OK. Well, it wasn't her business. Maybe Bethan

was out with her mates and Kieran was possessive and wanted her always with him. Tom had been the same irksome way. 'How's your dad?' she asked, as he came to mind as another source of Kieran's grumpiness. Tom's brusque, bossy nature could rub anyone up the wrong way.

Kieran let loose an inelegant snort. 'Much as ever. Loud, opinionated and critical.'

'Who, Tom?' she asked, trying to make him at least smile. The attempt failed and when Kieran had eaten a sandwich and her crisps as well as his, he hugged her goodbye and said he had to go.

Though still perturbed at her stepson's dark mood, Judith went to visit her mum. Unfortunately, Wilma proved to be out of sorts, too.

'That Mrs Yeats,' she whispered, indicating with a glance a woman who sat in the chair opposite Wilma in the lounge, 'has just got a really nice walking frame – and on the National Health.'

Unable to get a handle on her mother's dissatisfaction, Judith lowered her voice to a murmur. 'Is that a problem?'

'She didn't need a new one,' Wilma responded uncharitably. She tapped her own walking frame. 'Mine's even older but I've made sure to keep it nice.' Then she laughed, returning in a twinkling to her usual sunny self. 'Listen to me being a moaning Minnie. Tell me what's going on with you, duck.'

So Judith told her about lunch with Kieran – omitting the moodiness – Molly, Brinham and the new benches they were putting in the market square, and made her laugh with her story of Caleb's party and the escape of Fingers. After an hour she kissed Wilma's soft cheek and left her striking up a conversation with Mrs Yeats, despite

140

the new walker. Probably she was going to one-up her with, 'My daughter's got a snake loose in her house.'

She called at her sister's house next but received no reply so Judith parked up in town and spent the final couple of hours of the afternoon roaming around The Norbury Centre. She bought two new pairs of jeans, one black, one indigo, and a host of mundane items for the house – bin bags, a washing up brush, spray polish, dusters, cling film, a basket of multi-coloured pegs, pens and a turquoise can-opener.

Then, hoping that by that time Fingers would be safely corralled, she made for home. Unfortunately, she found Adam's BMW, which he insisted was only just getting in its stride at ten years old, was still parked outside her house in Lavender Row. Judith sighed. Honestly, this having space to herself business was not working today.

'Hello?' She managed to turn the key in the door with one hand while straining the fingers of the other to grasp six carrier bags, and staggered into the hall. She'd be glad when the carpet was replaced. She didn't like that bit at the bottom of the stairs where there seemed to be the lingering of an unpleasant smell. She stepped over it. 'Adam?'

He appeared from the sitting room, hands in pockets, smile sketchy, his shoulders hunched, expression guarded. 'I need to talk to you.'

She dropped her bags in dismay, disregarding the contents spilling out around her feet. 'What's happened now? Can't you find that bloody snake?'

'He was under the kitchen units.' He stood back and indicated a glass tank on the floor near the sofa and a red-and-russet shape coiled in a corner of it, half under a piece of wood.

She turned her eyes hurriedly away. *Coiled*. Urgh. Under the kitchen units where he could have slithered out at any time. *Urgh urgh*. 'Thank goodness. Thank you very much. Is something else the matter?'

His voice was very gentle. 'Come and sit down, Judith.'

Ignoring her spilled shopping, she flopped down onto the sofa and groaned. 'Oh, Adam is there some new disaster created by Leblond and son? Lost your tarantula or arranged a rave for next Saturday?' But when he just waited, very still, very grave, his eyes fixed on hers, she tailed off. 'What?' she asked softly, his manner making her realise this wasn't the time for jokes.

His voice became low and very soft. He even took her hand in his good one. 'I'm really sorry. But there's some bad news.'

The hairs on the back of her neck prickled. She had an absurd desire to stroke them flat with her hand as if that would make bad news go away. 'What?'

He hesitated. 'Someone left a message on your answer machine. I didn't answer when the phone rang, of course, but the machine kicked in and I couldn't avoid hearing the message.'

Her heart flopped. 'And how do you know what kind of news it is?'

His mouth twisted down at the corners. 'It wasn't difficult to recognise as bad news.'

She turned her head and regarded the phone. New and shiny, palest grey. The message-waiting light blinked red on the base. She swallowed. Shakily, she rose. Her heartbeat seemed to be in her eyes. Her throat. Her head. Vaguely, she was aware of Adam leaving the room, the sound of water whooshing into the kettle coming from the kitchen.

With an effort, she pressed the play button.

'*You have one new message.*' It was difficult to breathe while she waited out the statement of time and date, then the tone. A second's silence before gentle crying. Then Cass's voice, husky with tears. 'Judith, I ring to give you news. This morning . . . this morning, Giorgio died. They think a clot blocked his heart. He felt nothing, of course, he died suddenly but calmly with his mama beside him.' Cass began to sob in earnest. 'May he sleep peacefully.' Click. '*End of message. You have no more messages.*'

Dimly, over the rushing of blood in her ears, she became aware of Adam's return and the shifting of the sofa as he lowered her onto the cushions, the clunk as he deposited coffee on the low table. The pungent smell hit the back of her throat. She reached out and pressed play again. And again. Then he gently stayed her hand.

Rather than face the truth of what she'd just heard, she let her mind slip off in pursuit of inconsequential thoughts about Adam using the china mugs she liked. They were Royal Albert; she'd bought them as seconds from a shop in London's Piccadilly. He'd given her the white one with roses and taken pale blue with birds for himself. He knew how she took her coffee from the photoshoots they'd done together.

He held his left hand over hers on the mug until he was certain she was holding on securely and capable of lifting it to her lips. Then he was silent. Sipping his drink, watching her over the rim as she tried to drink.

'You were close?' he asked eventually.

She nodded. Despite the hot fluid, her teeth chattered, clicking on the rim of the mug. He slipped off the denim shirt he was wearing over his T-shirt and dropped it around her shoulders but even this warmth he tried to lend her seemed to simply drain away, leaving her shivering so hard it felt as if the sofa was vibrating.

'Was he . . .' He hesitated. 'Was Giorgio the one?'

She nodded, again. Nodding too hard, like a child.

He breathed out a sigh and ran his hand over his hair. 'So this is a terrible shock. I'm so sorry.'

For several moments she couldn't speak, couldn't swallow, couldn't breathe. It was as if a huge sob had turned to concrete in her throat. *Giorgio! Oh Giorgio, Giorgio.* Her eyes closed against dancing dots, red and black. Gradually, the sensation receded and her airway cleared.

She lifted her eyes to his. 'This wasn't entirely unanticipated.' She dragged in a deep, quivering breath and said the word she'd refused to use until now, substituting the more comforting 'unconscious'. 'Giorgio was in a coma.'

# Chapter Twelve

The words revolved around the hushed room.

Outside, children called to one another, a dog barked, a woman laughed.

She could almost feel Adam's shock as she ploughed on. 'The doctors had classified him as in a persistent vegetative state. I can give you chapter and verse on coma and PVS, how it's decided what constitutes what, which expert disagrees with which. The way the patient can twitch, grimace or groan without stimulus but react not at all to what's going on around him. I've read up on it.' A lot. Exhaustively. Absorbed the results of this test case, that campaign, what the Pope said about how victims must be cared for. 'He had a diving accident. It's why I came back here.'

Those months since Giorgio had been airlifted to St Luke's Hospital from the dive site at Ghar Lapsi, since Charlie Galea had turned up at her flat because he knew she had to be told, seemed both like only yesterday . . . and a lifetime ago.

All the if-onlys came crashing back. 'If only I'd been Giorgio's diving buddy that day, it could have been different. I'm more experienced and maybe I would have realised a motor craft was approaching. You can usually hear a whine from the engine and judge its proximity.' Conscious that she'd begun babbling all the old stuff she'd told herself so many times she made herself take another of those long breaths. 'But he surfaced and a jet ski hit him. There was a surface marker buoy to warn that there were divers down but some jet skiers are menaces. They aren't licensed or safety trained – they just buy the damned machine and hurl themselves about.'

'What happened to the jet skier?' His voice echoed with compassion and she realised that his good hand had taken hers.

Bitterly, she laughed. 'Nothing. He ran away in the confusion. You'd think you'd be safe from them at Ghar Lapsi – it's a steep descent to the sea and it would be murder to carry a bloody jet ski down the steps. It's not as if it were Mellieha Bay, a proper beach, where surface water sports are common. Accidents there are not unheard of – there was a girl killed last year. But some hooray had sailed his gin palace out from the yacht marina and anchored off Ghar Lapsi. Big boats often carry jet skis. The idiots came pounding in towards shore. They wanted to see the caves, I suppose. "*Ghar*" means cave. Probably they had no idea it was a dive site or that they shouldn't come within the arm of rocks. Morons.'

She stared into her now empty coffee cup. 'I finally got in to see Giorgio before I came home.' She drew in a quavering breath. 'To all intents and purposes, he'd gone. The damage where the jet ski hit his head was too much. He was a husk and only the machinery was keeping him breathing. His eyes were lifeless. So I left the island. Couldn't bear to stay.'

146

'I'm sorry.' His voice was rich with sympathy.

Freeing her hand from his she jumped up to pace the room. 'Before he met me, Giorgio didn't dive. If not for me, he'd never have had the accident. He'd still be alive, breathing, laughing, smiling—' Then she was crying, dry, painful sobs that scoured her throat and pleated her chest.

Warm arms threaded around her and her head fell forward onto Adam's shoulder, as she disproved her previous resolve to shed no tears for Giorgio and cried out the questions those left behind have always asked. '*Why?* Why him? Why did he have to surface right there, right that instant? A few seconds more, a few seconds less. That's all he needed. And I should have been there.'

The room grew dark around them.

Adam let her cry out her anguish in the depths of the sofa, fetching her a glass of water to ease her aching throat and a fat kitchen roll to absorb her tears. He squatted down beside her. 'Shall I fetch someone to be with you? Your mother?'

She blew her nose. 'Too old and frail.'

'Your sister?'

She managed a wobbly smile. 'Molly's wonderful but I'm not sure I can bear her particular brand of sympathy at the moment. She's a bit full-on.'

He hesitated before saying, 'Then I'll stay. I'd feel like hell, going home and leaving you like this.'

'I've stopped crying. I'll be all right.' But she couldn't get the words out without her face crumpling anew.

He made a deep noise of concern. 'I'll sleep down here, just so you're not alone in the house, tonight. I couldn't just abandon you.'

She blew her nose for the millionth time. A heap of

damp tissues was building on the carpet at her feet. No doubt it went attractively with a red nose and swollen eyes. 'I'm going to get drunk. Obliterate the pain.'

'Good idea.' Evidently choosing to view this as an invitation, he pulled the curtains and switched on a light. 'What booze have you got?'

She'd expected him to try to dissuade her rather than join in but, still trumpeting into a tissue, she led him through to the kitchen where they located a bottle of whisky in the fridge and two bottles of red wine in the under-stairs cupboard. He also discovered a tin of biscuits that Molly had given as a welcome-back-into-your-home gift and, back on the sofa, cajoled her into nibbling her way through two shortcakes. Then they began on the whisky, sloshing the twinkling amber brew into Judith's favourite cut-glass tumblers that were heavy at the base and fragile at the rim. Seated side by side on the sofa, they propped their feet on the coffee table.

Judith tossed back her first glassful and squeaked a gasp at the scorching in her throat.

'You unman me. Now I'll have to do the same.' Adam threw his back, too, then had to wipe his eyes on the back of his hand.

She poured refills, and sniffed. 'Life is sometimes very crappy.'

'Absolutely.' His voice was deeper than usual, hoarse from the whisky.

For the millionth time, Judith blew her nose. 'He didn't deserve to die. He had a lot of life left.'

Adam had kicked his shoes off and his feet alongside hers on the table were encased in black ribbed socks without holes or pulls. It occurred to her that he was a comfortable person to be in proximity to; nothing about him was worn or stale. His shoulder touched hers just barely. It was comforting.

She groaned, twisting her whisky tumbler in her hand. When she began anew with, 'I should have been with him that day, I could've—'

He interrupted her, turning in his seat so he could snare her with his gaze. 'Did you make him happy? Were you good together?'

She thought of Giorgio's face, the smile that had felt as if it were only for her, the way his dark eyes became darker as he pulled her into his arms. She nodded, biting her lip.

'Then don't "if only",' he suggested gently. 'It's pointless. If you loved each other, be glad. He chose to go diving without you that day and you can't change his choice.'

It wasn't bad advice. But so difficult to follow! Sombrely, she poured more whisky. When that had gone, she poured some more, talking incessantly about Malta and Giorgio, pouring it all out as she had done to no one else.

She wasn't sleepy. She might be hollowed out and exhausted, aching with sorrow, but she felt as if she'd never sleep again. She could talk all night. She could tell Adam everything and anything that came into her head. Adam yawned occasionally but Judith just drank steadily, watching the room turn to blurs, feeling her brain sloshing gently within her skull, hearing her voice stretching and contracting as her tongue struggled to cope with S and other difficult letters. She told him about the lack of divorce in Malta – although people were trying to change that – and the last time she'd seen Giorgio in his hospital room. By the time she reached the confrontation with Maria Zammit her ears were hearing Adam's replies slowly, making his voice thin and distant.

'Why wouldn't Giorgio's family let you into the hospital?' he asked.

She sighed. 'I have no status in their eyes. Giorgio's been separated from his wife for fourteen years but to them, and many others in Malta, marriage is for life.'

'So they acknowledged only Giorgio's wife who he hadn't lived with for years, even when he was so injured?' His voice held a note of disbelief.

She nodded. 'It was all about respectability. Maria, Giorgio's mother, was particularly hot on that. When Giorgio invited his parents to dinner and then produced me, Maria simply walked out. Agnello, his dad, shook his head and asked Giorgio why he had to hurt his mother like that – he had a wife till death, not till the marriage became difficult. After that, we carried on our relationship discreetly. Giorgio didn't want to cause any more pain to his family than necessary.'

Adam shook his head, probably trying to clear it of whisky fumes. 'He let you be treated like a dirty secret?'

She ran her tongue reflectively along the hard, thin rim of her glass. A dirty secret? It was an unusually blunt term, for Adam, but she could see why he'd say it. 'I suppose so,' she admitted. 'I was angry, in the beginning. But if we'd tried to force the issue, what would we have achieved? We'd have been together, but Giorgio would've been estranged from his family, possibly including his two daughters. I couldn't be responsible for that so I went along with the charade. I never met the kids,' she added.

'I see.' But Adam pulled a face as if the idea were sour.

She sighed. 'Don't be too judgemental; his family were acting on what they believed in. In their eyes, I was a despicable interloper. They're not alone in their attitudes – my own mother wasn't thrilled when I left Tom. Mum also thinks marriage is for life and she was very tight-lipped about me ending things.'

He opened his eyes wide. 'I'm getting confused about your relationships. You told me once you'd been married but I'd forgotten. Was that to Tom?'

'I like to forget it, too, but, yes, I was married to Tom until he fell for Liza and I shipped out. It's because of Tom that I have my lovely stepson, Kieran,' she reminded him.

'Tom must be stupid.' He swirled whisky unsteadily in the depths of his crystal glass. 'But at least you have someone else to blame for the break-up of your marriage. I don't.' He was in jeans today and his chestnut hair, in wings above his ears, fell over his eye, making him look laid back.

She wriggled to get more comfortable, slanting herself into the corner to face him. She remembered that he knew one or two things about separation and divorce. 'Want to tell me about your downfall? I've done all the soul-baring till now.' She'd drunk far too much to worry about being nosy.

He glugged some whisky, and reopened the biscuit tin. He'd been steadily feeding her biscuits without actually saying she needed to put something inside her stomach other than booze. After the shortcake, she'd eaten two bourbons, two custard creams and a digestive. Because he shook the tin at her again, she chose a ginger nut and a chocolate chip cookie then just held one in either hand with no appetite to eat them.

'Shelley and I were married for a long time. Since I was twenty-one.' He shrugged. 'We started out as good friends – and we are still. Friendship turned out not to be enough.' He gesticulated towards her with his chocolate digestive.

'It wasn't the love you've talked about, you and Giorgio. There was a lot of affection and when she brought the subject of marriage up it felt like a logical step. And I'd be able to sleep with her every night, which, frankly, was appealing. I suppose I mistook affection for love.' He creased his brow. 'Or it probably was love but not the right sort, the deep sort.'

She sniffed and blew her nose again. Her throat felt as if it were lined with hay and her eyes with sand. 'But she must've thought she loved you, or she wouldn't have wanted marriage.'

His eyes slid sideways, fastening themselves on her through a narrowing slit between his lids. 'Not necessarily. I think we were young and young girls twenty-five years ago, in the eighties, operated on a fixed programme. If they went out with someone for a certain length of time, they got engaged. They got the sparkly ring and the party – they were the centre of attention.'

It was true, that had been the norm. Judith had been thirty before she married, when the nineties had just begun, and some of her contemporaries had been on their second marriage already by then.

'And she's always joked that it was because "Shelley Leblond" sounded glamorous and was a big improvement on Shelly Dobben, which sounded like a cart horse.'

'Surely she didn't marry you just for a cool name?' Judith couldn't imagine that. She'd have changed her name via Deed sooner than do so.

He shrugged. 'She's artistic. An interior designer. Things like that are important to her.'

As the biscuits she clutched were getting sticky, Judith put them down on the table and tried to brush crumbs from her fingers. The crumbs shot in all directions and some worked their way between the buttons of her grey-green top. She tried to flick them out with her fingers but stopped when she realised he was watching. It felt odd to be ferreting around her boobs with his gaze on her. 'So did one of you find someone else?' she queried.

He drew his eyes back up to her face. 'No. But when I had my accident, Shelley found the whole thing very difficult.'

Judith shook her spinning head, trying to clear it, feeling that what he was telling her was important and required her to concentrate. 'How do you mean?'

His eyes flattened and became dark. 'She has a problem with ugliness.'

# Chapter Thirteen

In those few, carefully chosen words, Judith caught a glimpse of his pain.

He went on, 'Simply put, she couldn't bear the sight of my hand. And as for touching her – forget it!' He laughed, mirthlessly. 'My occupational therapist warned me that I might need to "rethink my position in the marital bed" and "get used to doing things with the left hand that had always been done with the right". Fat chance of that, as it turned out – Shelley didn't want me anywhere near her.'

With a dart of anger towards the unknown Shelley Dobben Leblond, Judith deposited her whisky glass on the table with a thump. She enunciated carefully. 'That's not nice. Not supportive.' She struggled for what she was trying to say. 'Not wife-like.'

He stirred restlessly. 'At least she was honest. Better that she told me candidly that she didn't want to sleep with me any more. Can you imagine how humiliating it would have been to realise she was suffering in silence? Pitying me? Gritting her teeth but shrinking inside?'

She frowned, watching him twirl his tumbler in the

fingers of his left hand. No wonder he tended to keep his right hand out of sight if his wife had done a number like that on him. She said, 'That doesn't sound very nice, either. But it's still big of you to be so . . . understanding.'

'It's more a case of bowing to the inevitable,' he said with a trace of bitterness.

He went to make coffee, leaving her hazily brooding on how bad things happened to good people until he returned with two mugs for each of them, fragrant and steaming.

'Two mugs at a time is a great idea. Saves getting up again. Wonder why I never thought of it.' She began her first mug. 'So how did you hurt your hand? Lawnmower? Power saw?'

He shook his head. He, too, had put down the remains of his whisky in favour of the coffee.

'You're a photographer,' she went on without giving him a chance to swallow his first mouthful of the steaming liquid and reply. 'I bet you were in a war zone and had to try to toss a grenade out of a vehicle careening across the desert, caught in a hail of cross fire?'

He raised his eyebrows as he licked coffee from his lips. 'You know very well that I'm neither the brave nor the glam kind of photographer. It was a stupid, freak accident.' Inhaling the steam from his coffee, he half-closed his eyes. 'I was helping Shelley. She'd taken on the interior decorating of this huge first-floor room, where the clients had knocked the walls out to create "a space". It was all wooden floors and Swedish furniture that didn't match.'

'Eclectic,' Judith put in helpfully.

He waved the terminology aside. 'She asked me to take pics. I often did that, so that she had a tip-top portfolio to show to clients. It was a nice house belonging to well-heeled

155

customers. They were keen to get their place into one of the glossy home magazines, so they engaged me to shoot some pics for them, too, so they could approach someone to write it up.' He paused for another sip of his drink.

He continued. 'The "space", as they all called it, had French doors opening onto a first-floor sundeck. They wanted photos of the family toasting one another with champagne on the sundeck. I was absorbed in what I was doing, trying to get the bloody woman client to shut up so I could get a photo of her not mouthing like a fish. And then someone let these dogs out.' He shook his head at the memory. 'Rottweilers, they were – half dog, half monster. They came flying out through the French doors, heading straight at me.'

Judith clapped a hand to her mouth.

He surprised her with a sudden smile. 'It turned out the dogs weren't aggressive but I didn't know that. Major heart attack time! I shot backwards. The wooden rails weren't up to twelve stone of Adam in a panic and gave way.' He drank steadily until he'd drained his cup. 'There was a conservatory underneath and I fell through it.'

'Oh, no,' Judith breathed through her fingers.

He nodded. 'It just *exploded*, shattering into my palm and fingers like razors. And my back and my neck.' He pulled down the neck of his T-shirt to show her a white, curving scar. 'But those were relatively superficial and healed OK. It was the hand that really suffered.' He glanced down at it where it lay on his thigh.

She reached for his hand to examine the crosshatching of thin, white scars on the palm and the tiny dots where he'd been stitched. The three knuckles where fingers should have been were pink, shiny flesh.

He took the hand back and pushed it into his pocket. 'I didn't realise how badly hurt I was, at first, though I was all gashed to buggery and could see the fingers weren't exactly intact. We raced off to Northampton General, Shelley driving and me with my hand held up in the air and towels soaking up the blood.'

'Were you in a lot of pain?' she asked, trying to imagine the shock of that kind of trauma.

He took up his second mug of coffee. 'I could tell I'd lost a lot of movement. What little I did have sent what felt like electric shocks searing up my arm. It was nerve damage causing that awful pain but it turned out I had everything-damage – tendon, muscle, tissue, artery. Over the next weeks I had several lots of microsurgery but the whole hand looked as if someone had slashed at it with a big knife from my fingers down to the heel of my hand. Then I got a deep infection that resisted antibiotics. The fingers never worked and pretty soon began to wither from the nerve damage and turn pale blue.' He smiled thinly. 'Quite quickly I realised that it was about as good as it was going to get. I'd have greater use of the hand without the useless, immobile fingers getting in my way. I was offered amputation and I took it.'

'That's such a horrific thing to happen to you.' As he had tucked his damaged hand away, Judith stroked his upper arm instead.

Looking down at his coffee, he shrugged. 'Much worse things happen to people. Being in and out of hospital brings that firmly home to you. For everyone who loses a finger, there are others who lose an arm.'

Judith realised she was crying again and wiped her face with the back of her hand, not knowing if these were tears for Adam or for Giorgio. They just seemed to well up endlessly. She gulped. 'So Shelley couldn't cope with the amputation?'

He shook his head. 'She turned white at the very word. Couldn't cope with the injury and gave up completely once she realised the fingers were never going to "be better". The disfigurement made her skin crawl. That was more painful than the injury and all the operations.'

Judith tried to imagine if it had been Giorgio instead of Adam who'd suffered like that. Surely she'd have mourned the loss with him? Then she tried to put herself in the place of a woman who loved beauty and couldn't bear mutilation near her. She failed. Surely love should have transcended the loss of physical perfection? 'When you compare it to what happened to Giorgio—'

'Yes.' His eyes were bleak as he accurately divined her thoughts. 'In comparison with death, my disability's pretty minor. And that kind of illuminates the quality of her feelings.' He jettisoned his mug roughly onto the table and it rattled around in a circle, almost spilling the remaining contents. 'Finishing the marriage was a similar process to deciding on the amputation. A clean end. Cut away what can't be saved. No point hanging on to something that's never going to work. Shelley cares for me a lot, but there's a gulf between "a lot" and "enough", and you can't bridge it artificially. She has someone else now and I wish her well.'

She thought aloud. 'So that's why you always hide your hand away.'

His head whipped around as he fastened a scorching glare on her. 'I don't do any such thing. My occupational therapist said people who don't hide their damage feel better about themselves.' Then he immediately contradicted himself. 'But yes, it's emotionally quite difficult to have it on display. Some people like to have a good stare and others avert their eyes. I don't know which is worse.'

She wondered what he'd thought about her trying to stroke it earlier. The fact that he'd taken the limb back probably told her. 'What about a prosthesis?'

'There's actually more for hands than fingers and I didn't like the idea. There are quite a few of us who'd rather put up with the loss of body parts than wear artificial replacements. I do exercises to assist with strength and symmetry, I have one or two gadgets and gizmos and I apply the problem-solving strategies I've been taught. I make the best of things.'

Judith nodded. All that fitted with what she'd seen of him. 'Like using your left hand a lot?'

'Yes, but not for everything. I can write with my right hand – untidily. I can drive – although it's better if the car's modified. I tend not to wear too many buttons but use my left hand for those that I do wear. I use my left hand for the computer mouse, to hold a spoon and clean my teeth. And one or two other things you won't want to discuss.'

She managed a watery smile. 'Yet you've done all the decorating here since you lost your fingers?'

'I have a gizmo to help hold things like paintbrushes.' His response was short, as if he'd had enough of the subject. He was probably only allowing this discussion to give her something to focus on other than Giorgio. The thought gave her a warm feeling. It would be fairer if she let him go to sleep but something inside her quailed at the thought of being completely alone with her grief. It might swallow her up.

He yawned again and changed the subject. 'You've mentioned a stepson to me. Have you got kids of your own?'

She shook her head. 'Tom wasn't keen and I felt we had enough with Kieran, my stepson. Your Caleb seems

159

such a lovely lad. I know I was furious at him about the party but it was bad judgement rather than malice. He's very pleasant and personable. A live wire.'

'Live wire,' he repeated drily. 'Polite-speak for Caleb ricocheting from one disaster to another. As you say, there's no malice in him but from the moment he could crawl he's been getting into strife. A big shock for us after his brother, Matthias, who was a golden child, bright but with common sense.'

Judith smiled. 'I half-forgot you had another child. Tell me more about Matthias – fabulous names your kids have, by the way.'

Hunkering down more comfortably on the sofa, Adam folded his arms. 'You know Matthias is in Plymouth finishing his doctorate. He didn't come home for the summer because he's got a work placement with some marine biology outfit. Northamptonshire's too far from the sea for his tastes so I usually go and see him, these days. The boys' names were Shelley's choices – I wanted Patrick and Mark. But what can you do against a woman who gets up out of her hospital bed and visits the registrar herself?'

She gurgled a laugh. 'Did she do that?'

'Yes, she did.' His smile was caustic. 'Patrick and Mark are their middle names.'

She absorbed the idea of someone who didn't view the names bestowed upon shared children as joint decisions.

He let his head tilt back, his jawline a firm sweep. 'I always indulged Shelley. I laughed at the more outrageous pieces of selfishness and quite admired her for doing what-ever it took to get her own way. She got used to it.'

It was deep into the night, now. Lavender Row wasn't a main road but all the houses were terraces and so cars parked on the street. When you couldn't hear any car doors slamming you knew it was late. Feeling guilty at keeping him up now, Judith wondered if she should find him a quilt and leave him to sleep. But Adam suddenly seemed in the mood to talk.

He crossed his legs comfortably. 'My mother mutters darkly that Caleb takes after Shelley. Does that mean Matthias takes after me? I'd like to think so, but Matthias is impressive. He's intelligent, motivated, good-looking and engaged to the most amazing girl. Davina. The divine Davina.'

Because he'd shut his eyes as he talked, Judith could study him properly. The tightness of the skin across his cheekbones under the fans of his lashes, the burst of deep laughter lines at the corners of his eyes, the cleft in his chin. Where many men, like Tom, sagged and slackened with age, somehow Adam, though she knew he was a couple of years older than her, seemed to have tautened and become wirier. 'How is she amazing?' she prompted.

One of Adam's eyes opened slightly to look at her. 'Apart from being frighteningly clever and hardworking, she's as gorgeous as Lara Croft. Honestly, she's a goddess.'

Judith pulled a mock-scared face. 'Personality?'

'Definitely personality-plus; cheerful, interesting and caring. They're going to have the most phenomenal children.'

She found herself relaxing. 'But is Caleb more fun?'

The eye shut again. 'Certainly less predictable.' He gave several huge yawns, covering his mouth with the back of his hand. 'My boys are like the anecdote about the guy with two really good friends. The guy gets drunk and ends up in jail. The first friend gets him a solicitor and hides the escapade from his wife. But the other friend is beside him in the cell, saying, "*Damn* that was fun!"' He yawned again.

Adam was a little like the second friend as they'd got

161

drunk tonight. Nothing fun about it but he'd stayed by her side. 'I ought to go up and let you sleep,' she said softly.

'Will you be able to sleep if you go to bed?' he asked.

She shook her head then, realising his eyes were still closed said, 'Probably not, but I can read.'

He smiled. He had a really nice smile. It could be gentle or sympathetic, and, sometimes, wicked. 'Sleep's overrated. I can sleep anytime. I'll stay with you a little longer.' He pulled himself more upright and opened his eyes to gaze at her. 'You and I went to the same school, didn't we?'

It was the first time he'd indicated that he knew. Maybe Melanie had reminded him. Cautiously, she said, 'I believe we did.'

'I recognised you the instant I walked into the kitchen when you first called. Judith Morgan, you were. We had a conversation once outside the school gates about Polos and if they'd rot your teeth.'

He remembered all that! She would never have admitted remembering the detail, in case it led him to suspect the gigantic crush she'd had on him. Weakly, she offered, 'I still like Polos.'

'Me, too, the mint ones are my favourite. And the fruit, of course. I'm not keen on the butterscotch or the citrus.'

'New-fangled inventions.'

'Absolutely. And the spearmint, with those flecks, they look as if they're made of washing powder.' His eyes drooped again. 'You always insisted on being called Judith; the guys used to sing out, "Hey Jude!" after you, and you'd get sniffy.'

Her own eyelids were actually feeling heavy now. Maybe she ought to go up to bed after all and leave him to what was left of the night. 'Paul McCartney sang it so much better.'

And despite everything, despite the heavy, gluey despair in her heart, despite the gallons of scalding tears waiting behind her eyes for the moment when she stopped thinking about other things and thought again about Giorgio, she couldn't help feeling pleased that someone had noticed and remembered things about her.

'I always thought it was kind of a shame,' he murmured, drowsily. 'I thought it would be nice to call you Jude. The name conjures up someone who dares to be different, fun. Interesting.'

While she wondered what to say to that she watched sleep steal up and claim him. As if in sympathy she felt her own eyes close and decided to let them. Just for a minute.

# *Chapter Fourteen*

Morning. Early. Judith opened her eyes to the sun-filled sitting room despite the drawn curtains and discovered that she'd spent the night with her legs curled and cramped and her head on the sofa arm. Her face felt creased, her mouth and eyes dry.

Adam was asleep at the other end of the sofa, feet on the table, arms folded, head propped against the uphol-stered wing of the sofa, as if he'd just dropped off for five minutes during *Grandstand*.

He'd stayed, she remembered, because of Giorgio.

*Giorgio*.

Nausea swilled over her, but her eyes were finally too dry for tears. Her mind had cradled the knowledge of his death while she slept, ready to thrust it back at her now with sickening clarity. Giorgio was dead and very soon would be committed to the ground of the island he'd loved.

Feeling as if the floor was heaving like the deck of a boat beneath her feet, she went to her computer in the alcove and left it to start up while she visited the bathroom, brushed her teeth and showered away the worst of her hangover. Sliding into an enveloping cotton robe, she returned quietly to the computer. Whatever whirrs and bings the computer had made as it booted up, Adam slept on.

The World Wide Web was a wonderful thing, she acknowledged, contemplating the elegant website of the *Times of Malta*. The *Times* could be accessed as easily in Brinham as in Sliema.

Clicking on the correct link, she watched the social and personal page flicking onto her screen. She scrolled down and, even though she was expecting it, Giorgio's name leapt out and stopped her breath.

*ZAMMIT. On 27 July 2004, at St Luke's Hospital, GIORGIO, aged 34, passed away suddenly, comforted by the rites of Holy Church. He leaves to mourn his irreparable loss his wife, Johanna née Grech, his daughters, Alexia and Lydia, his parents, Agnello and Maria, his uncles, aunts, nephews, nieces and friends – Rest in peace.*

*The funeral leaves St Luke's Hospital on Tuesday 29 July at 1.30 p.m. for Stella Maris Parish Church, Sliema, where Mass* praesente cadavere *will be said at 2.30 p.m., followed by interment in the family grave at the Santa Maria Addolorata Cemetery. Family flowers only.*

She'd guessed Maria and Agnello would place the obituary in the *Times* as well as in the Maltese papers, *In-Nazzjon* or *L-Orizzont*. Giorgio had been a businessman; his death would need announcing in both of the island's languages. She stared at the stark words that confirmed the loss of her lover.

Adam stirred, and she realised he was awake.

She had to clear her throat in order to speak. 'Obituary.' She nodded at the screen. 'I must go.'

He frowned for a moment, levering himself to his feet and crossing to where she sat to read over her shoulder. 'To the funeral?' He didn't precisely try to dissuade her but he rubbed his unshaven chin, making it rasp. Slowly, he said, 'If you're sure then somebody ought to go with you. I volunteer, if you can't scare up anyone better. You'll need an ally. The family will shut you out. Feelings will be running high. A mother and father have lost their son; children have lost their father. The wife will act with wounded dignity and ignore you.'

It was an uncomfortable picture. And, unfortunately, a realistic one. 'You're right,' she whispered, her heart sinking to the pit of her stomach. 'What was I thinking? It would be a horrible intrusion. But thank you. You've been really kind, Adam, especially considering that I threw you out of your home.'

Awkwardly, he reached out and patted her shoulder. 'You're having a rough time.'

Then the doorbell shrilled. They raised their eyebrows at each other. Judith pushed her chair back from the computer workstation. 'Half-past seven? Strange hour for visitors.'

Adam turned, then winced and lifted a hand to his head. It was the right hand so he must be feeling rough. 'Do you want me to answer it?'

'No, I'll do it.' When she reached the front door Judith opened it on the chain and squinted out into the light, pain lancing across her eyes as they were attacked by the cruel morning sun.

The small figure on the doorstep snapped, 'It's me,' and resolved itself into the shape of her sister.

'Molly?' Hastily, Judith unchained the door. 'What are you . . .? I mean, come in.'

Molly's Lexus was pulled up at the kerb, glinting gold in the early sunlight. Judith frowned as she made out solid shapes stacked on the back seat. Suitcases?

'Can I stay for a bit?' asked Molly, calmly, taking off her cardigan and smoothing her hair. 'I've left Frankie.' Without even waiting for Judith's jaw to drop, she slipped past into the sitting room then halted, spinning to look between Judith in her robe and bare feet, and Adam with his slept-in clothes. 'Who's *he*?'

The morning grew hazy with heat. Judith opened the back door to let the soft summer scents of grass and honeysuckle float in from the garden as she filled the kettle.

Molly was upstairs, unpacking her things into the spare wardrobe while Judith occupied herself with small chores, wondering what was going on with her sister at the same time as feeling nauseous and headachy. It was a long time since she'd been drunk enough to have a hangover but the whole unpleasant process had not improved.

From the alcove in the dining room the computer hummed gently, the 3D design on the screensaver rolling slowly through its contortions. She didn't need to click the mouse and let Giorgio's obituary beam again from the screen and jolt her with fresh pain. It lurked behind the screensaver because she hadn't quite brought herself to close the page. She felt more like lighting candles around it, like a shrine.

The sounds of Molly's purposeful movements in the spare room above filtered through the house; the wardrobe door opening, shutting, opening, shutting, the drawers of the chest groaning in and out.

It was a kind of inverted déjà vu. A few short weeks ago she'd shut herself in Molly's spare room to unpack her life methodically from her suitcases. And now here was Molly, returning the favour. She hadn't told her about Giorgio yet. It had felt wrong, even aggressive. *You've left your husband? I can trump that because my lover's dead . . .*

Shading her eyes against the sun, Judith sniffed back fresh tears and stepped out onto the patio, the flagstones warm beneath her bare feet, and looked up the long narrow garden at the lawn and Adam beyond it, cutting back a shrub that grew in an enormous spray of cerise flowers against the ochre tones of the back wall. He had far too much alcohol in his system to drive straight home. She was so incredibly touched that he'd kept her company last night when she hadn't even realised how much she needed someone. She'd refused to let him wait outside on the pavement for Caleb to fetch him just because her sister was taking her turn to have a crisis. Diplomatically, though, Adam had elected to 'make himself useful', which she'd translated as, 'I no longer have a garden of my own and really miss it.'

'Drink, Adam? Something cold?' she called.

He screwed up his eyes to look down the garden at her. 'Tea would be nectar.'

'OK,' she called back. Borrowing his pragmatic approach of the evening before and to show him she hadn't been too drunk to remember, she made two mugs and took him them both. She'd wait for Molly to come down to have her own.

He grinned appreciatively. 'The only thing better than a cup of tea is two cups.'

They chatted for a few moments before she headed back to the kitchen. She jumped to find Molly waiting for her, composed and neat in black trousers and a cherry-red short-sleeved jumper, hair brushed loose and shiny over her shoulders. Her smile looked forced. 'Sorry that I didn't feel like talking straight away,' she said.

Judith slid her arm around her sister, looking down at the pale face. 'I'm the last person to complain about that. How are you doing?'

'OK.' Molly didn't look OK. She looked drained and miserable. 'I'll get the kettle on, shall I?'

She was going to take over the kitchen, Judith could see; Molly putting herself in charge of the kettle was the first step. However, realising that Molly probably needed something to do and refusals to let her perform simple tasks was exactly the behaviour that had prevented Judith from feeling at home at Molly's place, she just said, 'It's just boiled,' and watched her sister search in vain for a teapot before giving up and dropping teabags in mugs and then pouring in the steaming water.

As she felt slightly less hungover in fresh air, Judith carried both out to the bench so that Molly had to follow. Adam being at the far end of the narrow garden, she knew they wouldn't be overheard. 'So.' She looked into Molly's eyes. 'Do I have to go round and smash Frankie's face in?'

Molly didn't raise a smile at this unlikely image. 'As long as I don't have to stay with him any more, I don't care what happens.' Her entire body was loose and still.

In the hush following this flat declaration, bees buzzed around the honeysuckle and children's voices came from a garden nearby. Judith linked her sister's soft arm and drew her closer. 'I don't want to poke my nose in but I think you're going to have to give me a few hints. He hasn't been knocking you about, has he?'

Molly shook her head.

169

'Having an affair?'

She shrugged. 'Not that I know of.' Then Molly sighed, her shoulders drooping. 'I just can't bear him any more, ruling the roost like a Victorian and trying to treat me like a skivvy. It's four years into the twenty-first century but he acts as if women are yet to get the vote. He never shows me affection but he thinks it's OK to ogle other women. When he told me that I bored him and he wouldn't . . .' She blinked fiercely. 'He wouldn't be able to *do it* if we tried because I don't arouse him, I packed my bags.'

Judith gave Molly's arm a sympathetic squeeze. 'Good for you. If he can't perform in bed then he shouldn't blame you.' She didn't directly comment on the rest. Frankie had always ruled the roost and always treated Molly like a skivvy. Equality at work had come thirty-odd years ago without Frankie ever taking out his subscription but saying that he couldn't get an erection for her, well, that was just nasty.

Given recent history, when Molly had unquestioningly taken Judith in with only a days' notice, Judith felt she had to hide the fact that it wasn't a good time for Molly to land herself in Judith's newly acquired space. She was sympathetic – of course she was sympathetic, she loved Moll to death – but it was tough to 'be there' for her just at this exact moment, when all she wanted to do was sit in the sunshine and think of Giorgio. She blinked away an ominous prickling behind her eyes. It was hard to listen sympathetically to Molly describing how empty and diso-rientated she felt without saying, 'Me, too!' and pouring out the horrible, terrible news about Giorgio.

With a quavering sigh, Molly put her hand over her eyes. 'Honestly, Judith, you can't know what Frankie's like! He's so grumpy all the time . . .'

To try and prevent her tears from spilling, Judith stared at Adam, who was squinting against the bright light.

Molly went on. '. . . dictatorial, criticising and carping . . .'

Adam had his back to them as if trying to preserve their privacy, his wiry legs planted firm against the earth as he worked his way methodically over the shrub, snipping off a leggy branch and snip, snip, snipping it into smaller pieces into a garden refuse sack. He seemed to be able to work the secateurs OK with his right hand – he'd slipped on his 'gizmo' from the car that he used for driving – leaving his thumb and finger free to lever against a projection where his fingers used to be.

He'd been so kind last night. Judith would be forever grateful at the way he'd seemed to understand the depth and futility of Judith's pain, and how it was amplified because her grief would forever go unacknowledged by Giorgio's family.

Judith's heart gave such a squeeze she thought she might pass out. *Oh, Giorgio! Will it always hurt this much?*

'. . . and he should've found someone else years ago if he's found me unexciting for such a long time. Shouldn't he? Judith?' Molly concluded.

Stricken that she'd obviously zoned out while her sister was trying to have a heart-to-heart, Judith turned. 'I'm sorry, Moll, I didn't—'

Molly's face flooded dull crimson and her eyes blazed. She made a theatrical show of following the direction Judith's gaze had been taking. 'I'm sorry if I *interrupted something* with my obviously inopportune appearance, but is it too much to ask that you stop lusting after the gardener just long enough to attend to my woes? Honestly, it's different when it's you, isn't it?' Molly's voice was tight and hurt. 'It's not like you to be as self-orientated as you've seemed since you got back from Malta.'

Misery closed in so hard Judith felt crushed. She had to swallow hard before she could speak. 'I'm sorry. But I'm not "lusting after" Adam. He stayed last night because . . .' She sucked in a big wavering breath but still her voice dwindled. 'Because Giorgio died yesterday.'

'*Died?*' Shock dragged down Molly's jaw. 'Don't be silly,' she denied uncertainly. 'How could he?'

Wearily, Judith let her head tip back. Her voice emerged thick with tears. 'He had an accident, he was in a coma, which is why I came home. And now he's been released.'

Molly burst into tears and threw herself into Judith's arms. 'I'm sorry,' she wept. 'I'm sorry, I didn't know. You should have told me! I knew there was something wrong but not that it was so terrible. Why do you keep everything hidden?'

Judith clutched at Molly's shaking shoulders. She could have said, 'Because I tell you my lover has died and you're the one crying and seeking comfort,' but she held it back. Kieran and Wilma had told her she kept everything inside so she obviously did . . . and it obviously hurt people's feelings. People she loved. She was just too dazed, grieving and hungover right now to resolve to strengthen her relationships by being more sharing and therefore caring.

Molly continued to cry. 'But please can I stay for a bit, Judith? It's been horrible, hardly speaking to Frankie and sleeping in the spare room.'

*That explained the underwear Judith had seen there.* 'Of course you can.' Hopelessly, Judith closed her eyes as her sister cried in great soaking gulps.

Maybe she shouldn't have come home. Her family skills were rusty from living in a different country.

Tomorrow, she should be standing on the rock of Malta as Giorgio Zammit became part of it forever. How, from green, leafy Brinham, could she feel close to him? Sense him in the golden stone and blue sea of the place he'd lived, the place they'd loved, and gain comfort that he'd existed? That she'd meant something to him. In Malta she would have been able to talk to his friends about him, Charlie, even Anton and Gordon, and bring his sense of humour and his boyishness back to life in their stories. Perhaps that would have overlain the inner vision that haunted her, of Giorgio, helpless and empty, like a big baby in a white gown, on a white hospital bed with a dressing on his forehead and his life lived for him by tubes and machines. Perhaps she'd be able to forgive him the fecklessness or recklessness that had left Judith in a financial hole.

Even as she patted Molly's heaving back and framed soothing sentences about Molly staying with Judith as long as she needed, other words were forming in her head, despite her earlier decision to stay away.

*I must go back.*

# Chapter Fifteen

It was the day of Giorgio's funeral. Judith sat on the clifftop at Ghar Lapsi and stared at the glittering sea where Giorgio had been hit by a jet ski more than three months before. The cliff here formed a broad shelf before rising again behind her. She'd seated herself on a sun-heated slab of rock amongst the scrub, well away from the restaurant and green-painted tables on the terrace, concrete pathways and the steps to the sea. Here it was quiet. She could gaze down into the bay sheltered by its arm of rock and not be bothered by tourists or fishermen.

She'd hired a car and driven to Ghar Lapsi straight from Malta's airport, making no attempt to see the funeral cortege set out from the imposing buildings of St Luke's Hospital. Nor had she tried to slip into the church to hear the mass said for the repose of Giorgio's soul or skulked between the mourners among the imposing marble monuments of Santa Maria Addolorata cemetery.

Instead, she mourned here, privately, watching the delicate movements of the sea where she and Giorgio had dived together and been happy, hugging to her the memories of loving a man who'd had a joyful heart, even if he'd proved to be a bit of a butterfingers with insurance premiums and her money.

Out of the respect for the power of Malta's summer sun, she'd brought a big bottle of water in her bag and she wore a big-brimmed black straw hat. Sunglasses guarded her eyes against the sight of blue waves shattering the sun's reflection into smithereens of blinding light. The sea was calm, rippling and sighing against the dark craggy rocks below. It was when there was a swell that the currents became treacherous and divers could be dragged out past the reef or trapped, slapped about somewhere in Ghar Lapsi's underwater cavern system.

Today was a beautiful day for a dive. The light would filter through the turquoise sea and into the mouths of underwater caves; rainbow wrasse, rays and morays would flit through weed that swayed with the motion of the sea. Divers would fin through the near-silent world in pairs, communicating with hand signals and instrument checks.

Out to sea, looking closer than it actually was, stood the dark shape of the tiny island of Filfla, a nature reserve and possibly, depending on what you believed, the home of two-tailed lizards. Beyond it, a couple of blue, red and green fishing boats surged across the waves. The rest of the sea within eyeshot was empty.

This was probably how Ghar Lapsi had looked the day Giorgio was injured, the squatting presence of Filfla and one or two boats. One, at least. One that carried jet skis.

It was almost evening by the time she roused herself from her private mourning and rose stiffly from the heated rock, her skin tight and burning from the sun and the salty breeze. She could have stayed all night, watching the sun set and the sky turn shrimp pink, purple, then black but her water was finished and she had something she must do.

Stiff from her long vigil, she retrieved the hire car from the car park and drove towards Tarxien and the Santa Maria Addolorata Cemetery, the many flat-roofed buildings she passed turning tawny as the sun angled low, a forest of television aerials glinting above.

Tiredness began to steal over her. The day had begun early – she'd only just made her flight because the southbound M1 was closed owing to a chemical spillage. Tense with anxiety she'd had to find a way onto the M11 and then M25 and pass London to the east.

She'd left without telling anybody but her uncle Richard, as she'd be staying with him and Erminia tonight.

No doubt she'd catch hell from Molly. Molly didn't understand that Judith had to do things her own way. And if that way included booking a flight and leaving for Malta before Molly was awake . . . She could almost hear her elder sister's scandalised complaints. 'Fancy just going off like that without telling a soul! Leaving me a note to say make myself at home and that there's plenty of food. What a way to treat a guest. That's just like you, Judith . . .'

What was surprising was that Molly should expect anything else. Who else would she be like? Molly had had Judith for a sister for forty-four years.

Once outside the black wrought-iron cemetery gates that were patterned to echo the Gothic stone arches beyond, she parked the car. It would be dusk soon and the flower stalls in the car park were closing up, the stallholders calling to one another as they worked. Judith stopped at the nearest and was just in time to buy a single white orchid.

The ornate gates to the hilly cemetery would be closing soon but the man who stood at the gates allowed her to slip inside. All was still except for the grumble of nearby traffic and the rushing of the wind. Funerals were over for the day and the dust had settled. There was no rolling grass here as in an English cemetery, just clumps of trees among the broad paved walks. Mausoleums and graves marked by sculpted figures terraced the hillside. Having only been to Addolorata once before, she'd forgotten how vast it was, stretching away in all directions as far as she could see.

She knew where the recent graves were and followed a succession of pathways towards them but she found nothing to indicate any connection with Giorgio. Elaborate wreaths, yes, but the names were wrong – Borg, Debono, Gatt. Her heart began to thud in panic as she hurried up and down.

Where was he?

And then she remembered the words 'family grave' in the newspaper, and relief seeped in. She returned to the older area, eyes skinned for the multitude of recent floral tributes that would indicate a recent burial, up and down the paths. It was quite an area to cover, her nails digging into her palms and her legs feeling as if they belonged to someone else. She passed between the ranks of marble, the occasional black to punctuate the pale grey, plots arranged close together like terraced houses and some edged with wrought iron or with posts and chains. Too many of the graves were graced with sprays or candles burning in glass lanterns for her to make the rapid progress she desired because she had to check every one. Already the sky was turning lavender, the precursor to the brief Mediterranean dusk.

She was just thinking that she'd have to return tomorrow or be shut in for the night when a burst of colour caught her eye. She dashed between the stone crosses and exquisitely carved saints to a blaze of fresh flowers that spilled onto the graves on either side.

At the head of the plot, beside a marble angel crying marble tears, were the words she was looking for. *Zammit Familja.*

The grave had been closed; gravediggers, obviously, were prompt in hot countries. The floral tributes were arranged between a series of marble plaques angled and ranked like pictures on a shelf. On each, the names of the Zammit family already passed were inscribed beneath small oval photos.

Reality hit her like one of Sliema Z Bus's buses: Giorgio was separated from her not just by death but by six feet of soil and stone. It was all too bald, too raw and real. Instead of the comfort she'd been searching for . . . this was a place of horror.

*Forget his twinkling eyes*, the monument seemed to say, *no more laughing mouth and hungry lips. No more searching hands. It's all ended down here with a box thrust into the ground, and Giorgio trapped inside it.*

She closed her eyes and told herself a proper death was better than to be a shell of a man in a hospital bed, not truly living.

Then a woman's voice broke the silence. 'I knew you wouldn't be long.'

Judith's eyes flew open. She staggered on the sloping path in shock as she spun around. '*Cass!*' she gasped. 'Oh,

178

Cass, how good to see you!' The relief at seeing someone connected to Giorgio who'd been friendly towards her was enormous. She lifted her arms ready to enfold Cass in a glad embrace.

In a black dress overlaid with lace that fluttered in the evening breeze, Cass clutched a white handkerchief. She'd aged ten years in the last months. Her eyes, washed with too many tears, were pink rimmed in the deepening folds of her face. Instead of stepping closer to Judith and accepting the offered embrace, she edged nearer the grave, crossing herself as she gazed down. 'They don't know I'm here,' she whispered, as if 'they' lurked behind a gravestone. 'I pretended I needed medication I'd left at home. Maria was watching for you all day. She was so very relieved that you didn't show up. Thank you for letting the family mourn.'

Judith let her arms drift down to her sides, shocked at being thanked for not inflicting herself on others. It was an odd thought, and one that made her feel hurt and distant. She hadn't fainted since she was a teenager but now her ears rung. Her voice emerged reedy and weak. 'But I'm mourning him, too. I loved him, too.'

Cass's smile was thin. 'I know. *I* know, believe me, I know how it was between you. But they don't care. They want him for themselves.' She made a gesture as if clutching Giorgio to her heart.

Judith was too distraught to summon a reply. Dumbly, she watched as Cass took out a brown leather purse and extracted a small item that glinted gold.

She recognised it with a jolt. Giorgio's crucifix. He'd worn it always against his skin.

Cass reached out for Judith's hand and dropped the crucifix into her palm, closing her fingers gently around the gold. 'And he loved you. Only his body is here. You have his heart. Take it with you.'

Then she turned and hurried away, leaving Judith beside Giorgio's grave alone, feeling the gold warming against her flesh as once it had warmed against Giorgio's.

It was three days later when Judith pulled up once again outside her house in Lavender Row, in her own car now, which she'd left parked at Birmingham airport while she'd paid her flying visit to Malta. She'd rung home to tell Molly where she was then spent a couple of days with Uncle Richard before coming home and his avuncular presence had calmed her. 'You stay as long as you want,' he'd said. His wife, the lovely Erminia, had smiled her big, warm smile and appeared serenely unmoved that Judith had been unwilling to join in dinners with her cousins Raymond, Lino and Rosaire and their families. Molly and Wilma should be that restful, Judith thought, struggling to open her front door with one hand, the other occupied with her suitcase.

Molly bustled to meet her in the hall with a ready embrace and a combination of pleasure and exasperation. 'I can't believe you went all that way just to go to a funeral.'

Judith didn't bother explaining that she'd been 'all that way' *not* to go to a funeral. It was too complex. She was just grateful that today Molly wasn't launching into a critique of Judith's strange ways. 'Hi, Moll. Good to see you.' She dropped her case.

Molly stepped back and clasped her hands. 'I went shopping when you said you were on your way home. There's a casserole in the oven because no doubt you'll be hungry.'

180

'Um, thanks.' Casserole sounded stodgy and worthy – very Molly – and Judith didn't particularly fancy it, even though it was true she hadn't eaten much recently. She thought longingly of an empty house and a full wine bottle. It didn't sound healthy, but it did sound attractive.

Molly tilted her head. 'That's a pretty cross on your necklace. Is it antique? It looks it.'

Judith touched the crucifix, which she'd worn around her neck since it had come into her possession. 'It was Giorgio's. His aunt gave it to me.'

'Oh.' Molly actually gave her a hug. 'I'm so sorry about Giorgio. If you got a keepsake then I suppose it wasn't too tricky coping with his family?' Molly didn't seem to expect more than vague answers so Judith was able to make her way to the kitchen without going into detail, her sister chatting amiably in her wake. She just couldn't bear to delve into the way Cass had sneaked around to give her something of Giorgio's and listen to Molly wonder aloud whether Judith should give it back. Instead, she located white wine in the fridge and red in the cupboard below the stairs. Excellent. She'd begin with the white. 'Wine, Molly?'

'Oh, no, thank you.' Molly looked faintly shocked, as if drinking wine were a disgraceful thing to do.

Judith poured herself a big glass – one of those enormous glasses meant to be quarter-filled with red wine to allow for breathing. She filled it right to the top and it took almost half the bottle. On the kitchen table lay her mail and, on top, a white envelope with *Jude* written large and untidy across the front. After a few sips of the cold, clear wine she opened it, letting Molly burble gently on about herbs in the casserole.

*Jude,* the letter said.

*Your ferocious sister grudgingly told me you'd be home tonight. You evidently decided you didn't want company on your odyssey but you know where I am if you need anything.*

*Don't forget to eat.*

*Look after yourself.*

*Don't get drunk alone (ring me and I'll get drunk with you).*

*Adam.*

Unaccountably, the short missive lifted her spirits. She sent Molly a smile and gave her another hug – one-armed this time so she didn't have to put down the wine glass. 'What's in the casserole?'

Molly smiled, on solid ground when it came to hearty meals. 'I've just told you – chicken, leeks, carrots and potatoes.' She reached for a pair of oven mitts – Judith was sure there had been no oven mitts in the house when she left for Malta because she tended to use a wadded-up tea towel – and took the casserole from the oven.

'Smells delicious,' Judith said, feeling the first tendrils of appetite unfurl. She reached down the plates and took cutlery from the drawer then accepted a ladle full of fragrant casserole. It steamed on the blue plate and she breathed it in. 'Lemongrass?'

Molly looked pleased. 'And thyme.'

Judith began to eat, because if she didn't make an effort she'd soon be as thin as a witch and Molly had gone to the trouble of cooking and even though Judith had kept her wish to be alone to herself, she felt guilty about it.

As if she'd read her thoughts Molly took Judith by surprise by asking in a small voice, 'Can I stay?'

Judith laid down her fork, seeing the way Molly gazed fixedly at her food and wasn't eating at all. With a melting feeling of love for her sister she reached out and patted her soft shoulder. 'Of course you can. You'll need somewhere until you decide what you're going to do.'

Molly's expression relaxed, though her eyes reddened as if tears weren't far away. She sniffed and smiled, then reached for a phone message pad – Judith didn't think there had been one of those before, either – and tore off a note and handed it to her. 'Kieran called. He's coming round in a while. Desperate to talk to you about something, apparently and I wouldn't do.'

With a ripple of unease, Judith set her wine aside. If Kieran was 'desperate' to talk, she might need a clear head.

# Chapter Sixteen

'Can we stay?' Kieran asked. He had a new eyebrow ring, silver with a red bead. It jarred with his otherwise clean-cut looks.

Kieran and Bethan were sitting together like a pair of cuddly toys on Judith's sofa, their hands clasped tightly and their eyes shadowed. Molly had ostentatiously taken herself off to her room, although slowly, perhaps hoping for an invitation to remain and be part of whatever was making Kieran and Beth so solemn.

Now Judith knew an urge to ask if she could leave, too. 'Stay here?' she repeated. That would fill every bedroom in her house, further compromising the peace to mourn that she craved. She'd have to ask Molly to move from the spare double room to the box room. She'd be able to hear Kieran and Bethan through the wall. Giggling, and no doubt making the unmistakable sounds of sex. Embarrassing her while probably quite unembarrassed themselves.

There would be a morning and evening queue for the bathroom.

The television on non-stop. Music at headache volume. She was too fragile for this. But with an effort, for Kieran, she managed a smile and to make her voice gentle. 'Why would you want to move in with me?'

Bethan gazed down at her trainers, oversized things that had once been white. 'I'm not getting on with my parents.'

'Is there a reason for that?' Judith switched her gaze from Kieran to Bethan and back, trying to read in their expressions what they seemed reluctant to put into words.

The two turned to gaze at each other. Kieran whispered to Bethan, 'Be best to explain.' He slid an arm around her narrow back.

Bethan's eyes filled with tears but she nodded. Her voice squeaked. 'Tell her, then.'

The caramel flecks in Kieran's eyes were very bright as he turned back to Judith. 'We're going to have a baby.'

Oh.

Frozen, Judith stared at him, taking in his boyishly rumpled curls that made him look younger than his twenty-two years. She had to force herself to remain calm. No good would come of yelling, '*Oh you stupid, stupid little buggers!*' however much it was her first instinct. It was far too late to ask them if they'd been careless or just unlucky. It was pointless to preach that unplanned pregnancies were life changing and that young people would be better off enjoying their youth while they found their feet in the world. It might even be optimistic to expect their relationship to last, but they didn't need to hear it.

Her lips felt stiff. 'So you told Bethan's parents, and they were furious?'

Two slowly shaken heads.

Understanding dawned. 'You haven't told them? You've just assumed that they'll be furious?' So they'd come to her.

Two nodded heads.

'You don't know what they're like,' Kieran added, earnestly. 'They're awful. They'll murder Bethan when they find out.'

'She's going to tell them!' squealed Bethan, bouncing to her feet like a frightened rabbit. 'We can't stay here, Kieran – I can't bear it if she goes and tells them! They'll go mad.'

Kieran jumped up too, expressive eyes wide and uncertain, his complexion very white against the bright red bead on his eyebrow ring. 'I won't let her tell, don't worry.' He drew Bethan into the protective circle of his arms.

Judith sat still. Leaping to her feet would take energy she couldn't summon. She felt weighed down by a new great sadness to add to the one she carried already. Obviously, pregnancy outside marriage didn't mean the same shame or economic difficulties that it had when she was seventeen. But what would happen to their youth? They were hardly more than babies themselves, it was too soon to give their lives over to parenthood and putting themselves last all the time. 'Don't panic,' she suggested, without raising her voice. 'Bethan, I can't tell your parents because I don't know who they are or where they live. And I think we three need to talk some more. Could you please sit down? You're giving me neck ache and dramatic outbursts won't help anyone.'

Looking deflated, Kieran and Bethan sank slowly back onto the sofa.

With many hesitations and prevarications, they began to tell Judith all about their frightening situation. Bethan was eight weeks pregnant. She'd both done a home test and seen a doctor. 'I can't tell my parents,' she repeated miserably. 'They don't even know I'm going out with anyone.'

'Why not?' Judith asked gently, blankly astonished at this information.

Bethan leant forward earnestly, her blue eyes seeming to beg Judith to be on her side. 'It's one of their rules that I can't go out with anyone more than two years older than me. They have loads of rules. Loads and loads. Dad's very strict.' Then she launched into a tangled explanation about the deceptions and subterfuges she'd felt obliged to employ so that they wouldn't realise she was seeing someone five years older.

Judith wondered how any parent at the beginning of the twenty-first century expected to make rules like that stick with a seventeen-year-old. Such blanket dictates seemed to fairly invite deception. Diplomatically, she said, 'Their rules are meant to ensure your wellbeing and safety, I expect.'

Bethan fixed Judith with big, tragic eyes. 'You don't understand.'

Sympathy twisted in Judith's chest. Bethan was so young to give her life over to bringing up a baby. She made her voice gentle. 'I think I understand pretty well. You find their rules unreasonable so you find ways to get around them.' She thought furiously, caught in the age-old parental conundrum of wanting to act in a way most likely to benefit the kids but not scare them into reckless behaviour. They were like overwound springs, poised to boing off in some wild direction. They'd probably surf sofas in the homes of friends rather than face Bethan's family. She didn't suppose for an instant that the youngsters had spoken to the council about what accommodation might be available for a couple expecting a baby or found out what financial benefits they might be entitled to. Kieran had been in his junior job with the water board for about a year and Bethan was still at school. Their reserves were probably non-existent. As she pondered, the clock ticked, and Kieran and Bethan held hands in silence and stared at the carpet.

Judith could see no real choice other than to make a qualified offer. 'You can stay here provided you ring your parents and tell them where you are.'

An enormous smile of relief burst over Bethan's face. She jumped back up and started for the door. 'I'll ring from my mobile.'

The poor girl must think Judith was simple.

Rubbing her forehead wearily, she disabused her of this notion. 'What, *pretend* to speak to your parents, do you mean? And then come back and declare that they don't mind a bit that you're moving in with an unknown woman for no particular reason? I'm sorry, Bethan, but that's not on. You'd be putting me in an untenable situation and it's not fair to your parents, no matter how hard you find it to stand up to them. Ring them from this landline and then they can speak to me as well.'

Silence. Slowly, Bethan sank down again, making no effort to make the call.

Kieran gazed at Judith pleadingly. 'You don't know how awful they are.'

Judith's patience began to stretch and her retort came out more sharply than she'd intended. 'Awful for minding that she's changing her whole life for the sake of a condom or a pill she could get free from the doctor? That she's kept you a secret because you're precisely the person they've asked her not to go out with? That she's lied to them and abused their trust? That she's forcing a grandchild upon them in the most difficult of circumstances, robbing them of all the joy a grandchild ought to bring?' It was an effort not to let her voice rise. 'And how do you know how awful they are, darling? You've never met them.'

Kieran looked stricken. Bethan went deadly quiet.

Judith looked from one of them to the other. She was upset. She recognised that it was about all the reasons she'd just outlined but also because they were making her deal with this when she had so much else on her plate already. And she still had the task hanging over her of telling Kieran that Giorgio was dead. Kieran didn't even know about her flying visit to Malta, let alone that she had heartbreaking news. Now could scarcely be considered the appropriate time.

Still, she could do nothing about the life that had left this world. The life coming into it took precedence and she'd do whatever she could to help with Kieran's baby. She forced herself to concentrate. 'Does your father know, Kieran?'

Kieran contrived to look sheepish and horrified both at once. 'No.'

Taking a deep breath, she focused her efforts on dealing with things as calmly as possible, making her voice sensible, reasonable. 'You've made a baby. I'm afraid you can't just run away from facing at least Bethan's parents because she's not eighteen.'

'That's not true,' Bethan said, though her voice quavered. 'The police won't make you go back once you're sixteen.'

Judith suspected Bethan was right and changed tack. 'However you feel about them, Bethan, they love you and they're entitled to the truth, even if their reaction makes you unhappy.'

Bethan began to sniffle.

Judith frowned as she swept through alternatives in her mind. 'I'll come with you,' she offered, heavily, not feeling particularly qualified for the role of peacekeeper but recognising Kieran needed her support and definitely needed encouragement to talk to Bethan's parents. 'You have to grow up tonight and learn to think of someone other than yourselves. If you're bringing a child into the world, you'll find you do a lot of that. I'm afraid it's time to face reality.'

It wasn't a textbook counselling session – but it got Bethan and Kieran into her car.

Bethan's family lived in a nice new part of town in a detached house, overlarge for its plot but not actually big. The bricks were yellow, the roof tiles red, the window frames had been stained with a too-red mahogany and would soon need doing again.

Her parents, Hannah and Nick Sutherland, looked bewildered and suspicious when their daughter arrived home with two strangers in tow. Hannah was small and mousy with blonde streaks that might have once brightened her up a bit but had now almost grown out. Nick was chunky with thinning brown hair. They stared from Bethan to Kieran to Judith. Nick demanded, 'What's going on, Bethan?'

Silence. Judith wondered with alarm whether the youngsters expected her to do the breaking of the news and wished she'd established earlier that it was their job. But then, with a noise like an elephant's sneeze, Bethan burst into tears and threw herself into her mother's arms. 'Mum, I'm so sorry. You're going to be so sad and angry!'

Judith would have loved Bethan's parents prove Bethan wrong about their reaction to her pregnancy . . . but Nick and Hannah Sutherland turned out to be both sad and angry. Very angry. Also:

'. . . horrified!' spluttered Nick.

'. . . hurt,' cried Hannah.

'. . . gutted—'

'. . . disappointed—'

The list of their emotions was long.

Judith did what she could to keep everyone calm and focused on the problem rather than on parental shock and anger. She tried to reassure them. 'You probably can't see it now, but Kieran is a lovely boy. Immature, of course.'

'Am I?' Kieran demanded, looking hurt.

She smiled at her stepson. 'You allowed yourself to be kept a secret and somehow you didn't protect Bethan from pregnancy. And,' as an afterthought, 'you haven't confided in your father.'

Kieran paled at her words.

After a long conversation in which Judith tried hard to be the voice of reason and support she realised that they were talking to her over Kieran's head, as if he were a child. Gathering her resolve, she gave Hannah and Nick, stunned and flabbergasted, poor souls, her telephone number – 'In case I can be of any help to you' – and prepared to take herself off home after giving Kieran a hug. 'If you want me to see your father with you, ring me. But I think you need to stay and talk to Bethan's parents, tonight. There are a lot of decisions to make.' Exhaustion was beginning to bow her down. She'd been up about twenty hours, hadn't slept much prior to that and had to deal with grief over Giorgio as well as the evening's emotional maelstrom.

Kieran looked shocked to be left to face the music. 'Can't you stay a bit?'

191

Judith turned back to press three kisses on his forehead. 'I could,' she admitted. 'But I think that this is where you begin to prove yourself by talking to Bethan and her parents about how you're going to support Beth through this. You know I'll always be on your side, darling, but I think you have to take charge now.'

Nick cleared his throat. 'Your mum's got a point, young man.'

He sounded so forbidding that Judith almost changed her mind and sat down again. Leaving Kieran to take charge of his own life was one of the hardest things she'd done, but she still said goodnight.

In her car, she suddenly became aware of Giorgio's crucifix touching the skin below her throat. She held it, kissed it and closed her eyes very tightly. Anyone watching might think she was engaged in private prayer but she just wanted it against her lips because it had lain so long against Giorgio's flesh. 'I hope I've done the right thing,' she murmured, then she started the car. She needed alone time. If only Moll would be in bed when she got home, then she could get back to that bottle of wine.

But it wasn't to be. Though it was midnight, Molly was waiting up for her, buttoned up in a pink candlewick dressing gown that didn't suit her and looked as if it should have been cut up for dusters years ago. Not that Judith ever cut things up for dusters, but Moll did.

'Hot chocolate?' offered Molly. The drinking chocolate powder waited in the cups, ready.

Judith retrieved the huge glass of wine she'd abandoned earlier and drank half of it quickly so that no one could expect her to do anything else responsible for a few hours. 'Not for me, thanks,' she said and headed for an armchair. Molly followed, perching herself on the sofa.

Because Moll knew something was up, and even though she was aware that Tom ought to be told first, Judith broke the news of Kieran's impending fatherhood.

Molly curled up tightly in a corner of the sofa. Her voice was small when, instead of commenting on Kieran's situation, she asked, 'You've got a lot on your plate, haven't you?'

Judith quelled the desire to thank her for noticing. 'Quite, yes.'

'I ought not stay.' Molly looked forlorn. For a big sister, Molly took some surprising detours into the territory of little sister, looking for help and comfort and, chiefly, support.

Judith felt her heart melt. 'Of course you must stay. You need to decide what to do next.' She reached out and took her sister's cold little hand. 'But it won't work long term, darling. You won't like it when I want to read for hours or stay on the computer all day. Or invite Adam round to get drunk.' His face flashed into her mind, his half-smile, the concern in his eyes. Adam was the one person who'd offered her unselfish support during her intense grief.

Judith caught the grimace on Molly's face and felt a flash of impatience. 'You see! You don't like my attitudes. You'll warn me about Kieran not being my birth son and grumble about Adam or Melanie and you'll expect me to consider you, your likes and tastes. Well, you'll think that's OK for a while, but it'll soon get old for you. You need to sort out your life.'

Molly sniffed. 'Me? If anyone needs a life sorting it's you—'

'Molly,' Judith interrupted, firmly. 'My life is sorted. I live alone in this house from choice. There's no mortgage, so a small amount of income is enough to get me by and I'm perfectly capable of earning that.'

She let her voice soften. 'I accept that I need time to recover. To grieve. To adjust. But it's you who needs to decide either to attempt to save your marriage or to abandon it. You who needs discussions with Frankie and to see solicitors if necessary.'

She slurped up the rest of her wine, conscious that Molly, for once, wasn't arguing. She added, 'All that's wrong with my life is that Giorgio's gone. And I've been left behind.'

# Part Two

The Road Gets Steep

# Chapter Seventeen

*January 2005*

'Why have you got the hump with me?' Judith demanded.

She watched Adam's profile as he steered his car through the centre of Ashby-de-la-Zouch in Leicestershire, his eyes on the road, face giving nothing away. Although only mid-afternoon, winter's early dusk was turning the world purple and making brighter the Christmas lights that surely should be taken down now that it was the end of January.

'I haven't got the hump with you. I just asked why you see Tom's happiness as your concern,' Adam said.

Judith snorted. 'Same reason you see Shelley's as yours, I suppose.'

He shook his head, his mouth quirking up at one side, as it did when something wasn't actually amusing him. 'Shelley and I are still friendly but that's as far as it goes. She runs her own life. Just as Tom's capable of running his.'

Judith turned away to gaze through the steamy car

window into the bow window of a shop full of intriguing glass decanters.

In the last six months – could it really be six months *since Giorgio*, as she'd begun to think of his passing? – she'd become used to zipping all over Northamptonshire and the surrounding counties with Adam. It was now second nature for her to take responsibility for a host of details on a shoot, especially the fiddly stuff that was easier for her hands than his, leaving him free to talk to his subjects or prowl around considering light and angles.

Judith had never got around to getting another job and nor had Adam got around to advertising for someone to replace her. The work had turned out to suit her; sporadic, varied enough to harness some of her energy and intelligence but not so much as to tie her down to a full week of regular hours.

She'd become attuned to his quiet directions. 'Jude, gold umbrella, please. We need warmer skin tones.' He even referred to her, teasingly as his umbrella girl. She was au fait with his admin – OK, she'd reorganised it – and had taken over the phone calls that made him cross, like wheedling accurate addresses from magazines' picture desks or chasing up late payments from accounts departments. People skills, she thought, yawning as the car picked up speed again and the display of pretty glass slid out of her view, Adam had loads. He just didn't always bother to harness them when it came to editorial assistants who sent him incomplete briefs or didn't put his invoices through for payment. The subjects of his photographs, on the other hand – 'victims' as he jokingly termed them – got the full benefit of his charm. That's how they were persuaded to change clothes and jewellery for the fourth

198

time or shunt enormous amounts of furniture in and out of their rooms to suit his shots.

Adam was so easy to get on with that he was now firmly a part of Judith's life. As well as their working relationship, they'd created a mutual aid society, from which Judith was certain she profited most.

Oh, the relief, for instance, that he'd taken over her rampaging garden. She considered it a more than fair exchange for her undertaking his household correspondence and bill payment – tasks that she could perform in minutes but irritated Adam like an attack of scabies. Adam painted Judith's front door; Judith ironed Adam's dress shirt, tied his bow tie and fastened his cuff links when he had to go – scowling – to some magazine's awards evening with a pocketful of business cards because it was a networking opportunity that couldn't be missed. The list of exchanged favours was long and complicated. When she'd brought Wilma to Lavender Row for lunch one day and found Adam there taming the garden, he'd ended up servicing Wilma's wheelchair. His smile and warm manner had wowed Wilma so much she'd allowed him to do her little favours ever since.

Judith considered Adam her best friend and whether their discussions were bantering or serious, few subjects were off-limits so she finally answered his question.

'I feel bad for Tom,' she explained. 'He's lonely, and he realises that his relationship with Kieran is poor. I feel guilty that Kieran came to me when they found out Bethan was pregnant, putting me in the position of colluding with Tom's son against him.' Then, because she could seldom resist winding him up, 'You don't mind if I care about Kieran, do you, if I'm not allowed to feel bad about Tom?'

He flicked her a wry glance. 'I completely understand

you caring for Kieran. You and he weren't the ones who got divorced. He's your stepson and it's natural you should still love him.' His attention returned to the jammed traffic, the red brake lights in front of them blurred by the rain. 'But hasn't Tom got a more recent wife to feel bad for him?'

She grinned. 'Liza? No good, though, is she? She ran off and got her own life.'

Suddenly they were clear of the last traffic light in Ashby town centre, and Adam put his foot down. 'Haven't *you* got your own life?'

She turned to study him as she swayed with the rhythm of the car, curious at the irritation he was displaying. 'Look, I'm sorry Tom rang my mobile during the photoshoot – I forgot to turn it off, and I can see why that annoys you. I tried to get rid of him but he didn't want to be got rid of. The fastest way was to agree to meet him tonight.'

Adam took the road for the motorway and shrugged. But he still frowned.

After her usual stint in front of Adam's computer then calling in at home for a shower and a meal, Judith met Tom in a pub called The Child and Queen. She'd rather that than visit the home where they used to sleep together and where Tom later slept with Liza, or for Tom to call at Lavender Row. She liked to have the option of leaving if Tom got tricky.

Tom hadn't liked her decision. To him, pubs were for guffawing over dodgy jokes with his mates, pint in hand. So far as heart-to-hearts were concerned, they lacked privacy. Still, he waited at a corner table for her to step into the welcome warmth of the pub and then bought the drinks.

'I've had poor old Frankie bending my ear over your sister,' he said as he set the drinks on the table and sat down. Over the past few months, he'd taken every opportunity to coax Judith to petition Molly to return to 'poor old' Frankie, who was, by Tom's account, utterly miserable since he'd failed to persuade Molly to give their marriage another go.

Judith gave Tom short shrift, if in an amiable way. 'Better Frankie be miserable separated than Molly be miserable married, so far as I'm concerned.' Molly was living in her own place now, working in the café of a garden centre and the most content Judith had seen her for years.

Tom harrumphed. 'OK, let's leave the subject of Molly and Frankie alone. I'm worried about Kieran.'

'Oh?' Judith felt a chill wash through her veins. She was still keeping Kieran's secret, though Kieran continued to stay with Tom and a heavily pregnant Bethan had been prevailed upon to remain with her parents, to Kieran's dismay. The baby was overdue now and yet Tom didn't know he was about to be a grandfather. Judith was generally straight with people and Tom's unease over his son only increased her sense of guilt.

From a wine-red velvet banquette, she faced him across the smoky atmosphere of The Child and Queen; he'd taken a stool and was crouching like a bullfrog over his first pint. She knew he'd drink a pint and a half of John Smiths because he insisted he could drink that and be safe from the breathalyser. He regarded her from beneath whitening eyebrows that seemed to beetle more busily each time she saw him. 'I don't know what to do with my boy, I really don't.'

Judith sipped her grapefruit juice. It had a gin in it. She

didn't trust the breathalyser to concur with human judgement on safe limits so it would be her only alcoholic drink of the evening. 'Do you have to "do" anything with him? He's nearly twenty-three.'

Tom snorted. 'But he's my son, living in my house. I ask why he's so damned miserable and he gets all defensive.'

'Perhaps he doesn't wish to be asked?' she tried.

'But he's living in my house.'

Judith smothered a sigh. 'That doesn't mean he can't run his own life.'

Tom, as always, simply ignored opinions that didn't chime with his. 'Do you know what's the matter with him?'

Judith dropped her eyes. *Yes*, said her inner desire to confess. *He's got his young girlfriend pregnant. You know nothing about her but she's Bethan Sutherland, not even eighteen till March. I reluctantly said they could move in with me but Bethan's parents browbeat her into staying with them. They hate Kieran for spoiling her life, but when they try to keep him away from her, Bethan threatens to run away with him. Neither Kieran nor Bethan want to be parents, they're screwing up their courage to have the baby adopted, but feel wretched and guilty. Kieran's hushing it all up because he's never really stopped being scared of you. He'd like to move to his own place but he knows he's not good with money and has trouble running a car and a mobile phone, let alone a flat. So he's stuck with you. I'm resisting the temptation to invite him to live with me. That would* cause you pain *– but Kieran believes in your bluff exterior and thinks you have no feelings . . .*

'Well?' Tom prodded.

Judith shrugged. 'Why would I know?'

'He's always confided in you.' He drank the last of his pint of bitter and glared at the glass as if it had betrayed him by being empty, his frown lines deepening to furrows. 'You were the one who did the lion's share of bringing him up. Pity you didn't stay and see the job through.' As he so often did, Tom introduced anger into what had been a perfectly amicable situation. His eyes lifted accusingly. 'You act so goodie-goodie, with your cross and chain and your sincere expression. But you gave up on us too easily.'

Judith pushed aside her empty glass. The trick in dealing with Tom when he turned unreasonable was to remain calm. His irascibility was getting markedly worse as he aged, though. 'I know you long ago excused yourself from blame over our marriage ending and that having your cake and eating it was a little mistake rather than a divorcing offence, in your opinion. But it's not the case, Tom, not for this cake.' She indicated herself.

He glared. 'No one made you go – I didn't want it, Kieran didn't want it – it was your choice. Sometimes things go wrong in a marriage and you have to be strong and—'

She rose and stretched unhurriedly, refusing to get embroiled in this same-old, same-old. He'd had an affair with Liza and married her once Judith was out of the way. He always conveniently forgot that bit. 'Goodnight, Tom.'

He did a big, exaggerated tut-and-sigh, throwing his thick, rough hands into the air. 'Don't be so sensitive! I was only saying.'

He watched as she felt for her car keys, then sighed again like a gust of wind, his shoulders dropping. 'Judith . . . People keep telling me they see Kieran out around town. With a girl. And she's pregnant.'

Her heart accelerated and she paused, casting around for an answer.

The face he turned to her bore pain and anxiety in every furrow. 'Why don't I know what's going on?'

'Ask him,' she suggested, gently. Despite her irritation of a few seconds ago, her heart went out to this angry man who found it so difficult to get close to his son.

His eyes narrowed. 'You know, don't you?'

'Ask him,' she repeated. But she felt her cheeks heat up.

His face sagged. 'Why didn't you tell me?' he asked sadly.

She sank back into her seat and covered his big, rough hand with both of hers. '*Ask him*, Tom.' She hesitated before adding, 'Ask him as if you want to help. Try not to shout.'

He snatched his hand from under hers with a growl and Judith knew, with despair, that a mushroom cloud was going to appear over Brinham now that Tom knew about the baby.

What a day it had been, she mused after patting her ex-husband's shoulder with mixed sympathy and exasperation and quitting the noisy, smoky atmosphere of the pub. She strode back to the market square, where she'd parked the car, thinking longingly of the peace and quiet of Lavender Row. She could have a long, hot bath and read her book . . .

But then, when she drew up outside her house, she found Caleb and Matthias Leblond waiting on her garden wall, hunched into a thick army parka (Caleb) and a red Marmot Alpinist jacket (Matthias). She knew Matthias now. He was staying with Caleb while he was on garden leave between jobs, as Caleb had his own place these days. Soon Matthias would join his new company on the Scottish coast, just after fiancée Davina became his wife. She had a new job to go to in Scotland after their honeymoon, too.

The brothers slid from the red brick and onto their feet with matching grins as she climbed from her little car. 'Seen Dad?' Caleb called into the chilly air, his breath turning white.

'I was hoping for a last chat about the wedding photos, but we can't find him,' added Matthias, the wind ruffling his neatly cut hair. Matthias was completely calm about his wedding, though the great day was less than two weeks away. Not for him half-meant jokes about only being able to sleep with one woman for the rest of his life or grumbles about not wanting to hear another word about bouquets, bridesmaids and black cars. Judith had never met a bridegroom so happy with his situation.

Caleb, as usual, looked crumpled and bemused, as if he'd come from a rock festival. The upper section of his dark hair was pulled into a tail at the top of his head and his jeans were slashed. In contrast, Matthias, with his sharply short tawny hair and ironed jeans, looked as if he'd just stepped from a Next catalogue.

She locked the car with the remote. 'I saw him at a shoot today, and left him at his flat after I downloaded the pics.'

Caleb's forehead furrowed. 'Wonder where he's gone.'

Huddling further into her coat against a wind that felt as if it were slicing her to shreds, Judith frowned. 'Is his mobile off?'

Matthias nodded. He really was a terribly good-looking man; he had Adam's cheekbones. 'Mobile off, answer machine picking up at his flat.'

'Maybe he's with a woman?' Caleb grinned and waggled his eyebrows.

205

Matthias shrugged. 'No reason why not. Mum's had boyfriends.'

Caleb gave Matthias a nudge. 'He's such a gent, he's bound to turn the phone off during—'

'Have you tried your mother's house?' Judith interrupted, making for the front door. The street was too chilly for her. No fan of cold weather at any time, this first winter back in England was proving particularly unbearable, even after the purchase of an enormous duvet-thickness coat in emerald green that Adam laughed at and called her cocoon.

Caleb allowed himself to be distracted from prurient speculation. 'He's not there.'

Both young men hovered as Judith wriggled the key into the lock. She grinned at their transparently hopeful expressions. 'Coffee?'

'Brilliant!'

'Cool!'

They jumped up the two steps and crowded into the warm house behind her, bursting with young-man energy. 'Tot in the coffee?' suggested Caleb, extracting a half-bottle of whisky from one of the many pockets of his khaki parka and wagging it in front of Judith.

Judith tutted in mock disapproval but nevertheless slid it from his hand. 'You're a lot like your father.'

'Dad puts a tot in his coffee?' he asked interestedly.

Judith decided it might be better to be vague on that point. She and Adam had a shared liking for whisky and found a tot warmed you through when you got home after a chilly outdoor shoot.

Once coffee mugs were steaming fragrantly on the low table, she pressed play on the answer machine as she dropped into a chair.

206

'*You have two messages. First message*: "Oh, *Mum*! Aren't you there?"'

She rolled her eyes and addressed the voice on the machine. 'I can't be here all the time, Kieran.'

The second message began with a lot of clicking and beeping. And then Adam's voice, measured and deep. 'Jude, I tried your mobile, but it went straight to voicemail. I'm at the hospital. Bethan's in labour and panicking like mad. Kieran's gone to bits and has asked me to try to locate you. Bethan's parents are being hostile towards Kieran. I'll hang around till you get here.'

After a second's shocked immobility, Judith snatched her mobile phone from her pocket and was met with a blank screen. She must have forgotten to put it back on after the shoot.

'So that's where Dad is.' Caleb sounded pleased to have the mystery solved.

Matthias looked interested. 'Who's Bethan? Does Dad mean your Kieran, Judith?'

But Judith, a sudden victim to the shakes, was handing back the whisky and hunting down the emerald-green cocoon.


She whizzed her car through the frosty evening to where the blocky grey shapes of the hospital buildings huddled at the edge of town. At least there were parking spaces available at this time of night, she thought, reversing raggedly into one. Parking was murder during the day and if you eventually found a space it cost you three quid.

Gathering her bag, she fumbled to press the lock button. If she was nervous, Kieran must be strung up with excitement and nerves. Amazing to think of him as a father. She felt too young to be even a step-grandma . . . She sighed.

If the baby was to be given up for adoption, she wouldn't really be. Did she have a sneaking wish that they'd change their minds and keep the baby? Excitement and regret warred in her at the thought of Kieran's baby as she hurried over the windswept car park.

Adam awaited her in the brightly lit lobby of the maternity building. He met her with his usual calm smile as she dashed into the serene cloying warmth and antiseptic smell of hospital. 'He rang my flat, trying to find you.'

'My phone was still off from the shoot.' Judith laughed, dragging off her coat at the onslaught of the powerful central heating of a public building. She felt like a fizzy drink that had just been shaken, ready to explode in a fountain of bubbles. 'You're a saint, Adam, thanks for being with him. Is he in the delivery room?'

'Bethan's parents have been doing their best to freeze him out but he's hanging in there. I expect he'll be out looking for you any time now.' His eyes looked dark in the night-time lighting. 'When he called me he was in a state so I offered to drive them both to the hospital, as I was only a few minutes away.'

'Both? They were together when she went into labour, then.' She found herself bouncing on the spot, her words falling over themselves. 'You are kind, Adam. Thank you. Crikey, this is exciting, isn't it? Although I still feel for poor Tom . . . I think Bethan and Kieran will keep the baby once they've had it in their arms, don't you? How could they not? A baby will bring joy and perhaps the tension between Kieran and the Sutherlands could fade as they realise they all have the same baby to love.'

Adam picked up his jacket. He looked tired and strained, she thought, noticing the deep lines beside his eyes and mouth. Maybe he was feeling under the weather? It would

208

explain his crankiness earlier this afternoon, after the shoot. But then he gave her a hug, taking her by surprise. Adam wasn't a casual embracer; they didn't kiss cheeks when they met or link arms if they were walking. She wasn't certain whether he'd always been reserved or whether it was the after effects of Shelley's disgust for his maimed hand.

Uncertainly, she watched him turn away. 'Matthias and Caleb were looking for you. Matthias wants to talk about the wedding photos.'

As he headed towards the big glass doors he raised a hand and nodded to show that he'd heard, but didn't turn around. She guessed he felt not connected enough to the birth to hang around.

The lobby, which was also the waiting area, was very still after he'd gone. Still and almost silent. Judith caught a bustling midwife, who promised to tell Kieran that she was there, then settled herself on a blue plastic chair to study her surroundings. Twelve blue chairs, the hard kind that bit into the buttocks until they found bone. A broad green line leading from the front door to guide labouring women to the sanctuary of the delivery suites, a silent understanding that brains sometimes turn to custard under the onslaught of childbirth and following a floor plan might be too difficult. Judith turned to a stack of creased magazines to pass the time.

Periods of silence were punctuated by the sounds of doors swishing open and closed. She caught the faint groan of a woman and then another, crying jaggedly. The drinks machine gurgled, making her realise she'd come out without any change.

And suddenly there was the glad sound of the wail of a newborn baby, thin and wavering.

Was it . . . *Kieran and Beth's* baby?'

But then half an hour passed slowly.

And another.

Where was Kieran? He'd asked for her, why didn't he come to tell her what was going on? And, now she had time to think about it, why had he asked for her at all? What was Judith doing here? Surely the place for her was at home, on tenterhooks for news? If Bethan had only just gone into labour it might be twenty-four hours before the baby arrived. Maybe she should assume Kieran had asked for her as a knee-jerk reaction, and go.

Then she heard low voices heading towards her and looked up. The Sutherlands! Nick's arms were around Hannah. There were no beaming grins of joy or even relief but still her heart leapt with anticipation and she hopped to her feet. 'Any news?' She heard herself adopt un-Judith-like hushed but soppily thrilled tones.

The couple sank into seats, both of them looking strained and drained. Nick glanced up at Judith. The only colour in his face was the blue of his eyes and the purple shadows beneath. He hesitated as if not sure if he wanted to answer. Then, 'I'm afraid the news is bad. You'd better sit down.'

*Bad.* Bad? Dread formed in her chest, ice cold and solid. Her knees weakened and she plumped down heavily, her voice emerging as a croak. 'What?'

'They can't find the baby's heartbeat,' Nick stated baldly. He licked his lips and ran his palm over his thinning hair. 'They went for a quiet drink, Bethan and your lad.' That would be Kieran. 'Her waters broke. Me and Hannah were out for the evening, near Cambridge. Bethan rang in a flap and I told her it would take us about forty minutes to get to her, so to phone an ambulance and we'd

210

meet her at the hospital.' He glanced at his wife, as if he needed her confirmation of his story.

'But Kieran rang your friend,' Hannah put in.

'Adam.' Judith nodded. 'He told me he kindly drove them to the hospital.'

Hannah cleared her throat. Her face was chalky, her eyes bright with dread. 'Things started out OK but . . .'

Nick blew out a broken sigh. 'Suddenly there was no heartbeat on the monitor or the portable scanner. They've gone in for a full scan.'

'Oh, no.' Judith felt as if her own heart was trying to flutter to a halt in sympathy. 'Kieran's with her?'

'Yes,' said Nick stiffly. His expression suggested he'd rather Kieran wasn't. Whether he liked it or not, though, Kieran was the baby's father and what Nick Sutherland wanted didn't count.

# Chapter Eighteen

Judith felt as if time had ground to a halt but, eventually, a midwife came to fetch Nick and Hannah. The full scan had only confirmed the worst possible fears.

There was no foetal heartbeat. No foetal movement.

Nick and Hannah disappeared back into the delivery suite. Judith felt she couldn't follow without a summons. She sat on in the lobby, drinking machine-made coffee as the maternity wing awoke. Cars or ambulances brought in women in the throes. Some were serene, some were frightened, some were joyful. Their partners' anxious arms hovered or friends trotted alongside, bright and heartening, and all followed the green line on the floor as if it were the yellow brick road.

Judith sat on as morning visiting hours began and visitors made a track up the open-tread stairs out of the lobby to the wards, clutching bouquets in pastel colours for new mums and cuddly toys for new babies.

But there would be no celebration teddy for Kieran's baby.

No ceramic clown for Bethan, his hat stuffed with glossy yellow freesias.

An excited new grandma chattered by, clattering her court shoes, clutching flowers clustered around a white wire stork. 'Isn't it *beautiful*?' she asked her male companion. 'I told the florist to fill the basket with pink rosebuds and white baby's-breath. Baby's-breath makes all the difference . . .'

Judith flinched and her fingers found their way to Giorgio's crucifix. It was unbearable to be a spectator to the joy of others this way. A sympathetic auxiliary came along but when she heard Judith's relationship to Kieran the best she could offer was the chance of joining the Sutherlands in a proper waiting room, one that seemed to be set aside for those needing privacy. Though initially glad of the offer, when Judith found the Sutherlands clasping hands and muttering, 'Bethan shouldn't have to go through labour when they know it's going to be a stillbirth,' and wasn't certain she hadn't been better in the foyer.

So far as Bethan's parents were concerned, Kieran was the black villain, the utter bastard, the cavalier rogue. Judith didn't point out that he couldn't have made a baby alone because she sympathised. Kieran should have taken responsibility.

At nearly midnight, the ordeal finally ended. A midwife came, very grave and sympathetic, to confirm the stillbirth.

Hannah wept for her daughter's sorrow in great gulping sobs that threatened to wrench her slight frame apart while Nick looked as if he'd like to kill someone.

Then suddenly Kieran came bursting in through scarred blue doors, red blotches and swollen eyes of endless crying marring his pallor. 'Mum? Oh, you *are* here!'

'Of course, darling. What a horrible time for you and

Beth. I'm so sorry.' Judith jumped to her feel and pulled him fiercely to her, his chest heaving as he gave in to hopeless, roaring sobs; her son, no matter what the lawful status, who needed her.

He choked, 'He was already dead, like a statue baby, all white and silent, but perfect. We've called him Aaron.'

'I'm so sorry,' she repeated tenderly, heart wrenching at the thought of the young couple sitting in the delivery room and choosing a name for the child who'd never answer to it. She was conscious of the Sutherlands watching on without making a single attempt to communicate with Kieran, let alone comfort him.

'I kept hoping the doctors were wrong.' Kieran gave a great, snorting sob.

'So did I, darling. So did I.' Judith couldn't have hugged him any harder. Hot tears streamed down her face.

His shoulders heaved. 'I left a message for Dad. Have you seen him?'

'Not yet,' Judith murmured, wondering how on earth Tom would deal with such an emotional situation.

After several minutes of hugs, Kieran gathered himself, blew his nose and went back to his poor Bethan. The sympathtic midwife returned to ask Bethan's parents if they'd like to see the baby now that he was dressed. When the midwife glanced enquiringly at Judith, Nick murmured something about 'not actually her grandson' and, stunned, Judith watched Bethan's parents follow the blue uniform away. Her heart contracted painfully.

*Not actually her grandson?*

Kieran was shut into that nightmare of a room with his young girlfriend and his dead son. She imagined the Sutherlands continuing to give him the silent treatment, or spitting agonised accusations at his young, bewildered head. She clenched her fists, pacing in frustration as she tried to decide what to do.

If they couldn't acknowledge her right to be there for the baby, couldn't they find it in their hearts to let her be there for Kieran?

But her parenthood was *ex*.

And *step*.

And she didn't know where that left her.

But then a familiar figure was shown through the door and came to an abrupt halt before her. Tom's furious eyes seemed to have shrunk into his puce face, his hands made big fists at his side. 'What are you doing here?'

She rubbed her eyes, weary of his resentment. 'Kieran asked for me. Oh, Tom.'

Suffering her sympathetic hand upon his arm, his voice hoarse with grief, he nodded. 'They've just told me. About the baby. I was away, I didn't get Kieran's message until now. And it's all over?'

She nodded. 'Beth's parents have gone to see the baby and be with Bethan.'

Tom charged off immediately, of course, to demand that he be allowed to see the baby, too. Minutes later, a midwife at his side, he thrust open the door to the waiting room. 'Come on,' he ordered. 'Kieran will want you there, too.'

So, finally, once Tom was there, Judith was admitted. She and Tom comforted their son, who'd just lost a son of his own, for once able to push aside all acrimony and emotional baggage.

When she finally emerged from the hush of the delivery room and the beautiful, soundless baby, Judith was dazed by grief, by the unfairness that life could peter out for no apparent reason.

She dragged one foot in front of the other until she

stood beside Tom on the edge of the car park that stretched away from them. 'Thank you for letting me see Kieran. And Aaron.' She felt now the unreality and lightheadedness that comes with missed sleep and being wrung by emotion. Every inch of her ached and she suspected the base of her spine wouldn't be the same for weeks after so many hours on the moulded plastic seats of that grim waiting room. Probably none of her would.

The Sutherlands drifted past like ghosts, without looking across or speaking. A harsh ray of light pierced the silver clouds on the horizon over the distant houses on the main road.

Tom thrust his hands into his pockets and stared over Judith's shoulder at the silver clouds heralding a cold dawn. Grief and anger laced his voice. 'It's always you. Always you he wants.'

So they were back to the animosity, evidently. Judith wiped her eyes, blew her nose and refused to be drawn into a spat. 'You're exhausted.'

He brushed that away with a gruff, 'I'll live. Shall I see you to your car?'

'No need.'

'Awkward mare,' he said tiredly. He hunched his meaty shoulders and shambled off like a bear seeking its cave.

# Chapter Nineteen

A letter trembled in Judith's hand.

It was ten days since the heartbreaking day at the maternity unit and this morning the family was to gather at the crematorium to say goodbye to baby Aaron. She'd been thinking about Tom, about the catastrophic thing that had happened to Kieran and whether it would push father and son together or further apart when the letter dropped onto the mat and worries about Tom faded away.

The letter had the kind of heading designed on computer software with phone numbers and an address and was printed on white paper, plain, an economy buy for printers and photocopiers.

*Dear Mrs McAllister,* it read, in navy ink and a font that looked like copperplate.

*My father was Giorgio Zammit.* Judith's heart gave a great kick.

*After his death, it was discovered that my father's gold cross and chain had gone missing, causing great distress to the family.*

And then, ingenuously: *Should you know the whereabouts*

*of this valuable treasure, please send it to me without delay.*

*Alexia Zammit*

And, at the foot of the page, *Giorgio Zammit RIP*

Automatically, Judith's fingertips twitched upwards towards Giorgio's crucifix. She wore it all the time, touching it occasionally through her clothes, reassured by its weight and its associations with Giorgio.

A part of him she'd been allowed to keep.

The letter was obviously designed to cause her to feel like a grave robber, to make her snatch off the crucifix and send it to Giorgio's daughter.

She thought of Cass in her black lace dress, standing on the hillside beside Giorgio's fresh grave and pressing the crucifix into Judith's hand. *'Only his body is here. You have his heart. Take it with you.'* The gift of the crucifix had given Judith comfort by acknowledging and validating her status as someone important in Giorgio's life. But, for the first time, she wondered by what right Cass had acted. She couldn't imagine Johanna or Maria authorising Cass to give Judith such a personal keepsake, and one that had a monetary value, judging by the hallmark imprinted in its yellow Maltese gold. Probably it was only Cass's soft heart that had urged her to do something for the woman Giorgio had loved.

The muted chime of the clock in the hall jerked her out of her thoughts, reminding her that something else needed her full concentration right now.

Shakily stuffing the letter inside her bag, she swept on a mac that belted at the waist – the only black coat she owned and nowhere near as warm as the unsuitably vivid emerald cocoon coat – and let herself out into the chilly day. She'd arranged to pick Molly up at the modern and bright semi-detached house she'd bought on a neat estate on the edge of town.

'We look like a couple of waitresses, all in black,' Judith observed half an hour later as they drew up at the crematorium. Molly had dressed as suitably as Judith.

'The car park's nearly empty.' Molly tucked her long hair inside her coat to keep it from the wind that swirled leaves across the tarmac as they emerged from the warmth of the car.

Judith hunched her shoulders against the cold. 'Kieran and Beth kept it to close family because they didn't want hundreds of their friends turning up. I can understand that.'

Inside the modern building, a tile marked *Aaron McAllister Sutherland* hung on the glass of a door. It was the smallest, most intimate room, but still their footsteps echoed as they entered.

The others were already there. Bethan's parents flanked her as if concerned someone might contaminate her with their presence in the same wooden pew. Kieran stood across the aisle in the dark grey suit he'd bought for his new job. Tom stood beside him, eyes front, as if on parade. Judith and Molly slid in alongside.

Seven mourners for baby Aaron. Just seven. It couldn't have been sadder.

There were no hymns. In fact, no one but the vicar made a sound at all. He took the short service in a hushed voice from a spot just in front of the two occupied pews, and the funeral seemed to be over in minutes.

When he'd finished and shaken everybody's hands with expressions of concern and offers of comforting chats, Hannah made a frigid announcement without meeting anyone's gaze. 'We're taking Bethan home – she's not fit

219

to stand about.' And in seconds they were gone, leaving Judith, Molly and Tom with Kieran, who sent an anguished look after Bethan, then turned his gaze to the blue velvet curtains that had shut between them and the tiny coffin. He gave one long, quiet sigh, then allowed himself to be herded out, his face set with misery.

'What was that all about?' he asked no one in particular, hunching his shoulders against the chill as Tom held the door for his slow, gangling figure to pass.

At first Judith misunderstood him. 'She's very pale, she's just given birth. They just wanted to get her home, I expect.'

Kieran grimaced. 'I know that. She needs looking after and I knew they'd clear off the instant the ceremony was over. They've made it very plain that they don't want me around while she heals. No, I mean . . . Aaron. What was he about? The pregnancy. All the pain and hate it created. For months it felt like we were part of some major disaster, a train crash or a bomb. Like things couldn't get any worse. But then, when . . . when he died, we realised how bad things actually can get.'

Kieran stared around the crematorium grounds, the formal gardens impressive even in winter with cushions of pansies and polyanthus between the shrubs and conifers, the memorial garden for stillborn babies a quarter circle in a sunny corner. 'It feels as if we're being punished, taught a lesson. *You weren't fit to look after a baby. You didn't deserve a son.* But I would've loved him. Even when we considered adoption it was because we thought it might've been, like, best for him and we'd be no good at it. We'd just about decided we couldn't let him go to someone else and then he died, as if we didn't make up our minds in time.' He sounded bleak. Hopeless. He looked less boyish now, his face aged by pain.

'Of course you would've loved him.' Judith squeezed the words out past the lump in her throat.

Tom's voice came suddenly, deep and gruff, making Judith jump. 'Will they try to keep the girl away from you, now, boy?'

Kieran's face screwed up bitterly. 'Of course. Protect her from me because I've ruined her life, given her a dead baby, mucked up her A-Level year. Their idea's to move away, taking Beth with them. They say it will give her a fresh start.' He shivered suddenly, thrusting his hands into his trouser pockets. Hopeless, angry, he turned up his collar against the onset of chilly drizzle. Judith wondered how – if – he'd ever become his usual self.

She linked his arm. 'Come with us. We'll get coffee together. Maybe a snack.'

'I'm not hungry, thanks, Mum. And I don't want company.' Kieran managed a smile and squeezed her hand against his side with his arm. As if to pre-empt any argument she meant to put forward he added, 'Yes, I really do think that's best. But thanks for coming. Thanks, Dad. Thanks, Aunt Molly. I'm glad you were all here.'

Judith watched, heart aching, hair blowing in a spiteful wind, as his drooping figure folded itself into his car and drove away.

When he'd gone, she turned to say her goodbyes to Tom but she looked up into his face and her conscience smote her at the bleak expression of loss in the gaze he sent after his son. On impulse, she tucked her hand through his elbow. 'I bet you were just going to offer us a cuppa at your place, weren't you, Tom?'

'If you like.' But he turned with such alacrity for the car park that Judith knew, despite the daggers Molly's eyes launched in her direction, that she'd done the right thing.

'What did you say that for?' Molly demanded, as they strapped themselves into Judith's car and followed Tom's navy Volvo out through the gates.

Judith checked for oncoming vehicles, indicated and pulled into the traffic. 'Because he's sad.' Her tone was mild. 'And when you were sad, you appreciated a bit of company. He's no different.'

Molly sniffed but she turned to gaze out of the window without further argument.

In Tom's kitchen that once had been hers, too, Judith sat herself down on a beech stool at the table and watched Tom shambling about, assembling boiling water, teabags, sugar and milk into the correct combinations. He didn't, as Molly had probably anticipated, try and put in a good word for Frankie.

When he'd delivered steaming mugs to Judith and Molly he sat himself down and drank his tea at a temperature that would've scalded most people, his eyebrows twitching like corpulent caterpillars above his eyes. 'Never had a chance,' he observed gruffly.

Judith put down her own tea, untouched. 'I'm afraid not,' she said, quietly. 'As Kieran said, it's difficult to understand.'

'Only a babby.' Tom's face worked, his complexion deepening to the brick red it seemed to be so much of the time. 'When Kieran was a babby, I used to watch him in his cot. Make sure his little chest was moving. And Pam. She'd get up in the middle of the night sometimes, just to check.'

Molly joined the conversation. 'I used to, too, with Edwin. I think all parents do it.'

Tom let out a huge, wavering sigh. 'I've been thinking a lot, lately. How different things would have been if Pam hadn't died.'

Judith knew this wasn't a barb aimed in her direction. She'd always known Tom and Pam's marriage had been strong and Judith would never have been in Tom's picture if Pam had lived. The thought had never hurt her, even when she and Tom had been together. If anything, she understood that better since she'd lost Giorgio. 'I know what you mean. But you still have Kieran.'

Tom stared into his empty cup. 'Are you sure?'

An hour later, Judith was back at Lavender Row, having been firm with a protesting Molly that she would be perfectly OK to go home for lunch.

'OK,' Molly had said. 'I'll see you later when we take Mum out.'

Judith had confirmed she'd remembered this arrangement before driving off. Now she'd eaten a sandwich she was lounging on her sofa, enjoying the feel of a hot drink in her cold hands. Recently, she'd painted the sitting room walls a dignified pigeon grey. She'd been going for 'understated' but ended up with 'disappointed' at a dull result. Then Adam, who, like many photographers, had an arts college background, took a flamingo pink and a deep cream to the ornate white plaster ceiling roses and patterned coving. With the lightest touch of his paintbrush, highlights to a flower here, a teardrop there, and the whole room took on fresh life. It was stylish and unusual and she loved it.

The fire was roaring as it fed on the wind blowing down the chimney when her doorbell rang and then she found Adam on her doorstep, coat open over a midnight shirt that accentuated his spare frame. He said, 'I was passing and saw your car.'

'Come in. The kettle's just boiled.' She ushered him in

and he gave a whistle as he followed her up the passage. 'Jude, you have legs! I suppose it's not funeral etiquette to tell you that they're nice?'

'Probably not.' But it was quite pleasant to be noticed as a woman.

Over the second mug of tea, and after she'd given him an account of Aaron's funeral, she dug the letter from Alexia Zammit from her bag and showed it to him.

His eyebrows shot up into his hair as he read. 'This is extraordinary.' His eyes moved over and over the page. 'What do you intend to do?'

She leant closer to reread the letter over his arm. 'She's made me feel like a thief.'

'She meant to, obviously. But you were given the crucifix – you didn't steal it or even ask for it. Even if you suppose, just for a minute, that you're not entitled to it – how can you be sure that Alexia is? It could've been left to anybody: Giorgio's other daughter or his parents. Or the local cats' home. No one's offered you sight of the will.'

Letting the page flutter to the coffee table from her fingers, she scratched her head. 'So what do I do? Just grimly cling on to it and see what happens?'

'Get a solicitor.' He hesitated, looking faintly embarrassed. 'If the fees are a problem, I think there's assistance available. Or I could . . . you know. If you were stuck.'

She picked the letter up again, folding it neatly between her fingers, troubled and uncertain. 'Thanks, but it's not the money. I just hate the thought of setting a solicitor on Giorgio's family.'

'And being proved to be in the wrong isn't your strong suit.' He grinned and tugged a lock of her hair.

She acknowledged his point. 'True. But I probably am

the one in the wrong because I doubt that I'm in the will, if one exists. The executors would've written.'

He frowned, his mind obviously working. 'Where would they get this address?'

Judith stared at him. 'For that matter, where did Alexia get it?'

Diagonal frown lines appeared on Adam's forehead. 'The aunt? Cass? The only explanation for the whole thing is that she admitted she'd given you the crucifix and coughed up your English address.'

She shoved her now empty mug onto the table. 'But surely Cass would've rung to warn me that trouble was on the way?'

He yawned and stretched. 'Your faith's refreshing.'

She frowned. 'Cass wouldn't drop me in it.' But she heard the uncertainty in her own voice.

He took her hand. It was his unharmed hand, of course, the fingers strong and healthy as they curled around hers. 'Think about her husband being furious, and probably all the rest of the family too. It might have been difficult for her to resist the pressure. Then, having given way, she might not have been in a rush to own up to you.'

She sighed and let her eyes close. 'So you feel I'm presuming too much upon Cass's loyalty.' The thought hurt. When Giorgio had been alive Cass had been their one supporter and Judith had called her a friend.

Adam's voice came very close for a moment, his breath brushing against her cheek. 'I think, realistically, she might've had to choose – loyalty to you, or loyalty to her husband and his family.'

She sighed again. 'And she'd have to choose her husband Saviour and the rest of the Zammits, obviously.' Covering her eyes with her arm, she groaned. 'I bet the damned thing's valuable.'

It was several seconds before Adam replied, carefully, 'Actual monetary value might not be Alexia's main motivation in trying to get the crucifix back.'

'No. The family just doesn't want me to have it,' Judith concurred miserably.

They chatted for a little longer then Adam confirmed the arrangements for the next photoshoot and pulled on his coat as he prepared to leave the warmth of the fire.

'Friday, eight sharp,' Judith noted. 'And, of course, I'll be assisting you at Matthias and Davina's wedding on Saturday.'

Adam stuffed his phone in his trouser pocket. 'I wish they hadn't asked me to do it. I'm no bloody wedding photographer.' He frowned.

She threw him a sympathetic grin. 'A photographer's a photographer to them, I expect. Would you enjoy the wedding more if you were simply a guest?'

He pulled a face. 'Probably not. I'd be criticising whoever was doing the photos instead. You are staying for the reception, aren't you? Shelley's going to be with her new bloke – I don't want to be all on my own, ain't-it-obvious-Adam-has-no-date.'

She laughed. 'Get a date, then.'

'You forget how long I was married. I've forgotten how.' He gave a crooked grin as he moved towards the hallway and she rose to see him out.

She gave a disbelieving sniff. 'I bet your mates' wives are always inviting you to dinner parties. I bet they line up divorcees and you could get eight dates, if you wanted.'

He lifted his eyebrow in mock-hurt surprise. 'I do get invited to dinner parties, do you think that's the only reason? Shelley was always dragging me out to sit at someone's ugly dining suite and talk to people I didn't know. I took it as a perk of the separation that I could give those evenings a miss. Anyway, a date would expect phone calls, after.'

'Dire,' she observed gravely, watching him push his feet into the shiny black shoes he'd jettisoned on the tiled floor when he came in. The laces were elasticised and didn't need tying. 'How do you know that I won't?'

His eyes gleamed with laughter as he straightened. 'But that's what I like about you, Jude – you never expect me to phone unless I've got something to say. Neither do you dredge up grudges from a week last Thursday and leave me to guess what's wrong. You don't create tenuous cases to make things my fault, you don't tell me what to wear, you don't put on stupid heels and then bitch because your feet hurt, scream over a broken fingernail or sulk because your hair's only ninety-nine per cent perfect.' He grinned. 'In fact, you're not like a woman at all.'

Somewhat to her surprise, Judith felt herself flinch. 'Is that meant to be a compliment?'

His grin faded. 'Um . . . it was *meant* to suggest that you're pleasant, easy company. But it came out a bit . . .'

'As if I have no feminine attraction?'

This time his smile blazed right from his eyes. 'Not that. My compliments might be skewed, but my sight is excellent.' He smoothed his shirt collar neatly beneath his jacket, thoughtfully. 'I've annoyed you, haven't I?' He sounded surprised and intrigued and Judith noticed he didn't actually say sorry.

Then he swung back, an expression of alarm flashing

across his face. 'Just don't say you won't come to the wedding.'

Later, as Judith showered, she reminded herself that frowns and pouts would only add unwelcome lines to those she owned already, but, nevertheless, kept finding herself frowning and pouting, Adam's words circling annoyingly in her mind. Seriously? Not like a woman at all?

After dressing in new black trousers and a cream jumper ready to pick up Molly so that they could take Wilma out for a meal, as was already arranged, she made up her mind to make a phone call. She glanced at her watch. The person she wanted to talk to needed time to get home from work so Judith awarded herself a soothing hour with the latest Harlan Coben thriller.

The thump of the book sliding off the sofa forty minutes later woke her, crick-necked and left foot burning with pins and needles. Easing her head upright and the foot painfully into motion, she glared at the baroque silver clock on the mantelpiece, a rare extravagance from a jeweller in Valletta. 'Blast.'

She definitely hadn't intended to sleep. Naps seemed so middle-aged. Pins and needles so *unwomanly*.

Maybe because she wasn't a woman at all . . . She thought of again Adam's surprise when he'd seen her in a skirt and his inference that she didn't care about her hair or nails. She glanced down at her neat, unpainted nails.

Oh, for goodness' sake! It was madness to take any notice of Adam's teasing. Didn't she know how he loved to wind her up?

What was more important right now was that she'd soon have to leave to get to Molly's. Wilma thought the sky would fall in if she weren't home by nine o'clock and would therefore be in a fluster if they hadn't collected her from The Cottage by seven.

Judith had two minutes to get the phone call over with. Decisively, she found the number, reached for the phone and dialled.

Click. Click. Silence. Then the single ringing tone, sounding far away. In contrast, the voice that answered unnerved her with its clarity. 'Hallo?'

She caught her breath at the sudden realisation that she was breaching the citadel of Giorgio's till-now-unseen family and had to concentrate to make her voice work. 'May I speak to Alexia?'

The voice became guarded. 'I am Alexia.'

'This is Judith McAllister.'

A pause. 'Yes?'

Judith swallowed and moistened her lips. 'I'd like to speak to you about your father's crucifix.'

Alexia's English was excellent, no doubt she practised it every day in her job in the pharmacy where, Judith knew, she'd gone to work straight from school at sixteen. She must be eighteen, now. 'You have it,' Alexia said, with steady satisfaction. 'Please send it to me. My address is on my letter.' And the line went dead.

Swearing, Judith redialled, speaking the instant Alexia answered. 'I don't know whether I can do that. I need information.'

The voice that came across the miles was just as controlled and dispassionate as before. 'Please send back my father's cross. Thank you.'

Gritting her teeth and thinking of Giorgio, Judith dialled a third time, trying not to think of her phone bill. She made her tone gentle and reasonable. 'The crucifix was given to me by a member of the family, I accepted it in good faith. I—'

For the third time, the dialling tone cut her off.

'Bugger you,' she snapped, then fetched her cocoon of a coat – this English winter was killing her – and slammed her way out to the car, wishing Molly was picking her up for once so she'd have time to ring a fourth time. Taking her mood out on the absent, she fulminated at her sister, shoving the grape-coloured car into first gear, checking over her shoulder for traffic and peeling out. Molly always expected to be picked up. Molly never drove if she could get someone else to, never attempted to move furniture or take something apart to see if she could mend it. She cooked casseroles. She'd made all the floral curtains for her new Frankie-less house.

The estate was off Fairbank Street and Molly's cul-de-sac was named Fairbank Close. Bloody close, Judith thought as she whipped into Molly's narrow, shared drive a few minutes later. Without Judith having to toot, the door opened and Molly stepped out, coat fastened, handbag on her shoulder as she locked the door after her. As she slid into the car, she looked pointedly at her watch.

'Evening.' Equally pointedly, Judith made no apology for her tardiness.

In five minutes, they were at The Cottage, a glaringly inappropriate name for a three-storey brick townhouse of some magnitude. Judith zipped into a parking space and yanked on the handbrake.

Indoors, they found Wilma waiting on one of the rose-pink vinyl chairs beside the reception counter and pigeonholes covered in chipped, off-white Formica that was the staff station. 'You're late,' she observed politely, accepting simultaneous kisses, left cheek Molly, right Judith, and moving a boiled sweet around her mouth.

'Nothing to speak of,' breezed Judith. 'I'll get your chair.'

Wilma pulled her hairy maroon coat more tightly around her. 'So we're still going?'

'It's only seven minutes past seven, Mum – we can easily get you back for nine.' Judith suppressed her impatience. She didn't want her mum to end her days institutionalised and unwilling to go out into the world, crying off from outings at the least excuse.

Wilma pulled herself up onto her walking frame with a little grunt at the effort. 'I don't want to be any trouble.'

'You won't be. We're going to drive you to a new café by the embankment where you can see the river.' Trying to sound encouraging, Judith hooked the wheelchair with one hand and with the other made an entry in the book that recorded taking out a resident after six p.m., signing it, *J McA-wiggle-wiggle*. She didn't feel like waiting for Molly to sign it clearly *M R O'Malley*, with the capitals, the apostrophe, a loop on the Y, a curly flourish below, and a careful full stop at the end.

Once she'd gained her balance, Wilma hitched her way down the hall that was carpeted in a funny shade of honey, pushing the walking frame out in front of her and shuffling to catch up to it, her handbag swinging from a hook at the front. 'Isn't it too dark to see the river?'

'They have lights shining on it. It's pretty.'

Wilma chuckled creakily and rattled her sweet against her dentures. 'Pretty wet. Is it raining outside?'

'No, not at the moment.' It was Molly who offered the reassurance, this time. She took up station beside Wilma, ready to catch her arm if she wobbled. This was the way they usually divided the responsibilities: driving and wheel-chair, Judith; giving an arm, Molly.

'Is it going to?' Wilma persisted.

Judith wheeled the folded chair. 'Perhaps later.'

Her mother halted, and Judith almost ran her over. Wilma sucked vigorously. 'Do we want to go if it's going to rain?'

Judith patted her back to gently encourage her on. 'It's not raining yet. The car's right outside – I'll put your chair in the boot while you hang on here with Molly, then I'll open the car door. You wouldn't feel more than two drops, even if it poured.'

Wilma didn't budge. 'Only, I've just had my hair set. It was a new girl came round, and she's done it lovely, hasn't she?'

'Lovely.' Judith joined Molly in chorus. Making their mother happy was getting increasingly difficult. Wilma was losing her confidence about being taken out of The Cottage but didn't always want to be left in it. She worried if her daughters phoned instead of visiting but she admitted that their visits tired her.

'Do they do scones at this new place of yours?' she queried.

'Yes.' Judith paused for effect. 'With oodles of jam.'

'One oodle will be enough, dear.' Spurred on by the promise of jam, Wilma set off again. Then, hovering in the doorway with Molly, she observed Judith's struggles to fit the wheelchair in her boot. 'Pity you didn't bring Adam – he's good at lifting the chair.'

And better at charming her mum out of capriciousness, Judith thought, exchanging a look with Molly. Molly, having long ago conquered any antipathy towards Adam, often teased him that Wilma had a crush on him. Wilma never seemed as tired when Adam was there to make her laugh and never checked her watch and wondered if she'd be back in time for cocoa.

'There,' Wilma said, when she was settled in the front passenger seat of the car. 'Now, Judith, how's Kieran? He hasn't been to see me for weeks.'

It sounded as if Wilma had forgotten for the moment about the pregnancy and stillbirth. It would distress her to be reminded, so Judith just said, 'He's doing OK, Mum,' and drove off to the café by the river where Wilma ate heartily and said at the end of it, 'Lovely. I wish I could get out more often.'

The sisters exchanged glances, unified by exasperated amusement. Judith offered, 'Then we'll take you more often.'

Wilma looked pleased. 'We can celebrate New Year.'

Molly patted her mum's hand. 'OK, but it was nearly two months ago. It's February 2005.'

'Yes, I know dear.' Wilma cast her daughter a puzzled look as if Molly were the one who got muddled.

A couple of hours later, Judith pulled up once again outside Molly's house at Fairbank Close. Molly rubbed her forehead as if easing tension. 'Gosh, Mum's exhausting these days. Not her fault, of course, bless her. Coming in for a cuppa?'

Although she'd planned to go straight home for a couple of hours with her book, Judith found herself wanting to accept the invitation. Home meant not only the seat-edge thrills of author Harlan Coben but a lot of time to think about Alexia, the crucifix and who it actually belonged to. About today's tiny funeral. About Kieran, his face floating in her imagination, eyes empty and shattered.

Earlier, she'd texted him a simple, *Hugs. You know where I am if you need anything*, but otherwise Judith had left him in peace to mourn.

She followed Molly into the dead neat, dead plain home that was decorated in beige and peach. She could certainly do with a cosy sisterly chat – and Molly could occasionally be cosy, as well as being convinced of her duty to volunteer opinions on Judith and her life. They made for the kitchen – beige units, peach walls – Molly fussing over her long wool coat as she slid it on a hanger and hung it in the coats cupboard.

Judith tossed her emerald cocoon over the newel post. 'Do you think I'm blokeish, Moll?'

'"Blokeish"?' Pausing in the act of washing her hands, Molly's eyes grew round. 'What, butch do you mean?'

Judith considered as she hopped up onto a stool. 'Not butch, exactly. But . . . unfeminine?'

Molly shrugged. 'Depends which definition of unfeminine.'

Judith felt her eyebrows fly up in horror that Molly hadn't shrieked in protest at 'unfeminine' and 'Judith' arising in the same sentence. 'Using any definition!'

Molly whipped a broderie-anglaise apron around her waist and fastened it in a bow. 'You're very independent, of course, and you're often – almost always – natural.'

Judith's voice sharpened. 'What do you mean, "natural"?'

Molly looked surprised at Judith's tone. 'Without make-up. Also, perhaps because you're quite tall, you stride everywhere.'

'Being tall gives a naturally long step,' Judith protested.

Molly crossed to the mug tree. 'You hardly ever wear heels.'

'They'd make me taller.'

'You overtake a lot when you're driving—'

Judith gave up. 'And overtaking makes me blokeish?'

Molly dropped two teabags into a pretty white-and-peach china teapot. 'I never said blokeish – you did. But I always queue behind any traffic but men rush by, even when they can't really see what's tearing up to meet them.'

Judith sighed. If Molly considered it a male trait to overtake, this conversation was never going to evolve as she'd like. 'I don't think I meant the way I drive or walk. Go back to "independent".'

'Overly independent,' said Molly folding her arms and regarding Judith thoughtfully as the kettle made its first grumbles and hisses. 'Fiercely independent. Not requiring advice. Some people call it being bloody-minded.'

Judith ignored the bloody-minded bit. 'But it's good, isn't it, not to cling?'

Her sister shrugged shoulders that had grown plumper since she'd left Frankie – although Frankie, conversely, looked thinner the few times Judith had caught a glimpse of him around town, undoubtedly because he had no one to cook him dinners and puddings each evening.

Molly began clattering in drawers and cupboards, finding a small pair of scissors to slit open a packet of shortbread – the expensive, thick and delicious kind – and set out the fingers on a plate like the hands of a clock. 'Depends. When I left Frankie, there was no one I'd rather have had in my corner than you. You were encouraging and supportive, you have a built-in scanner to detect lies and nonsense and you're overawed by no one and nothing.'

'So? I still don't see a problem.' Judith watched her sister, reflecting that she would probably have just opened the shortbread packet and slapped it on the table.

Molly adjusted the space between her pieces of shortbread with military precision. 'I didn't say there was a problem. I lean on you, Mum leans on you, Kieran does, even Tom still would if you'd let him.'

'But?'

Molly sighed and rinsed crumbs from her fingertips at the tap, instead of licking them off as Judith would have. 'But if I was a man who liked women to be frilly and girly, I suppose I wouldn't be yearning after a Judith. I'd be after something more malleable, someone who'd demand my attention and look to me to solve things for her.'

Judith's stomach clenched in shock. 'You'd be looking for a Liza?'

'Oh gosh.' Molly's hands froze in mid-air and she sent Judith a stricken look over her shoulder. 'Sorry. That was a bit close to home, wasn't it? I didn't mean to go there.'

Judith pursed her lips. 'Anything else?'

Molly dried her hands, joined Judith at the table and passed her the shortbread. She smiled wickedly. 'You could do with tidying up. But that's just you, Judith. Your hair needs cutting, you stride about in your jeans and boots, efficient and practical. But men's eyes still follow you.'

'Except men who like feminine women?' Judith groused, taking the biggest piece of shortbread to punish Molly for telling her things she didn't really want to hear.

Molly took the second-biggest piece of shortbread. She patted Judith's hand. 'Well, you can't expect to attract all of them.'

# Chapter Twenty

'There – first exit from this roundabout . . . don't miss it, dummy,' Judith cried, waving the roadmap in her hand.

By cutting up the car behind, Adam just managed to steer his car into the turn in time, muttering darkly about late instructions and 'dummy' and lifting an apologetic hand at an angry honk from a Toyota almost on his bumper. On the other side of the roundabout, the traffic braked once more to a halt. Adam muttered some more and glanced at his watch.

'Yes, we're going to be late,' Judith confirmed. She took his mobile phone from the centre console and made an apologetic call to the day's photoshoot 'victims', the Donlyns, a family in a mag feature about childhood sweethearts. When the call connected she identified herself into the phone and said, 'I'm so sorry we're late. The traffic's a nightmare.'

Nigel Donlyn, the father in the family, snorted into the phone. 'I took a half-day off work for this, you know.'

'I know.' Judith was gravely sympathetic. 'We *do* appreciate your co-operation. But the M1 is closed and we're having to navigate the A-roads along with all the rest of the motorway traffic. We won't be a moment longer than we need, I promise. I can only ask you to hang on just another half-hour for me.'

Sounding mollified, Nigel Donlyn agreed. 'Well, all right.'

'You're an ace crawler,' Adam observed as she shut the phone, the traffic actually allowing the car up to thirty miles per hour for a short stretch. 'That bloke didn't stand a chance against your "for me" and "promise" in that soft, sexy voice you put on.'

'It's a talent,' she owned complacently. 'When I was in project management on construction sites I used to leave all the yelling to the men. I won more arguments with my syrupy voice than I lost.'

Adam launched the car into a gap on yet another roundabout. 'I've had no problems with picture desks since you took over my queries. You just sugar them into submission.'

'More like saccharin,' she observed, cheerfully. 'Artificial.'

Finally, they arrived at a 1970s chalet bungalow, liberally clad with overlapping semi-circular tiles the colour of wet bark. 'Ugly,' Adam remarked under his breath, jumping out to grab his photography case from the boot. Judith followed him and loaded her arms with tripod, stands and umbrellas.

A middle-aged man flung open the door as they knocked. Judging by his clothes, the only concession he'd made to having his photograph taken was a recent visit to the barber's. 'Nigel Donlyn. You only just caught me. I was going to give you up and go to work,' he growled, tugging down a too-short top.

Judith summoned her best smile. 'We can't thank you

enough – we're so grateful. We would've flown if we could.'

Grudgingly, Nigel Donlyn stepped back to admit them to the house. 'Is it you what's been ringing me, then? You don't look how I thought.'

'Sorry, were you expecting a twenty-five-year-old dolly?' Judith made a comically dismayed face.

Mr Donlyn looked discomfited. 'I didn't mean . . . Anyway, the others are in here.' He showed them to the sitting room where the other Donlyns waited: his wife, Hayley, generous of figure and dark of hair, and two teenage kids, Samuel, a loud show-off, and Jemma with a practised line in rolling eyes and petulant tuts. Both teenagers gazed open-mouthed at Adam's right hand as he opened his silver equipment case. Judith gauged by the deepening of his frown lines that he was uncomfortable with their stares.

As he needed both hands and therefore couldn't jam the right one in a pocket, he ignored their fixed gazes and got down to work, moving a Christmas tree out of sight as it was now February, shoving chairs around, murmuring, 'Jude, see if you can get Hayley's blouse and lipstick changed or her skin tone's going to look horrible.'

While Adam got into conversation with the kids, probably to try to put them at ease with him, Judith coaxed Hayley out of an unflattering lime-green top and into a soft raspberry pink that brought out the roses in her creamy cheeks.

'It's not you,' she fibbed reassuringly. 'But certain colours argue with the camera. We want you to look lovely, don't we? That blood-red lipstick's gorgeous but have you got anything softer?'

Next she chatted Nigel out of the England football shirt

239

that rode up to exhibit the underside of his hairy paunch and into a hyacinth-blue polo shirt that covered him more respectably.

First, Adam requested shots of Nigel and Hayley washing up together in the kitchen. Hayley didn't hide her disappointment with this idea. 'But the kitchen needs decorating,' she objected. 'Why can't we be taken in the lounge? The wallpaper's lovely in there, and the suite's only a year old.'

'It's the spirit of the feature.' Judith turned up her palms, as if she totally agreed, but what could you do? 'To give the reader a glow, you know, the idea that you deal with everyday life together and stay happy.'

'I wouldn't be happy drying up in this new shirt,' protested Nigel.

'You wouldn't be happy just 'cos you've got hold of the tea towel,' pointed out Hayley comfortably. Then she launched into the story of how she and Nigel started going out together at the third-year Christmas disco and had never looked at another person, '. . . not neither of us.'

Judith slotted a flash unit onto a stand while Adam got the couple laughing guiltily about how their parents had been outraged when they got engaged on Hayley's sixteenth birthday without seeking permission. The parents had accused Hayley of being pregnant. 'I wasn't, but we'd had our moments,' she giggled.

Nigel went red but added a, 'Heh, heh.'

It was typical for the subjects to believe that the photographer would want to hear their story, although that was firmly the province of the freelance writer who'd identified the Donlyns as a case history in the first place. The feature writer must have conducted the interview, which the editor must have already decided to run or they wouldn't have briefed a photographer.

Then Judith's mobile phone went off with a loud rendition of a Mexican dance, distracting Nigel and Hayley just when Adam was beginning to get them relaxed and to forget they were the subjects of a photoshoot. He looked at Judith sharply, brows raised as she scrabbled for her phone. That, from Adam, was like a ferocious scowl from anyone else, and she felt herself flushing. 'Sorry, sorry,' she muttered as she whizzed out into the hall, embarrassed to be guilty once again of disturbing the shoot by forgetting to switch off her phone.

Having answered the call, she whizzed back. 'It's for you, Adam.' Her voice was solemn but her eyes danced as she offered him the phone. 'It's Matthias. He says do you know your phone's off?'

With a curse, Adam swiped the mobile from her hand. 'It's switched off because I'm on a shoot, Matthias! . . . No, *obviously* I haven't forgotten about your wedding day tomorrow, son, and *obviously* I'll be on time . . . Whatever else you have to worry about, it's not me.' He listened a while longer and then said, 'Oh.' He rolled his eyes. 'Can that be changed? No? No point worrying, then.' He switched Judith's phone off and returned it to her, grumbling, without heat, 'Flaming boy.'

Judith winked at Hayley and Nigel. 'It's his son's wedding, tomorrow. Sounds like a few nerves are creeping in.'

The rest of the shoot went without incident. Adam was quiet on the drive home, twin lines engraved between his eyes and his expression troubled. After trying unsuccessfully to make him smile, Judith touched his arm. She knew that Matthias's wedding had preoccupied him recently, but he'd been uncharacteristically short with Matthias on the phone. 'You're not wound up about shooting Matthias's wedding, are you?'

He negotiated the next swarming roundabout before making a morose reply. 'No. I'm wound up about Shelley.' He flexed his fingers on the steering wheel and sighed.

Judith studied his profile, watching his gaze move from the windscreen to the mirrors. 'Why?' she asked eventually. 'You and Shelley get on OK.'

He tutted and muttered at a driver trying to muscle into the traffic from another lane. 'Yes. But Matthias says because you're not my actual partner she's seated you down the room somewhere, not with me at the top table. I'm sorry.'

'Oh.' She digested this. She didn't think she'd ever actually agreed to be Adam's plus-one at the reception when he'd asked her but she hadn't said 'no' either and she'd fulfilled the same role at a couple of formal dinners he'd had to attend at Christmas. 'Seating plans are always a pain. I expect it's just expediency.'

He nodded as he slowed for traffic lights. 'Maybe.'

# Chapter Twenty-One

Shelley Leblond was a striking woman, tiny and glamorous. At Matthias's wedding the next day, Judith marvelled at how Shelley carried off peach-blonde hair and clothes that were too young for her. Surely most women nudging fifty wouldn't choose a short, tight wedding outfit in grass green and daffodil yellow? And, if they did, they wouldn't look so damned good in it? Shelley had a big laugh and a great smile and posed on the imposing steps of Brinham Country Club between her tall, attractive sons with proprietorial pride, talking easily to Adam while his whirring camera captured the shot.

They were presently what felt like hours into the wedding photos and the beautiful bride in blush satin and her chatty bridesmaids in cornflower silk were having a break while Adam took shots without them. The end-of-February breeze seemed to come from the ice caps and their lips looked on the verge of turning as blue as the bridesmaids' dresses. Matthias took stunningly to the stark formality of a morning suit, hair groomed, jaw shaved, trousers pressed.

Caleb, a cheerfully laid back best man, his ponytail hanging down his back, hands in pockets, looked as if he were wearing the matching outfit for a bet. Adam had elected to wear a lounge suit and looked understated but handsome in the winter sunshine that he was muttering was 'shit for wedding photos'.

Shelley's latest boyfriend, apparently, had made a late choice not to attend the wedding after all, which probably explained why Judith wouldn't be seated with Adam for the wedding breakfast. Shelley had waved the question of her boyfriend's absence away by saying she'd never be able to spare him any attention but it seemed likely they'd fallen out and Shelley didn't fancy navigating her son's wedding alone.

Now she called gaily, 'Adam, you've got to be *in* some of these photos. Get the shot set up and then come and look gorgeous. I'm sure your assistant can push the button.'

Adam gave Judith an apologetic look. 'Um . . .'

She grinned. 'Go on, get the other side of the camera.' She 'pushed the button' for a few shots with Matthias and Caleb, then with Matthias and bride Davina, Shelley's hand tucked lightly through his arm throughout.

Then, as Adam moved to disengage, Shelley tugged him back. 'Adam, we've got to have some together with the best man, too.' She called to Judith. 'Take two or three and then just of Adam and me.'

Judith let a few shots run while Shelley tossed her hair and smiled up at a rock-like Adam, unsure whether Adam looked uncomfortable at being the 'victim' in the photos or because it was always tricky for divorced parents at the marriage of their child.

But Adam was soon back behind the camera and in photographer mode. 'Got an empty memory card, Jude?'

'Yes, I'll change it.' She took the camera off the tripod then flipped open the back and slid the empty card in place, stowing the full one safely in a wallet in a pocket of the silver equipment case.

Adam lifted his voice as he took back the black, expensive camera. 'Matthias and Davina, please.' Then, to her again, 'We'll finish out here with the bride and groom by that towering weeping willow. I'll need some reflectors or their skin tones will be green and gloomy.' Absently, he fired off three candid shots of Caleb and Matthias laughing together, Matthias's hand at his new wife's waist. 'Can you manage the smaller case, Jude? Then we'll go indoors for the cake.'

'We're doing the cake shots before the meal?' Judith queried.

'That's the plan – so I can enjoy the reception and circulate. Not my plan,' he added in a lowered voice, with a significant look in Shelley's direction.

Hiding a grin at his long-suffering air, Judith filled her arms with equipment and set off awkwardly across the grass. When she reached the willow, she discovered that she was alone and turned to see that Shelley had intercepted Adam and was laughing up into his eyes. He was stooping slightly to listen to her, hand in pocket. She looked petite and feminine, which made Adam appear as if he were looming over her protectively.

Cursing the fact that, as a plus-one, she'd to dress like a wedding guest, Judith made a return journey for the large case and the tripod. Her newly purchased dress spangled with meadow flowers was pretty but suitably elegant heels were hell on the ankles when traipsing over the winter-softened lawns. And the wind cut through her. She missed her trousers and boots and especially her coat.

'It would've been better if I'd worn a suit and flat shoes,' she grumbled, when Adam finally joined her. 'And whenever I bend over, I have to hoist up my neckline.'

The corner of his mouth twitched as he assessed the sky and then the willow. 'Don't hoist on my account.'

They finally escaped into the warmth of Brinham Country Club for the cake shots, then Shelley dashed up as the final flash popped, beckoning to Adam and the parents of Davina and looking pointedly at her watch, leaving Judith to pack away the camera equipment. By the time she had, in several trips, lugged everything to the car, Adam was involved in greeting guests.

If Judith had found the photos turgid, the wedding reception was worse.

The food was good and the speeches entertaining, but after that . . . For what seemed like hours, she watched Matthias and divine Davina in one another's arms on the dance floor, Davina a vision in her wedding dress. The barely pink satin made her look like an angel at daybreak and Matthias, tall and handsome, his silver cravat still neatly tied, gazed at her adoringly, ignoring the other dancers and some children tearing around the dance floor in endless games of chase.

To occupy her mind as she sat alone amongst chattering groups of people she didn't know at the tables of The Magnolia Room, the glittering pride of the country club, Judith tried to establish who was who among the family. Adam's mother was easy enough – Judith heard both Matthias and Caleb call her Grandma, and Adam call her Mother. She was stooped and leant on a stick as if afraid she'd tip over without it. Two tall, rangy men just had to be Adam's brothers, Terence and Guy, similar enough to him in appearance even if she hadn't heard them also call the stooped woman Mother. A woman with improbably platinum curls seemed to be Mother's sister.

Judith smothered a yawn and, from habit, lifted her hand to toy with Giorgio's crucifix around her neck. Her fingertips encountering the beads she'd worn instead today set her brooding about Alexia's letter, now tucked into the drawer of her dressing table. As Adam had teasingly pointed out, Judith was none too keen on being in the wrong and it was beginning to seem to her that the wrong was exactly where she was. Sending the crucifix back to Alexia sounded a simple fix but how could she establish that Alexia was the one who was entitled to it when Alexia refused to discuss the matter?

She wrestled with the problem until a conviction grew in her that she knew what it was she had to do. She'd have to check with Adam when it was best to take time off.

She searched him out with her gaze and caught a glimpse of him across the room between table decorations of silver and blue balloons and great displays of sea holly with tortured hazel. Shelley had commandeered him for hostly duties, which could be viewed as reasonable, Matthias being just as much his son as hers. However, Shelley was acting as if she and Adam still belonged together. Judith couldn't be peeved as she had no claim on Adam herself, but it rankled when he'd asked Judith to stay for the reception so that he wouldn't be Adam-no-date. She suppressed another yawn and tried not to notice Shelley not only linking Adam's arm but leaning her head against it. Shelley was petite and pretty and the epitome of femininity. A girly girl if ever Judith had seen one.

Caleb was the only other guest Judith knew and he was part of a scuffling crowd in the corner, jacket off, shirt ballooning from his trousers as he shared in gusts of laughter and tipped pints of beer down his throat. Briefly, she considered joining the mob around him but, as she'd be roughly twice the age of anyone else in the group, immediately discarded the idea.

Judith watched Shelley tug Adam around to face her as she laughed up into his face. It was an intimate, familiar gesture . . . and Judith had no idea why it made her feel as if she had ants crawling beneath her skin. Not stopping to analyse the unwelcome feeling, she unhooked her jacket from around the back of her chair and wriggled into it, picked up her bag and jumped to her feet. Skirting the dance floor and threading through the press of bodies she escaped The Magnolia Room. In the privacy of the ladies' cloakroom she was able to switch on her phone and dial a cab. A minute later she'd retrieved her coat and was ready for a discreet escape.

But outside the cloakroom she found Adam lurking. He frowned. 'I spotted you skulking off in this direction. You're leaving?'

She wondered whether she should feel guilty that she'd intended to melt away without telling him. 'Yes, I've just rung for a car.'

He cast a hunted look towards The Magnolia Room. 'I've talked to almost every guest at this bloody do except you – the one I actually want to speak to. And you're *my* guest. I'm never normally guilty of such atrocious manners but I just couldn't get away. Are you totally fed up with me?'

She grinned, but said, firmly, 'Totally. Next time you need a date for the sake of appearances, ask Mum.'

Then, seeing his face fall, she gave his arm a pat. 'I'm joking, don't worry. I understand you've got to talk to everyone. You're the father of the groom.' She zipped up her coat.

Disconsolately, he fell into step with her, his sleeve brushing hers as she crossed the softly carpeted foyer to the big double doors where she'd arranged to await the taxi.

'I feel a proper shit,' he said morosely. 'Every time I turned to look for you, Shelley found someone else she decided I just had to talk to. I don't suppose you'd change your mind, and stay? One dance?' he wheedled.

Smiling, she shook her head. 'You don't even like dancing.' Adam's intentions might be pure but Shelley was so good at taking his arm and steering him off in the name of father-of-the-groom duties that she was pretty sure she'd be on her own again within ten minutes of returning to The Magnolia Room.

Adam hunched into his jacket as the doorman opened the door and let them out into a frigid evening. 'Matthias is about to slip off to the bridal suite with a bottle of champagne in one hand and Davina in the other. My father-of-the-groom duties must be over. Do I really have to stay here on my own?'

A car turned in between the stone gateposts and up the drive, its tyres crackling over the gravel. 'Here's the taxi,' Judith pointed out unnecessarily, stepping forward to signal her whereabouts. When the car drew to a halt she opened the back door and turned to wish Adam goodnight . . . only to find him racing around and getting in the other side. She gasped, 'Adam, you're not supposed to be getting in it!'

'No one will miss me,' he said cheerfully as he clambered

into the back seat. He grinned at her as he gave the driver her address.

'You're supposed to be staying the night here,' she protested.

'I didn't make that booking,' he pointed out. 'I'll fetch my car in the morning.' He leaned back in the car seat, pulling off his tie with a huge sigh of relief.

Fifteen minutes later, the taxi deposited them outside Judith's house in Lavender Row and drew quietly away into an evening that was fast becoming misty. 'I'm sure you should've stayed,' Judith said for about the tenth time, teeth chattering, and struggled to open her door, which seemed to swell a little more with every wet winter day that passed. She thought longingly of the hot, dusty country she used to live in where freezing, dank evenings like this were unknown.

'For whose benefit?' Adam asked, hands jammed in pockets because his coat was back at the country club along with his car. He turned up his collar against the damp as he fidgeted on the step below hers. 'Matthias and his divine wife will by now be tucked away in the honeymoon suite. Caleb is in his favourite spot, the middle of a crowd, getting thoroughly and mortifyingly drunk. Neither of them needs their old man around.'

'And Shelley?' she couldn't help asking, still fighting the recalcitrant door.

He paused. 'I hope she's enjoying the party. It's more her kind of thing than mine.' Then he reached over Judith's shoulder and struck the door a swift blow from the heel of his hand. The door flew open.

Judith shuffled into the inky black hall, wishing that she was like Molly and always remembered to leave on a light when she expected to return after dark. 'I think your presence was required for her to enjoy herself.'

He sighed, stepping in close behind her as she wiggled the door key to free it from the lock. His voice was neutral. 'You noticed, did you?'

The key came free, making her jerk backwards. 'Difficult not to.'

He said, 'She tells me it's time for us to talk about our future. See what can be salvaged now that we've both had time to think.'

'Oh?' Judith concentrated hard on not letting her heart sink. But it was selfish of her to let her mind fly to the conclusion that Adam would have no time to be her friend if he returned to being Shelley's husband.

Shelley had hurt Adam, but maybe now she'd had time to get used to Adam's altered physical appearance and realise what she'd lost. If so, and that's what Adam wanted, good. He deserved to be happy.

Judith turned in the narrow confines of the hall to give him a beaming smile and a brief kiss on the cheek to go with her enthusiastic, 'What a surprise! Congratulations! I hope it works out for the best.'

He touched his cheek, lounging against the wall as she felt for the light switch by the meagre light of the street lamps outside. 'Oh, come on, Jude – we both know it's not going to happen,' he chided, softly. 'She scuttled the ship, and it sank too deep to salvage. Obviously, her latest boyfriend has moved on to pastures new, making her temporarily insecure. I'm just an old habit she's tempted to take up again, for comfort. You know how hard it can be to break habits like that.'

He extended a hand to shut the door behind them but stopped abruptly and hesitated, swearing under his breath. Then he swung it open again with an exaggerated air of resignation so that Judith could see the large man slamming his way out of the pick-up truck slewed to a halt half on the opposite pavement. 'It seems to be the night for exes. Here's yours.'

Surprised, Judith peered past him to see Tom barrelling across the road towards them, chest out and fists clenched. From ten feet away he began bellowing. 'Judith, there you are! I'm going to part your bloody head from your shoulders, girl.'

'Normally I'd offer to give you privacy but I can't leave you alone with a man with murder written so clearly on his face,' Adam murmured, squaring his shoulders.

Judith groaned. 'Thank you. He looks plenty angry. I'm not scared of him but he can be as unpleasant as a snapping pitbull.'

Tom arrived with a clumsy jump up the two steps to the front door. '*Bitch,*' he swore, slamming his two powerful fists either side of the doorframe. 'I can't believe what you've done.'

Resignedly, Judith tried to usher Adam a step back. 'Tom, you'd better come in.' Adam stayed where he was.

Tom was actually shaking with fury. His voice dropped to a malevolent hiss as he talked rudely over Judith's courtesy. 'This evening I've been harangued and insulted by that Sutherland bloke. He was trying to find Kieran. After blood, he is. Because Kieran, who got the man's young daughter pregnant, a girl who subsequently suffered a stillbirth,' he said with heavy emphasis, as if Judith needed these reminders, 'has now run off with her.' He face worked as he struggled for control. 'And you *knew.* You knew, just like you knew about my grandchild and you didn't tell me.'

Pinpricks of sweat sprang out on Judith's face. Kieran and Bethan had run off? 'I didn't.' Then, seeing Tom's glower, she amended hastily, 'Yes, yes, I did know about the baby, but I know nothing about them going away together.'

Punctuating his words with his fists against the doorframe, Tom blazed, 'He's *my* son! *Not yours!*'

This inarguable truth made her stand very still. 'I was in a difficult situation about the baby,' she said shortly. She met Tom's infuriated glare.

His face was puce and his eyes bulging; he looked as if he might be flung to the floor by the giant hand of a heart attack at any moment. His eyes narrowed meanly. 'And Aaron was my grandchild, not yours. You meddling, interfering mare.' His breath bunched up and began to come in gasps between insults. 'It was you who spoilt Kieran rotten.' Gasp. 'Made him so wishy-washy he was too scared of me to bring me his troubles.' Gasp. 'Well, I hope you're happy now. Because they're gone. Both of them. She's disappeared from her home and Kieran's room has been emptied. Neither of their phone numbers are working so they must have changed them. Her poor parents are out of their minds.'

He paused, heaving for breath, spittle dotting his livid lips, teeth bared. 'Be truthful. Do you know where they are?'

Too stunned by what he'd said to take exception to the way he'd said it, she shook her head. 'I haven't seen either of them since the day of the funeral.'

Snorting his scepticism, Tom actually shook his fist under her nose, making her jump. 'If I ever find out you knew where they were and didn't tell me, by Christ I'll—'

'Enough.' Adam coolly put his arm between Tom and Judith. 'You're crossing boundaries. You need to calm down. You're lucky Judith hasn't called the police.'

Tom crowed for breath. 'Calm down? I could kill her—'

'No, you couldn't,' Adam corrected softly. 'Not while I'm here.'

Tom glowered into his face. Then he lowered his head towards Judith like an animal considering a charge. 'Who's this joker? A new boyfriend?'

'That doesn't concern you.' Adam didn't back down. 'Judith's told you she doesn't know where Kieran and Bethan have gone. If she doesn't know, she doesn't know.'

Tom glared at Judith over Adam's arm for several seconds. 'Bloody bitch.' Then he swung away, stumbling down the steps like an enraged rhino, slamming into his pick-up and roaring away.

A silence enveloped them. Adam gently steered Judith away from the door, pushed it shut and bolted it. He turned to Judith, concern written on his face. 'That was pretty awful. You OK?'

She nodded, fearing to speak in case it let a sob out. She thought she'd seen Tom angry before but nothing like tonight. Though she'd maintained an outer calm, the violence of his outburst had shaken her. If she'd been alone, she truly thought he might have struck her.

'You're shaking.' Adam slid his arms around her, giving her shoulders a reassuring squeeze.

She nodded again and let her head tip forward to rest against the warmth of his shoulder. Shock shook through her as she clung on to his mist-dampened jacket. Tom had been so venomous.

In the unlit hall, the smell of the winter's night rose from their clothes, mingling with the wedding fare of sherry, champagne and wine, and Adam's aftershave. 'You're OK,' he murmured, slipping his arms around her. 'You're OK. He was scary, but he'll calm down.'

Her head jerked up, recalling the reason for Tom's fury. 'But where can Kieran and Bethan have gone? What if something happens to them?'

Adam tightened his embrace. 'Try not to worry. They're probably supremely happy in some love nest bedsit at this very moment, snug and safe from all the endless parental outrage, eating chips from the paper because they haven't got plates, finally able to comfort each other over Aaron.'

'He's not very good with money.' She let Adam's warmth comfort her as she breathed him in. His good sense made the picture he painted reassuringly credible. Kieran was of the generation that thought: *made a mess of things? Throw that life away, and begin another . . . Go on, mate, no one can stop you. You got rights, you know. The police won't drag your girlfriend home at her age. You're not doing anything against the law. And no one knows where you are, do they?*

Gradually she relaxed, her mind clearing. Tom was angry. Well, that was nothing new. Kieran had 'done a moonlight'. Not altogether unexpected, she supposed – a bit underhand, not very brave, but he wasn't good at confrontation. 'I wonder whether Tom's right, that I brought Kieran up too soft?'

Adam stroked her hair. 'If all his life he's had to face uncontrolled rages like the one we've just witnessed, I don't blame him for developing ways to avoid conflict. He's not wishy-washy. He's just gentle.'

She sighed and lifted her head, slowly this time. She'd never got as far as pressing the light switch and illumination from the street shone through the fanlight of leaded glass above the door, highlighting the planes of Adam's face, light then shadow on the taut cheekbones and angular jaw, creating gleaming lights in his eyes.

255

His arms slackened, as if he expected that she meant to step away. But the prospect of putting the customary distance between them made her feel hollow and bereft and instead of letting her arms slacken, she tightened them. Without consulting her brain, her body softened against his. He was solid and safe, but it wasn't a search for security that made her nestle against his warmth.

For several moments, Adam seemed to hold his breath.

And then his embrace shifted subtly and, somehow, the way he was holding her was no longer that of a friend. And the contact between their bodies wasn't incidental.

'Jude?' His whisper was a caress, holding a note of hope.

She looked into his shadowed face. Their heads hovered closer together until their lips touched. Softly. The merest brush.

Then he swooped, and pleasure prickled over her at the sensation of his tongue seeking hers while his urgent hands pressed her so close that she struggled for balance as the rhythm of his heartbeat gathered her up and made her head spin. No heart had beaten against hers since Giorgio's. No one since Giorgio had taken pleasure from her mouth.

But it didn't feel like a betrayal. It felt . . . well, like a welcome home. One of Adam's hands cradled her head and his hot, hard body lifted her clear of the floor as if she were a lightweight. She was being kissed – she was kissing him back. And her bones were melting.

Suddenly unbearably hot and uncomfortably encumbered, she dropped her arms and shook off her coat. It made a scratchy, synthetic sound as it slithered down her arms to the tiled floor.

It seemed to bring him up short. He paused, his breathing all over the place. Like hers.

She could hear a smile in his voice as he steadied himself. 'I didn't mean to do that.' Another pause. 'At least, I didn't mean to do that *yet*. Because Giorgio—' Then, gently, 'You're not wearing his crucifix.'

'It's the first day I've left it off.' She shook her head. 'I don't know . . . The letter made me feel different. It reminded me that he was gone.'

His embrace began to slacken. 'I leapt on you. If you want me to apologise, then I will. It's been a long time, and I miss—'

Her embrace tightened, her voice husky. 'You miss human contact, the affection and pleasure of it. You miss being held. It's typical of you to kindly take the blame. But I leapt on you, too.'

Then he kissed her again, this time with extraordinary tenderness. 'I've wanted you since you were a stroppy fifth-year. I've built up quite a yen.'

Her face heated. 'You hardly noticed me when we were at school together.'

He laughed, stroking her hair, the back of his hand brushing her cheek. 'I noticed all right. I noticed whether you wore a ponytail or a plait, black shoes or brown. I also noticed that after our riveting conversation about Polos, you looked away whenever I tried to catch your eye. And you were more than two years younger. They were pretty sinful thoughts I had – about a fifteen-year-old.'

He flicked his tongue to the corner of her mouth and she heard a tiny groan that must've come from her. 'I couldn't look at you,' she confessed. 'I wanted you to talk to me again so much.'

His lips moved to her eyelids, her temples, exploring her in the dark. 'Tell me how you're feeling.'

'I'm attracted to you and tired of being in limbo,' she

whispered, giving in to the honesty of the moment. 'And so weary. Of Tom's fury and Kieran's despair, Molly's unhappiness. Mum's defencelessness. I'm tired of being strong for them all. I want . . . to be comforted.'

Adam was more frank. 'I want to go to bed with you.'

She hovered her mouth closer to his, feeling his breath against her skin. 'I want to go to bed with you, too.'

Adam made love to her with total concentration and all of his body . . . apart from his damaged hand, which was pretty much excluded from the party.

In her bedroom that used to be his, he undressed her slowly beginning with forest-green ribbon lacing the bodice of her dress. 'There's a zip,' she pointed out, trying to guide his hand. 'You don't have to struggle with the ribbon.'

He smiled, easing her hand away. 'But I've been fantasising about this all day.' He plucked at the ribbon, pulling it slowly through each loop with a whisper of sound, fumbling sometimes with its slipperiness, pausing to kiss the swell of her breasts as each fresh millimetre was exposed. 'Have you any idea how erotic it is, unwrapping you?'

She shuddered, letting her head tip back. 'Pretty much.'

He laughed, pushing back her hair so he could kiss her hard then kiss her gently, continuing to unfasten every possible fastening that would reveal her – including a left-handed struggle with her cream satin bra – before sliding out of his own clothes until there was nothing left to prevent the delicious heat of flesh on flesh as he rolled her down to the lemon-yellow pillows.

Judith gave herself up to pleasure of Adam. He was tender but not shy. At all. He absorbed himself, engaging all of her senses, his lips coasting around her body as if to compensate for the loss of sensation from the missing fingertips on the right hand that he held away from her.

His body was all bones, hollows and sinewy muscles. She enjoyed the warmth of him beneath her palms and the tickle of his body hair against her skin.

And when he poised himself above her, he looked down into her face as if checking that she wanted him to go on. Then he dipped his head to kiss her. And let his body sink into hers.

It wasn't really daylight until seven thirty at that time of year. When thin, pearly light stole around the curtain edges Judith had been awake and staring at the ceiling for an hour, the duvet pulled to her chin.

Fingertips trickled across her ribcage, raising a swathe of goose-pimples in their wake. She turned her head on the cool cotton of the pillow to find Adam smiling at her, his hair falling in his eyes and the bedclothes dropping away to display whorls of chest hair. 'You're transparent,' he observed. 'I can read every thought rolling around your beautiful head: where do we go from here? What have we done? What have we changed or sacrificed? Did I want to wake up with him? What will he think this means – that he has some rights over me? Will he expect to make love again this morning?' His smile twitched. 'He's nice and warm to put my feet on?'

She hadn't noticed that the soles of her feet had found a cosy home against his warm flesh. She flexed them, feeling the brush of his leg hair.

He slid closer, smile fading. 'Where *do* we go from here?'

She looked away. And tried not to hear the tiny change

259

in his breathing that wasn't quite a sigh. 'It was too soon for you,' his tone was suddenly flat. 'The cold light of day has made you wretched. You're thinking of Giorgio. The guilt's killing you.'

She wriggled around to face him, trying to be honest with his grey-eyed gaze. 'I'm not wretched, and I certainly don't regret the lovemaking. In fact, I feel . . . at peace. It's as if for months I've been wound up in elastic bands and now you've picked them all off. As to guilt . . .' She drew a breath. 'I think my only guilt is in not feeling guilty. I understand that Giorgio's gone and that I'm still here. What about you?' she challenged him. 'Shelley was pretty possessive, yesterday.'

His eyes smiled. 'We're over and there's definitely no guilt,' he declared firmly, his hand moving on to the round-ness of her stomach and beginning to make tiny circles. 'I feel strange. Special. As if I'm beginning a clean slate and that was my first time.' His hand slid lower.

She put her hand on his wrist, feeling the softness of the underside. 'You didn't perform like a first-timer.' She smiled. 'But what do you want? Because we might not want the same things. I'm afraid you might be more ready than I am for a normal relationship.'

His hand continued to caress her. 'There's no rush to decide where we go next.'

She groaned, seeing a yawning pit opening at her feet. She should have explained before this. She only hadn't told him because she wanted to get her motives straightened out in her mind. She reached up to stroke his face, gently. 'Adam . . . I'm going back to Malta.'

His hand stilled.

She hurried on, wanting to make him understand. 'I want to speak to Giorgio's daughter about the crucifix.

It's becoming a burden instead of a comfort. I owe it to him and her to do the right thing.'

'Debatable.' He rolled away from her, to his feet, and headed to the bathroom.

'Then I owe it to myself,' she murmured to his departing back.

# Chapter Twenty-Two

While Adam showered, Judith went downstairs to begin breakfast, more to occupy herself than because she was hungry. As she reached the hall she noticed a folded piece of paper on the floor. It was scuffed and dirty. They might have walked over it in the darkness last night.

She opened it out as she turned towards the kitchen. Then halted at the sight of Kieran's hurried handwriting.

*Mum, I came round to see you but forgot it's Adam's son's wedding today. I wanted to tell you that me and Beth are going off before Beth's mum and dad drag her away to some new place to try and make her forget me. She says the only way she can stop being a wimp with them is to leave them. We need to be together and don't want any more hassle. I'm dead sorry I didn't get to see you and will be in touch.*

*Don't worry about me. Love you.*

*Kieran. x*

Sadness soaked through her, followed by a hot wave of fury. She continued to the kitchen and sliced bread and broke eggs mechanically, lips set, her heart banging angrily.

Between Tom McAllister and the Sutherlands, they'd shoved Kieran away, and he'd gone without trusting her enough to tell her where. Did he and Bethan even have somewhere safe to go? Her eyes prickled threateningly, and she wiped the corners with the back of her hand. Guilt struck her that it was at her insistence they'd 'done the right thing' and told Bethan's parents about the baby.

And look what a mess her parents had made with the knowledge, forcing Bethan to choose between them and Kieran. If she could go back to that night when Kieran had come to her for help she would let him and Bethan move in and argue with Tom and the Sutherlands later. At least she'd know they were safe now.

She always seemed to be regretting something – her relationship with her mum, with her sister – even bringing the question of Malta up with Adam while they were still in bed – and now she regretted not listening to Kieran properly when he told her what Bethan's parents were like.

What if those two tender young kids weren't safe in the kind of love nest Adam had depicted? They might be trying to live in Kieran's small car, surrounded by their belongings, chilled to the bone. Or battling to stake a claim to a corner of a horrendous squat. Kieran wasn't the type to stick up for himself in such a hurly-burly environment and Bethan would be scared to back him up because she was as much a softie as he was. Judith had a sudden vision of herself having to track them down to some squalid terrace with boarded windows and extracting Kieran from under the noses of the lawless and the hopeless.

She set about scrambling the eggs with unnecessary force, splashing her hands and wrists as she beat.

Of course, technically, crucially, Kieran wasn't actually her son. That's what Tom said. Despite all those years of cuddles and bedtime stories, bruised knees kissed better and homework explained, Kieran had only been on loan to her. Well, sod Tom, she wouldn't have driven Kieran away if she'd been able to influence the situation.

Adam came down in yesterday's suit trousers and white shirt, hair damp and jaw stubbled, his eyes wary till Judith showed him the note saying, 'Poor kids. I hope they'll be OK. I should have let them move in here when they asked.'

He squeezed her waist and kissed her hair. 'You can't put everything right for everyone, Jude. If they'd lived here, they would've been under constant attack from Tom and Bethan's parents. And so would you. You might've stood it, but could they?'

She sighed. 'It's just so wrong they feel they have to leave to be happy together. That people who love them have driven them away.'

After making tea to go with the food, they ate facing each other at the table. Adam cut the corner from his toast and scooped up fluffy eggs. He didn't have what he called his gizmo to fit around his hand and the knife was obviously a struggle. 'So you're going back to Malta?' he asked bluntly.

She sighed, dragging her mind from whether, by slipping off together, Kieran and Bethan could actually have done what was best for them. 'For a while.'

'How long's that?' He waited, clear grey eyes fixed steadily upon her.

She sipped her tea, aware that it was the person who

264

filled a silence with explanations who was the weaker negotiator. However obliquely, they were negotiating. Last night with Adam had caught her unawares but it hadn't changed what she knew she had to do. 'Until last night, I didn't have any reason, aside from fixing up time off, to consider you when I made the decision to go.'

He asked, 'You couldn't make your enquiries from England?'

'Probably,' she acknowledged. 'But it would prove to be frustrating and unsatisfactory. Also, I didn't tell you because you had the wedding to worry about as well as a busy work schedule, but Richard rang last week. He's organising his retirement. If I'm not going back to the business he wants to buy me out so he can pass Richard Elliot Estate to his children. The development the business invested in is up and running now and providing a nice reliable stream of income. It's a good time.'

Adam narrowed his eyes but his voice was as matter of fact as if he were planning a shoot. 'Do you also have the option to return to the business and keep your stake? Reclaim your old desk?'

She chewed mechanically, picturing herself back in her corner of the office at Richard Elliot Estate with the constant flow of traffic beyond the window and the sea beyond that, bobbing with colourful small boats. She admitted, 'I could pretty much reclaim my entire old life.'

He paused, thoughtfully. 'Except Giorgio.'

She swallowed. 'Except Giorgio. But now the rawness of losing him is fading I miss Malta. I miss the sea, the people and their approach to life. I miss hot days and warm evenings, the food, the beer, the fireworks at *festa* time, the amazing amount of traffic in the tiny streets. I even miss the storms.'

'And you'd feel closer to him, there.' He laid down his knife and fork.

She flinched. His calm couldn't disguise the hurt in his eyes but still he remained the same decent Adam. He didn't bawl or glower or throw things or crash his fist on the table to make her jump.

She tried to be truthful but gentle. 'I don't know. It might be comforting. Or it might be torture, as it was before. I'll find out.'

They finished the meal and Adam's brows cut thoughtful lines above his eyes as he helped her stack the dishes into the washer. Then he leant against the table and folded his arms. 'Can I go with you?'

She felt her jaw drop. 'To Malta?'

'For a couple of weeks, anyway. I realise you might stay longer. Months. Forever. But I think you could do with someone for a while, a friend. I'm your friend. You know that?' Despite the hurt that still lurked in the grey depths, the expression in his eyes was compassionate.

She nodded, unable to speak for the lump in her throat. Instead, she picked up his hand, the one with only the finger and thumb, and turned it over to examine the white scars and the pink knuckles. Casually, he changed hands so that he could curl a full complement of fingers around hers.

'You're one of the kindest men I ever met,' she said when she'd conquered the urge to cry. She shifted her gaze to his. 'No one treats me with the same consideration that you do, no one is so much in my corner. It's probably harder to find a friend like you than a lover.'

He stiffened. 'You're suggesting I ought to be *pleased* to be your friend rather than your lover?'

She fidgeted, uneasy at this unfamiliar hint of anger. 'I'm not trying to tell you what to feel. But let's think of you for a minute. What do you want? Where are you on the road to recovery? What comes next? Forget making me happy, tell me how you'd arrange your world if you could.'

He squeezed her hand, his expression softening, facial lines shifting so that they crinkled around his fine eyes. 'I'm ready to go forward. I wish we could do that together. But, so far as I can see, I'm still travelling on my own. I'll settle for dawdling for a while. See how steep you find Recovery Road.'

Her voice cracked. 'I might never catch you up.'

He nodded. 'You might even turn back. I'd have to give up on you.'

'It seems a bad bargain for you because I can't offer much.' Her heart lurched at the realisation that she was opening the door wide for him to leave, to give up on her, at any time.

But he said, 'I don't expect much. Are you going to Malta immediately?'

She dropped her eyes. 'Not straight away.'

With one finger, he lifted her chin. 'Because you'll be like a dog with a tick up its bum until you find out something about Kieran and Bethan?'

She managed a smile, viewing him through a sparkle of tears. 'You reveal me.'

The pad of his thumb wiped gently beneath her eye. 'I particularly liked that part. If you fancy it, we could go back to bed and I could reveal you again.'

She blinked away her tears and slid her hand onto his thigh. 'Bring it on.'

The winter ground along throughout March, wet, cold, windy, and it felt like forever.

Judith didn't get any fonder of cold weather. Adam declared, 'You'll need surgical intervention to prise you from your cocoon coat when the warmer weather eventually arrives.'

'If it ever does,' she sighed, checking the weather forecast for Malta and seeing it was seventeen degrees and sunny. She hadn't made arrangements for her return visit, yet, but it was constantly on her mind.

Adam was in a quiet, reflective mood, these days.

He said it was because his boys' lives were diverging steadily from his. After their honeymoon, Matthias and Davina had moved into an apartment on the west coast of Scotland. Adam had gone up for a week to help them decorate what he deemed upside-down rooms – coloured ceilings and white walls.

And Caleb, to everyone's surprise, landed a city advertising job and bought a grey suit and five white shirts. Then he put cobalt-blue streaks in his hair to celebrate becoming a London commuter.

Shelley asked Adam round to 'talk about the boys' then put her heart on the plate with the fresh cream cakes she'd bought him and asked him to go back to her. Gently, he told her that he couldn't and that he had feelings for Judith.

Judith felt sorry for Shelley but couldn't help being glad for herself.

However, to her bewilderment and dismay, Adam then took a unilateral decision to return his relationship with Judith to platonic. It wasn't a decision he voiced before he put it into practice but, after them sleeping together regularly, one day Judith tried to kiss him, he gently drew away. 'It'll be less confusing, for the time being,' he explained.

She knew he meant, 'I can't just let you jump about on my feelings while you decide what to do about Malta.' Though her eyes brimmed, she didn't protest, and they stepped back into their old ways, without touching, without sex. Apparently, Adam having 'feelings for Judith' didn't mean he had to act on them.

His resolution wavered only once. He'd come round to help Judith move her sofa and chairs around, wearing his usual grin along with a blue sweatshirt that brought out blue flecks in his eyes. Judith discovered an old cannabis stash of Caleb's tucked into the frame of the sofa and tried to dispose of it by chucking it on her open sitting-room fire. Adam flung himself full length across the carpet to snatch it from her hand. '*Are you mad?* What are you trying to do, Jude? Get the entire street stoned?'

Then he laughed so much that he went weak and somehow she ended up in his arms on the floor, her shirt open to her waist and two of the buttons on the floor as a testament to his impatience with his own lack of dexterity. They threw the cannabis in the wheelie bin later.

But that hot, sweet interlude on the floor became their swan song so far as sex was concerned.

Their old friendship was intact. It didn't keep Judith warm these frosty nights but she knew it wasn't fair to want a loving relationship to comfort her while she decided what to do with a life that may or may not include Adam. But that didn't stop her wanting it.

April brought snow to Northamptonshire, which Judith hated more than the rain. In her opinion, snow should come from December to February, not when trees were trying to blossom and birdsong had begun. Tramping through a cotton-wool-like six-inch layer had yesterday broken the heel of the only elegant pair of boots she owned and today was putting white streaks in her new chocolate suede trainers as she slithered through the salted pedestrian area in town, the late afternoon as dark as winter. It didn't cheer her at all to glance up and see Tom ploughing past in clumpy steel cap toe work boots, looking dry-shod and certain of his step.

Nevertheless, feeling that she should make an effort now he'd had time to cool down, she called, 'Tom!'

Ignoring her, he flung through the aluminium-framed doors of The Norbury Centre.

She pulled a face after him. Awkward sod. Then she watched him pause to attach a hanging orange flyer more securely to a post, one of many flyers the Sutherlands had scattered through the town. *Have You Seen Bethan?* it asked. There was a picture of Bethan, laughing into the camera in happier times. The posters had been up for weeks and were already shredding and blowing away. They'd been a forlorn hope but parents got desperate when it came to the fate of their children.

Judith had received two visits from Nick and Hannah Sutherland. The first, only a couple of days after Kieran and Bethan had left, had been hostile. They'd refused to step over her threshold but just bristled on the doorstep, insisting loudly, 'You *must* know, you *must* know, you *must*!' The next visit, a few weeks later, had been more conciliatory. They'd accepted Earl Grey in the sitting room and addressed her earnestly. 'If you know anything, anything at all, if you can just reassure us that she's all right . . .'

Judith had shaken her head sadly though she showed them the note from Kieran telling her not to worry. 'Apart from that, I've heard as much from my son as you've heard from your daughter. Nothing.' She hadn't been able to resist the little dig about Kieran being her son, after the way they'd excluded her at the hospital, but it didn't afford her much satisfaction. She missed Kieran. A constant heartache, daily misery. Even when she'd lived in Malta, they'd shared weekly phone calls and emailed in between. There hadn't been this awful, yawning silence.

She missed his trick of rushing his words together when he had a good story to tell, the way he laughed so much he could scarcely get the funny bit out. Even today, she couldn't help cocking an eye for him as she fought to keep her footing through the slushy town centre, as if he might suddenly emerge from a shop or a pub, laughing with friends as the cold pinkened his face.

Not unexpectedly, she failed to spot him. No news was supposed to be good news but whoever came up with such an optimistic view had never lain awake at night picturing her son sleeping rough, being beaten up for his cardboard box and left shivering in a shop doorway.

Hoping that if anything like that was happening he'd have the sense to contact her, and then trying to banish such images from her mind, she swung left at the edge of the precinct, stepping off the broken block pavers and onto the simpler flagstones of Henley Street as she made for Rathbones, the leather goods shop that had been on the same spot ever since she could remember. Wilma had asked her to buy her a new purse.

'The zip's gone on this one,' she'd said, when Judith and Molly had visited her yesterday afternoon. 'Can you get me a black one to match my bag, with a zip not a clasp – you know my hands – and a separate bit for the notes? But don't pay much, duck, it's not worth it. Go to the pound shop.' Wilma had taken to insisting on buying the cheapest available, in case she didn't last long enough to get the wear out of anything of quality. It was a habit that saddened Judith and she had no intention of shopping for her mum's new purse at the pound shop.

She entered Rathbones just before they closed. She told the man behind the counter, smart in his maroon smock, what she was looking for and he slid a drawer full of black purses from beneath the glass counter. Judith fingered rapidly through them and selected the one she thought Wilma would like most and paid £9.99 for it. Roomy and soft, it had chunky zips that should be easy to grip and smelled satisfactorily of leather.

Once outside, she picked off the price tag and discarded the thick, pale-blue paper bag in favour of a thin, pink-striped carrier she had in her pocket, knowing that was what Wilma would expect from the pound shop. She felt like a teenager preparing elaborate lies to pull the wool over her mum's eyes but Wilma was so staunch in her refusal to let Judith or Molly 'treat' her to nice things that a little subterfuge was called for occasionally.

Slithering on through the slush to the car park, she sighed over the lacy fingers of the bare trees that protruded through the pavements and longed for spring to act like spring and clothe the trees in frothy dresses of pink blossom. At the car she swore when she dropped her car keys in the snow and had to locate them by feel. Finally, she drove to Molly's house with numb fingertips. It took two big mugs of her sister's 'real' coffee from a filter jug to warm her through and biscuits to keep her from fading away before Judith was ready to take Molly on to visit Wilma. Knowing Wilma would refuse to leave the sanctuary of The Cottage in the snow, she and Molly had already agreed to eat together later.

When they were ready, Molly drew on mittens and a

voluminous red cape. 'I'm glad you don't mind driving because I just can't be doing with this white stuff,' she grumbled, shuffling down the path in crepe-soled boots and angling herself cautiously into the passenger seat of the car as if she were at least Wilma's age.

'Me neither,' Judith answered seriously, hopping into the driver's seat. 'I hope we don't crash or have to get out and push.' Then she threw her head back and laughed to see her sister's horror. 'For goodness sake, Molly! Don't clutch the door handle, I was joking.'

But Molly hung on as if the car were a roller coaster about to dive down a precipitous slope and actually shrieked as the car side-slipped the corner into Northampton Road. Rotating the steering wheel rapidly to correct the skid, Judith shook her head at her sister's feebleness. Driving in snow was the only thing she liked about it, still childish enough to be exhilarated by the odd skating moment.

They found Wilma awaiting them in the residents' lounge. Her hair looked freshly done and she was wearing passion-pink lipstick that didn't suit her, probably meaning it came free on the front of a magazine. 'You made it without huskies and sled,' she beamed. 'Did you remember my purse, Judith?'

Judith settled into one of the high-backed chairs. They were the only visitors in the lounge but there were several unaccompanied residents. Watching other people's visitors was a bit of a spectator sport when there was nothing good on the telly and so several grey-haired ladies craned to see as Judith handed over the carrier containing the purse.

Wilma beamed as she fumbled the black leather out of its wrapping. 'Ooh, isn't it a lovely one?'

273

'Lovely!' chorused around the room.

'But you didn't get this from the pound shop?' Wilma demanded, narrowing her eyes suspiciously.

'Yes, I did,' Judith lied. 'I've kept the receipt at home in case you want me to take it back.'

'I won't want you to take this beauty back, m'duck.' Wilma creaked a laugh. With stiff fingers, she unzipped and examined compartments, dropping her voice. 'Did you put a coin in it? It's bad luck to give a purse without.'

'Of course.' Then, honestly, she added, 'Molly reminded me.'

Molly smiled at receiving due credit. She'd hung her cape tidily on a coat rack whereas Judith had just stuffed her green cocoon on the floor beside her chair.

Wilma discovered the lucky coin. 'Judith, it's a *pound*. That's all the purse cost. Here, let me give you some change.' She reached for her ever-present handbag by her feet.

Laughing, Judith protested. 'You can't give change for a good-luck coin, Mum – it's bound to stop the luck working. Adam put it in there, anyway. You can't hurt his feelings by refusing.'

Beside their mother, Molly's dark brows rose in big-sister reproof that Judith was slithering into bigger and bigger lies just as she had when they were children and she wanted to avoid being found out over some misdemeanour.

From across the room, a silver-haired lady in a bobbly oatmeal cardigan demanded, 'Was that purse really only a pound? My dear, I need a new purse. I don't suppose you'll be going to that shop again, will you? Could you get me one?'

'And me!' said another lady, reaching stiffly into her pocket for change.

274

Then a third lady called, 'And me, m'duck, if you're sure it's not too much trouble.'

With a sinking heart and a grinning sister, Judith found herself collecting three one-pound pieces that she was supposed to exchange for three genuine leather purses 'from the pound shop'.

When the other ladies had drifted off to their rooms or were nodding over newspapers, Wilma grasped Judith's hand anxiously, her flesh chilly despite the central heating. 'Were all them purses alike?' Her whisper was almost a wheeze.

Judith understood instantly. 'I think the rest were smaller.'

'Oh.' Wilma sat back, looking satisfied. 'They won't mind theirs being smaller.'

Judith reflected ruefully that her well-meant fibbing was about to cost her somewhere in the region of twenty-seven pounds and left much of the conversation to Molly. Her sister was good at talking trivia, storing up little nuggets of information about her neighbours – people Wilma had never met – what Molly's son Edwin had told her about his skiing holiday in his last phone call and that Molly might visit him soon, then what seeds she intended to grow on her conservatory windowsill. Molly was working now as a volunteer in a charity shop alongside her part-time job in a café and Wilma was even interested in what knick-knacks came in. She followed all these little details with fierce interest until the residents' cocoa was ready. Visitors were welcome to join in the nightly cocoa ritual at a cost of thirty pence per cup and Wilma used the pound from the purse to pay for them.

Judith waited until the frothing drinks had been served, then, knowing that once it was drunk visiting hours would be over, decided to break her news about possible travel plans.

Until the moment arrived, she hadn't given much thought to the actual words she'd use or having to watch Wilma's face as she delivered them. Faced with the reality her heart began to race. She found that the more she attempted to make her tone casual, the more falsely contrived it emerged and the fewer words she seemed to have at her disposal. 'I have something to tell you,' she began. 'I'm probably going back to Malta, Mum.'

A silence. Molly frowned, her face sharp with disapproval, glancing at Wilma and laying a comforting hand on her forearm. 'For good?' Molly demanded.

Judith realised that she'd been too blunt and wished she'd talked to her sister first. Molly would have done something to prepare the ground, used some of the endless comfortingly inconsequential chat she had at her disposal to talk around the subject, how much Judith loved Malta, how she wouldn't be surprised if Judith went back some day so that the seed of possibility was sown somewhere on Wilma's narrow horizon. 'I don't know,' she muttered. 'But I've got to see Richard, anyway, and discuss what's going to happen with Richard Elliot Estate.'

Wilma gripped her hands together. 'But it might be for good? Just when I'd got used to you again.' Her words were forlorn, and there was a hint of a tremble about her round chin. Then, hurriedly, 'I've got my new glasses, did you notice? The frames are called "Amethyst". That means mauve.' The tremor gaining strength, she removed the glasses to display them, using the manoeuvre to surreptitiously blot her eyes with the back of her hand.

Dismayed, Judith gazed at the teardrop glistening on the soft white skin. Gently, she rubbed it away with one fingertip before taking her mum's hand, swollen with age, in both of hers. 'They're lovely glasses. Even if I stay in Malta, I'll come back often to see you, Mum.'

'Of course you will, dear.' Wilma sniffed. 'But I just thought . . . I thought you might settle here, now, so that I could carry on seeing you all the time. Adam's such a nice man.'

'He is.' Judith didn't pretend not to understand. 'He's coming to Malta with me for a couple of weeks.'

Wilma fumbled to push the new glasses back on her face. 'Lucky for you, he's patient,' she observed sagely. But she didn't smile.

The sisters got a quiet table at The Three Bells in the little dining room. Molly didn't like to eat in pubs unless it was in a separate dining room so The Three Bells was her choice.

A log fire roared in a stone fireplace ornamented with a companion set, andirons, bellows, horse brasses and a warming pan. The beams were hung with corn dolls and more horse brasses. A young lad with red hair and a serious expression wiped their table and presented them with cutlery wrapped in white paper napkins and a little round pot of sauce sachets.

Usually, Molly seemed to enjoy sitting across the table from Judith and talking about the charity-shop customers, those who came in every week to stretch their budget by trawling the clothes and the middle-class matrons who couldn't resist Royal Doulton tea services at one-tenth of their value. Normally, Molly would go on to sniff about the man from Brinham market's thriving antiques corner, because he liked to buy cheap in charity shops and sell dear on his stall.

But today she could scarcely wait for the first sip from her Coke before starting in on her sister with a huge sigh. 'Just when I thought you'd settled here. But, no, you're off again.' She folded her arms with a little huff of annoyance. 'You can't keep shuttling backwards and forwards for the rest of your life, you know, Judith.' She didn't sound cross so much as anxious.

Judith couldn't resist jibing back. 'Actually, I can. I wish you wouldn't talk as if I need your permission or approval. The days when Mum used to put you in charge of me have gone.'

'Pity,' Molly snapped.

'Come off it, Molly—!'

But then Molly's eyes glistened with tears. 'I'm just thinking about Mum.'

Judith sighed and drank half her lager in one swill instead of making it last as she normally did when she was driving. 'I'm sorry I handled breaking the news badly. I didn't think she'd take it quite so hard,' she admitted gloomily. 'I lived there for over four years before.'

Molly picked up the menu as the red-haired teenager returned with his pad and pen and ordered herself chicken and chips. 'I'm afraid she's feeling her age,' she said when he'd returned to the kitchens. For once she didn't sound judgemental or bossy. Just sad. 'Now, every time she sees you, she'll upset herself over whether it's the last time.' She lifted her hand to halt Judith's attempted interruption. 'And I know that the same could apply wherever you lived – but when you're in Lavender Row you're only ten minutes from her. Malta, in Mum's mind, is an inconceivable distance away. She can no longer grasp the reality of it, a little country in the middle of a big sea. The longer you're away, the further it seems to her. And don't waste

278

your breath trying to convince me otherwise. I spent those four years you mention being cheerfully comforting when all she wanted was to see you.'

Judith sank into guilty silence.

Molly unrolled her cutlery from the paper napkin to inspect it for water marks. 'How much was that purse?'

Judith groaned. '£9.99.'

Molly burst out laughing, Schadenfreude diverting her momentarily from worrying about her mother. '£9.99? And you've got orders for three more? You'll have to pretend they've sold out, won't you?'

'No, I'm not disappointing those ladies.' Suddenly, Judith wanted to cry at the thought of old ladies watching other people's visitors and waiting for their wonderful one-pound purses.

Or was the indigestible lump of emotion lodged in her throat at the memory of Wilma trying to blot her tears?

# Chapter Twenty-Three

But it was a week until Judith's tears finally fell.

She'd been with Adam on a photoshoot, capturing images of twin brothers who'd married twin sisters. Now the sisters were each expecting babies – single births, disappointingly – during the forthcoming summer. A magazine was doing a feature on this convoluted family branch and intended follow-ups in one year and two years, keen to see how alike or unlike the children would prove to be.

The shoot had been an easy one and they returned to Adam's flat by mid-afternoon to download the images. When the last had saved, Judith shut his machine down. 'I've got the ingredients at home for a Thai green curry, fancy joining me?'

Adam took off the glasses he'd begun wearing sometimes for close work and rubbed his eyes. 'You get me where I'm most vulnerable. You know I love Thai curry.'

'Play you at paper-rock-scissors for who's going to cook it?'

Adam studied his right hand thoughtfully. 'I can only make a rock.'

Judith grinned. 'Don't try that stuff on me – we'll both play left-handed.'

Adam still lost, leaving him to cook a curry in an iron wok in Judith's kitchen while, free of domestic responsibility, Judith switched on her computer to download her emails. She clicked on send and receive, and watched four messages download. A message from Richard. One from Microsoft. And from her book club. Then an unfamiliar email address.

*Kierycakeeater@yahoo.co.uk.*

It was a moment before it made sense; a moment of her mind hunting for the right memory to tune into like a hound circling for the scent. Kiery Cake Eater. Her heart kicked into a gallop as she was assailed by a memory of playing a silly, raucous game of chase around Tom's sprawling house, she roaring, troll-like, 'Where is Kiery Cake Eater?'

Kieran, breathless from giggles and the delicious panic of the pursued, 'Eating all the cake!'

The silly nickname had been used only between her and Kieran in the days when Kieran was young and life was simple and Judith always knew his whereabouts and that he was safe, her greatest problem likely to be how to prevent him from sneaking a third slice of cake. The scalding tears welled as she fumbled over the two simple clicks it took to open the message. She had to swipe the moisture away before she could read.

*Hey Mum,*
  *Me and Beth are fine. We live in a house we rent from a bloke. I got a job and Beth's doing her A-levels at a college next year so she can go to uni. She's temping till then.*

Impatiently, she used her sleeve against her eyes again so she could read the rest.

> *Sorry I haven't been in touch, I could've emailed u earlier, but we needed 2 get our heads round things. U know how it is! Clearing off and coping on your own is sometimes the only way. I know all the things u r going 2 ask, so here are the answers:*
> 1) *Yes, Bethan has sent a letter to her parents so they know she's ok. But she posted it when we went away on a coach trip two days ago so they won't know where she is. They should receive it today or tomorrow.*
> 2) *Leaving was her plan but I wanted the same.*
> 3) *No, I haven't contacted Dad. If you want to tell him I'm ok, that's up 2 u. He'll be completely peed at me, anyway.*
> *C u again,*
> *Love you, Kieran x*

Judith wiped her cheeks with the backs of her hands and then dried her hands on her jeans. *C u again!* It didn't matter so much when, just so long as it happened. So long as she knew he was safe and one day she'd see his brown hair sticking up at the front and his lip creasing when he smiled.

Shaking, she began to type a reply, careful to let him know how much she loved him, how much it meant to hear from him and know him to be out of harm's way. Not giving even a hint that her cheeks were wet and her fingers rubbery with emotion, as she ended: *I shall certainly let Dad know that you're OK, darling. He was distraught when you left. I'm glad Bethan wrote to her*

282

*parents – they will be so relieved . . . Any chance of you doing the same for Dad? Please? Tons of love forever, Mum xxxxxxxxxxx*

And then Adam arrived beside her, sliding his arms around her and pulling her head onto his shoulder, not asking any questions, just stating gruffly, 'I don't like it when you cry.'

But she only sobbed harder. 'He's OK. Adam, he's OK. He's living in a rented house and he's got a job . . .'

He rocked her while relief shuddered through her, stroking her hair and letting her tears soak his shirt while the curry stuck and burnt and the rice he'd been watching like a mother with a baby, boiled dry.

They ordered a takeaway while the pans containing the ruins of Adam's green curry steeped in hot soapy water.

Adam watched as she ladled rice from The Oriental Garden – never as fluffy as his – and creamy green curry out of the foil cartons and onto hot plates. 'Are you going to ring him?'

Judith didn't have to be told that 'him' meant Tom. She blew on a steaming, fragrant spoonful of curry that she was by now ravenous for but which scorched her lip when she approached it. 'He'll hang up on me before I can tell him why I'm calling.'

Adam nodded, annoyingly managing a spoonful of succulent chicken and plump sultanas as if it wasn't hot at all. 'And if you knock on his door?'

Judith sucked air into her mouth in inelegant whoops as she put the curry sauce in anyway and it stung her tongue. 'Big risk of having the door slammed in my face. I'll have to write the stupid man a note.'

'Perhaps then he'll thaw. He'll realise that you didn't

have to put yourself out to give him information about Kieran.'

Blowing gustily on her second spoonful, she shook her head. 'Not Tom. He bears a grudge. But at least if he doesn't want anything to do with me, I won't have to worry about him any more. It'll be a relief in a way.'

'You haven't had to worry about him since you separated.' Adam put the slightest emphasis on the 'had'.

'True. Maybe I should've accepted that sooner.' Then she added, honestly. 'I hope Kieran does write to him, though, and that they make up at some time in the future. Tom ought to be happier than he is.'

Adam got up to grab a cold can of Strongbow from the fridge, cracked it open and shared it between two glasses. 'I hope you still worry about me when I'm as old and grouchy as Tom.'

'Of course.' Warmed by the hint that they might have some kind of relationship going forward, she took the glass up and toasted him. 'To the coming of your grouchy old age.'

He clinked his glass with hers. 'But not too soon.'

Old age that was occasionally grouchy had already come to Wilma and Judith was glad Adam was with her on her visit that evening because Wilma wasn't in one of her sunnier moods. She awaited them in her pink-and-white room rather than in the lounge, her walking frame before her chair like a barrier.

Her first words were, 'Did you get them purses?'

Judith was ready for the question. Experience told her that Wilma wouldn't want the shine being taken off her lovely – cheap – new purse by her companions getting newer ones the same. Petty jealousies and one-upmanship

284

seemed to feature large in her life now she was living communally. 'Well, I have, but they're not as nice as yours,' she said with faux regret and displayed three purses without the section for cards or the stitchery design on the front that Wilma's boasted. 'Do you think the ladies will mind?'

Wilma bridled. 'I'm sure they won't have to. Goodness me, if they send you out for their shopping, they'll have to put up with what you bring them, won't they, duck?' Wilma took a purse in swollen hands, turning it over and slowly unzipping compartments. 'Smaller than mine, aren't they? Same price?'

'That's right,' Judith agreed, feeling that one more lie in the Great Purse Deceit was scarcely important. They had been £7.99.

Wilma looked sharply at Adam. 'You haven't put a pound coin in all of these, have you?'

Looking slightly surprised but forbearing to enquire why the devil he should, Adam shook his head. 'No, Wilma.'

'I put two pence in each, that's all.' Judith dropped the purses back in the carrier. 'Shall I hand these out, or will you?'

Wilma became more gracious. 'I will, duck, to save you the bother.'

Hiding her grin, Judith handed the carrier over, knowing Wilma wouldn't be able to resist reminding all her friends that they must remember to thank Judith.

'So,' Wilma turned to Adam. 'You're letting her go off back to Malta, then?'

Adam raised a rueful eyebrow. 'I'm afraid I have no power to *let her* or prevent her.'

Rattling her dentures around her mouth, Wilma looked thoughtful. 'I thought you might try.'

He raised both eyebrows this time and seemed to consider carefully. 'I don't think there would be much point.'

Wilma sighed. 'No, there never was.' She shook her head dolefully, folding her knobbly hands over the buttons of her maroon cardigan. 'But you're going with her, aren't you?'

Adam nodded. 'For a couple of weeks.'

Wilma went on discussing Judith as if she wasn't there. 'You're a good man. I hope she'll let you look after her.'

'Shouldn't think so.' Adam gave Wilma a big wink.

Judith perched on the corner of Wilma's bed, listening with rising irritation. 'I've lived in Malta before – it's a safer environment than Brinham,' she pointed out.

Wilma lifted her stick and used it to push her Zimmer aside as if it might interfere with her fixing Judith with a level look through her glasses. 'Do you miss Kieran?' she demanded.

Taken by surprise at Wilma's swerve to another subject, Judith hesitated. Why would she ask that? Judith hadn't told her mother that Kieran and Beth had run off, wishing to be in possession of a happy ending in the form of hard information of Kieran's whereabouts first, as she now was. Kieran's visits had always been sporadic and Wilma hadn't complained about not seeing him lately. 'Yes,' she agreed, cautiously.

'I know about him and his young lady doing a moonlight.' Wilma ruminated over her dentures again. 'He came to say goodbye.'

Distantly, the rattling of the cocoa trolley beginning its evening circuit could be heard above the loud and clear voices of the carers talking to other residents. But in Wilma's room the hush swelled until Judith's ears buzzed with the pressure.

'I see.' Judith's voice somehow sounded as if she were under water. So her mum had known before her and before Tom, who only knew now because they'd stopped on the way so Judith could stick the note she'd written through his letterbox. She minded, she realised, with a rush of mixed anger and surprise. She minded that Wilma had seen Kieran to say goodbye when Judith hadn't been able to, because he'd called when she was at Matthias's wedding. She particularly minded that Wilma had been sitting on the information. Dimly, she was aware of Adam leaving the room, of the murmur of his voice, of him returning with cocoa for three. Automatically, she let him pass her a cup and saucer. The crockery used by The Cottage had a matt feel to it that she disliked and now it positively set her teeth on edge as she sipped to ease her rigid throat.

Wilma, apparently unaware that she'd upset Judith's applecart, took saucer in one hand and cup in the other. 'He told me all about the baby. Poor little dot, wasn't he? Poor, poor little dot.'

Though she was telling herself that her mum's grasp on time and the order of events wasn't to be relied upon these days, Judith's voice seemed to be coming from someone else. 'And what did you say to him?'

The light reflected off Wilma's glasses. 'I told him how much you'd miss him, duck. Have you heard from him?'

'Yes. I've just got an email. He says they've rented a place and he's got a job.' Judith swallowed more of the milky cocoa. 'Did he tell you where he was going?'

'Back to Sheffield.' Wilma said it as if there should be an 'of course' at the end of the sentence.

The cocoa was gone and Judith felt sick. It had been too milky, too sweet. Kieran hadn't trusted her enough to tell her where he was going to live. Of course, Sheffield – where he'd been at university and knew the area, had friends – was an obvious choice. Easy for him to organise accommodation and a job. Why had she never thought of it? And what possible use was the information now that she had it?

When the visit was over, in the darkness of the car Adam delayed starting the engine and took her hand instead. 'He may have been trying to protect you. He knew his father's temper – he probably felt that you'd be more comfortable facing Tom if you genuinely didn't know where he'd gone.'

'You're probably right,' she agreed, dully, but still the feeling of betrayal persisted.

His fingers squeezed hers. 'I don't think Wilma realised she might hurt your feelings.'

'Of course not.' It was raining now, the droplets on the windscreen shattering the car-park lights into fragments in the navy-blue evening.

His thumb stroked her knuckles. 'I think she was just hinting that she'll miss you in the same way that you miss Kieran.'

'I expect so,' she muttered. She knew only too well the leaden emptiness of missing someone. The way you got used to it and learnt to live around an absence.

'She's bound to miss you. So will Molly,' he murmured. 'And so will I.'

She stirred, feeling as if something were sliding out of control, going too fast, carrying her along when she wasn't sure yet where she wanted to go. 'I'm only going for a recce this time,' she reminded him weakly. 'If I decide to live there again, it'll take time to organise.'

His breath came out in a heavy sigh, steaming up the

windscreen. 'I suppose . . .' He considered his words, then began again. 'I suppose none of us can see quite what would keep you here. We feel the "recce" is just a formality. And that you're humouring us.'

# Chapter Twenty-Four

Adam pulled up outside Judith's unlit house a few minutes later.

She screwed up her eyes and stared through the rain to a point across the street. 'Hell's blood, is that Tom waiting in his truck?'

He turned his head to follow her gaze. 'Looks like it. Shame. I quite liked it when he wasn't speaking to you.' His tone told her he was only half-joking.

They sat in silence, listening to the hiss of the rain as the warmth the car heaters had generated seeped away. The rain increased until the hiss became a grumble. Adam offered, 'I suppose I can stay out of earshot while you talk to him.' His tone was grudging and the inference was that he intended to remain within eyesight.

Judith unfastened her seat belt and let it slither over her shoulder and snap against the side of Adam's car. She was only half-joking too when she observed, 'Or, as it's peeing down, it would be perfectly natural to make a run for the house.'

Adam laughed. 'Put a real spurt on, in that case.'

Of course, Tom spotted them, even if they did scurry through the inclement weather. By the time Judith had jiggled the key in the lock and Adam had hit the door to make it open, Tom was on the garden path behind them, huddled against the sting of the rain. 'Oh, hello,' said Judith unenthusiastically. 'You'd better come in out of this downpour.'

Switching on the hall light and hanging her wet coat over the newel post, Judith faced Tom in the hall while Adam went down the passage to the kitchen, discreetly absent but not out of earshot. 'Not cutting me dead, tonight?' Judith challenged, when Tom didn't speak.

Rain dripped from the peak of his navy baseball cap with the name of a builders' merchant embroidered on the front. He ignored her question. 'Do you know where he is?'

She didn't have to ask who 'he' was. 'He didn't tell me,' she answered truthfully.

In the kitchen, Adam coughed.

Tom glanced in the direction of the sound and scowled. 'I suppose it's too much to ask that we do this privately?'

Judith folded her arms. 'Yes, actually. You got pretty physical last time you came to my house.'

Without responding, Tom stepped closer to loom over her. 'Did he phone or write? Where's the letter?'

She felt her temper rising. 'Get out of my face – you really are lacking in all manners!' she challenged. 'Allow me to breathe or leave my house.'

Another glower . . . but Tom stepped back.

Judith made herself remember how let down she'd felt less than an hour ago to realise Wilma had known where Kieran was and hadn't told her. That was almost certainly due to age but Judith didn't have that excuse. She softened her voice. 'I can't tell you more than I did in the note. He contacted me. He gave me permission to let you know he's all right. I encouraged him to contact you directly. That's it.' She omitted the word 'email' as Tom would instantly demand Kieran's new email address.

In the kitchen, the kettle bubbled to the boil and clicked off. Adam could be heard turning the pages of a newspaper, making them crackle. Tom removed his sullen stare from Judith and narrowed his eyes in Adam's direction. 'Do I have to worry about him?' he asked abruptly.

'In what way?' Judith hadn't quite meant to inject the level of astonishment that coloured her voice.

He turned his basilisk stare back to her. 'Are you *together*? A *couple*? An *item*?'

Incredulously, she laughed. 'Mind your own bloody business. The days when who I slept with was your concern are long gone – very long gone, you ridiculous arse.' The insult came out almost affectionately. She heard footsteps behind her and knew Adam had come back into view.

'I don't like the way he hangs around,' Tom persisted obstinately, ignoring Adam's presence.

Adam snapped, 'I was just thinking the same about you.'

With an exasperated tut, Judith slipped past Tom and yanked open the door. 'I like Adam hanging around,' she said with deliberate calm. 'There's nothing else I can tell you so goodnight, Tom.'

On Thursday, Judith assisted Adam at a photoshoot. Podraig Mahoney, the subject, had lost his short-term memory and had to be constantly reminded of his surname. He was highly reliant on his dark-eyed wife, Loraine, because if he left the house for too long alone, he forgot his route home.

He treated his highly unusual and frustrating condition with humour and had to be constantly reminded not to beam into the camera lens as the magazine was looking for a pensive mood.

By the time the shoot was over, Podraig had to confess that he'd forgotten why it had happened at all. Helplessly, he smiled at his wife. 'You'll have to remind me. I forgot to write it down.'

Seated at Adam's computer later, downloading the pics into a fresh folder ready for Adam to select his submissions to the commissioning magazine, Judith mused on how often Podraig asked his wife to be his memory and how often his wife patiently complied. How strong did love have to be to withstand the constant drip of a frustration like that? Podraig and Loraine had seemed truly happy together.

Adam concentrated silently on the images he was working on from an earlier shoot. He'd been almost morose since Tom's visit.

From her pocket Judith's mobile began to ring, vibrating disconcertingly against her hipbone. An unknown number flashed up on the screen.

But the voice that went with it when she answered the call was achingly familiar. 'Hey, Mum.'

Judith swallowed. A rush of love surged through her, making her hot and dizzy, and any resentment that he'd confided more in Wilma than in her evaporated.

'Mum? It's me.'

'Hello, Kieran,' she managed. Her voice cracked. She was aware of Adam looking up suddenly, a smile clearing his frown like magic. She closed her eyes, the better just to absorb the sound of Kieran's voice as he told her about the house they'd rented. 'Red bricks, black roof, white windows. Nowhere to park.' And his job. 'I left the one in Brinham without working my notice, so they wouldn't give me a reference. I'm working in a shop, now, but it's cool. It's a big shop so I'll be able to work my way up. They've already put me in charge of ordering stuff for the CD section.'

'That's wonderful,' she bubbled. 'Darling, it's just wonderful to hear from you and know you and Beth are OK.' Her heart expanded in relief. He had a roof over his head and a way of keeping it there.

'Luckily, Bethan's good with money.' Then Kieran cleared his throat awkwardly. 'So, I've rung to ask a favour. You know . . . at the cemetery? We ordered this little . . .' He cleared his throat again.

She said it for him. 'The stone tablet? For Aaron?'

She heard him take a couple of deep breaths. They whooshed down the line. After a moment, his voice unsteady, he said, 'Yeah. We've had notification that it's been laid in place. We were wondering . . . could you ask Adam to take a digital photo of it and email it to us? Bethan's a bit stressy about whether it's been done right, so when we've seen it, we'll be cool.' His voice became gruffer. 'Well, we might be upset, but we want to see it. We need to.'

'Of course.' Without waiting for the conversation to be over, she passed the request on to Adam.

'Tomorrow, as soon as the cemetery opens,' he promised. 'The light will be pretty decent – this rain's due to pass over tonight.'

'Cool.' Kieran's relief was audible. 'You're both cool. Thanks.'

They talked on for ages and Judith went to bed happy that night.

Next morning, the cemetery was silent apart from the breeze through the naked trees and cautious, is-it-finally-spring

294

birdsong. Adam's camera bag containing the black Nikon swung from his shoulder as he paced at Judith's side.

The stone, set into the grass, was easy to locate; the grey veined marble was lettered with gold. Adam took shots from above so that Kieran and Bethan would be able to read the inscription, *Aaron McAllister Sutherland*, and then a couple of Judith laying white roses beside it, her hair blowing back from her face.

Crouching, touching the engraved inscription, the bleak, single date that reflected the baby's failure to draw breath, Judith felt claws of pain around her heart.

Adam extended his hand to help her to her feet. 'Let's go back to my place and send the pictures straight away.' He kept her hand all the way back to the car. He knew exactly when she needed small expressions of support. She might get a bit of silent disapproval from him where Tom was concerned but he stepped up the instant she needed him.

The next day, it was Adam who found a message from Kieran in his inbox.

*Really cool. Thanx mate. Tell Mum we're really, really ok – don't think she believes me. Thx again. Means a lot. K&B*

Reading the mail for the fourth time when she should be typing invoices, Judith mused. 'It sounds as if he's truly growing up. As if they both are.'

Adam nodded as he cleaned out one of his equipment cases with the brush on the nozzle of the vacuum cleaner. He didn't like dust on his equipment. 'Tough breaks tend to chase immaturity away.'

She clicked to print out the invoice she'd been working

on and began a fresh one. 'I think they will be OK. It's still hard to accept that Kieran's chosen not to confide whether he is living in Sheffield or whether that's just what he told Mum, and I expect Tom's still livid, but if a young man decides to resign from his job, pack his clothes and leave, there isn't very much you can do about it. The Sutherlands have discovered there isn't much you can do about a seventeen-year-old girl doing the same thing – or is she eighteen by now? I think she must be.' She looked outside to where rain had begun to fall in a cold, heavy curtain. Again. She sighed and turned to look at the quiet, gentle man beside her. Softly, she said, 'Adam, I think it's time for me to plan my trip to Malta.'

Adam fitted the crevice nozzle to clean out the smallest compartments where the brush wouldn't reach. When all was satisfactorily dust-free, he switched off the vacuum, wound up the flex, and went out to stow the machine in the cupboard in the hall.

He came back into the room and picked up his diary.

'I can clear the first two weeks of May,' he observed, after quickly flipping through the pages held within the navy-blue cover. It wasn't a question or a hint, just a statement of a fact she could take advantage of or not. He shut the book with a snap.

She smiled to herself as her rapid fingers opened another invoice template. 'I'll ask Richard if we can stay with him.'

# Chapter Twenty-Five

It was the second day in May when Judith stood, motionless in the soft darkness, and listened to the sounds of Malta and its overwhelming feeling of 'home'.

The crickets, *werzieq,* were making their endless background buzz. Sliema Creek lapped at the edge of the pavement, a gentle noise that soothed and comforted. Late-night cars whooshed past between the silent shops and the broad pavement where she stood, headlight reflections wheeling over those of streetlights that lay across the black water like golden scribbles. The smooth railings that edged the harbour were cool beneath her hands. She breathed in salt water and boat oil, pine trees and dust, listening to the pull and suck of the water, feeling the utter peace.

Quiet footsteps made her turn.

Hands stuffed in the pockets of his black canvas jacket, Adam had the creased appearance of someone who'd just woken up. 'Are you safe out here at two in the morning?'

She smiled at his disgruntled air. 'Probably. There's not much crime here – not that I have any valuables on me

– and any self-respecting Romeo would be looking for someone younger.'

'Good thinking,' he said drily, and yawned. 'And maybe even Romeos are put off by madwomen who hang around alone in the dark.'

'I couldn't sleep and I like the dark.' With a long, slow, even breath, she inhaled the essence of Malta, the perfume from the oleanders on the promenade and the brine from the sea.

He stifled another wrenching yawn.

'Go back to bed,' she suggested gently. 'Erminia's given you a lovely room, and she's wonderfully hospitable. I expect your sheets are scented with lavender and your pillows plump and inviting.'

Groaning longingly, he leant his forearms on the rail and studied a rowing boat that rocked beside a faded red buoy. 'Richard heard you leave and made me come out to look after you.'

She tutted with exasperation. 'Don't say he's waiting up for me too?'

He yawned again, saying sourly, 'Not now I'm out here.'

Her laugh was loud in the still air. As he didn't seem inclined to leave her to a private wallow in the Maltese atmosphere, she decided to tell him about his surroundings, nodding first to a bulk of land across the narrow ribbon of sea. 'This is Manoel Island, here in front of us. It is an island, but only just – it's joined to this road, The Strand, by a bridge. This part of The Strand's called *Triq Marina* or Marina Street on some maps, but everyone still calls it The Strand.'

She looked left. 'Those are the ferryboats – see the little one with *Lowenbrau* on the side? That shuttles all day to-and-from Valletta. We can go across in the morning. Or stay in Sliema. Whichever you prefer.'

He turned, resting his backside on the rail, regarding her curiously. 'Can we? I thought you had plans? Giorgio's family?'

Slowly, she nodded. She did have plans involving Giorgio's family, of course. Wasn't that the main reason she'd come? 'Now we're here, a little rest and relaxation won't hurt. I'd like to show you some of Malta and I need a couple of days of thinking time.'

He didn't comment that she'd had weeks to think but glanced around with weary interest, as if resigned to the fact that sleep wasn't immediately in the offing. 'So where's Richard's office?'

She pointed down The Strand the other way, towards Ta' Xbiex. 'Just about in sight – see the restaurant with the bright yellow sign? Immediately past that.'

'And your apartment?'

She swung the other way. 'Behind the ferryboats and the bus stops. Second floor.' The outside of her old home – although someone else's home at the moment – was so familiar. She remembered the warmth on the soles of her bare feet when she stepped onto the balcony the evening she waited for Giorgio, but then Charlie Galea showed up instead. She shut out the recollection. 'You were supposed to be seeing all this in the morning.'

He gave her a wry look. 'Yes, I remember the idea being to go straight to bed after our late flight. I missed the bit where it got changed to wandering about half the night.'

She let her exasperation show. 'Go back to Richard's without me.'

He adjusted his position on the railings and showed her a peeved scowl. 'You are a bloody awkward woman, Jude. At one time if a man put himself out to protect a female, she used to damned well let herself be protected.

Now he has to be apologetic, in case he offends her. Go on, you carry on with your tour guide bit. I'm sure I can cope indefinitely without sleep.'

*Tour guide.*

*Giorgio, standing at the front of the bus and making all the passengers smile with his easy charm.*

She let the pang of sorrow fade and made herself relax. 'If you're going to pout about it, we'll wait till morning.' She took his arm and they crossed the road, turning up the tiny street further up The Strand that led to Richard's house with its courtyard behind. A traditionally Maltese house of limestone with tiled floors and staircase, a scroll of wrought iron swelled over each window like a belly. On older buildings it would have signified that the building had needed to be defended, the bulge at the bottom to allow a lookout to be kept down the street for enemies and fire arrows at them if necessary. On Richard and Erminia's house it was an ornamentation filled with potted red geraniums lovingly tended by Erminia.

'Look, lizards.' Adam pointed up at geometric shadows on the pale limestone, legs making right angles against still bodies that ended in long pointed tails.

'Geckos,' she corrected. 'Wall geckos. You'll see plenty at night because they hang out near a light to eat the insects it attracts. Geckos have shorter, broader bodies than lizards and are dull, like speckled sand. Geckos are nocturnal but lizards like to bask in the sunshine and have shiny scales, sometimes a beautiful dark green.'

'Beautiful?' he queried. 'Geckos and lizards are OK but snakes, like poor old Fingers, are not?'

She snorted. Happily, Fingers lived in the spare room at Adam's flat and she never had to look at him. 'The geckos are up on the wall. Fingers was in my kitchen.'

She let her explanations fade away. Adam was watching her mouth.

Geckos weren't that interesting a subject when your one-time lover was looking at your lips with a particularly intent expression that started desire uncoiling inside her. She reached out. Her fingertips collided with his scarred palm and she let her hand close around his. 'Adam . . . why don't we sleep together any more?'

He betrayed by only a blink that her bluntness had caught him off guard. 'Self-preservation,' he offered, with a quirk of his lips. And he inserted his left hand into the cradle of her fingers to take the place of the right as they walked into the lofty, cool interior of Richard's house.

The next three days became a holiday.

Full of pride in her once-adopted country, Judith showed Adam up and down the steep golden streets of Sliema with the shops packed tightly from corner to corner and the pavement cafés overflowing with customers. The following day, they borrowed Richard's car and drove to the beautiful beaches of Paradise Bay and Ghajn Tuffieha, where the Mediterranean had never looked so blue, and then onwards to the impressive silent city of Mdina in all its medieval splendour. Despite the fact that it was far from silent, as extensive cable laying works were going on and the air was full of the noise of road drills, Adam shot so many photos of the carved-stone buildings and tiny streets that he had to use a computer in Richard's office to download the pics and email them to himself in order to free up his memory cards.

It was in the after-hours quiet of the office that Judith sat down at her old desk and said simply, 'Richard took me aside, this morning. He's met with the liquidators of

Sliema Z, Giorgio's old company. I won't see a lira of my investment back. Nothing left after paying off the preferential creditors and my loan was unofficial, anyway.'

Adam crouched down to put a sympathetic arm around her. 'That's terrible.'

Wordlessly, she nodded. There wasn't much left to say.

On the third day, she took him on the ferry to the lovely, unspoilt ancient capital city, the citadel of Valletta, pointing out the landmarks as they approached. 'That tall steeple is St Paul's Anglican Cathedral – known as the British Church – and the dome is Our Lady of Mount Carmel. You can see the turret of the Grand Master's Palace, too.' The way up into the walled city that seemed to hang above them was steep but Judith was merciless as she steered Adam onwards and ever up to one of her favourite spots: the heights of the Upper Barrakka Gardens, on the other side of the compact city.

There they leaned on the painted railings and stared out over the glinting blue splendour of Grand Harbour, watching the far-below ant-like passengers disembark from a towering white cruise boat that had its own swimming pool on deck. Adam gazed silently over the depths of incredible blue to the church domes and bell towers of the three crowded little cities of Vittoriosa, Cospicua and Senglea on the opposite shore, their fingers of land creating the creeks that sheltered the clutter and clatter of the docks. 'I can see why it's called "grand",' he breathed. He was so dazzled that he didn't even start taking photos for several minutes.

They strolled back along the paved paths of the gardens then she took him into the city and showed him the central thoroughfare, Republic Street – a particularly pleasant place to shop as no traffic was allowed. The streets were beautifully decorated for a saint's feast, the *bandalori* or bunting showing the city at its best. They lunched on pasta and calamari at Caffe Cordina in Republic Square.

Judith chose salad and beer. 'In the sixteenth century the Ottoman Turks laid siege to the Knights of St John in Valletta, floating the knights' dead comrades back across the harbour waters to destabilise them,' she told him, munching on slices of chicken and romaine lettuce leaves. 'La Valette, the grandmaster of the time, gave the grisly order to fire back the heads of Turkish prisoners in response.'

Adam pulled a horrified face. 'Brutal times.'

After lunch, they strolled between the golden baroque buildings along dusty streets so narrow it seemed impossible to survive the cars whipping past, and others where they felt safe from vehicles because the road was actually a giant flight of steps.

She showed him the city gate in the huge ramparts that had protected the city for so long. They bought cake and ice cream from stalls standing around the circular bus terminus and he took photos of her sitting on the coping of the Tritons' fountain in the middle, laughing, her face dusted with icing sugar and crushed almonds, her ice cream melting over her fingers.

Judith enjoyed playing tourist with Adam, watching his face as he drank in the buildings and the views of deep blue sea to be glimpsed down almost every street. Finally, she looked at her watch. 'We'd better go back to Richard and Erminia's house. Family dinner tonight – cousins, their spouses and all the children they've brought into the world.'

When they returned they found the family had already assembled around the long table beneath the chandelier in the dining room, ready to catch up with Judith and learn all about Adam.

Adam looked a bit shell-shocked at the advent of so many people but joined in an evening full of laughter and finger-licking food such as *lampuki,* peppers and sausages. Richard beamed as he carried on conversation with every member of his large family. Silver-haired Erminia, always more reserved, listened, but she, too, wore a constant smile. Children clambered down from the table between courses to let off steam, Lino, Rosaire and Raymond competed to entertain Adam with unflattering cousinly stories about Judith.

It was late when the party broke up, and eerily quiet. After Judith had hugged her aunt and thanked her for a fantastic meal, Richard and Erminia went to bed, Erminia calling behind her, 'We are not so young as you.' Judith and Adam went out to sit in the courtyard among big dusty pot plants, the May night air chilly enough that Judith needed her jacket. Adam entertained himself by spotting geckos on the house walls.

Tentatively, Judith said, 'Will you be able to look after yourself tomorrow? I have stuff to do.'

Slowly, Adam laced his hands behind his head and trained his gaze on the moths battering themselves against the orange light. 'You're beginning your mission?'

'If you want to call it that,' she agreed, aware of tension in his voice.

'And you want to do it alone,' he stated.

She frowned as she tried to interpret his mood. 'For the moment.'

A pause. Adam continued to observe the night-time wildlife. Judith continued to observe Adam. At last he asked, 'Are you any nearer knowing what you're going to do?'

She blew out a breath. 'The office is evidently running perfectly well without me and I know it would suit Richard and his family if I simply sell out to them. Richard's spending fewer hours in the office and Rosaire, Raymond and Lino are doing fine without me. It's fair enough. I was the one to go home to the UK.' She shrugged. 'On the other hand, if I want my old position back I think it's possible.'

He rocked his chair back on two legs. 'Thanks for the last few days. I've enjoyed being with you.' His tone was so polite that Judith couldn't quite tell whether he was being sarcastic.

They lapsed into silence and for a while she thought he'd fallen asleep. But then his voice came suddenly. 'How does it feel to be back in Malta?'

'Nice,' she answered carefully.

'Nice,' he repeated. He sounded as if he had no idea what that meant.

# Chapter Twenty-Six

The sun was getting some real heat into it, making Judith roll her shoulders in satisfaction beneath the butterscotch-yellow cotton of her light shirt as she approached where her cousin Raymond's blue Peugeot was parked. As he was tied to the office all day today, he'd said she could borrow it and she'd already called in for the keys. After a brief tidy up inside the vehicle, which involved throwing all the papers from the front into the back, she drove cautiously out of Sliema. She'd decided to begin her 'mission', as Adam termed it, by re-establishing her connection to Giorgio.

That connection hadn't quite happened just by returning to the island, a little to her surprise. Even in Sliema, where she and Giorgio had lived, her present life intervened. Perhaps it was because she wasn't in her own apartment.

Or perhaps it was Adam. Their familiar, easy way of being together.

She'd certainly expected more of a reawakening of grief than she'd so far experienced. On her last visit, Giorgio's loss had been new and shocking and Malta had seemed full of memories of him, ringing with his voice, bright with his smile, unbearable without him.

The roads were no quieter than she remembered and she felt nervous of the lanes of weaving traffic on the regional road as she tried to re-accustom herself to the Maltese driving experience. It seemed rapid and busy after Brinham. Dust blew in through the open car window on a breeze that held a firm edge of heat, auguring the rigours of the summer just beginning. The sun bounced from the pale new limestone blocks of a building under construction, the site hemmed about by other buildings and the road. A precarious-looking crane lorry swung the large blocks into what would be the building's basement.

Construction in this style was a particularly Maltese skill. A building would be cut from between its neighbours and the site excavated into a yawning hole into which a new building was erected. She was sure that the occupants of the houses on either side must breathe a sigh of relief when the construction was complete.

Joining the queue of traffic threading past the crane, she began to relax as she left it and the busier roads behind in favour of uncrowded residential areas with prickly pear trees lolling over dry-stone walls like spiky green Mickey Mouse ears. She began to enjoy her drive.

The cemetery, when she parked the car, was enjoying an early-morning peace. The flower sellers were still setting out their stalls on the sloping car park and she paused at one to buy a single orange gerbera. Stepping through the tall, decorative gates, she had no trouble remembering her way up the avenue on the left, uphill under the pine trees to the Zammit family plot. Her previous visit was pretty well scorched into her memory.

But having searched the monument out, she came to

307

an uncertain halt before it, eyeing the weeping marble angel.

Nobody was there to observe her but still, somehow, she felt like an uninvited guest. Perhaps it was because she could imagine the fury of Maria and Agnello Zammit if her visit happened to coincide with one of theirs.

The plot was tidy. Fresh white and yellow flowers stood in a central vase. A new plaque had been created and placed in front of the older ones, pale compared to their weathered tones. An oval photograph of Giorgio made her flinch. It looked like the photograph that had appeared at the back of his tour company's brochure. The inscription on his plaque read:

*Giorgio Zammit*
*1970–2004*
*Rest in Peace*

Her stomach hollowed. Already it was almost a year since the accident in the twinkling waters of Ghar Lapsi. At the other end of the summer, it would be a year since his death. She would be *another* year older than Giorgio as he lay here alone, the flowers nodding in the breeze, the carved angel standing guard.

After a further glance about her, Judith lowered herself to the dusty floor. She sat cross-legged, propping her forehead on her fist and closing her eyes, preparing herself to remember Giorgio, trying to feel close to him and talk to him as she used to. She tried to tap into the grief from the familiar point of lament.

If she had been there to keep him safe, she thought, struggling to keep her eyelids shut in the bright and inappropriately cheerful sunshine, she'd presumably have a completely different life now, still living in Malta with Giorgio.

Her thoughts interrupted themselves. Should the two parts of that statement be separate?

She might still be living in Malta . . . but 'with' Giorgio? Only behind closed doors.

Letting her eyes open, she gazed at the flowers. Perhaps it was always difficult to envisage one life when living another? Having now accepted Giorgio's death, it made it difficult to imagine him alive.

But specific things had brought her back and she'd come here to focus on one of them. Fishing in her bag, she brought out Giorgio's crucifix. It gleamed in the palm of her hand, some of its lustre lost now that it was no longer worn every day against warm skin. She closed her eyes again, reaching out determinedly to Giorgio with her mind.

*What am I supposed to do with this? Cass gave it to me so I'd have something of you. And now Alexia says it's hers.* The memory of her conversation with Giorgio's daughter intruded. There had been positive dislike in the young woman's tone and no echo of Giorgio.

She sighed. There were so many things she had regrets about that she badly wanted to do the right thing about the crucifix, the right thing by Giorgio's daughter. She just wished she knew what that right thing was. Maybe she should have let Adam come with her, as he'd so obviously been prepared to, because he was a rock in a crisis. All she'd had since she'd met him was one crisis after another. He must be used to coping with them by now.

For goodness' sake, she wasn't meant to be thinking about Adam!

Pushing herself to her feet, she brushed glumly at the dust and dead pine needles that now coated her jeans, dropping the crucifix into her bag, feeling foolish over sitting cross-legged like some old hippy and attempting to gauge the opinions of a dead man. And an insect had bitten her ankle into a white lump with a pink halo and it itched already.

She tucked the orange gerbera in with the other flowers. It blazed out from the tasteful muted whites and yellows. She hesitated. When his family brought fresh flowers, they'd surely notice this floral stranger.

Oh, let them.

It was unlikely to be Johanna, Giorgio's estranged wife – she hadn't even liked her husband. If it were his children or his parents . . . well, they'd just have to accept that she'd loved him too, no matter how they'd frowned.

*I wish I knew what to do.* Giorgio's grave had brought her no answers.

She swung away and started down the hill, legs swinging like pendulums, until she could pass through the towering black gates and climb back into the hot interior of Raymond's car. Disappointment and dissatisfaction crept over her like a black cloud. Only Giorgio's name remained at Santa Maria Addolorata Cemetery, beside the posed photograph that would keep him smiling and forever thirty-four.

She thrust the car into gear and drove away.

Ghar Lapsi was an area of outstanding beauty by any standard.

Sauntering along the cliff top from the car park, Judith made for the same slab of rock where she'd waited out the day of Giorgio's funeral. She squinted past the glitter of the sun on the ocean, almost too much for the eyes, at a red fishing boat and the dark shape of the rock of Filfla. The sea was much rougher today than last time she'd been here. She shaded her eyes to watch the blue-green, frothing waves and listen to them crash onto rock. Then, changing her mind, she returned to the steps to jog down to the foreshore.

She passed no one on the way but there were a couple of families at the restaurant at the bottom. A pretty waitress with melting brown eyes and a ready smile took her order for cappuccino and Judith settled down to watch the waves from a green chair on the terrace as she drank. Substantial waves thrashed the shore. Divers would be foolhardy to go down today. The rip would carry them away or fling them against rock without warning. Smash, dash, flip, tumble, hold you down, drag you out into angry, jade-green depths. The sea had a soft belly but a hard head, as the Maltese saying went, and only the experienced and the incautious went down when it was so restless.

Gently, slowly, she closed her eyes and listened to the crash of the waves and the boom of water falling back on itself, salt scenting the air. She remembered the feeling of being down there, finning along above the weed and rocks to the sand fields, brilliant fish darting away, octopus reversing into rocky crevices, red starfish prone on the bottom, the sun filtering into the water in diagonal bars and the Darth Vader sound of breathing loud in her ears.

But she couldn't make Giorgio emerge in the shape of a diving buddy.

When her cup was empty, Judith paid then picked her way right down to where the water boiled inside the arm of rock and the sea was forced through a tiny fissure in spouting spray. The wind rattled in her ears. It was like standing on the edge of a cauldron. On a projecting rock stood a loan fisherman, his bait in a white plastic box at

311

his feet. He glanced around and she saw it was Paul Vella, his skin glowing golden from the spray-laden breeze. 'Pawlu', the men called him. Giorgio had fished with him from a boat sometimes for the local big catch, *lampuki*. They'd thought it a great joke to cast near the baited floats laid out painstakingly by commercial fishermen, effectively intercepting their catch.

Pawlu's silver hair was damp. He raised a hand to her, then secured his rod and stepped back over the rocks.

'Catch much, Paul?' she called to him as he neared.

His smile transformed his face. 'Sure. Little silver fish, big red eyes. *Vopi*.' He gave the Maltese name for mullet.

'What are you using? Shrimp?'

'No, just damp bread, smelly cheese, and patience.' They gazed at the bubbling sea together for several moments. 'You OK?' he ventured.

She nodded. She'd shared many a beer with Paul and the rest of his boat's crew after they had returned from an excited day's pursuit of yellowfin tuna or Mediterranean marlin. One of the funniest, sweetest men she'd ever met, he'd made her cry with laughter with his knack for telling stories; there was nothing he liked better than to have a crowd in stitches. Those laughter-filled days seemed a long time ago now, another lifetime. Another life. 'I'm OK.' She hesitated, then added, 'I came to remember Giorgio. But I can't seem to feel close to him.'

His eyes shone with compassion. 'You find him some-where, maybe not where you're looking. I think of him today too, at Ghar Lapsi. A good man, Giorgio Zammit, and we always raise a drink to him on the boat.'

She could imagine them, some of Giorgio's many friends, joking in the sunshine over their rods and nets and noisome

312

bait as they raised their cans of beer to Giorgio and fished from the little boat that lurched on the waves.

He said, 'It's good to see you in Malta again. I remember you when I attend mass.'

'You're kind.' She managed a smile at the thought that he was praying for her. 'Give my love to your wife Massie. I hope she doesn't mind cooking all those fish.'

'You want some?' He gestured towards his keep net, his mischievous eyes twinkling now. 'Put them in your handbag. They stop wriggling by the time you get home.'

The echo of his gentle humour helped her ignore aching knees as she climbed the steep rock steps back to the car.

Once she'd driven back to Sliema, she left Raymond's car in his parking space in the street behind the office but when she went to return the keys she could see Raymond through the large windows and he was talking to Richard and Adam, who was perched sideways on a desk. After a moment's hesitation, she turned and strode away without letting any of them know she was back.

A twenty-minute walk through the Sliema streets brought her to The Chalet, Ghar id-Dud, its pier-like skeleton still reaching into the sea and meeting the waves as it had done for decades, letting the sea gradually wear it away. Her hair writhed in the wind that blew on-shore, stinging her eyes as it obstructed her vision, and she zipped up her jacket.

There was an even bigger sea on this side of the island than there had been at Ghar Lapsi, green rollers smashing angrily against the pilings. The waves submerged the surrounding rocks, spewing spray that rose high enough to be blown onto the promenade thirty feet above, one wave subsiding with a hiss of streaming water as the next roared over its head. It wasn't calm enough for teenagers to leap joyfully from The Chalet today.

Judith selected one of the green-painted benches furthest back, out of range of the spray, and sat down.

It had begun here.

Giorgio had materialised at her elbow one day to enjoy her fascination with the kids and their perilous descent into the sea. Then he'd started lingering to intercept her. She'd begun to watch for him. He'd enchanted his way into her heart with his brown-velvet eyes.

But there was no sense of him here now.

Back at Richard and Erminia's house, Erminia had made *kawlata*, a thick stew of pork and sausages with vegetables. 'Mm,' said Judith, kissing her aunt. 'My favourite.'

Erminia twinkled. 'Really? I had forgotten.'

'Ha. She made it for you especially,' said Richard, packing a generous portion into his rotund body, talking cheerfully about the day, the weather, the rough wind. Erminia chimed in occasionally with tales about their grandchildren.

Adam ate quietly.

Despite the gorgeous *kawlata*, Judith could scarcely eat at all. Her insides fluttered and her head ached. She'd got precisely nowhere today and was no nearer to knowing what to do about the crucifix.

When the crockery had been cleared away, Adam thanked Erminia charmingly for the wonderful meal, then his eyes went to Judith. 'Fancy a walk to the marina? I thought I'd get a look at those floating palaces.'

She managed a quick smile. 'I'm afraid I have to see someone and I think they'll be coming home from work

314

about seven.' Maltese shops commonly stayed open into the early evening.

His expression closed down. He turned away.

She pressed the cool back of her hand against her aching forehead and touched his arm. 'I could use some company, though.'

After a moment, he smiled. 'That would be me.'

# Chapter Twenty-Seven

The house Judith led Adam to was set back slightly from the pavement and was packed tightly against its neighbours. It had one upstairs balcony and square windows with green shutters. A few stone steps led up to a front door of varnished wood and a longer flight went down to the basement. Judith had known on which street Johanna and Giorgio's daughters lived and Erminia had discovered for her which house was theirs.

Now, standing outside, heart thumping, Judith took a deep breath. Throughout her time with Giorgio, the figures of his estranged family had lurked in the shadows; part of Giorgio's past that, she'd been shown quite plainly, didn't concern her. But now she was about to make them real, give them faces and voices. Feelings.

The wind was gusting, bringing the temperature down to one that was low for a Maltese May. In fact, it was quite like being back in Northamptonshire. Adam's warm fingers slid around her chilly hand and she looked up to see concern in his eyes.

'Don't put yourself through this – you don't have to,'

he said. 'Why should you challenge these people who feel antipathy towards you? The time for that was when Giorgio was alive and there might have been some purpose to it. You can keep the crucifix – it was given to you – or send it to them by messenger. Or stuff it through the letterbox and run away! Whatever you feel is right.'

'But I don't know, that's the point,' she murmured. 'I used to be certain about things. Giorgio was trapped in a state of separation; it was unfortunate and unfair but he'd parted from Johanna a long time before I came on the scene. That had been her decision, too. So far as I was concerned, we were blamelessly in love. When Cass gave me the crucifix, I took it as my due. It was a part of Giorgio when I needed a part of him most, he'd worn it every day and it was as if it represented his heart.' She shivered. 'But now . . . I'm not quite sure why I was so convinced I was due anything.'

He pulled her lightly to him, sharing his body heat. 'Then take a little more thinking time,' he suggested.

She let herself sag against his tall, lithe body, closing her eyes and thinking how good it was to have contact with him. Then she straightened. It wasn't common in Malta to get physical in the street. She raised her chin. 'No, I have to do something about this. It's a weight on my shoulders. Will you wait here for me?'

When he nodded, she climbed slowly up to the front door. A small, thin woman in her mid-thirties answered the bell, her eyes turning to black pebbles the instant they lit on Judith. She made a show of looking down her nose. 'Yes?'

Judith pushed her hands into her pockets in case they began to shake. Facing her lover's widow was less easy than she'd supposed it would be. 'Johanna Zammit?'

The slightest of nods.

'I'm Judith McAllister. May I see Alexia, please?'

After a long stare, Johanna turned away, shouting into the depths of the house in Maltese. Judith caught the words for 'now' and 'woman'. Then a young woman, barely more than a girl, clattered down the stairs into the hall and stood, staring with hostility at Judith. She and her mother were very alike: slight and small, cheeks hollow, lips narrow and held in straight lines, hair glossy with chestnut lights.

Judith began, 'I'm—'

'I know who you are,' the young woman said.

Judith swallowed. 'You wrote to me—'

'And you've brought to me my father's crucifix? Thank you.' The girl was icily polite.

Slowly, Judith pulled the familiar weight from her pocket, the chain pooling in her palm.

Alexia reached out – but Judith closed her hand.

The young woman's eyes flashed angrily. 'My mother says I am to have it! You have no right.' She made a move almost as if she were going to grasp Judith's hand and prise it open.

Judith thrust both her hands back into her pockets. Her voice shook. 'I can see why your mother would like you to have it. But, of course, I must see the will, just to check *in law* who it belongs to.'

'That is me.' Johanna spoke suddenly. 'As he left this house to me. Us.' Then her eyes moved to a point behind Judith. 'You have a . . . friend with you?' Her voice was soft with scorn.

Judith glanced around. Adam had moved closer, his hair blowing over his eyes, his brows straight lines of concern. Johanna's tone contrived to make it sound as if Judith had, inappropriately, brought her new lover to this delicate

318

meeting with her dead lover's wife and child. It didn't make her any more comfortable that, basically, it was what she'd done.

'He's . . .' She searched for an explanation that wasn't exactly a lie. 'He's my friend.'

She turned to the Zammit ladies. 'I'll give the crucifix to the person it belongs to but you must agree that I need proof. What if Maria or Agnello or Saviour tell me it belongs to them?'

Sharply, Johanna said, 'It is not your business—'

She broke off as a car pulled up outside and a girl in her mid-teens bundled out, calling thanks in Maltese and leaping for the front steps. Pulling up suddenly, she giggled as she realised she'd almost run full-tilt into a stranger. '*Skuzi*, madam.'

'*Ma gara xejn.*' *It's of no consequence.* Judith managed a smile, moving aside to let the girl through.

With a word of thanks, the girl darted indoors, past Johanna and Alexia. Then she turned to smile again.

'Oh!' The smile was replaced by surprise, realisation, curiosity as the identity of this evening visitor obviously dawned on her. But without the hostility of her mother and sister. 'Oh . . .' she breathed, again.

'You must be Lydia?' Judith's heart clenched as she studied Giorgio's youngest child; the laughing eyes and a smile that made people smile back, the round chin and wide cheekbones. The thick, black hair. Even the angle at which she held her head.

For the first time since coming back, she felt Giorgio's presence.

Johanna rounded on her daughter with a flurry of Maltese; Judith caught '*tard*', late, and '*xoghol*', work. Probably she hadn't done her homework today. With one

319

last candid appraisal of the visitor, Lydia disappeared into the house.

Judith gazed after her. Then she returned her attention to Johanna and Alexia. 'No doubt you have a copy of the will? I expect it's in Maltese but what I can't understand myself I can certainly get translated by my aunt Erminia.'

Johanna shrugged. 'I don't have it.'

'That's a pity.' With a smile, Judith turned away.

Walking down the street, she finally allowed herself to tremble. Adam took her into a bar on the corner of the street and bought her brandy, curving her hand around the balloon glass and helping her to lift it to her lips, his leg against hers, his arm along the back of her chair. She dropped her cheek against his shoulder. 'That was horrible.'

He said again, 'You don't have to put yourself through this. Cass gave you the cross as something to remember him by.'

She groaned. 'I've been thinking hard about that. It's a romantic premise, but . . .' Her voice was muffled by his jacket. 'I have other things he bought me when we were together. A necklace, a picture. I'm afraid I may have had my share of Giorgio.'

Beneath her cheek, his shoulder rose and fell on a sigh. 'Difficult, hmm?'

She pulled back to look into his face to see if she could decipher the feelings that went with that neutral response but Adam had carefully cleared his expression. She straightened up. 'Let's have a couple of drinks before going back to Richard's.'

The following day, Judith went on foot to see Cass. This time she went without Adam, knowing the conversation would flow better if she were alone. The wind had dropped and the sunshine on her shoulders felt good as she trod the bustling narrow pavements up to High Street, off Tower Road, the gracious area where Giorgio's uncle and aunt lived. Both Maltese and English filled the air, along with the rumble of slow-moving traffic.

Cass, when she saw it was Judith knocking at her highly polished door, looked as if she'd swallowed a scorpion.

'Sorry,' Judith offered, not particularly apologetically. 'But I'm back.' Today, she made no effort to embrace the older woman.

They studied one another. It was the first time Judith had seen Cass without make-up, although her dress and sandals were as smart as ever. Running a smoothing hand over her neat chignon, Cass frowned and plunged into the conversation she obviously knew to be coming. 'I should never have given it to you.'

'I expect you've regretted it,' Judith acknowledged carefully.

Wariness was replaced by Cass's wry smile, the one that Judith remembered from happy evenings in restaurants with Giorgio. 'Many times. I was emotional but it was a stupid thing to do. I should have known that Maria would notice it was missing – she would count the tea leaves in the pack to make sure they're all there, that one.'

Judith relaxed at the warmer expression on Cass's face. 'Did you get into lots of trouble?'

Cass rolled her eyes. 'Enough.' Her hand was hooked onto the door handle but she made no effort to invite Judith in. 'Saviour was not pleased with me. He said I'd embarrassed him.'

Judith was sorry to hear it. 'How did he know it was you?'

Cass flushed. 'Once she realised it was missing, Maria

321

talked of nothing else for weeks. Saviour began to notice how guilty I looked every time she began. He says he can read me like a book.' She almost smiled at this last, as if quietly pleased.

Judith shifted her position on the step, trying to peep past Cass's shoulder to the tiled hall. 'Is Saviour here?'

The wary expression flashed back onto Cass's face. 'He's working on his old car.'

'I was hoping to see him.'

A long hesitation, Cass's dark eyes fixed on Judith's face as if trying to read her mind. Then she stood back. 'Please come in.'

The house was beautiful. A pale-grey marble staircase swept upwards from the square hall past round windows. In the *salott*, the formal sitting room, the furniture was either heavy and polished or of painted wood. Two stuffed birds stared down from atop a cabinet and turquoise glass ornaments shone like the sea. Cass led her through the *salott* and then a central courtyard dotted with spiky palms, back into the house and through a formal dining room, then out again to a tall gate. Judith almost reeled from the gleaming grandeur of Cass and Saviour's dwelling. It felt like a little palace. They must be pretty comfortably off.

Once outside the gates, they approached a garage that seemed to have been built under the side of another house with a drive that was so steep it was almost unfeasible. The black-painted doors were concertina-folded inside against the white walls.

A man was up to his elbows in the engine of an elderly white Mercedes, oil making black gloves on his hands and smearing his forehead. His clothes, old and baggy, were equally soiled, especially where his shirt strained to contain a belly that suggested a love of food. He didn't seem a natural match for neat and polished Cass but he had the look of someone happy and absorbed in his task.

Until he saw Judith.

He stared for several moments, his hand unfaltering as it worked in the depths of the car engine. He awarded her a cautious nod and then shifted his gaze to look hard at his wife.

Hoping she wasn't dragging Cass into deeper trouble, Judith plunged straight in. 'I'm Judith McAllister.'

He nodded again, straightening, picking up a rag every bit as dirty as the hands he wiped with it, all without speaking.

She held his gaze. 'I'm looking for information. I've come to you because I believe you're a man to give me an honest answer.'

His expression narrowed and he tilted his chin. 'Maybe.' His tone suggested: *or maybe not*. His tone was cold.

Behind Judith, Cass whispered, '*Giorgio kien ihobbha*.' *Giorgio loved her*.

After another pause, Saviour inclined his head. 'My wife take you to the house, Mrs McAllister, and I wash my hands.'

It was ten minutes before he joined them, by which time Judith was seated with Cass at a beautiful mosaic table of rich reds and greens in the shade of the courtyard, the *bitha interna*, a drink of cold peach juice beside her.

Saviour sat down in a dark-grey iron chair that wouldn't be stained by contact with his oily gear and regarded her. His eyes were unsettlingly direct, as if he knew more than she was aware.

With a deep breath, she began her explanation. The crucifix, how comforted she'd been to receive it when grief was crushing her and how it had reassured her for many months, shifting against the skin at the base of her throat. 'But then I had a letter from Alexia Zammit.' She paused in case he'd like the opportunity to join the conversation.

He just waited, silently.

Judith eased her throat with the deliciously cold juice. 'Alexia asked for Giorgio's cross back and for the first time I questioned my right to it. Perhaps I should have done that sooner but I was caught up in my own grief. But now that Alexia's claimed it, it's worrying me. I need to know what to do.'

Finally, Saviour spoke. 'The crucifix is valuable.'

'I suppose so. It's gold.' She nodded. The monetary value wasn't the issue and they all knew it.

'But more, it is old. When my wife wish to give you a thing of Giorgio, she no realise this belong to Giorgio's *nannu*. My father. Agnello give to Giorgio when he become a man. And before that?' He shrugged eloquently. 'Perhaps the father of my father.'

Judith felt instantly that he was speaking the truth. There was something direct about Saviour Zammit that made instinctive trust easy. She chose her words. 'I've visited Johanna and Alexia. They tell me the crucifix has been left to Johanna, who wishes to pass it to her daughter.' She allowed the merest suggestion of cynicism to creep into her tone.

She waited. He waited longer.

She looked into his olive-skinned face, the creases and folds of age and met his gaze. 'I asked to see the will. They said they couldn't show it to me. I need to be convinced of who owns the crucifix before I hand it over. So I came to you. Who does the cross belong to?'

The sun was bright across his face, engraving the lines

more deeply. Bright flecks glowed in his dark eyes as he stared at her with surprise. 'You come to Malta to ask this?'

She nodded.

'*Is-Sagramewt!*' An old man's exclamation of astonishment.

Honesty got the better of her. 'Well, partly, that's why I came. And to decide whether to stay in England, or to come back here.'

'You let Maria think you go live England.' He sounded curious rather than accusing.

Faintly, she grinned. 'I went. I didn't go because she told me to and I didn't say I'd stay.'

He gave one of his slow nods and sank into his thoughts, sipping juice from a thick tumbler, the oil of many hours of playing with engines edging his fingernails and defining every grain of the skin of his fingers. At length, he stirred. 'You give money to Giorgio for a bus?' He sounded suddenly tired.

She felt her cheeks warm. 'I was a private investor in the company, yes.'

'And me.' His voice had become deep and sombre.

She stared at him. It hadn't occurred to her that Giorgio might have involved his family with his business. In fact, she hadn't given a thought to any other investors.

'You lose a lot a moncy?' he asked.

She debated telling him to mind his own business. But, if he'd invested himself, there didn't seem much point in hiding anything. She shrugged. 'Very nearly everything except for my house in England and what I invested in my uncle's business.'

He grunted, glaring ferociously, shaking his head. 'He is a silly man when he do this. A . . .' He looked at his wife and spoke in Maltese.

'An optimist,' she supplied.

'And *sappitutto*!'

'Know-all,' Cass translated.

Saviour tossed up his hands and his eyes grew moist. 'But still, he does not mean this bad thing to happen to us.'

Judith smiled, painfully. 'I know.'

Sorrow took charge of Saviour's face. 'But he know, before he die, that he make a mistake with the insurance.' Saviour held up an admonishing finger. 'A mistake, only. Not a cheat. When, after the company was involved in an accident and he discover no insurance, he has horror. Horror, yes?' He checked with his wife. Silently, Cass nodded. Saviour turned back to Judith, a sheen of sweat beneath his flashing eyes. 'And scare. He has scare. He come to me . . .' Saviour's voice broke and he pushed his finger and thumb fiercely against his eyes.

Quietly, Cass excused herself.

Judith looked away to let the proud old man compose himself. Consolingly, she said, 'I'm glad it was a mistake.'

'He no mean to cheat you,' he repeated in a voice that rasped. Saviour wiped his eyes and stared absently at the houses that rose around, the balconies and outside staircases made of stone, the sky above, china blue. He let out a long, long sigh, spreading his gnarled and grimy hands. 'He come to me, but too many money is needed. Those last days he has . . .' He hesitated, searching in the air with his fingers for the word. 'He has the mood. Not so many smiles.' He demonstrated with a smile of his own and Judith felt that it was something not seen too often.

Shakily, she drained the last of her peach juice. 'You must be right. He was awkward – moody – with me because I couldn't dive with him on Saturday. Unnecessarily moody. He refused to wait until Sunday and said he had to work.'

'If he wait for Sunday, he lives now.'

She didn't need reminding.

Cass reappeared with a tray of small cups and coffee in a chrome pot. Saviour tossed his cupful back in one steaming draught, then said, abruptly, 'Possessions, they go to his parents.'

It took several moments for Judith to appreciate what he was saying. 'His parents?'

Saviour nodded. 'I know how Giorgio left his matters and his possessions belong to Agnello and Maria.'

'Thank you,' she managed, slowly absorbing the knowledge that she'd have to speak to Giorgio's parents. A heart-sinking thought.

Examining his grey hands, Saviour spoke in Maltese to Cass, too rapidly for Judith to pick up any of it. Then he rose. 'Goodbye, Mrs McAllister. I wish you well.' He nodded and crossed the courtyard with a rolling, bandy-legged gait, back in the direction of the Mercedes.

Cass waited until he was out of earshot. 'He said, you have honour.' She sounded awed.

Judith needed time to think. She spent the next day quietly with Adam, wandering around the yacht marinas to admire the sleek craft bobbing on the waves, chatting and pausing to take photos.

In the evening, Richard and Erminia had to go out to a party at Birzebbuga, down in the south-east corner of the island. The party was to celebrate the engagement of one of Erminia's legion of great-nephews to a girl who they both agreed was beautiful and accomplished but

327

neither could remember her name. At any other time Judith would have joined the celebration but tonight preferred to eat at a *pizzerija* along The Strand, with Adam. They sat on the first floor, beside an enormous plate-glass window overlooking the creek, and shared pizza, dough balls and several beers.

Adam was quiet. In fact, it seemed as if quietness had become a permanent state with him.

Judith tried to bring him out. He smiled when she made jokes and listened when she spoke but, as they strolled back beside the slack, black, rippling water of the creek, she had to accept that he wished to dwell on thoughts of his own rather than listening to another airing of hers.

She let them into Richard and Erminia's silent house, shutting out the *zirzar* of the cicadas as she closed the tall door and led him into the large and homely kitchen where an enormous window dominated one wall. She turned and reached for his hands. 'I've been neglecting you and you're getting fed up with it.'

His answer was light. 'That's what you get for inviting yourself along on someone's quest.' But he didn't manage a smile.

As usual, she felt him slide his right hand out of her grasp. She settled her hands on his chest, instead. 'It's true that I've had a lot on my mind.'

He shrugged, staring past her and through the window into the black night. 'It's more than that. You're a different person in Malta. At least, you have been since you focused on the crucifix problem. You wanted to sort your life out, I understand that. It was my fault, I offered to come, to be available when you needed me. You never promised that the reverse would apply.'

Guilt flushed through her. 'I am sorry. It's just this decision's been on my mind. I didn't think it'd take so long—'

Abruptly, he stooped and shut her words off with his lips.

Surprised by the swift, brief kiss, she tried to explain. 'I'm not a different person, not really. It's more that I have an unusual situation to deal with. Different and difficult and unhappy. I thought the way forward would be obvious if I was back on the island but . . .'

His forehead was scored by a frown and he looked almost angry. Once again he stopped her words with a quick, hard kiss.

She got the message. He'd had enough of hearing about her problems and was too polite to snap at her to shut up, for crying out loud. Perhaps she ought to be thoroughly affronted but she could see his point. She'd been self-absorbed and she couldn't blame him if he was sick of hearing her whine. Every problem she had, she took to him: her pain over Giorgio's death, worry for her mother, emptiness and fear over her son, even her exasperation with a well-meaning big sister.

Deliberately, slowly, she fitted her lips back to his. Soft lips, parted, offering a different kiss altogether. For an instant she felt the muscles in his shoulders gather as if he might pull away. But he stayed, opening his mouth as her tongue tip explored, participating, sliding his hand into the small of her back and pulling her close.

Her heartbeat kicked up several gears. She let herself wallow in his embrace and the feel of his firm body against hers. She tightened her hold on him, murmuring against his mouth, 'Take me to bed, Adam.'

He groaned, thrusting against her and making her gasp.

'It's not the right time. You're caught up with Giorgio and his family. Your head's with them.'

'All of me's here,' she hissed, thrusting back. 'From the neck up as well as from the neck down.'

Against her mouth he murmured, 'You shouldn't make me want you like this, Jude.'

She kissed his neck and nuzzled beneath his ear. 'I've never really understood why not.'

There was no long, delicious disrobing. Adam just grabbed her by the hand and raced her upstairs, hustling her into her bedroom, hauling her shirt over her head, snapping off the button at the waist of her trousers with his impatience. 'I want you,' he murmured, as if she might not have gathered that. His breathing was hot and uneven, gusting out of him and fluttering back in. He flung back the covers and lowered her to the sheet, then shucked off his jeans and T-shirt in two seconds.

She gasped as he let himself down on top of her, kissing, nibbling, rubbing against her, pulling impatiently at her underwear, whispering her name, kissing her eyelids, cheekbone, collarbone, breast, stroking his jaw against the softness of her stomach and touching her with his tongue to leave a cool trail.

Afterwards, moonlight shone into the room. Adam lay on his side, facing her.

She wriggled closer to him, seeking safe harbour in the curl of his body. 'I was beginning to think that would never happen again.'

'I've had the same thought.' He did his off-kilter half-smile.

Cautiously, she smiled back, made unsure by an odd note in his voice. 'You seemed fairly enthusiastic. Do you wish . . .?'

330

He kissed her forehead, then her hair. 'Wish you didn't make me want you? Perhaps,' he said enigmatically. 'I dragged you up here like a caveman. Had I better go back to my own room? Will you be embarrassed if Richard and Erminia realise we're in bed together?' Now the passion was over he seemed tired and beginning to withdraw.

She shook her head. 'They're so late that I should think one of Erminia's relatives has offered overnight hospitality.' She slipped her hand around his waist. 'I'm sorry I've been preoccupied.'

'I understand.' But he made a sound suspiciously like a sigh. 'It's what you came here for.'

She tried to be honest. 'Tomorrow, I must try to speak to Giorgio's mother, Maria.'

He began kissing her again, giving her mouth something to do other than tell him her plans.

Much later, when Judith was sliding off heavily into sleep, her back spooned against Adam's front, his bony, warm arms looped around her, she heard his voice in the darkness. He said, 'It's a small country.'

'Malta? Of course.' When she was less sleepy, she could quote him facts about the Maltese archipelago, size at widest and longest points, population, visitor numbers and even rainfall.

'A small world,' he added. 'Far away from Britain.' He sounded wistful and she wanted to talk, to reassure him if he needed it.

But her dreams whooshed up to carry her away.

# Chapter Twenty-Eight

When morning came, Judith found herself in bed alone. Even before opening her eyes she knew that Adam's warmth was absent.

She unglued her eyelids and stretched, gingerly waking muscles that had been exercised by a night of lovemaking. She smiled.

'About time.' His voice came from the doorway. 'I was going to wake you, if only to check that I hadn't killed you.' Dressed already in black jeans and a black shirt with the sleeves rolled up, he'd brought her a late-morning brunch of ham, cheese and crusty bread, with tea for them both in two of Erminia's pretty butterfly-strewn mugs.

She laughed, hoisting herself up against the headboard, letting the dawn-pink cotton covers fall to her waist. 'I thought I stood up to the action pretty well. It wasn't me who had to leap out of bed and cavort about the room because of cramp.'

'No, I suppose somebody was needed to stay in bed and giggle.' He leant forward and kissed her naked breast, his lips hot.

She caught the back of his head, stroking his hair into his neck. 'Come back to bed. I promise never to giggle again.'

Slowly, he freed himself, kissed the corners of her mouth and smiled, crookedly. 'Jude, if I get into bed with you again, I might never get out. And I don't want you to think that all I'm good for is no-strings sex.' He pushed himself back to his feet and left her to eat, shower and dress, pondering his words and his air of vulnerability.

When she caught up with him he was out in the midday sunshine, rocking on two legs of a chair and studying a book of drawings by M. C. Escher. He was fascinated by the work of Escher, that master of mathematical mosaic, optical illusion and reflection. It was one of his favourite Sunday treats to listen to The Hollies or The Eagles while he gazed at the masterly work.

'Lizards or geckos?' he asked, indicating a drawing where unlikely-looking reptiles appeared to walk in and out of a mosaic. His hair blew over his forehead and he pushed it back.

She laid her hand upon the strength of his forearm. 'Adam, I don't want you to think that I only want you for—'

He covered her hand quickly with his and squeezed it. 'Don't let's do this now.'

She squeezed back, wanting, needing to make him listen. 'But I just want to—'

'Please, don't.' He snatched his hand away and turned a page so roughly that it should have ripped from the book's spine.

He'd never raised his voice to her like that before, and she recoiled. 'Why are you angry with me?'

His voice softened, but his gaze remained fixed upon

his book. 'I'm angry at myself, not you, which is why it's not the time to talk. I shouldn't have let sex cloud the issue. I turned basic, and I wish I hadn't.'

She waited for further illumination. 'You wish you hadn't because . . .?'

'Because it was amazing.'

She yearned to loop her arms about him but his rebuff kept her standing stiffly apart. 'Yes, it was. Absolutely amazing, and I don't regret it at all.' She was aware that she was using what her mother would call her 'difficult voice'.

He turned a page to a drawing of a single drop of water capturing a world of reflections. Gruffly, he said, 'Judith's satisfied with the way things turned out, so that's OK, then.'

She'd never encountered him in this mood before: prickly, rueful and troubled. Until now he'd seemed prepared to go at her pace, to wait for her while she traversed a rockier road than his. Misery clouded her vision. She'd hoped their return to lovemaking was a breakthrough, a step forward, but he was treating it like . . . like an error of judgement. 'That's not what I meant.'

With deadly calm he said, 'How many times do I have to repeat myself before you believe that I don't want to talk?'

There was no point persisting while he was churning with anger. It was better if she went to see Giorgio's parents and got that over with. She longed for the saga of the crucifix to be done. When she returned, hopefully he'd be his normal self. They could talk honestly without ghosts and missions hanging in the air between them. She'd already made up her mind to tell him that she loved the island but she'd realised that, for her, it was part of the past. It was hard to get any of that over when he refused to talk. Stiffly, she took a step away from him. 'I have to go out for a while.'

He turned a page slowly to a picture of a house with an enormously bulbous balcony in its centre. 'Thought you might.'

Softly, she said, 'I don't think I'll be very long.'

A silence drew out. As she turned away, he said, 'I'm going to see if I can change my flight. Leave a bit earlier.'

She hesitated. 'I'm sorry you feel like that.' And then, when he didn't respond, she added, 'Change both tickets, won't you? I'll go when you do.' He quirked an eyebrow so she took that for assent.

The sun was pounding the crown of Judith's head by the time she climbed the hilly section of Tower Road to take the turn-off for the house of Agnello and Maria Zammit, not far from Cass and Saviour's home. She was surprised how the temperature was making her head throb, considering it was only May. She was reacting like an English tourist, wiping sweat from her forehead with exaggerated care in case she increased the pulsing ache that was building there, making squinty eyes at the sun and cursing herself for not wearing her sunglasses and hat.

The Zammit residence was in a tall and narrow street built of creamy limestone near the twin bell towers and cupola of the charming Stella Maris parish church, 'the star of the sea', built so that long-ago sailors coming to and from the harbour could always have it within their sight. Although several houses in the street boasted a traditional *gallerija* or enclosed balcony painted dark green or plum red, there was no comparison between these residences and Cass and Saviour's. Agnello evidently hadn't made the money that his little brother had. His house looked as if it would fit into Saviour's four times.

She sighed as she approached, remembering Maria Zammit's barely contained fury at their last meeting and wondered, wryly, whether she ought to check that Stella Maris Church offered sanctuary to non-Catholics.

The front door of the Zammit house was panelled. The highly polished brass knocker was in the shape of something that looked like the result of an intimate moment between a sea monster and a dolphin. Before she had a chance to change her mind, Judith seized it by its bulbous head and rapped sharply.

And, in a few moments, she was face to face with Giorgio's mother.

Maria looked first shocked and then irritated when her gaze rested on Judith. Her dress bore a small, eye-aching geometric design, her hair was almost entirely silver now and she wore small wire-framed glasses that matched it. Her dark eyes narrowed into the lined skin around them and she gave a small, ladylike sniff of disapproval.

The sniff made Judith feel like just giving the whole damned thing up. She was tired of being a target for antagonism. Why should she continue to knock on doors and force people to speak to her who blatantly didn't wish to? She could return to Richard's house and spend whatever time was left being a tourist with Adam before getting on the flaming plane for England whenever he'd arranged. Perhaps she should have done as Adam had suggested and shove the crucifix through the letterbox before running away.

But that was ridiculous. For goodness' sake, she was a perfectly respectable woman and not prepared to act as if she were ashamed of her existence. She pulled herself up to her full height – considerably more than Maria's – and lifted her chin. 'Good morning.'

Maria Zammit's muttered, 'Good morning,' was icy.

It had been in Judith's mind to suggest that they take coffee and cake together in a café, like mature and civilised women with a matter to discuss. But seeing Maria's expression, she decided to save her breath.

Instead, she reached inside her pocket. 'I've brought you this.' The gold cross and chain, getting duller by the day, hung between her fingers.

Slowly, as if she couldn't quite believe it wouldn't be whisked away again, Maria Zammit reached out and took Giorgio's crucifix. Kissing the suffering Jesus upon it she crossed herself, closing her eyes in an obvious moment of pain, as Judith had done so many times. The eyes reopened and she frowned, plainly baffled.

Judith frowned back, shading her eyes against the harsh sunlight slicing into the street. Her headache was growing more intense by the second. 'For a while I believed it was OK for me to keep it but I'm told it belongs to you. Saviour explained what was in Giorgio's will.' She turned to go.

Then she swung back, ignoring the way her headache seemed to move separately, painfully, as anger fuelled a sudden desire to make her point. 'I know that you blame me for his death but I made your son's life happy for his final few years. Perhaps, in time, you'll come to think of that.'

Decidedly, Maria shook her head. 'You take him under the sea.'

Letting her breath out on a long sigh, Judith hunched her shoulders in frustration. 'Not that day, I didn't. I asked him to wait for me but he refused.' And then, more gently,

'I agree that if I'd been there, it wouldn't have happened. I believe that, as you obviously do. But I asked him . . .' Her voice caught in her throat as a sudden vision of Giorgio blazed across her mind, the angry frown lines digging grooves between his black brows as he'd shrugged off her pleas to postpone his dive. She cleared her throat. 'I tried to make him see he was a novice and would be safer with me. But he'd made up his mind. *He* made up *his* mind. If you want to blame me, I understand that it might help to make me a focus for your grief but I tried my hardest to keep him safe.'

She'd probably said too much and said it too rapidly for Maria's instant comprehension. And what use was there in pounding over the same old ground again, anyway? Maria hadn't believed her a year ago in the hospital so why should she be more receptive now?

Hitching her bag up on her shoulder, Judith thrust her hands into her jacket pockets, her fingertips finding the empty corner where the crucifix had lain in a tangle for the last days. She wasn't sure yet whether it was a loss or a relief but she'd drawn a line under the whole saga, and would, in time, feel better.

As she turned away, the ache in her head became a dagger of pain and the world suddenly shimmered and pooled around her.

She halted, screwing up her eyes. The air was sparkling as if Tinkerbell had just flown around the edges of the buildings, making them glisten and warp. Her heart sank. It was a feeling she hadn't had for a long time but . . . oh, no. Migraine. The sunshine on the fairy dust made her eyeballs hurt but she forced her feet to move, left, right, up the street, their echo launching lance-like pains above her eyes, across the bridge of her nose and her cheekbones. Her ears began to ache, the chatter of nearby children making them hurt, car engines pounded as they passed in low gear and the voices of three women calling to one another from their upstairs windows sounded like howls.

She hadn't had a migraine since her teens but she hadn't forgotten how savagely they used to attack. Shading her eyes, she felt the pavement turn to sponge beneath her feet. Bile rose up into her throat.

Putting a hand to a wall to steady herself, she breathed in through her mouth, trying to quell the nausea as the world dipped and swung. Hopefully, she wouldn't suffer the humiliation of being sick in the street. If previous attacks were anything to go by, she had a couple of hours of this misery before the sickness that would signify the end of the migraine swept over her. Sweat burst out over her face, in the hollow of her throat and down her spine. She swallowed hard and breathed deeply.

Engrossed in her own discomfort, she didn't notice that Maria had followed her until her voice came from behind. 'Hey!'

Pain cannoned about Judith's skull as she half turned.

Maria was holding out the crucifix to her. Agnello waited a step behind his wife. He'd lost a lot of weight since Judith had seen him last and deeper lines had dug themselves into his weathered skin. Grief did that to you.

Dumbfounded, Judith squinted at the glint of gold, then at Maria's expressionless face. 'What . . .?' She winced as the pain above her eyes grew boots and kicked at the top of her head.

Impatiently, Maria shook the crucifix in Judith's direction.

Slowly, Judith put out her hand. Maria dropped it into her palm. The chain pooled with the cross lying crookedly on top.

'But . . .?' Nausea pulsed in rhythm with the pounding in her head. Focusing through the fairy dust became harder. 'Are you giving it to me?'

Maria gave a tiny nod, then a huge shrug, reminding Judith sharply of Giorgio. 'It was give to you.'

Judith tried to think through a band tightening around her forehead. 'But should it have been given to me?'

Maria began to turn away. 'Perhaps yes. Perhaps no.' Agnello sent Judith a curious look, nodded, and followed his wife.

Shaking, Judith managed to cross into the shade but her pain increased until she felt as if massive talons gripped her head and her vision danced and fizzed. She sank down against the base of the wall, legs like water, desperate just to be still, to be out of the sun, to close her aching eyes. She prayed that the church bells wouldn't begin to peal. Even the thought made her stomach heave.

She was so taken up with her discomfort that she jumped as a hand grasped her shoulder. The movement made her feel as if her skull had broken into shards and rasped sickeningly against her brain.

'You are ill?' asked a gruff female voice.

Judith opened her eyes to slits to see Maria Zammit had returned and was frowning over her. The pattern of her dress made Judith feel as if she was spinning. 'A little,' she mumbled. 'Migraine, I think. I'll have to wait for it to go off.' She let her eyes close again.

Maria clicked her tongue and made a noise, '*Tsh, tsh.* You don't stay here.'

'I'll go soon. It'll pass. I just need . . .' Judith covered her eyes with her hands, craving darkness.

With another click of her tongue, Maria turned away

and then there was a man beside Judith. Agnello. 'I put you in my car?' he said.

Judith swallowed convulsively at the thought of being shaken about on Malta's busy roads. 'Thank you, but I'm afraid of being sick.'

'OK.' She felt a hand under her elbow. 'Come, you have a quiet room and lie down. Yes? We phone your friends.'

She forced her eyes to open slightly to check it was really Maria and Agnello helping her as, one either side, they pulled her gently to her feet. All she could think about was the blinding headache and vertigo that was the migraine. It was certainly no time for a prideful refusal. 'That would be . . . a relief. Thank you.'

They helped her across the road, through their door and into a small room with a long sofa. She was pathetically grateful just to lie down and close her eyes as her unlikely white knights closed the thick russet curtains with stealthy movements and fetched her a blessedly soft pillow for her poor head. She managed to give them Richard's home phone number, but they received no answer when they called. Adam must have gone out. She elected not to phone Richard Elliot Estate, although at least one of her cousins would no doubt be there. She could live without their cousinly ministrations. She wanted Adam.

As she couldn't get him, she closed her eyes and gave herself up to simple gratitude for the cool, dim room. Gently, gradually, she relaxed. Once she was motionless the pain in her eyes, temples, cheekbones and the top of her head settled to a lancing throb and the rolling nausea began to subside.

She dozed uneasily, torn between appreciation and anxiety. She'd found a haven but it was in what had, until now, been hostile territory. Fervently, she wished she could click her fingers and find herself back in the bed she'd abandoned so late this morning . . . preferably with Adam's comforting arms around her.

The church bells began, sliding into her dreams as she dozed.

Visions flickered through her mind. The graceful Stella Maris parish church. Giorgio's funeral mass, which she'd only seen in her imagination. Dark suits and dresses. Solemn faces, lines of grief, tears.

And, back down the years, Johanna beautiful in a white lace dress, Giorgio handsome in a new suit, impossibly young and smiling despite Johanna's pregnancy lurking beneath her dress. Family members proud that they were doing the right thing. Nobody knowing that Giorgio and Johanna would grow to dislike each other and one day the implacable sea would take Giorgio away.

Her eyes flickered. A frightening image formed of the sea welling up onto shore after him . . . Fresh pain banged through her head as she moved unwisely on the pillow. No. The sea wasn't to blame but the jet ski, roaring, racing into a diving zone. And Giorgio surfacing at the wrong instant . . .

Giorgio hadn't taken every precaution possible. She swirled the idea around her mind, testing it for soundness. No one could argue with the fact that he'd committed the sin, for a diver, of not respecting the boundaries of his own limitations. Armed with his brand-new open-water certificate, really quite a basic qualification, he'd put himself in peril and flouted advice.

Giorgio had known all about the consequences of the lapsed insurance policy. Perhaps fear at the consequences of his own mistake was what had made him reckless?

They'd never really know but he'd risked a life that was good, a life containing her love. He'd paid the price. They all had.

Because she'd blamed herself she'd let others blame her, too. The burden had been impossibly unwieldy.

Giorgio's image swam into her mind.

She smiled because the image of Giorgio was smiling. Of course, it would be; he smiled so often. The smile the image wore was the apologetic one he employed when his enthusiasms had overcome his common sense and everything had gone wrong – when he'd tried to speed up the cooking and burnt the meat; when he'd tried to force his way into traffic and pranged the car.

Sighing, she frowned, trying not to move her head although she was growing cramped, anxious not to reawaken the blinding pain.

Something felt strange because she was used to abrading her wounds and making certain that she could still feel the blame.

Forgiving herself was a new sensation. A relief. She smiled at the Giorgio of her imagination and said goodbye.

# Chapter Twenty-Nine

It was an hour later when Judith awoke from restless, fitful dreams of headache, heartache and Giorgio.

The tolling of the church bell was just reaching a resonant end and the house was filled with the aroma of frying onions. She could hear the murmur of voices, water running in a sink and the sawing of a bread knife. Experimentally, she opened her eyes. To her immense relief, the glittering fairy dust had gone. She tried rolling her head on the pillow. Bearable. Cautiously, she pushed herself upright. *Error!*

Nausea rose like a tide. Desperately, she launched to her feet and staggered from the room, following the smell of cooking to the kitchen and surprising Maria into dropping a wooden spatula. Mutely, Judith slapped a hand across her mouth and Maria immediately grasped the urgent nature of the problem.

'*Hawnhekk!* In here!' She hustled her into a downstairs shower room and Judith fell to her knees in front of the loo as the door closed.

Finally, when the last spasms had passed, Judith found

the migraine had passed also. She felt a residual giddiness and a sort of hangover but her vision had steadied and the violent headache had subsided. Sleep was still beckoning but that could come later.

Self-consciously, Judith made her way out to the kitchen. Maria turned away from wiping the table. She didn't smile but she didn't glare or frown either. Her voice was considerately soft. 'Do you recover?'

Judith's voice sounded thin. 'I'm much better, thank you. You've been so kind. I'm very grateful.'

Maria shrugged and clicked her tongue dismissively. Any kindness on her part was not up for discussion, evidently.

In the corner, Agnello shook out his newspaper and Judith noticed him for the first time. 'It is good. You are not ill. You want food?' He indicated a big saucepan.

Judith looked away hastily, despite not having eaten since the brunch she'd eaten with Adam. 'Really, no, thank you, I couldn't.' But she was grateful when Maria got her a tall glass of clear, cool water, which she made herself sip.

When she'd drunk a little, she put down the glass. 'Thank you for your kindness. I'll leave now.'

Maria nodded and walked her out to the street. 'You know the way to go?'

'Yes, thank you.' And Judith did. During this uncomfortable day and the ones that had preceded it, her way forward had become wonderfully plain and simple.

'We say goodbye.' Unexpectedly, Maria held out her hand.

Judith took it, gaining a curious comfort and feeling of closure from taking the small, rough and wrinkled hand of the woman who'd given Giorgio life. 'Goodbye. And thank you. Really.'

Maria took her hand back with a shrug, though her voice quivered with pain. 'I think of Giorgio.'

Judith settled her bag on her shoulder and prepared to head back towards Tower Road. 'Of course. So do I. He'll remain in our hearts and memories.'

Maria almost smiled as she turned away.

In a few minutes, Judith arrived once more at Johanna's door. The impact of knocking on the wood stuttered up her arm and into her fragile head.

She'd slept longer than she'd first imagined and it was evening now, mild and balmy. The sky had faded to the beautiful, ethereal lavender dusk Judith remembered so well. She waited on the top step. It probably wasn't as long as it felt before Johanna answered, gazing suspiciously out, her features sharpening.

Judith didn't bother trying to summon a smile, but ensured that her voice was pleasant and polite before letting it out to duel with Johanna. 'Would it be possible for me to speak briefly with Lydia, please?'

'Why?'

Judith evaded the question. 'A very quick word. I don't need to be alone with her but I do need to talk to her directly.'

Johanna looked thoughtful and didn't turn to call her daughter to the door. She stared silently at Judith, instead, as if trying to read her mind. Perhaps she would never have replied if Lydia hadn't come running downstairs as Judith waited on the well-swept steps.

'Hello,' said Judith, carefully.

'Oh!' said Lydia, exactly as she had last time. She looked intrigued, eyes agog.

Judith ignored Johanna's impatient tuts and addressed

Lydia, extracting her hand from her pocket, the crucifix looped between her fingers. 'Lydia, you know who I am. I've been to see your grandmother, your *nanna*, this afternoon, and she said I could keep this. But I'd like you to have it, instead.'

Pleasure blazed from Lydia's face as she took two rapid skips closer. 'It is for me?' She took what Judith offered unhesitatingly and with joy, her thick, dark hair framing her huge smile as she clutched her prize.

Judith smiled back. 'I think it's better if it stays in your family. Your uncle Saviour tells me it belonged to his father, and perhaps *his* father, too.' Then she turned to a wooden-faced Johanna and offered as much of an explanation for her actions as she was going to. 'She has a smile just like her father's.'

# Chapter Thirty

By the time she reached The Strand on the way to Richard's house, Judith was beginning to feel stronger.

Her headache had faded to tenderness, her legs had rediscovered the bones that were meant to be in them, her vision had cleared of fairy dust and the giddiness and sickness had vanished with it. Tourists were crowding the pavements and filling the cafés but the sound of their clatter and babble was bearable, even over the roar of the evening traffic.

Her detour to see Lydia had made her feel as if she'd put down a burden.

Strolling along beside the gently lapping sea creek, watching the boats bob at their moorings, she felt as if every step was one in a new direction. The right direction. The no-more-regrets direction.

The house was quiet as she let herself in through the warm kitchen redolent of the cosy evening meals. In the *salott,* she found Erminia knitting at great speed in the pool of light from a tall lamp, her eyes more often on the television than her red wool, which was nevertheless forming into the correct shape to clothe a grandchild next winter.

Her needles slowed when Judith walked into the sitting room. She exclaimed, 'Have you been lost? Adam has waited for you.'

Judith yawned as she dropped into a comfortable chair and explained about the migraine. She decided recounting her emotional and unexpected interactions with Giorgio's family could wait for another time. 'Isn't Adam here?' she asked. 'I suppose he's sloped off for a beer with Richard? I'll just make a sandwich, then, and have an early night.' It was frustrating that she wouldn't be able to speak to Adam tonight after all, to rest her fast-recovering head on his shoulder and tell him about her day. And, of course, that they must talk about themselves, now. However, she couldn't blame him for not hanging around all day for her to turn up again. He'd been fed-up enough with her and her mission before she'd left.

Erminia raised her eyebrows and began to cast off stitches with quick, agitated movements, her gaze fixed on Judith. 'He left a letter in your bedroom. Go read it now.'

'OK. Thanks.' Reluctantly, Judith clambered out of the depths of the comfy chair that had nestled her in its cushioned arms and yawned her way up the tiled stairs, desperately tired. She was forcibly reminded of the strength of the craving for sleep that went hand-in-hand with the misery of migraine. Her eyes began watering with every jaw-wrenching paroxysm.

Maybe she wouldn't even bother with a sandwich. If she just cleaned her teeth she could fling off her clothes and collapse into a comfy bed. Close her eyes. Stretch out, naked to better appreciate the welcome of those smooth, cool sheets.

349

In her room, the first thing she saw was a pale blue envelope waiting for her on her bedside table. *Jude* was written large on the front in Adam's familiar scrawl.

She ripped it open, still yawning, shaking out the folds of the note even as the fingers of her other hand began on the buttons of her shirt. Her room seemed considerably neater than when she'd left it this morning and she felt guilty if Erminia had felt the need to tidy up after her.

*Jude, I waited as long as I could because you said you wouldn't be long. But you were. No doubt you've been busy with things that don't concern me . . .*

Her latest yawn died mid-execution.

*Do you remember, last night, that I said Malta was a small world? I think I was coming to realise that you're going to stay safely within it. I'd love you to come back to the world that we've lived in together but I don't think you will. I'd love to think that someday you'll be ready to care for me in the way I care for you – but that seems unlikely too. Is it Malta that's called you back? Or the memories of Giorgio? I don't know. But your head has been somewhere else for the past few days and the rest of you seems poised to follow.*

*I suppose Malta was the life you chose and returning to Brinham was a knee-jerk reaction to a horrible episode. When I asked to spend this time with you, I thought there was a decent chance you'd put Giorgio behind you but, instead, I've watched you getting more and more involved in your past. Maybe I should have stayed at home and waited to see whether you returned.*

*Of course, we were very much together last*

*night in bed, and it's a night I'll carry with me forever – even though I'd sworn to myself I wouldn't sleep with you again unless things changed.*

*Lovely as the island is, I'm unhappy in Malta and have rearranged the flights for tonight.*

TONIGHT! Judith stared at the word, thunderstruck.

*But now you've stayed away all day, it seems as if I should've left your ticket as it was. If you don't make it, I'll pay for your replacement flight. I hope I'll see you when you're in Brinham.*
*Adam x*

Judith gazed at the sheet of paper in her hand. Her heartbeat halted and then started again with a giant pulse that almost burst her heart from her chest. Adam had gone home without her. She'd been so absorbed in the unsatisfactory business of trying to feel close to Giorgio in order to decide what he would have wanted her to do with the crucifix that she'd managed to push Adam away.

The single kiss beneath Adam's signature wasn't much comfort. After last night? The way his mouth had fed on hers? In a moment of painful clarity, she realised what last night had been about. Why Adam had broken his own rule to sleep with her.

He'd suspected that their lovemaking would prove to be a goodbye.

He'd gone back to Brinham *without her*.

Judith ran downstairs and burst back into the living room. 'When did he go?' she demanded of her aunt.

'More than half an hour.' Erminia had obviously been

351

waiting for her to reappear, and her brown eyes were pools of sympathy. She even laid down her knitting to hand over a scrap of paper bearing the flight number in her neat writing. 'Flight KM-one-eight-four-five. Richard took him.' She hesitated. 'I packed for you, in case you want to catch him . . . Shall I order a taxi?'

'Yes, please!' Judith was already snatching up her handbag, realising now, why her room had seemed so tidy. Erminia had known what Adam had doubted. Judith would be leaving, too.

In ten agonising minutes, Judith was hugging Erminia then leaving her behind with her knitting and the TV. She clambered into the back of a Ford Focus and gasped to the driver, 'The airport, please.' Moments later, they were whizzing towards Gzira to join the regional road.

The traffic was hell – it always was when you really needed to get somewhere. She gritted her teeth and gripped the seat as they sliced past other cars, ruthlessly feeding into the flow of traffic in scary games of Chicken, the taxi driver unconcerned when others blew their horns in long, angry blasts or treated him to angry gestures.

Judith clung to the door handle as the car changed lanes or flew around roundabouts, refusing to look at the dashboard clock as the minutes slid by. From fireworks sparkling in the navy sky she gathered there was a *festa* going on. The traffic flowed through the tunnel at Hamrun well enough though, and as they picked up the signposts for the airport, the going became easier.

At least Malta's international airport was small and accessible and there was no long, slow approach and miles of car parks as at Heathrow or Gatwick. As they neared in grim silence, she felt a gust of panic to see the lights of an ascending aircraft then she scolded herself for a

352

stupid leap of her heart. He couldn't have taken off yet.

She knew it wasn't Richard's way to hang around waiting for visitors to queue up for check-in so Judith wasn't surprised not to see his car in the drop-off zone. She threw ten liri at the taxi driver with her thanks, waited impatiently for him to pull her case from the boot, then fought her way through a disembarking minibus-load of tourists, all displaying typical end-of-holiday grumpiness, and on beneath the arch and the big glass doors signed *Departures*.

She normally liked the airport. Bright and clean in relaxing speckled shades of sand and honey, it reminded her of happy events such as meeting Kieran from the plane. But she'd never seen it so *busy*. A million tourists waited before her in snaky lines, each as long as a football pitch. What the hell was going on with the check-ins? Tour reps patrolled the queues, loud and jolly despite the holiday-makers' peeves about hanging about and the weight of their cases, as if it were someone else that had stuffed the luggage with Mdina glass and books about Malta's part in World War II.

'Excuse me, excuse me, please.' Judith tried to wiggle through the tail end of the lines that blocked the door.

A broad lady with a red face turned sharply. 'It's a *queue*, lovey.'

Her travelling partner fanned herself with her passport. 'I don't know why they don't open more check-ins.'

The first lady sighed. 'That's why they tell you to be here two hours in advance, if you ask me. They've no intention of opening enough.' The tourists turned their stolid backs on Judith as they grumbled, consigning her to her position in the space by the doors.

Judith tapped the nearest on the shoulder. 'I don't need to

check in! I just need to get through to find someone,' she fibbed. 'And their flight's being called,' she added more accurately, her heart giving a giant lurch as she caught the announcement of Flight KM-one-eight-four-five from the booming PA system. As there was no movement in the wall of turned backs, she took a breath, aimed for a weak spot, and jostled her way through.

'Charming!' she heard behind her as she burst into the area beside the queues. 'Don't mind our ankles with your damned luggage.'

She rushed along the length of the queue, gripping the handle of her suitcase as it bounced along on its inadequate wheels, craning her neck, searching for the familiar tall shape with the hair that slid forward over his eyes. Tiptoeing, stretching, she tried to look over into the next bunched line and the four beyond that.

She slowed. It was hopeless.

He'd probably checked in by now anyway and was through security. With such a queue to check in, she doubted that she'd make the flight and join him. She tried his phone but it was off.

Heart a ton weight in her chest and searching for a way to damage limitation, she swung around, aiming for the Air Malta desk. Perhaps they could page him and get him to a phone, wherever he was in the airport. Then, even if he'd gone through the departure gate and up to the first floor, she'd at least be able to talk to him, tell him she'd be on a later flight.

The airport was heaving with reps in red or blue blazers, tourists with bulky luggage, airport staff, and what looked like a delegation of businessmen making their farewells to their hosts.

And then she saw him.

He was at the head of the queue filtering between the barriers into departure security, the enclosure where hand luggage was scanned and passengers stepped through the metal detector before taking the escalator up to the departure lounge. His black camera bag hung over his shoulder and he held a newspaper. Any moment and he'd step out of sight.

'Adam!' she called.

Her voice was lost in the swirl of conversation and echoing public address announcements as Adam shuffled another couple of paces between the barriers.

Abandoning her suitcase – strictly against the advice of the posters – Judith took a deep breath and began battling her way towards him, hollering, 'ADAM! ADAM LEBLOND!'

The sea of humanity began to part for her, shocked and surprised faces turning her way.

And Adam stopped in his tracks, his head moving, eyes searching.

'*Adam!*' She windmilled her arms, trying to side step and dodge her way around the teeming mass of people. 'I'm here!'

Adam's gaze locked with hers. He cast a glance at the looming archway that signalled entry into the security check area and the point of no return, spun on his heel and began thrusting his way against the flow of human traffic, not noticeably bothered by the annoyance of passengers he shuffled aside. The barriers either side of the queue were made of several tiers, like steel ranch railings, and he couldn't just duck beneath them.

The crowds continued to part under the onslaught of Judith clawing her way across the polished floor. Then she saw uniformed security staff bearing down on her, frowning, plotting a course to intercept hers. Forcing strength into her legs, she put on a spurt.

Adam had become locked in a dispute with a red-faced tourist whose size didn't allow easy passage past him. His eyes began measuring up the waist-high barrier.

She jinked around a family who were arguing in German and broke into a sprint. Her heart sank to see a man in uniform had got in front of her to intercept her, holding up a forbidding hand and shouting simultaneously at Adam in an effort to stop him slinging a long leg over the barriers.

She pretended to halt in front of the uniformed man but then swerved around him, evading his hands. Nearly there! Five, four, three, two, one . . . 'Adam!'

But as she tried to skid to a halt where Adam was still trying to scale the barrier, the highly polished tiles caught Judith out. Her feet scrabbled, trying to gain purchase, but they were heading for the gap beneath the barrier – a slot too small to allow the rest of her to follow. 'Oh, no,' she gasped. Her knee folded, and she grasped fruitless handfuls of air.

And then a hand caught hers. She felt ridged scars against her skin.

Her slide arrested, she was yanked upright, her left arm almost dragged from its socket, and hauled up against a long body. The uniformed man stormed up to bark at them as he snatched his walkie-talkie from his belt. But Judith didn't care. Even with the barrier still between them and digging into her stomach, Judith was safe within the warmth and comfort that surrounded Adam.

His eyes had fastened silently on her face and it took three good breaths before she could dredge up some words. 'You're wrong,' she gulped, gripping the hand that had caught hers tightly. 'I was delayed by a migraine. I came home to talk when it had passed but you'd gone. I couldn't believe it. I got a taxi but the traffic was a bastard.' She paused to suck in air, ignoring exasperated tourists wanting to shove past to get security and passport control over so that they could spend the last of their liri in the shops.

The security guard was growling insistently at them but Judith zoned him out.

Adam's grey eyes were intense, his voice quiet. 'What am I wrong about?' His hand tightened around her wrist so hard that she had a job not to wince.

She tried to organise her scrambled thoughts. 'I had to go back, to tie up loose ends. I couldn't be happy until I had.'

'And?' he prompted. His voice was tense.

'And I've done it.' She beamed. 'I gave the crucifix to Giorgio's youngest daughter Lydia, because she reminds me of him and, although it's not very nice of me, I don't care for Alexia. I told Maria I didn't accept the blame for what happened.' She thought about that, frowning. 'I think she may even have accepted my point, to some extent. But I got this incredible migraine and I'm not completely sure how much was actually said and how much just happened in my head.' She leaned into him. 'But Giorgio's parents took me into their house and let me lie on their sofa in a dark room until I felt better. Which was nice of them, considering.'

'And?' he asked, again, more gently this time.

'So you're wrong that I want to stay here without you. I choose the world in Brinham,' she said, as if it were the obvious thing. 'And you.'

'What about Giorgio?' His voice was tight.

She looked down, suddenly becoming aware of the hand holding hers, the tightness of the pincer grip. For the first time he was letting her hold his right hand. Trusting her with the damaged part of himself, for once not withdrawing and hiding it away.

She smiled, savouring his touch. 'I've said goodbye.'

Then he, too, looked down at their hands clasped between them, as if he hadn't been aware until that moment that he'd used his imperfect hand to hold her. His smile twisted. But he didn't try the usual left-hand-for-right exchange. Instead, gently, he tilted her face to his and kissed her. 'I think we've finally ended up on the same bit of road.' He kissed her temples and her cheekbones, her eyelids and the crook of her neck. 'We can go home together.'

She let her head fall back and closed her eyes, feeling his lips on her flesh and the beat of his heart through her hands upon his chest. 'I haven't got a bloody ticket.'

He laughed. 'It's waiting for you at the Air Malta desk.' He peered around her to where the uniformed man with the walkie-talkie was still watching them but calmly now, almost smiling. Two of his colleagues surveyed them from a vantage point at the top of the escalator before passport control, obviously prepared to be tolerant of these mad English. 'I wonder if this nice man will help hurry you through?'

Judith felt happiness filling her up and her face stretching into a massive, beaming smile. 'Bound to. The Maltese are terribly kind.'

He turned her gently towards the security man. 'OK. Let's see if we can go home together.'

Loved

## A Home in the Sun?

Then why not try one of Sue's
other sizzling summer reads
or cosy Christmas stories?

The perfect way to escape
the every day.

This summer, join Zia as she sets out to uncover her past...

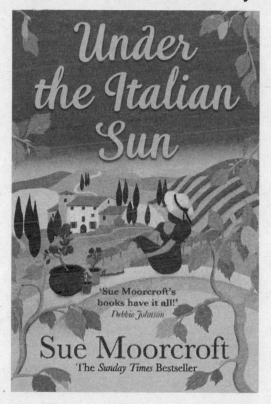

The #1 bestseller is back with an uplifting, escapist read that will brighten the gloomiest day!

# Sparks are flying on the island of Malta . . .

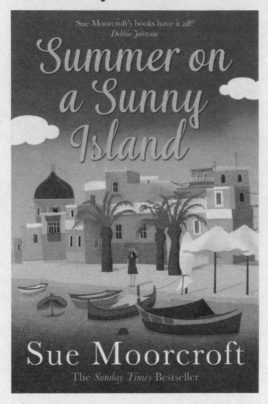

An uplifting summer read
that will raise your spirits and
warm your heart.

# Come and spend summer by the sea!

Make this a summer to remember
with blue skies, beachside walks and
the man of your dreams . . .

In a sleepy village in Italy,
Sophia is about to discover a
host of family secrets . . .

Lose yourself in this uplifting summer
romance from the *Sunday Times* bestseller.

What could be better than a summer spent basking in the French sunshine?

Grab your sun hat, a cool glass of wine, and escape to France with this gloriously escapist summer read!

*Hannah and Nico are meant to
be together. But fate is keeping
them apart . . .*

'Sue Moorcroft's books have it all!'
*Debbie Johnson*

# Christmas Wishes

## Sue Moorcroft

The *Sunday Times* Bestseller

**A heartwarming story of love,
friendship and Christmas magic
from the *Sunday Times* bestseller.**

This Christmas, the villagers of Middledip are off on a very Swiss adventure . . .

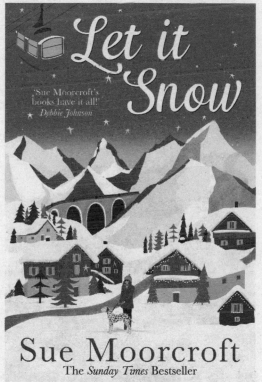

Escape to a winter wonderland
in this heartwarming romance from
the *Sunday Times* bestseller.

# One Christmas can change everything . . .

Curl up with this feel-good festive romance, perfect for fans of Carole Matthews and Trisha Ashley.

It's time to deck
the halls . . .

'I love all of Sue Moorcroft's books!' *Katie Fforde*

The
*Little Village*
*Christmas*

S**UE** M**OORCROFT**

Return to the little village of
Middledip with this *Sunday Times*
bestselling Christmas read . . .

For Ava Blissham, it's going to be a Christmas to remember . . .

'I love all of Sue Moorcroft's books!' Katie Fforde

The Christmas Promise

Sue Moorcroft

**Countdown to Christmas
as you step into the wonderful
world of Sue Moorcroft.**